Kidnap

on the

Mekong

A Declan Finney Thriller

Gregory O'Neill

oneill.gregory.e@gmail.com

Logo by Malina O'Neill

Photo Images by joephotoimages.com

1st edition 2024

ISBN 978-1-7637481-0-1

DECLAN FINNEY ADVENTURES

The Golden Triangle is a rugged region of Southeast Asia where Thailand, Myanmar and Laos meet at the confluence of the Ruak and Mekong Rivers. Known for its notorious history as a centre of opium production and drug trafficking, the area once supplied massive amounts of heroin right across the world during the latter half of the 20th century.

It is also home to ethnic minority groups including the Shan, Karen, Akha, Lisu and Lahu with their rich traditions and customs. The landscape is lush and mountainous with fertile soil, high in plant and animal diversity. It is a truly beautiful part of the world.

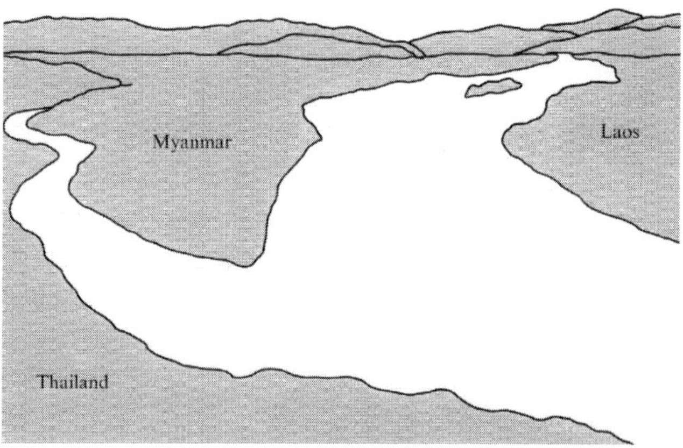

Pain is inevitable, suffering is optional

The Buddha

Prologue

The crash of a metal pipe shattered the boy's skull. His attackers abandoned him face down in the river as they bundled the girl into the back of a pick-up truck. This trickle of a river which separated Myanmar from Northern Thailand was once again the site of brutality. It wouldn't be long before he was found, but there would be no witnesses. The recent return to power of the generals would not help matters. Don't ask too many questions, his friends had said. He had ignored them.

His friends across the river in Mae Sai were oblivious. As far as they knew, he had slipped across the border again to interview a few more freedom fighters, taking their new friend Jane with him. The coup in February 2021 shocked only those unaware of Myanmar's political landscape since 2015. While some questioned the Generals' sudden change of heart, most were too swept up in the euphoria of seeing The Lady take the reins of power, they couldn't see the obvious. Why would the Generals give up so much for so little? Did they crave Western approval? They had China on their side and indifference from ASEAN. After all, were the Thais or Cambodians really in a position to criticize the democratic conventions of the Burmese generals?

Bound and gagged with three young Burmese women, Jane Gordon was already halfway to a small village on the east side of Myanmar where it borders Laos in the famous Golden Triangle. The Shan State was a rebel stronghold where the government had virtually given up. The rebels came and went as they pleased and supplied the insatiable appetite for methylamphetamines in Thailand and beyond. The rebels had to pay for their weapons somehow.

This trip her parents had paid for as a break from her troubles in Australia had been intended as a way of getting Jane back on track. It did not look like such a great idea right now.

Back in Sydney, several weeks earlier, a car full of international students careered toward an intersection full of pedestrians. The light was red, and the driver was drunk. As they sped on, the elderly pedestrian was flung over the top of the car and landed violently on the pavement. It was instant, he was dead. The car slowed and then accelerated suddenly, but not before pictures were taken and a registration plate number recorded by other pedestrians on the street. They would not get far.

Two suburbs away, Declan Finney occupied a corner of the Newtown bar. He was hunched over a glass of beer with a vodka chaser. 'This is the last one Declan,' said the barman, as he handed over another drink. 'I count that as number six and that is enough for anyone, even a seasoned drinker like you.' Finney looked at the image in the mirror behind the bar, contemplating his years working undercover. The little nicks and scars on his face told the stories of close calls and narrow escapes. The worst scars were those that were invisible.

Sydney Life

Declan Finney's descent from monk to madman had been swift and brutal. Three days earlier, he'd been resolute in his vow to stay off the booze for six months, a penance, a reset after a string of bad decisions. But his resolve had crumbled within hours, and now he found himself on the familiar, treacherous path of self-destruction. The looming suspension from the force weighed heavily on his mind. With it, the prospect of meeting his nemesis, Detective Chief Inspector Peter Burrows, only darkened his already stormy mood.

DCI Burrows, known among the ranks as 'Shifty-Eye,' was on a meteoric rise through the police hierarchy. He had the perfect pedigree for the job. His father, Detective Charlie Burrows, had been a tragic figure in Melbourne's infamous gangland wars, gunned down in a brutal execution-style killing that was splashed across every newspaper in the country. The image of a young Peter standing beside his grieving mother at the funeral had been seared into the public's memory, making him a natural successor in the eyes of many. From the police academy to detective, and now a step away from the top job, Burrows' trajectory had been inevitable.

For Finney, the road had been far more arduous. He'd clawed his way up to detective sergeant, each promotion hard-won through sheer grit, often at the expense of his personal life. But his most recent misstep proved to be his undoing, an informant dead, and the blame lay squarely at his feet. The suspension was a certainty and expulsion from the force a looming spectre.

The meeting with Joey Lonsdale had been routine, just another exchange in their carefully choreographed dance of information and secrecy. Joey was a regular, reliable, if somewhat unremarkable, informant. Finney had cultivated the relationship for two years, drawing on Joey's knowledge of the drug scene in King's Cross. It was a dangerous line of work, and they both knew it. Finney had often voiced his concerns, but Joey always brushed them off with a casual confidence bordering on recklessness.

'They trust me, Mr. Finney. It's cool,' Joey would say, with a nonchalance that was almost comforting.

Their meetings took place far from the prying eyes of King's Cross, in the upscale, quiet suburbs on the north side of the bridge, Mosman, Palm Beach, Killara. Places where Finney hoped the tentacles of the underworld couldn't reach. But the underworld had a way of seeping into even the most unexpected places, and this time, it had found them.

Now, with Joey dead and Finney facing the fallout, the familiar pattern of his life played out once more. The booze was his only escape, a way to drown the guilt and the fear that gnawed at him. But it was also the thing threatening to drag him under completely. The meeting with Burrows was just two days away, and he knew his future hung by a thread.

Joey had been a typical user. A bit of small-time dealing to support his habit, he had started young, as a street kid, weed, coke, and then of course onto meth. When he was 'well' Joey was bright and lucid. High on meth he was mad and manic, coming down off it he was abrasive, sometimes violent, and best avoided.

Finney was playing the long game with Joey. He needed intelligence on the network. Who was at the top? How was the drug coming into Sydney? Years ago, there were cooks and precursors, the ingredients, ephedrine and pseudo-ephedrine in various forms were brought in and then 'cooked' in meth labs. More recently, however, it was simply cheaper to just bring ready-made pills or a powdered form of methylamphetamines. Much of this came from Myanmar via Thailand or Laos. The precursors came across the border from China into the northern Shan state of Myanmar, where it was manufactured and then sent onwards around the world.

As a result, places like Thailand also had a big meth problem. The drug was cheap and plentiful and retailed for less than US $1 per pill. The same pill could be sold for US$10 in Australia and, as a result, Australia had become a prime destination because of the high profit margins. The Australian Federal Police (AFP) and the state authorities were trying to work together to stop the drugs before they came into the country. To achieve that they had to work their way back to the source, the Mr. Bigs. This was not so easy.

Finney had been working with his informant unofficially. He knew this was risky, but he had given information resulting in some busts so those higher up the food chain were prepared to let him run with it. Of course, they would, that was how it worked. Until it didn't. Burrows knew what Finney was doing but of course, would deny any knowledge if things went south. Joey ended up in a dumpster in King's Cross with his mouth stapled shut and Finney's phone number carved into his emaciated chest. Finney had been running him without authority. Suspension was inevitable.

Of more immediate concern to Finney was the impending coffee with his daughter, Ella. The coffee date was set for less than two hours from now, and he was in no state to be seen by anyone, let alone his fourteen-year-old daughter. It was 8 am, and he hadn't slept in days. His reflection in the bathroom mirror revealed a three-day stubble and bloodshot eyes, his mouth tasting like an ashtray after a night of chain-smoking and hard liquor. Finney only smoked when he drank, but that was little comfort now.

He couldn't show up looking like this, but cancelling wasn't an option. Sarah would never let him hear the end of it. A last-minute cancellation would be another glaring failure in the eyes of both his ex-wife and his daughter. It was yet another stick Sarah would use to beat him down, and he'd have no excuse. He deserved it, after all. He'd made a habit of disappointing those who mattered most, and the job had always come first, no matter the cost.

From the very beginning, his commitment to his career had been a source of conflict between him and Sarah, even before Ella was born. The arguments were always the same, his late nights, his dangerous assignments, and the constant tension of being a cop. Sarah had warned him this would drive a wedge between them, and she'd been right. Now, as he stared at himself in the mirror, he saw the physical manifestation of every poor choice he'd ever made.

He wanted to be a better father. He wanted to be the kind of dad who could be there for Ella, who could make her laugh, who could be a steady presence in her life. But somehow, the job always seemed to take priority. The pressures, the danger, the thrill of the chase was an addiction, and like any addiction, it had taken over his life.

But now, with a looming suspension and the real possibility of losing his job, the reality of his choices was sinking in. If he couldn't even manage to show up for coffee with Ella, what did that say about him as a father? As a human being?

He had less than two hours to pull himself together. He splashed cold water on his face, rubbed his hands over the stubble, and made a silent vow: whatever it took, he'd be there for Ella today. This time, he wouldn't let her down.

Sarah Hall, a splendid vision, walking through Durbar Square, Kathmandu, in flowing white cheesecloth. The sun shone through her blond locks and Finney was in love. He didn't know her name or where she was from, but he knew at that moment, she was the one. As it turned out they were staying in the same guesthouse down in the Thamel. The Tibetan Peace Guest House - or just TP Guest House, as it was known. Not quite in the jungle the Thamel had become, it was a few streets away in a quiet little cul-de-sac. Finney had been travelling through India and Nepal burning up the money he had made labouring across various building sites in Sydney. He planned to 'do' the sub-continent and then head over to Amsterdam for the European leg of his world tour.

Sarah, on the other hand, was doing the opposite. Funded by her doting, eastern suburbs parents, she was on an all-expenses paid holiday which had taken her through the UK, France, Spain, Italy, Germany, and now to Nepal and home via Thailand. Finney abandoned his plans for Europe and followed Sarah to Koh Samui in Thailand for a couple of weeks before ending up back in Sydney.

They spent two weeks together in a bungalow by the beach, where they barely left their love nest. They made love, they made plans to travel the world and build a life together. Sarah would be a human rights lawyer, saving those displaced by corrupt regimes, women in poverty, and children abandoned to struggle on the streets of the developing world. Finney, on the other hand, had no real plans for his future. He was content for Sarah to be his future for the time being.

By the time they got back to Sydney, they were well and truly inseparable. Sarah enrolled in law at Sydney University, and Finney returned to toiling on a building site. Back living with his parents in Coogee wasn't ideal but he was close to Sarah, who lived with her parents in Rose Bay. In a whirlwind of romance, they got married too young and had a daughter, Sarah put her university degree on hold, and somehow Finney ended up in the Australian Federal Police. A degree in criminology and a graduate employment program meant job security, boredom, and a strangling malaise.

Before they knew where they were, a trial separation was in place. It was the resentment Sarah had felt about having to abandon her dream of becoming a lawyer. It was the long days and nights apart, him working while she looked after a baby and struggling part-time through a law degree. It was her parents' disapproval; Finney just never measured up in their eyes. They were just too young. There was never any infidelity, no raging arguments or disputes, just a slow withering of love and affection. Regret was followed by bitterness, remorse, and then the feeling of numbness. Sarah moved back to live with her parents, taking a five-year-old Ella with her.

Sydney on a Saturday

Ella, at fourteen years old, had decided coffee with Dad on Saturday morning was essential. They had only done it a couple of times, but it seemed important to her. However, it sure played havoc if Friday night had been big, which it inevitably was. Declining one for the road from the barman at the early opener in Newtown, Finney slipped out the side door and shuffled the two short blocks back home. The daylight was the bright intensity that only Sydney could muster in early spring. An eclectic mix of goths, punks, and transgender couples thronged King Street in Newtown, queuing for an almond milk latte or whatever the latest beverage craze was at the numerous coffee shops in this part of town. When had coffee become such a big deal, Finney wondered. I might have a Nescafe instant coffee when I get home, he thought.

He was still in the apartment he, Sarah, and Ella had shared a decade earlier. Munni Street, Newtown offered up a motley collection of modest terrace houses, some were renovated, but most were not. His place was an eyesore, a nasty-looking 1950s beige brick building with ground-floor parking. It was the kind of bland structure where functionality and economy were balanced in equal measures, having squeezed out aesthetics altogether. Its occupants were a mix of owners and tenants. He kept promising himself he'd take some leave, throw on a coat of paint, and maybe even replace the tiles in the bathroom. The place was dated, drab, and musty ten years ago. Now it was just plain sad. Newspapers, magazines, and record CD covers littered the worn parquetry floor. A single tattered leather armchair stood as a solitary symbol of his bachelor lifestyle.

He had less than thirty minutes to clean himself up and get over to meet his daughter. He had offered to go and pick her up from her home with Sarah in Balmain. A modest little terrace worth more than two million dollars. Evans St., Balmain was a world away from Newtown. Full of renovated terrace houses, and plantation shutters offering privacy and self-satisfaction to their owners. A colour-coded picket fence capped off the neat little package of domestic bliss. A gift from her Mum and Dad, and way better than anything Finney could ever have afforded on his pay. Ella had insisted on taking the bus over to meet him. Sarah thought he should come and pick up their daughter, but Finney knew this was all part of Ella asserting her independence. He did, however, track her phone just to be sure she was OK. Fourteen-year-old girls on their own on the buses of Sydney, even in broad daylight, were vulnerable. He knew it better than anyone.

Hair washed, freshly shaved, and with a splash of cologne, Finney might just be presentable enough for the coffee appointment. His façade of respectability would at least last a couple of hours before Ella went back home to her mother. That was about all he needed. The last thing he wanted was her reporting Dad smelled strange and had 'panda' eyes.

Café Newtown had been Ella's choice. It was right opposite the railway station at the junction of where King St. Newtown met the Prince's Highway, and was quintessential Newtown. People sipping coffee on the pavement, murals in the side streets, artists mixed with stockbrokers mixed with families. The neighbouring shops included a Vietnamese restaurant, a hipster barber shop, Dr. Hempire Organic Foods and a tax accountant. How was that for diversity? It had it all.

Here she is! A familiar pang hit Finney, the pang of seeing his daughter morphing from a little girl to a young woman. He was both proud and terrified in equal portions. The lift-off-the-ground hug had been replaced by a peck on the cheek and a little brush on the shoulders. He was fine with it. He knew hugs would be back in a couple of years.

Ella was about to begin the last four years of high school in a private girls' school in Drummoyne, paid for by her maternal grandparents. She had been a good kid with school, studious about the workload and enthusiastic about learning. Sport was not her thing, but she was just average enough to get by in a sport-obsessed country like Australia. She was a great reader, but not too nerdy and seemed to have just the right number of friends. Finney felt reassured on the one hand Ella was doing so well, and guilty on the other, he should have been around more. All credit for Ella's successes belonged to Sarah.

Sarah had been seeing a man named Charles Drayton, although Ella always referred to him as Charlie. He was a lawyer, of course, what else? Finney had met him several times. Slick, driving a smart car, wearing tailored suits, and boasting credentials from Sydney Grammar and the University of Sydney, he was everything Finney wasn't. He was a nice enough guy, but Finney hated him, and he knew why. It was all about Ella. Charles, Sarah, and Ella had just returned from a holiday in Hawaii. It seemed to Finney that Ella was being careful about how she talked about it, but he knew she had enjoyed herself. It was simple enough; Finney hated Charles Drayton because he was jealous. Not of his relationship with Sarah, but because he was slowly becoming de facto father to Ella.

It was hard enough at first when Charles came on the scene. There were weekends when Sarah would take Ella away with Charles. Skiing in Thredbo, theme parks on the Gold Coast. He could tolerate those things, but when Sarah announced Charles was moving in with them, it really hurt. He said nothing, of course, how could he? He took it on the chin, as he had done with so many disappointments. You should stand up for yourself, his brother David had suggested. He was the confident and assertive sibling in the family. Not Declan, the older of the two.

Two hours sped by in a stream of anecdotes about Ella's school friends, complaints about her mother, and the usual exaggerated angst which only teenagers can generate. Finney had no reference point for *gotta go Dad, later.* And just like that, she was gone. He sat for a while and just gazed out across the café. Things could be worse, he concluded. Ella was doing OK.

Another long Saturday afternoon stretched out before him, and it was his turn to visit his father. Andrew, his younger brother by three years, had called him mid-week to remind him. Outwardly, very solid and successful, Andrew was an accountant with Price Waterhouse. He was married with two kids, a Mercedes Benz in the driveway, and doubtless a safe portfolio of shares.

He and his wife had recently purchased a three-million-dollar house on the lower north shore of Sydney.

He was only in his mid-thirties. His children were in private schools, his wife didn't work, and their latest holiday had been to Europe. There was something not right about his brother's rapid success. Finney hadn't quite worked out what it was, but he had a strong feeling it wasn't legal.

Finney's father, Hector, had endured a tough life. Dragged from Galway on the west coast of Ireland by his father in 1957, at age eight and dropped into a public school with a name like Hector, he was bullied his whole school life. During the first twelve months, the family were housed in a migrant camp on the outskirts of western Sydney before a housing commission place became available in Maroubra. Hector struggled through school, just dodged the Vietnam War draft, and fell into a safe government job.

After his wife died it was as if Hector just lost the will to live. His sons saw for the first time how much their father relied on their mother. Not just the practical things, washing, cooking, cleaning, but the things that mattered. A reason to get up in the morning. For the first few months, his sons had just put it down to shock and grief. Hector's wife, Maria, was the youngest daughter of Italian migrants. She had grown up in the inner western suburbs of Sydney, along with a swag of extended family members. Both her parents had died young, from sheer exertion and overwork. Determined to make a successful life for their children in their new country, both had worked seven days a week running a restaurant and a cleaning business. Heart attacks, both, before they reached fifty years old.

Hector Finney and Maria Rossi met in The Department of Community Services. Hector, a section manager, and Maria a children's care officer. It was shortly after her parents' deaths and Maria was looking to start a family. Hector came along and that was that. They married in 1976. Then there were ten years of torture and heartbreak, with Maria suffering numerous miscarriages. When Declan finally arrived on 29 September 1986, there was rejoicing, but mostly relief. He was doted on accordingly.

They were not overly affectionate toward one another, Hector and Maria. Their bond was built on mutual dependency, they just did everything together. Then came the lump in the breast, easily ignored. By the time it was diagnosed, it was stage four. One day she was functioning normally; a month later, she was in palliative care. Another month, and it was the funeral. It happened so quickly. Six years had passed since her death, but for Hector, it may as well have been yesterday.

'Knock, knock, anyone home?' he called out to his father. The screen door unlocked; the front door was wide open. 'Dad, you've got to lock the door. This part of town is not what it used to be.'

'Sure thing, son,' was his father's reply.

There was an unpleasant smell in the house. They had someone coming twice a week to tidy up, wash his clothes, and do simple cleaning. But it was not enough. His father had always been such a fastidious man. He would clear the leftovers, wash up, and wipe down the benches before the rest of the family had even finished their meal. His Dad was living on toasted bread. This was the smell. It had permeated every corner of the house. He unloaded the groceries and packed perishables in the fridge and toiletries in the bathroom.

The house looked tired: There were scuff marks on the floor, cobwebs hung from the walls and the furniture was frayed. It needed a deep clean. His father shuffled around the house in worn-out clothes, and he was unsure if he was showering every day. He had not shaved and there were food stains down the front of his crumpled shirt. He had always been so particular about his appearance, but not anymore.

'Put the jug on, son.'

Tea. It was always tea. His father had joked he would always be a tea drinker. He had tried coffee once, never liked it and he didn't see the point of trying it again a second time. Only ever tea leaves, never tea bags. There was a ritual. Heat the teapot and the cups. One spoon for each person and one for the pot. Swaddle the teapot and be patient while the tannin is released.

You cannot hurry a good cup of tea, his father had always said. Hector had applied the approach to most things in his life. He never seemed hurried. His son had often wondered what his father was like in the workplace. Was he the same man? Quiet and thoughtful. He realised he had never seen his father angry.

Declan had been separated from Sarah for almost ten years. Still, he waited for the inevitable question.

'Any chance you and Sarah will patch things up?'

'Very unlikely Dad,' he replied, 'but you never know.' He wasn't sure why he added a note of optimism because it was unlikely they would ever reunite. He knew the script and here it came.

'Sarah is the daughter we never had.'

'I know, Dad.'

'You know it would be much better for Ella if she had a mother and a father.'

'She has a mother and a father.'

'You know what I mean. All together under one roof.'

'I know Dad, it's just the way it is.'

'I miss seeing Sarah and I never seem to see Ella enough.'

'Well, Ella's a teenager now, she has lots of commitments to school and friends. I'll try and bring her over time.'

'That would be nice.'

Tea was poured and then they drifted into a silence, broken only by the perfunctory questions and answers about work, how great Andrew was doing, whether there was anything that needed to be done around the house, and on it went. They both knew this was just the way the conversation stumbled. Hector never had the ease of talking their mother had. Both boys seemed so at ease with her. With her gone, there was a gulf. Saying their goodbyes both men wished there was more warmth but accepted that this was as good as it would ever be. 'See you in a couple of weeks Dad,' he said.'

'Mind how you go, son,' replied his father. As he always did.

Saturday night as the hangover descended, the predictable ritual of penance began. Herbal tea and many cups of it. Loads of washing, cleaning his apartment, vacuuming the floor, changing the sheets on the bed. This was all part of the ritual for Finney. Ironically, the benders tended to occur during the week. On the weekends when everyone was out partying, he simply bunkered down. He knew the next day would be the more painful second-day hangover, always worse than the first day. That is why people say the best way to avoid a hangover is to stay drunk. His strategy was to keep busy.

No Church on Sunday

Finney, in his youth, had been a promising athlete. He played soccer for the first-grade school team and was a star swimmer, but his great love was athletics. He ran the one-hundred- and two-hundred-meter sprints. At fifteen he was 182cm, tall for his age with gangly legs. He had competed at the state level and had dreams of being a professional athlete. An ankle injury sidelined him for six months and put an end to the dream. He could still jog and occasionally swim laps at the Sydney University pool, but a future in professional sport ended abruptly.

This Sunday morning, he opted to swim. At 8:30 am. on a Sunday morning the pool was uncrowded, just how he liked it. The early morning crowd was mostly older folks, with Finney bringing the median age down considerably. The indoor, heated pool, thick with the smell of chlorine, brought back familiar memories of daily swimming practice, before and after school. His target was twenty laps which for him was easy enough to achieve. He alternated between freestyle and breaststroke. Finishing his laps, he made the twenty-minute walk back home and felt invigorated. Perhaps the second-day hangover would not be too bad.

He needed a strategy for his return to work on Monday. DCI Burrows, his nemesis, would be waiting for him. He had to have some answers ready. Of course, there had been an inquiry, but it was inconclusive, neither exonerating Finney nor condemning him. This was the problem because it left the door open for DCI Burrows to decide his fate.

He wasn't sure when he lost favour with Burrows or whether he never had it to begin with. They were both of a similar age and had gone through the academy at the same time. Their career paths, however, had taken very different turns. Finney was swimming upstream his whole career where Burrows was the golden boy. His strategy had to be simple, accept what came his way. It's still my day off, he thought, best make the most of it.

There were better places to shop than King St. Newtown, but it was close by, and he couldn't face one of those all-in-one shopping centres. So, he chose the Aldi store on King St. behind the Newtown train station. The usual staples of milk, bread, pasta, tea, and salad would have to do. Chances were half the milk, bread, and fresh food would be discarded as garbage at the end of the week, Finney having decided to eat out most nights anyway.

Was this why the life expectancy of a bachelor was ten years less than a married man, he wondered. Pathetic really, but understandable. It wasn't that he couldn't cook, many friends had remarked he made a good curry and his risotto marinara was restaurant standard. No, it was just that it didn't seem worth the effort to cook only for himself. So, most nights he simply ate out or bought in, or worse still, he didn't eat at all. People often asked him how he stayed so thin. It's simple, was his standard reply, just don't eat.

Late Sunday morning on King St., Newtown was a weird mix of shoppers, all peppy and ready to tick things off their list of achievements before hitting the treadmill of Monday-to-Friday monotony. They were joined by the stragglers who had done an all-nighter and stayed on for a late breakfast. Pop-eyed and slack-jawed, they struggled through a high-protein breakfast and faced a hangover that would last until they crash-landed on Tuesday. He knew only too well how it felt. It was called Blue Tuesday.

Leaving the grocery store and only ten meters away, Finney could see the girl struggling. She was standing at the ATM, with two men beside her. One was holding her left arm near her shoulder, while the other man's arm encircled her waist. At first, he thought the two men were supporting her but then he realised they were trying to force her to withdraw money.

There was a car parked by the curb, with the passenger door open, and the engine running. The driver shouted at the two men to hurry up. Both men wore black hoodies. Even in this part of town, in September, it was too much. The girl resisted and fell to her knees, screaming, and trying to break free.

He dropped the bag of groceries on the pavement, a broken bottle of passata, and oranges rolling across the pavement. Sprinting towards the girl, shouting as he went and scattering other pedestrians along the way. The two men looked around at the commotion and immediately let go of the girl. As they leapt into the waiting car it screamed away into the traffic leaving her sprawled on the ground, shaking, and crying.

She was trying to get to her feet, still crying and still flailing her arms. With his hands resting gently on her shoulders, he said softly, 'Police, I'm with the police, you're OK now.' As he did so he tried to get a look at the car. Black BMW, series 3, quite new. That was it. No numberplate. Chances were, it had been stolen anyway. The priority at hand was to calm the victim and look for any injuries. The training kicked in; it was all muscle memory.

As he knelt beside the young woman, his voice cut through the panic, shouting for someone to call an ambulance. The drawback of plainclothes police work was the public sometimes had trouble differentiating the good guys from the bad. This situation was escalating fast. He quickly pulled his badge from his pocket and raised it high in the air, to avoid a well-meaning bystander mistaking him for the perpetrator. The crowd gathering around them offered support, and a woman stepped forward and identified herself as a nurse. The girl resisted. 'Just help us get some space around her,' Finney asked of the woman. She obliged by pushing back the onlookers.

As he cradled the trembling young woman close, her tears mingling with his attempt to comfort her, he couldn't help but notice the stark contrast between her untidy appearance and the luxury of her accessories. It was a familiar sight; one he had seen many times before during his years in the force. The clothing was a deliberate attempt at a shabby look, scruffy torn jeans and a wrinkled T-shirt, all in black of course. But shoes and bags were always a giveaway. The sneakers were designer brand, as was the bag. Eastern suburbs girl, slumming it in Newtown. Her eyes were bloodshot and teary, her breath was putrid. One thing was certain, she was an active drug user. It was MDMA, Meth, or both.

'What did those guys want,' he asked, 'do you know them?'

'I don't know who they are,' she screamed at him. 'They just wanted my money.' The girl was in no fit state to answer any of his questions right now. He decided to wait for the uniformed police to arrive and hand her over to them. It was Sunday and this wasn't his patch. Wrong place, wrong time. Perhaps if he had gone to the shopping centre, he would have avoided this mess.

What followed was the usual mayhem of sirens and onlookers. The perpetrators had escaped. There were a couple of uniformed police in attendance as well, one male, and one female. The young female police officer took charge while the young man followed her lead. Names and addresses of witnesses were recorded, the crowd was dispersed, and they dealt with the ambulance officers who arrived shortly after. The girl was OK, but it was protocol that she would be seen by a doctor at the nearby Royal Prince Alfred Hospital, not five minutes' drive away.

Newtown Police Station was a landmark. A statement of authority. Perched and slightly elevated above Australia Street, the original building was erected in the mid-19th century. The newer, far less attractive building alongside it was where Finney was headed. The New South Wales Police Force was the product of the brutal conditions of early colonial settlement by the British in Australia and it had a reputation to match. Finney had done a brief stint at the Station early in his career. It held bad memories for him. As a junior police officer, he was answerable to almost everybody. He did not fit in there; it was a blokey culture with boozy lunches at nearby hotels in King Street, being a regular occurrence. He was happy when he was transferred to the city station and eventually into the Australian Federal Police after just six months. It was a mere two minutes' walk from the scene to the station, but the police had insisted on him travelling with them by car to the station.

The afternoon and early evening were consumed by the visit to the police station and a statement. Jane Gordon was taken to hospital but appeared not to have any injuries.

'You know who she is, don't you,' said one of the young constables.

'I've got no idea,' he replied.

'Jane Gordon, the daughter of Sir William Gordon, the governor of NSW. It's all about drugs you know,' said the young constable.

'Well, this is Newtown, most crimes are drug related. If that's it, I'm out of here.' With a wave over his shoulder, he left to salvage what was left of his weekend

It was almost 6.30 pm and the sun had disappeared, but the weather was still warm. Spring in Sydney brought people outdoors, especially to the outdoor bars and cafes which dotted King Street Newtown. Some patrons had been enjoying the balmy weather for the better part of the whole afternoon. There was a rowdiness, but it was measured. It was Sunday. For most of those enjoying the last of the weekend, it was back to work the next day. Some would carry a hangover through Monday.

Finney, get over here, he heard the voice and knew it straight off. His downstairs neighbour from his apartment block. He was one stride into crossing the road in front of Webster's Bar on King St., when the voice boomed out. He deliberately kept moving and turned back only after he reached the other side of the road. He looked across and up to the rooftop terrace bar where she was seated and tapped his watch. I've got to get somewhere, he mouthed and was on his way. If he stopped and engaged with Megan Styles, his evening would go downhill fast in a sea of alcohol. They had been neighbours for almost three years. Young, vivacious, and a hard drinker, Megan was the last person he needed to be around tonight. Evading her attention meant a detour back around King St. to get home, but it was worth it. He had managed to save most of his shopping, or at least he hoped to. He wouldn't know until he got home and unpacked it.

The apartment was in darkness, smelling clean after his chores earlier in the day. He emptied the remains of his shopping bag onto the bench. Despite a fully stacked fridge, he opted for instant noodles, yet again. You are just way too predictable Declan Finney; he thought to himself.

Leaving a half-eaten bowl of noodles on the bench top he staggered off to bed wishing he could start the day again and make it more interesting. Half his day had been spent at a police station, on the wrong side of the desk. Tomorrow loomed large in his mind. This time tomorrow, he thought, I might be looking for a new job.

Sleep overtook him eventually. It was fitful and spooked by frustrating dreams. He was always chasing but never catching those he pursued. He talked to Ella, but she couldn't hear him. Hand in hand, Sarah and Charles walked on a beach toward a sunset in the distance. Finney, on the other hand, was walking through a blizzard, in bare feet.

Jane Gordon

After being examined at the hospital, Jane Gordon accompanied by her parents in the official vehicle of the NSW Governor, rolled into the driveway of their home in the leafy eastern suburbs of Sydney. The official residence was in Macquarie St. in the city, but the Gordons only received visitors there. They preferred the comfort and privacy of their mansion. Jane didn't live with her parents. but they had insisted she stay with them, at least for the evening.

As they sat in their lavishly furnished house, Jane related her experience yet again. Despite the fact her parents had heard it a dozen times already at the police station in Newtown, they insisted on hearing it again. Did she know either of the attackers? Were they trying to steal from her or kidnap her? Did they speak to her? Jane threw her hands in the air as she burst into tears, not for the first time that day. She could not remember a thing, it all happened so fast, she screamed at them.

'Just leave her for now Bill, please. I'll get you something to help you sleep Honey,' said her mother. As she went off to get her daughter some sleeping pills, her father leaned over his daughter and brushed her hair softly. She flinched; they were not close. At sixty-eight years old, William (Bill) Gordon, was finding out parenting a second time around, and at this age, was proving tougher than he had imagined.

He had three children from his first marriage. All grown up and with children of their own. And here he was with a twenty-year-old who had left school a year earlier, had no job, and had a drug habit.

They had thought it best to set Jane up in an apartment of her own. She lived not too far away but they barely saw her. A regular payment was made to her bank account, but it was never enough, and her mother secretly topped it up every week. She had also noticed cash seemed to disappear from her handbag every time Jane came to visit, but Lady Susan Gordon could not bring herself to believe her daughter would steal from her. Someone else may have taken it, she told herself, or she had just imagined the money had gone missing. They had plenty of money. They could afford to lose a little here and there, she told herself.

Jane had been such an easy kid. She had been in school at Rose Bay Primary and then at the boarding school, Rose Bay Convent. Her mother, having studied there, insisted Jane live and study at a boarding school they could almost see from their living room window. William Gordon had initially objected but had caved in during the mayhem of juggling a divorce and two families. The bright young optimistic little girl they waved goodbye to at the gates of the boarding school, emerged years later as a brooding, introverted, and often hostile teenager. By the time they realised what was happening, it was too late.

They tried to have a routine of a weekly dinner together, but it didn't always work out. Bill Gordon's commitments were numerous, and his wife was expected to be by his side. They had drifted apart from their daughter and now didn't know how to bridge the gap. Was it even possible to get her to move back with them?

Jane had been in therapy for almost two years. She had scheduled appointments every week, but she didn't always make it. Even though the parents paid for the therapy they had no idea what kind of progress she was making. The counsellor had been very clear right at the beginning, Jane was an adult and entitled to her privacy. Jane's mother could accept it, but Bill Gordon was old school, we are paying for this therapy, and I want to know what's going on, he had said.

By the time her mother had returned from retrieving the medications, Jane was gone. 'Bill,' she called out, 'she's gone.' Oh, for Christ's sake, he muttered to himself. He felt disappointment yet again. He suddenly felt very tired and very old.

Susan had been a hostess in the business class section of a Qantas flight to Singapore. Bill Gordon was a passenger, travelling to Singapore in his role as boss of a big mining company. It turned out they were both staying in the same hotel. They bumped into each other in the hotel bar and the next thing he was ditching his wife of almost twenty years, moving in with Susan and expecting a child.

The divorce had been messy and spiteful. Friends were divided, his kids were resentful, and his work colleagues were shocked. The reality of moving out of the palatial family home and into a two-bedroom apartment with his pregnant girlfriend had been a nightmare. All of it of his own making, as numerous friends felt compelled to remind him. He didn't want sympathy, but he didn't want derision either.

Twenty years on, his children from his first marriage had all but forgiven him. They had embraced Jane as their half-sister, but the age gap was just too much for them to be close. The children, three of them, had each other. Jane Gordon felt like she had nobody. Her parents were just never around. Always at some gala dinner or award ceremony. She had few friends. The friends she did have were all drug users who were not friends at all.

The divorce scandal had initially affected Bill Gordon's career, but he was in the boy's club and soon enough he had an Order of Australia for services to the business community. The next thing, he was appointed governor of New South Wales. The governorship turned out to be harder than he thought. It was no fairytale. He had connections and influence, without authority or power. He missed the power and authority he no longer had. He would have given it all up for a fishing rod and a deserted beach. It's all self-inflicted, he thought to himself.

Monday morning came around faster than Finney would have liked. The meeting with his boss was scheduled for 9.00 am, but the call came at 7.00 am. 'Get yourself in here at 8 am sharp,' said DCI Burrows, 'and be dressed in a suit and tie'. This was it, the end of the line. His informant was killed in broad daylight and the body mutilated. His career was as good as over.

Finney made the meeting with a few minutes to spare, dressed in a suit. His usual attire was crumpled long-sleeved linen shirts, always blue, black Levi's 501 and black slip-on boots. He had, until recently, also worn an almost rusty earring in his left ear. Ella had bought him a shiny new one which he was self-conscious about, but he wore it anyway. Colleagues told him if he just made a little bit more effort with his choice of clothing his career would benefit. He retorted that he dressed this way because he was working undercover, but it was because he liked the way the linen felt on his skin. He didn't care if the shirt crumpled thirty seconds after he put it on, it made him feel good. Same with the jeans and boots. Shabby chic was what he called it. Sloppy was what his superiors thought of it.

Seated outside the office of DCI Burrows, he barely registered the older man with the much younger woman as they went in ahead of him. When summoned into the room some fifteen minutes later, he was greeted by the couple as they stood from their chairs with outstretched hands. Finney was introduced to Governor Sir William Gordon and his wife, Lady Susan Gordon. They were both charming and intimidating at the same time. Speaking softly, Lady Gordon thanked him sincerely for his actions in saving their daughter from the would-be thieves the previous day. Her eyes were puffy, red and glistened with tears as she spoke. She was very emotional. Consequently, Sir William Gordon did most of the talking. Finney was surprised the couple had bothered to meet him personally. He was to be awarded a bravery medal. 'I've spoken to the police commissioner myself this morning,' said the governor. 'Officially the medal will come from us by way of him,' he said. It was to be kept secret, for security reasons at this stage. Their daughter was bruised, and in shock, but she was OK. They would be forever grateful. He was a credit to the force. The meeting was over. The Gordons left the room.

Jane Gordon, the only child of Sir William and Lady Gordon, had lurched from one drama to another. Unknown to Finney, Jane had experienced brushes with the law before, when she had been present when a drug bust occurred two months earlier. While not charged, Jane had been cautioned. Privately educated, Jane had started several university courses after finishing school, but none were completed. To say her parents were worried about her was an understatement. This was cause for thought for Finney. So far, things were OK with Ella, but would the fact she was an only child, with divorced parents come back to haunt her as she grew older? He was jolted from his thoughts.

'You must have a guardian angel,' said DCI Burrows, with a look of genuine disappointment. 'I had your termination notice ready for you, but I can hardly give it to you now.'

This all seemed to cancel out his errors of judgment and the death of his informant, Joey Rivers. He was off the hook and reinstated from suspension. All was good, or better than expected. He was to be reassigned as soon as Burrows could find somewhere for him. He would remain in the AFP Drug Squad but in a less front-line role. He could sense Burrows was treading carefully. This event changed the dynamic, at least for the time being. 'Just tie up all the loose ends on this Joey Rivers thing and keep your head down,' were the last words uttered by Burrows as Finney was ushered out of his office.

There were expectant looks all around when he emerged. There were plenty who felt the same as DCI Burrows and would happily have waved Finney goodbye. He did of course also have his allies. Stacey Harmer was one of them. 'Coffee?' she said. And off they went. As they walked down the corridor and outside toward the coffee shop Finney put his finger to his lips, meaning they should get well clear of their colleagues before the debrief. They would normally have gone across the street, but they opted instead to walk the extra five minutes to Miss Carter, located in Castlereagh Street, a coffee shop rarely frequented by their fellow AFP officers. Their conversation was still part spoken and part murmured. With most AFP staff in plain clothes, it paid to be discreet.

'So, what's the story, are you in or out', she queried.

'Well, it looks like I have friends in high places.'

'You are one lucky bastard,' said Harmer. 'The consensus was you would be out on your ass. Everyone knows how the big boss feels about you.'

'Something happened over the weekend,' he said, 'and it seems to have changed everything.' She was given the abridged version of the events the day before.

Detective Constable Harmer was new to the team. A western suburbs girl, she called a spade a spade. An uncut diamond as some had described her. She had struggled through school in a one-parent household. Her mother was a nurse, working night shifts, and Stacey, as the oldest child, had virtually raised her two younger brothers. Some of her colleagues found her abrasive and very much a potty mouth, but she and Finney got along well. This had something to do with the fact he was one of the very few colleagues who had not tried to get her into bed.

'I'm not sure where I will go from here. I need to take some time and wrap up what I have so far from Joey. He's given me what looks like some good intel, but of course, it still needs to be verified.'

'So, what's with the suit', she laughed, 'a wedding or a funeral?'. She was happy he was sticking around. The only guy in the squad who treated her as a professional.

They headed back into the office. Finney did have a lot to do, but he felt like he also had some time and space to get it done. There were rumours about Mr. Bigs and the trend away from home-cooked meth to the big importations of ready-made gear. This was going to be more challenging. Meth labs could be policed more easily than the eastern border of Australia with more than 3,000km of coastline and dozens of ports where containers were delivered.

Added to that, the foreign biker gangs established in Thailand would be very active in working with the manufacturers operating out of there. Get the drugs down from Myanmar, onto a container ship bound for Australia and large profits were there to be had. Interesting times indeed thought Finney.

The bigger problem for him was his tarnished reputation. Many of his colleagues saw him as a cowboy, a loner, and hard to work with. He certainly wasn't in the boys' club. While he liked a drink, it was rarely with any of his colleagues in the force. In short, he had very few allies. He had thought about a change of career in the past but never taken any action. Perhaps now was the time for him to move on. It hadn't always been this way.

Finney's claim to fame was a conviction he'd engineered five years earlier – a case he had stumbled on in a Darlinghurst nightclub. Ironically, he wasn't even a clubber but had ended up in the Voicebox nightclub in one of those 'one for the road' moments. After leaving a couple of friends at the bar, he went to use the bathroom. Inside, he found three men doing lines of coke off a playing card perched on the basin top. He was invited to join them.

'You've got to try this,' said one of the others, 'it's straight off the boat from Colombia.'

The man in the expensive suit shot him a look that screamed: *Shut your mouth.*

He decided it was worth returning to the club a few nights later. Mr. Expensive Suit, as Finney had named him, stood at the bar with several other people. When the group dispersed leaving the man alone at the bar, he made his move. He walked to the bar and ordered a drink. As his drink was being poured, he casually looked over towards the man. 'Hey man, how are you doing, we've met before,' said Finney.

The man was reluctant to accept the outstretched hand.

'I'm Declan, nice to see you again,' he said. Finney had the gift of putting people at ease as he did with his new friend, James Doralo. Later in the evening, he was invited to a party in nearby Paddington. It was the home of his new friend in the expensive suit.

Over the next two months, he and Doralo became close friends. During this time, they had partied together with Finney keeping a close eye on the man's friends and associates. His colleagues had put a tracker on his car and had people watching his house along with all those who visited. Somewhere along the way, his superiors in the AFP began to get impatient with the progress of the case. He reassured them their patience would be rewarded. Sure enough, the taps on Doralo's phone paid dividends. A large shipment of cocaine was intercepted at Port Botany in Sydney. Two tons of cocaine worth an estimated street value of $800 million was seized along with a significant amount of cash.

The surveillance exposed a tangled web of large-scale cocaine importation. The network pointed to three key players, responsible for smuggling more than 75% of the cocaine flooding into the country. The shocking part? These operations were orchestrated by partners of one of Australia's most prestigious law firms, Hilmer, Steele, and Doralo. The cocaine was expertly concealed in shipments of computers originating in South America and coming via the USA. Finney's only disappointment was Doralo himself escaped prosecution through a legal technicality. 'Watch your back, Finney,' were the man's parting words, as he left Downing Central Court after his acquittal.

The case captured the attention of senior police, including the commissioner and even the minister for police. Finney received a commendation and a promotion in the Australian Federal Police. He was given a free run to go undercover, but somewhere along the way, his momentum stalled. Now, he felt like he was just treading water. He had often asked himself why he was doing this kind of work. He was not an anti-drug zealot; he understood addiction all too well. His vice just happened to be legal, and in a country like Australia, drinking was practically a national sport. He remembered being a young adult, underage, and how getting hammered was almost a rite of passage. He had seen the misery of drug addiction up close and the ruthless exploitation by traffickers. If decriminalization wasn't on the horizon, and it wasn't, then something had to be done about organised crime and its stranglehold on the drug trade.

He had thought about asking for a transfer, but where would he go? The more radical ideas included moving interstate to join another police force or even trying his hand at private investigations. But he knew he couldn't leave Ella behind, and he knew himself well enough to admit he didn't possess the self-discipline to be a private detective. He decided to wait and see what opportunities might come his way. For now, he knew he was safe in the AFP, if he kept his head down.

The first thing Finney decided to do was to visit the family of Joey Rivers. He felt it was the least he could do. He wasn't planning on explaining the nature of their relationship, only to say he knew Joey and he was sorry for their loss. He felt obliged to do so. Joey had often talked about his family. He had let them down, he said. They were just good, ordinary people.

Driving towards the Rivers' family home, he realised it was time to buy a new car. His twenty-year-old Peugeot coupe 206, affectionately known as Claude, was well past its prime. The brakes were shot, and the engine groaned as he struggled to keep up with the rest of the traffic heading to the western suburbs. Adding to his troubles were most mechanics didn't want to touch it, and spare parts were expensive and hard to come by. He could afford a new car; he just couldn't muster the energy or enthusiasm to find one.

He didn't get out into this part of the city very often. As a result, it was quite foreign to him. He didn't want to say it, but it was suburban, in a way the suburbs closer to the beach were not. It was the great divide that was Sydney, the proximity to the water. He parked outside the double-fronted brick bungalow, a modest house in a modest street, full of other public housing.

It was technically the job of the Police Family Liaison to visit the family. They had already done so. The family had already buried their son a month earlier. He felt an obligation to give them some explanation of what had become of their son, Joey. It was also a way of dealing with his own guilt.

The old man who answered the door looked beaten down and sad. Years on an assembly line, three kids, a failed marriage, and now his son, murdered, and left to rot in a dumpster. Finney introduced himself and the man graciously invited him inside. Accepting the offer of coffee, he followed the man into the kitchen.

The room was dark and dingy, used plates, pots, and pans littered the cramped space. Joey's father looked around as if he had never been there before in his life.

Finally, he found the kettle and began to rummage around for coffee. He took the lid off a bottle of milk, gave it a sniff, and decided it was still OK. Finney was doubtful.

With the coffee made, they moved to the living room and there was that smell again. It was so familiar. Toast. Cecil Rivers had something in common with Finney's father. They both ate a lot of toast. A convenience, but even more so, perfect when there was no motivation to prepare anything else. He recognised the feeling about himself. The living room was just as cluttered as the kitchen. Washing hung from the back of the chairs, a racing form guide lay on the floor, and an empty beer bottle teetered on the edge of a side table. The man did not attempt to clear anything, merely motioning for Finney to sit down wherever he could find space to do so.

He had identified himself as a policeman, but Cecil Rivers still asked him how he was acquainted with his son.

'Were you his friend,' he asked as he looked up from his coffee. Joey had mentioned to his father he had a mate in the police force. One of the good guys he had said.

'It was you, wasn't it?

'Well, I guess you could describe me as a friend,' Finney replied. 'I knew him for over six months. We caught up occasionally. He mentioned he was trying to get an apprenticeship as a carpenter.'

'He was always good with his hands,' said the father. 'When he was little, he'd help me around the house. Odd jobs, fixing things, you know. He was a good lad, helpful and kind. A bad crowd it was, back then though. We lived near Liverpool in the housing commission area. It was rough. He fell in with some bad kids and that was it. He can't have been more than twelve or thirteen. Next thing, he's stealing cars and breaking into houses. It broke our hearts, it did.'

'I know he had regrets about that time in his life,' said Finney. 'He was a good lad though, as you say. Joey wanted to make things right. He was helping us with our inquiries.'

They sat in silence.

Suddenly, and without warning, the man's expression changed. He had been slumped in the armchair, clutching his coffee. Suddenly he sat bolt upright. He glared at his visitor.

'Was he dobbing on the drug dealers,' the father asked. 'Were you paying him? That's why they knocked him, isn't it?' His face was flushed red, and his hands trembled. 'Well, was it,' he demanded. 'Did those low lives kill him because he was ratting them out?'

'Joey was trying to get clear of the drugs,' Finney explained. " He was doing well. He had a part-time job, even going to the gym and working out. He felt guilty about the hurt he had caused you and the rest of the family. It was his way of trying to make up for some of the mistakes he had made.'

'Bullshit,' the father shouted, 'you hung him out to dry. Get the fuck out of my house.'

This had been a bad idea. It was time to go. The old man followed him down the hallway and out into the front garden, shouting and waving his arms. Finney could see him in the rear-view mirror, shaking his fist in the air, as he drove away.

He brooded all the way back to the city. What did he think he would achieve by going out to visit the father? Joey Rivers was a junkie, and he had exploited him. Sure, like most junkies, Joey wanted to get clean. He had been to rehab and been ok for a short while, but as soon as he hooked up with his old friends he tumbled back down.

He had grown up in Liverpool, in Sydney's western suburbs in the late '90s. He was twelve when he first tried meth, and by fifteen, he was a drug mule for the gangs. He got his dope for free, but it kept him out of school. From there, he moved to Surry Hills, close to the city centre. But not the glamorous side with high-end fusion restaurants, trendy bars, cafes, and three-million-dollar terrace houses. Joey was in the public housing zone but being cheek-by-jowl with the well-healed residents made burglary and car theft very convenient.

By the age of seventeen, he had been in and out of youth detention for house-breaking and bag snatching. At his hearing, the judge had given him a chance. Go to rehab and stay out of trouble for two years and you will avoid a prison sentence. Joey followed the advice, mostly because he feared adult prison more than anything else. When he did come out of rehab he went to live in a small country town three hours from Sydney. His counsellor had stressed the importance of staying away from his old friends. His junkie friends. It worked for about six months.

Of course, Joey had to visit his parents, and when he did, he was just too close to old friends. It was part curiosity and part challenge. I can do this, he told himself, I can visit friends and still stay out of trouble. I'm clean and sober and strong, he told himself. Turns out, like many of his contemporaries, he wasn't. He never went back to Bathurst, even to collect his belongings. He never went back to say goodbye to the host family who had helped keep him clean and even given him a job in their commercial bakery. He just walked away and soon enough he was back in Surrey Hills, selling packets of meth, stealing cars, and breaking into houses. And sure enough, soon enough, he was in prison. The big house. As a scrawny little freak, barely 70kg, he was a soft target in prison. After the first few weeks of beatings and bullying from the hard men, he settled into a routine of running errands and cultivating protectors. He did at least have some survival instincts. He also made some useful criminal contacts to use on the outside and once released went into a more intentional criminal enterprise, but things soon came unstuck and when he was busted yet again, he made the deal with Finney. Six months later he was dead.

The deal was simple. Joey would provide names, places, and dates. Who was moving the drugs, when they were moving them, and from where? It all sounded so simple, but Joey was taking big risks. Finney knew if Joey was caught, the consequences would be serious. The problem was Joey's brain was addled from years of drug abuse and his memory was vague, at best. So, Joey started writing notes on his phone. When Joey was discovered dead in the dumpster, it was taped to his bare chest just under where Finney's phone number had been carved into it.

There was not enough evidence to arrest anyone, so the operation was shut down and abandoned. It had been deemed a failure and the blame sheeted home to Finney, and he knew it was his responsibility. He had let the boy down as well as his colleagues. All that effort for nothing.

As he headed back into the city, his thoughts turned to Ella again. How could he steer her clear of the drugs, boys, and the pain of growing up? He realised how little he knew of her life. Who her friends were, what she thought about, and what got her excited and motivated. He also needed a plan to manage Charles Drayton, the new Dad.

Sarah had hinted she and Charles might be buying their own house together. He had a house in Rosebay, the smart side of town. It wasn't big enough for the three of them, but he wanted to move back to the eastern suburbs. If that happened, Finney figured, he would see even less of Ella than he did now. He concluded he really could not object. He and Sarah had been separated for a long time, and she deserved some happiness. It was not about Sarah; it was about Ella. That was what hurt the most. He felt his blood pressure rising. Not for the first time, he promised himself he would try harder to spend more time with her.

The Big Mango

When his phone rang at 4 am on Saturday morning he knew it could only be bad news. Sleep-deprived and in a fog of vodka, cigarettes, and house music, he tried to sound sober. 'Finney, get down here right now,' and the phone went dead. This was all he needed. DCI Peter Burrows, having a last shot at taking him down. He tried to think of what he might have done. He had kept a low profile and his head down over the past two weeks since the incident with Jane Gordon. What could I have done? His brain wasn't functioning. He would find out soon enough.

Showered and dressed, but barely sober, it was best to take a cab to headquarters. It was still dark across the city and the night shift of police officers were attending to paperwork and looking forward to breakfast followed by sleep. He had never adjusted to the 'graveyard' shift, as it was known, and was relieved when his promotion to detective sergeant meant he rarely ever had to do it again.

Burrows looked like he'd also had a rough night. With large bags under his eyes, he looked like he had done the night shift himself. 'Sit down and listen closely,' he barked. 'I've had Sir William Gordon calling me on and off for the past three hours. His daughter is missing, and he wants you to find her. God knows why,' he went on 'if only he knew what a degenerate and a disgrace to this force you are. But you made an impression on him, so here we are. What is it with you,' Burrows continued, 'I can't seem to get you out of my hair. I should have sacked you when I had the chance.'

Finney began to speak but Burrows cut him off. 'I said listen closely. The daughter is in Thailand and hasn't been heard of for several days. She is up north somewhere in a place called Chiang Mai. They've had a tracker on her phone, and it went dead a couple of days ago. No action on the credit card, no calls, and no emails. The parents are beside themselves. Personally, I think she is probably just having fun somewhere, probably stoned off her head, especially now the Thais have decriminalized weed, and are selling it everywhere. You've met the parents and probably understand what they're like. You're a parent yourself right Finney? Anyway, either way, you're going to Thailand today. I think we've got you on a flight around 4:00 pm. A car will pick you up at midday. Are you still at that dump in Newtown?'

Shocked and lost for words, he blurted out, 'Thailand, and why me?'

Burrows simply stared at him, 'for some strange reason they want you on this case,' he said. 'I don't know why but it gets you out of here for a while and gives me a chance to work out what the hell I'll do with you, Finney. For the time being Thailand is far enough away and will do just fine. I've organised someone to be your liaison with the Department of Foreign Affairs and Trade. You will be dealing with them. As of 4 pm today you are officially on secondment to them so you will not be my problem. Are we clear?'

He nodded, still in shock and not knowing how to respond.

'Needless to say,' said Burrows, 'if you fuck this up you are finished. Part of me is hoping you will. In all seriousness, get his girl back here and get her back fast. This is Bill Gordon you are dealing with. Don't let him down or you will regret it. And one last thing, get some decent clothes to wear, for Christ's sake. Get out of my sight.'

Before he had time to ask any further questions, he was being ushered out of Burrows' office. His head was spinning, dawn was just breaking outside, and he felt like he had been up for days. He went to his desk to think. He opened his laptop and just stared at it. Eventually, he logged in and opened Google. Weather in Thailand, visa to Thailand, drugs in Thailand. He searched Google Maps for Chiang Mai.

Why am I bothering with any of this, he thought. Jane Gordon will turn up safe and well before I get on the plane. By now it was nearly 7 am. He found his way to the regular coffee shop around the corner, ordered a double espresso, and grabbed a seat in a quiet corner. He sent a text to his colleague Stacey Harmer. **Meet me for coffee - the usual place.**

The reply came quickly, **I'll be there in half an hour.** By the time Stacey Harmer arrived, he was on his second cup of coffee and was in the process of devouring a bacon and egg roll. He was feeling better but still very confused.

'You look like shit, have you been on the booze again,' she said. 'What's with junk food this early in the morning?

'Great to see you too Detective Constable Harmer. I may have had a late night, but I also had a very early morning.'

His colleague alternated between laughter and disbelief as he related the story to her. 'You should see this as a great opportunity,' she said, 'you get to escape from office politics and have a paid holiday at the same time. What's not to like? Thailand is cool.'

They parted with an awkward hug. 'Just see it as an opportunity to have a break, to have some time to think and reflect,' she repeated.

'I'll do my best,' he said, and they went their separate ways.

As he walked away, he remembered the parent-teacher evening, scheduled for Monday, two days away. Oh, Christ, he thought, Sarah will be furious, and this is another opportunity for Charles Drayton to step up and be Dad. He made the call, and he was right, she was furious.

She simply did not believe him. 'Who is it,' she asked. 'Who are you going to Thailand with? A little holiday? Is it anyone I know?' It was pointless to argue with her, so he sat quietly on the other end of the phone until she finished.

'Listen, Sarah, I know it sounds ridiculous, but it is the truth. I'm sorry. I'll get back as quickly as I can.'

'I do believe you, and only because this is just the crazy shit that seems to happen to you. You just attract trouble and complications. Why can't you just be like everybody else? Just be normal. So, I may as well tell you this now. Ella, Charles, and I are moving. I've talked to Ella about it, and she is fine. She and Charles get along well. He's been offered a partnership in the company, and they want him to go and manage one of the international offices. The destination hasn't been finalized yet, but it will be one of the Southeast Asia offices. It will be either Singapore or Hong Kong. It's a promotion. Ella and I will move at the end of the school year in December,' she said. 'So, it's not like we are moving immediately. I'll let you know the details. So, I guess we will talk again when you get back from your holiday. Take your time, you always have,' and she ended the call without a goodbye.

He knew it would always be like this with Sarah. She had made a successful career for herself as a lawyer in the Attorney-General's department. Sarah was always popular, with a sharp intellect and desire to succeed. She was all the things he wasn't, and now she had Charles Drayton by her side. The perfect couple. It was too much to process at the moment, on top of everything else which had occurred during the day. A call to Ella during this weekend wouldn't work. He knew she had friends staying over. It would have to be a text. It was hard to see how the day could get any worse.

He didn't have much time. The first thing he realised was he didn't even have a proper suitcase or even some clean clothes. He had no laundry at home and did his washing at a local laundromat. He headed to the nearest department store and purchased himself a suitcase, three collared shirts, and a pair of trousers. Everything else he might need he figured he could get when he arrived.

Returning to Munni Street, Finney emptied his recently stocked fridge into a garbage bag, closed and locked his windows, and made a perfunctory attempt to tidy his small apartment before packing his suitcase with his recent acquisitions. He had credit cards and some cash and no real idea of what else he should have; other than the briefing notes he had been given earlier that morning. The morning, which began with a phone call at 4 am., now felt like a lifetime ago.

There was a knock on his door right at noon. It was the taxi driver. 'Can I help you with your bags?' The man was heavily accented, perhaps from somewhere in the sub-continent. Passing his bag to the driver, he turned and looked around the apartment. Lights off, fridge emptied, lock the door. He felt like there should be more to do before leaving and more to carry. He had a small daypack with the briefing notes, his favourite notebook, and an over-ripe banana. My life in a bag, he thought. Pathetic really.

'Traveling anywhere special today sir,' the driver enquired.

'I'm heading to Bangkok.'

'Business or pleasure?'

'It's a work trip,' he said, indicating in his tone he didn't want a conversation. This was not his usual style. Finney was a talker. He liked friendly banter and did it well. Not today. He was trying to work out if he could fit in a call to Ella before he left. How would he find his contact at Sydney Airport? He couldn't check in without a passport. Too many things on his mind to engage in small talk with the driver.

One advantage of living in Newtown was the short distance to Sydney International Airport. It had been years since he had been near the airport, he barely recognized it. It was a giant construction site. The drop-off area adjacent to the terminal was a jumble of taxis, buses, Ubers, and private vehicles. His headache was getting worse.

Without valid travel documents, a temporary diplomatic passport had been arranged. Since the 'gap year' trip resulting in his marriage to Sarah and the birth of their daughter, he had never travelled overseas again. Finney had always planned to travel but something always got in the way. So, the trip to Thailand was also bittersweet as it was a place of happy memories. A tumult of intense emotional love and lust. Technically Bangkok was a stopover before the real trip to find Jane Gordon began.

There was to be a meeting with the Australian Federal Police at the Australian Embassy in Bangkok and no doubt plenty of advice from the foreign affairs experts. Sitting up in the members' lounge at the airport, he was still coming to terms with the pace of his deployment. One minute he was persona non grata in the department and likely to be pensioned off, the next he was a hometown hero being sent on a special mission.

The bespeckled young man seated next to him was a junior staffer from the Department of Foreign Affairs and Trade (DFAT). He had been waiting at the check-in counter. Finney didn't even catch his name. He handed the shiny new passport and a file of materials to Finney. The files included photocopies of Jane Gordon's passport and a background profile but very little else.

'Is this it,' asked Finney.

The young man nodded. 'There will be an embassy staff member there to meet you at Bangkok airport. You will be given a full briefing at the Australian embassy tomorrow morning.' The meeting was over, and the young man left.

By the time he'd checked in, navigated passport control and security, and finished his briefing, it was 3:15 p.m. No time to call Ella. Once again, his personal life was on hold, or had he just let it slip away, as always?

As he boarded the flight to Bangkok, exhaustion weighed heavily on him, uncertainty gnawing at his nerves. But he was caught off guard, pleasantly surprised to find himself seated at the pointy end of the plane, in business class. Two seats to himself, a cool towel, and a glass of champagne were offered to him as he settled in. Accepting the cool towel he declined the champagne. After the previous night's overindulgence, the thought of alcohol turned his stomach, and the reality of what lay ahead was beginning to sink in.

He looked around him at his fellow travellers and felt out of place, but he was just too exhausted to care. As the plane set off, he pondered what might have been. He concluded that this was an opportunity for a clean break, to get himself straight, to get himself sober, to think about the future.

'Off to Bangers eh, so is this work or pleasure,' the voice said.

Startled from his thoughts, he looked across the aisle at the man sitting opposite.

Clad in an ill-fitting suit, he was in his mid-fifties, his glowing red nose betraying years of heavy drinking. Overweight and with the weary air of a seasoned traveller, he looked like someone who'd seen too many miles and too many drinks.

'Just a quick work trip,' said Finney, who was yet to craft his final back story.

'So, who are you with,' said the man.

He paused, he wasn't about to admit to being a police officer, and certainly not with this stranger anyway. 'Oh, I'm with the state government,' he said, 'we're just doing a little bit of trade work up there.'

'So, are you a regular visitor to Bangkok,' the man continued, eager for conversation.

'Well, I have been there before, but I wouldn't say I'm a regular visitor. Just excuse me for a moment if you would, I just need the bathroom.' It was his way of getting out of the conversation before it even began. He stood up and moved towards the galley where two flight attendants were deeply engaged in giggly chatter.

'Bathroom,' he asked.

'Just on your right sir,' said one of the flight attendants, before going back to her conversation. Taking a moment in the cramped space to compose himself, he decided the full backstory would have to wait. For the time being he would just avoid conversations until he got to his destination. Emerging from the bathroom and stopping again at the galley, he requested a soda water.

'Certainly, sir,' said the chirpy hostess. 'I'll bring it to your seat.'

Sliding into his seat Finney immediately grabbed the headphones and put them on. He had no intention of watching a movie. This was simply a strategy to put an end to the conversation with his travelling companion. It worked. He was reminded of a movie he had seen many years before, The Accidental Tourist. The lead character Macon Leary had said when travelling one should, *Always bring a book, as protection against strangers.* If only I'd done that, he thought.

He didn't know how long he had been asleep but a gentle nudge from the air hostess brought him back to consciousness. 'Please put your seat back in the upright position, sir' she muttered, 'we will be landing in Bangkok shortly.' Soon after it was the pilot who came on the intercom, and it was his turn to give a running commentary. What was it about air travel with constant updates and notifications? You are driving the plane, just get me there safely, he grumbled to himself. There was also the weather update, 34 degrees centigrade, humid, with occasional showers. It was late September, smack in the middle of the wet season. On his last visit to Thailand, Finney had been mightily impressed with the power of the monsoon storms. He was looking forward to re-acquainting himself with these amazing downpours.

As he stepped off the plane onto the gangway, he had a moment swooning at the cocktail of aromas. The aviation fuel mixed with air freshener, perfumes wafting from the duty-free stores, and of course the collective body smells of his three hundred-plus travelling companions, as they shuffled herd-like towards the immigration counters.

The airport in Bangkok was immense, with an almost one-kilometre walk from the plane to the immigration counter. Like most new airports, it was full of overpriced duty-free stores, designer labels and shops selling fridge magnets and souvenirs. He was tempted to buy some duty-free hard liquor. Vodka. Common sense and fatigue got the better of him and he ploughed blissfully towards the sullen officials at the immigration counter. The Land of Smiles indeed.

Standing to one side he saw the Australian Embassy staffer first. The welcoming committee. The man was not holding a sign with Finney's name on it, but he knew who he was looking for. They made eye contact, and he was pulled aside and fast-tracked through immigration. Some small benefits, he thought, as he looked back at the snaking line of arrivals waiting to be processed.

It was 10.30 pm in Bangkok. Despite his fatigue, Finney felt invigorated to be back in the Big Mango. It had been more than fifteen years, but the memories were there, partly stored in his olfactory senses. The sights and sounds added to the familiarity. The traffic had, however, become worse. The black van with heavily tinted windows hurtled along the expressway, to begin with, and then exited into suburban streets and heavy traffic.

As they weaved their way through the back streets, Finney realised his life in Sydney was monochrome and suddenly everything was in technicolour. The streets were dotted with vendors selling all manner of foods. There were clusters of chairs and tables with patrons tucking into bowls of steaming noodle soup, satay sticks, fried noodles, and more. Gaudy fairy lights were draped around the stalls, and lamps illuminated the fold-up tables. The patrons were a mix of working people, either heading to or from their jobs and revellers who, after a few drinks, needed to fill their stomachs before making their way home.

This was Saturday night in Bangkok. The streets thronged with people. Pop-up markets lined the sidewalks while flashing neon lights signalled bars, clubs, discos, and restaurants, catering to every budget. Bangkok nightlife was the stuff of legend, but his experience had been limited to some timid bar visits in the backpacker's haven of Khaosan Road with Sarah all those years ago. Back then they did not need late nights in dance clubs, they had each other.

He was brought back to reality when he realised his companion had been talking the entire time. Richard Hanlon was part of a dynasty at The Department of Foreign Affairs and Trade, simply known as DFAT. His father had been ambassador in Malaysia years earlier and now his son was back in the region as a junior political officer. To say he was unimpressed at having to play minder to Finney was an understatement. But when you got an order from the Governor of New South Wales, you did as you were told.

By the time he was checking into his hotel, Jane Gordon was huddled under a makeshift shelter, shivering in the cold as rain hammered down on the corrugated metal roof. The girls around her sobbed softly, their fear palpable in the damp air. Nearby, their captors were drinking heavily and playing cards, their laughter cutting through the otherwise quiet night.

There was nowhere to run. The darkness outside was impenetrable, the kind that rendered an escape impossible. Jane glanced at the small portion of cold rice with a few scraps of fried pork they'd been given—the first food they'd had in over twenty-four hours. She forced herself to swallow a few bites, knowing she'd need strength to survive, but the pit in her stomach wasn't from hunger. It was the realization that no one was coming to save her.

Back in Bangkok, Finney was told to expect a driver to pick him up at 6 am. He had already been checked into the Intercontinental Hotel in Chidlom, Central Bangkok. It was three blocks from the Australian Embassy and better than any hotel in which he had ever stayed. The porter insisted on carrying his bag and then providing a full room tour, pointing out the location of light switches, USB charging ports, wardrobes, and all the features of the audio-visual system. There was an awkward silence as the porter waited expectantly by the door for a tip. I am sorry, Finney stuttered, I've no Thai money as he handed him a $10 note, in Australian currency. The boy smiled, grateful for the tip, which was triple what guests usually gave, albeit in a different currency.

He slumped on the edge of the bed, trying to take stock of his situation. Yesterday, he'd been stuck in limbo, his superiors unable to decide his fate. Now, he was in another country, holed up in a 6-star hotel, wearing a fresh set of clothes, with no idea what came next. International travel had never been his thing, and the disorienting fog of the long-haul flight clouded his thoughts. After more than nine cramped hours on the plane, he was tired and irritable. It was nearly midnight in Bangkok and 3 a.m. in Sydney. His body was gearing up for the day, but he desperately needed sleep.

He need not have worried. Fully clothed, he nodded off in seconds.

Finney awoke, having slept fitfully, like a man with a guilty conscience. His head was fuzzy, and his limbs were stiff. Despite having slept only four hours, the anticipation of his assignment soon sharpened his concentration. He knew a crash would come and he would need to sleep, but not just yet. He showered and was ready to go, well before his early morning call. He descended to the lobby at 5.50 am and waited for the driver to appear. It was then he realised he didn't know the driver's name or the type of car. It did not matter, the driver was already there and moved towards him as he exited the elevator.

A different vehicle and driver had picked him up from the airport the night before. Dawn was just breaking, and it was already hotter than he could remember. The city looked different in daylight; it was less forgiving. Like most places, it was prettier at night, the darkness masking everyday grit, grime, and monotony. Street sweepers were at work, garbage trucks lumbering along, collecting the debris left behind. Delivery trucks, heavy with fruits, vegetables, and livestock, rumbled past the early commuters. For a Sunday morning, it appeared very busy.

'We are not far from the embassy,' said the driver. They were at their destination in less than fifteen minutes.

The old Australian Embassy in South Sathorn Rd. had been replaced by a newly built fortress in Wireless Rd. five years earlier. It was tucked away quietly on a side street behind the Embassy of Japan. Further along the street was the much larger U.S. Embassy. The security gates gave way to a building comprised of a maze of lockable sections clad in bland brown bricks. It was state-of-the-art, but it had a brutal coldness about it which was so common in modernist architecture. Despite having won several design awards, Finney thought it looked like a five-story toilet block with tinted windows. The building had little connection to its surroundings and appeared as if it had been lowered into place without any consideration of the surrounding neighborhood. He understood the need for security, especially after 9/11. There had been bombings at Australian embassies, including in Jakarta, but he still wondered whether some more aesthetic features could have landed it more sympathetically into the landscape. Fortress Australia had spread to Bangkok.

Roger Clifton-Blythe, the Australian Ambassador, was old school. Even at 6.30 am on a Sunday, he was sharp and immaculately turned out. Gold cufflinks, monogrammed shirtsleeves, and a classic tie in navy and grey. All wrapped up in a double-breasted, tailored suit. He smelled of expensive after-shave, private schooling, and privilege. He was endowed with patrician good looks, and deep olive skin and oozed a natural charm that put you dangerously at ease.

'Please, Detective Finney, can we get you some breakfast, tea, or coffee,' the ambassador asked. 'Malee,' the ambassador instructed his assistant, 'please get our guest a pot of coffee if you would. We've got some intelligence which may be of use to you. I've asked our Senior AFP officers in the embassy to provide you with a detailed briefing.' He turned to a man who had stood silently near the door of the room. 'This is Barton Guthrie, our most senior AFP man here in Bangkok. The man, in his early fifties, was lean and well-built. He had the physique of a man who regularly visited a gym. Ex-military, with a close-cropped hair cut to match. He had steely grey eyes that made no effort to look at Finney, nor did he move to shake his hand.

Where is Barry Quinn,' the ambassador said, directing the question to Guthrie.

'He is on his way,' Guthrie replied, 'stuck in traffic.'

'What, at this early hour on a Sunday morning,' the ambassador scoffed. 'We will have to start without him. This is an important mission, but it must be kept top secret. We have no jurisdiction for such an endeavour and cannot afford to upset the Thais. If you don't appreciate the difficulties, then let me spell them out for you.'

Clifton-Blythe then went on to reiterate what he had been told before leaving Sydney. Technically, this was a matter for the Royal Thai Police, but unless someone was willing to shell out a hefty sum, this was just another backpacker who had smoked too much weed and temporarily dropped off the radar. The Thai Police had little incentive to follow up on this case.

What the AFP had been able to piece together so far was that Jane Gordon had been sightseeing in Chiang Mai and joined up with a group of young American Peace Corps volunteers. What neither the AFP nor Jane Gordon knew was the quiet young man named Jessie, who kept to himself, had been secretly crossing the border into Shan State in Myanmar to meet with the rebel freedom fighters. He had been interviewing them and posting stories, under an assumed name, on an online news site. Finney, unsure how they had gathered this intelligence in such a short space of time, was impressed with what they knew.

As the door opened and his coffee arrived, so did Inspector Barry Quinn. Ruddy-faced, overweight, and looking like he'd had a late night, Quinn apologized to Clifton-Blythe for his lateness. Helping himself to coffee he barely looked at the man from Sydney. As the ambassador did the introductions, Quinn didn't bother to shake Finney's outstretched hand. So, that's how it's going to be, he thought. Alerted by a colleague in Sydney he would be working with Quinn, Finney had done some discreet homework through a friend. Quinn had been in Bangkok for three years already and achieved very little. He was posted to work closely with the DEA from the U.S. Embassy. The rumour was he and his pals from the DEA in Bangkok spent most of their time in bars in the red-light district on Silom Rd, known as Patpong. They rarely bothered to leave Bangkok.

Barry Quinn offered a perfunctory briefing. Jane Gordon's parents had not heard from her for several days, which wasn't unusual. What was strange was there had been no activity on her credit cards during this time, leaving the parents anxious. They had sent numerous text messages and emails, with no response. Discreet inquiries had been made at her last known accommodation, a guesthouse in Chiang Mai. The AFP, with the help of the Australian Consul in Chiang Mai, had been able to determine she had checked out with the Americans and taken a bus to Mae Sai, on the Thai-Myanmar border. There had been no contact since.

Finney was starting to fade and lose concentration. He was jolted back to the present as the ambassador stood from his desk. He was issuing instructions to Barry Quinn to accompany Finney to Chiang Mai as soon as possible. It was clear Quinn wanted nothing to do with Finney, the case, and most of all a trip to Chiang Mai. Despite this, Quinn knew he had no choice. He glared across toward his colleague, Bart Guthrie, who nodded at him as if to say, *do as you are told.*

'This is the daughter of the Governor of New South Wales, let's find her,' said the ambassador as he walked out the door, leaving the men to share an uneasy silence.

'Fuck this,' said Quinn, staring at Finney, 'it looks like I'm your babysitter.'

It was just Quinn, Guthrie and Finney in the room now.

'Let's face it,' said Guthrie, 'she will turn up soon enough, maybe even before you get to Chiang Mai. Keep your fingers. If not, as the boss said, don't come back without her.'

Finney nodded.

Now it was Quinn's turn to rant. 'Come on Bart, this is a waste of our time, and you know it.'

Guthrie shook his head, 'I'm sorry Barry but my hands are tied. I suggest you two get yourselves up to Chiang Mai as quickly as possible.' Turning to face Finney, pointing at him and in a menacing tone he said, 'I've heard bad things about you. Don't mess this up or your career is over this time.'

He was ferried back to his hotel to retrieve his bags before making his way to the airport for the onward trip to Chiang Mai. Quinn would meet him at the airport.

It was nearing 8 am when they arrived back at the hotel. 'No hurry,' said the driver, 'your flight is at lunchtime. We can leave at 10 am.' Finney was overwhelmed by the number of tourists in the lobby as he made his way to the hotel's coffee shop. With almost four hundred rooms it was little wonder it was busy. Caffeine, he longed for caffeine and plenty of it. He also needed to load up his SIM card provided to him by Marlee, the ambassador's trusty assistant. Having done so he made a call to Ella.

'Hey Sweetie,' he said, as she answered the call.

'Dad! Where are you? Mum said you went overseas somewhere,' she squealed into the phone.

'I'm in Bangkok and I'm sorry I couldn't call you before I left, it was all very rushed.'

'It's all good Dad. Hey, can you bring me back some of those elephant pants like the ones Mum has?

He remembered the cotton pants from all those years ago. Every backpacker was wearing them and of course, Sarah had bought several pairs. Was she still really wearing them after all these years? 'Of course, I can Sweetie, he said, any particular colour?'

'One blue, one green. Would it be OK Dad? And some of funky silver jewellery. That would be so cool.'

'Sure, Sweetie, can I talk to you about this move your Mum is planning? How are you feeling about it?'

'I'm going to miss my friends,' she said. 'Mum says I'll make friends over there. I'm not even sure where we are going but wherever it is I think it will be OK. It's not until the end of the year anyway, I'll think about it then.'

He paused before speaking again, knowing he had to be careful. Anything he said would go back to Sarah and the retelling would be distorted. He couldn't afford it. So, he said nothing more about the move.

'So, it's just the elephant pants and some jewellery? I'm not sure how long I'll be over here. It might only be a couple of days. You can get me on this number,' he went on. 'Can you see the number on your phone there?'

'Sure Dad, I can see the number,' she said.

He could sense he had lost her attention already. Talking over the phone wasn't their thing. Ella preferred text messaging. It's the generation, Sarah had said, don't take it personally.

They ended their call. Despondent, he knew it was a losing battle. Sarah would be taking Ella to live overseas and there was nothing he could do about it. All he could hope for was not to antagonize Sarah any further. He sat and watched the movement of hotel guests, many tourists, businesspeople, and locals using the space for early morning meetings. The staff moved easily among the guests, taking orders, serving coffee, and cleaning tables. They glided around the room with pasted-on smiles and endless patience. He had no appetite and had declined the offer of a full buffet breakfast. 'It is included in your room rate,' the waiter said. Finney shook his head.

Having repacked his bag, he made his way to the cavernous lobby where he saw the driver hovering nearby. As he climbed into the van two marked police cars pulled up adjacent to them. One of the officers spoke to Finney's driver. Once in the vehicle, the driver informed him they had a police escort to the airport. One police car pulled in front of the van, the other behind it, both with flashing lights and sirens. By the time they exited the hotel, the traffic had thickened to the point of gridlock. Even with the convoy and using the expressways it still took almost two hours to drive thirty kilometres to their destination. They had less than thirty minutes till their plane departed. Finney was panicking but the driver was relaxed. 'The plane won't leave without you and Mr Quinn,' he said, with a broad grin on his face.

Quinn was standing by the curb with the ambassador's assistant, Marlee. How the hell did they get here so fast, he wondered, without asking. It was simple, Quinn drove like a maniac and Marlee had taken a motorbike taxi. When they boarded the plane, ten minutes after its scheduled departure time, it was full, with all the other passengers already seated and buckled in. The driver was right, they wouldn't leave without them. Phone calls had been made; the plane had been delayed accommodating the two VIP travellers.

Barry Quinn had started his career in the fraud squad, then graduated into the drug squad. Both squads had dubious reputations, and he could see Quinn had fitted in just fine. He was a man's man who liked to drink, had burnt through three marriages, and left a trail of kids and disappointment along the way. He had however made a couple of big arrests and enjoyed the patronage of several highflyers in the boy's club of the Australian Federal Police. He was only in his early forties and five years older than Finney, but years of hard living had him looking more like his late fifties. As he glanced across the aisle at his travelling companion, he saw a glimpse of what his future might be. He didn't like what he saw.

The Rose of The North

There to meet them at the airport was their driver from the previous evening. His name was Banjob, but Quinn had insisted on referring to him as Mr. BJ. The driver knew he was the butt of a joke but chose to ignore it with quiet dignity. The driver took care of their bags with practised efficiency and ushered them into the back of the van. 'There's cold water there for you,' said Banjob, gesturing to the bottles in the cup holders. 'I was also advised to get you one of these,' he said, passing over a new mobile phone. Fully charged with internet access and overseas calls, Finney nodded in appreciation, knowing this would make it easier to stay in touch with his daughter, provided she chose to pick up the phone. He could now discard the cheap SIM he had in his phone. As the van pulled away from the airport, he glanced at the driver through the rearview mirror. Something was reassuring about the driver's calm and steady presence, a small relief amid so much strangeness.

They travelled in silence until they reached the Honorary Consul's house on the outskirts of Chiang Mai. It was only 2 pm but it was clear the Australian Honorary Consul in Chiang Mai already had one or two drinks behind him. Finney remembered reading an article about the place of alcohol in expat life, especially in Asia. Expats were at high risk when it came to alcoholism. Maybe booze helped take the edge off culture shock or so much business networking and socializing included alcohol. Whatever it was, it was real, and he was about to see it firsthand.

Jamie Owens had been living in Chiang Mai for a decade. Married to a local Thai woman, he had spent his life working on oil rigs all over the world. He had been described as a '*knockabout kind of bloke'*. His sentences were peppered with expletives, and he had one of those permanent suntans, with wrinkled, leathery skin. He spoke with a broad Australian accent, reflecting his childhood growing up in a small town in rural Western Australia. Dressed in shorts and a T-shirt he was hardly the typical diplomat profile. Despite ten years of living in Thailand, he couldn't speak a word of Thai and so consequently spoke an annoying form of pidgin English to his wife. For some reason, he chose to speak the same way to the two AFP officers.

Jamie Owens insisted they both have a drink. Finney declined a gin and tonic or even a beer and opted for water. Quinn, on the other hand, happily accepted the offer of a cold beer. It was obvious their host enjoyed having an audience. Owens launched into a monologue, primarily comprised of criticisms of Thailand and the Thais themselves. 'The place is organised chaos,' said Owens, 'but somehow it still seems to work. The cops and most government officials are corrupt, and the people are bloody lazy. I blame it on the school system here,' he drawled on. 'It's all marching up and down each day in uniform and doing what you're told. Nobody can think for themselves.'

Quinn sat in his chair, sipping beer, and nodding in agreement with their host.

'So why do you live here,' asked Finney.

'Well, Mate,' said the consul, 'I can't live in Oz anymore, it's become a nanny state. The taxes are too high, and I hate all that bloody political correctness. Besides, it's cheaper over here and the women are good-looking.' He glanced over and winked at his wife, who sat quietly in the corner. 'The missus is a northern girl, so I thought we'd give it a go here in Chiang Mai,' he said. A northern girl, suffering in silence, thought Finney.

He tried to get him back on the topic of the missing girl, Jane Gordon. 'Have you heard anything at all about her,' he asked.

'Nothing at all Mate. These kids, you know they do many silly thing for no reason. They take drug, they ride motorbike. Ride motorbike in Thailand, very dangerous you know.' Jamie Owens rambled on in his annoying Pidgin English and provided very little useful intelligence.

What were the qualifications to become an Honorary Consul? This man was clearly a drunk, knew very little about what was going on here in Thailand, and was probably not a very good representative for his own country. He felt relieved as they left after a brief and unhelpful conversation.

The next stop was the VIYA Lodge Guest House where Jane Gordon had been staying before she disappeared. It was in the Old Quarter of Chiang Mai, which was surrounded by a moat, built centuries earlier, to keep out the marauding Burmese, and it was a mecca for backpackers and flashpackers alike. It was a crisp, and modern-looking two-story shophouse. Downstairs was the reception and coffee shop occupied by young travellers exchanging travel stories. The reception in the other corner was occupied by two young Thai women. They both looked like they should be at school, such was their youthfulness, but they were probably married with children and ten years of work experience behind them.

The older of the two, identified as Pat by her name tag, stood up and greeted the men with a Thai *wai.* The clasping of both hands in front of the face seemed universal in Thailand but Finney had a feeling it was a very complicated protocol. Unsure of the etiquette and following Quinn's lead, he did not reciprocate. Rather, he introduced himself and outlined the reason for their visit. This put Miss Pat immediately on the defensive. In a halting and heavily accented tone, she explained how Jane had checked out of the guesthouse three days earlier in very good health and had planned to travel to the town of Mae Sai on the border with Myanmar.

According to the receptionist, Jane had left with two Peace Corps volunteers, Jessie Cheeseman and Chuck Bowers. Both had been in the region for quite some time and spoke excellent Thai. Jessie also spoke Burmese and had many Burmese friends in Chiang Mai and other places along the border. She also indicated she thought Jane and Jessie were more than just friends. They had all left together to catch a bus to Mae Sai.

Leaving the guesthouse, Barry Quinn was about to have his second meltdown of the day. 'Fuck this, there's no way I'm going to Mae Sai,' he blurted. 'Fucking shithole. Been there once and never again.'

Finney realised there was no use, and no need to argue with him. The ambassador's instructions had been clear. Find Jane Gordon and don't come back to Bangkok until you do. So, Finney suggested they find somewhere cool, have a drink, and take stock of what they knew so far.

Down the end of a tree-lined street, strewn with randomly parked motorbikes, the small café was part bar, part restaurant with a strange mix of old wooden furniture and tattered movie posters. There was no air conditioning but it was full of plants and fans, which somehow made it feel cooler. Finney ordered soda with lemon and Quinn ordered beer. Not a glass but a large bottle and a glass of ice to go with it. He explained this was a habit he had picked up in Thailand. It was so hot the beer needed ice, and lots of it, to keep it cold. Finney decided to take his word for it. Watching him gulp the whole glass in one go, he felt glad he had chosen soda. He figured Quinn would be next to useless for the rest of the day, having already consumed one large bottle of beer at the consul's house. He was right.

Quinn knocked back another three large Chang beers before Finney suggested they visit the bus station to see if there were witnesses to the departure of Jane Gordon and her friends to Mae Sai.

Quinn simply shook his head; 'you are on your own with this one pal,' he said. 'I might just have a couple more drinks here and stay hydrated. I'll see you back at the hotel. Off you go with BJ,' he said,' and I'll get a taxi.' and he waved them both away.

He felt immediately relaxed as they departed, leaving Quinn nursing his beer in the bar. In the van on the way to the bus station, he took the time to get acquainted with Banjob. He was a farm boy from the northern part of Thailand who landed a job as a low-level helper at the Australian Embassy in Bangkok some twenty years earlier. Realizing the opportunity, he made himself indispensable and was soon a driver reserved for visiting staff and other VIPs, as well as a handy translator.

So, you're from this part of the world, he asked.

'I'm a local, I think it is the correct expression,' said the driver.

While Finney and Quinn had flown to Chiang Mai, Banjob had set off in the early morning and driven the seven-hundred-kilometre trip in the van. He had been there ready to collect them when they arrived at the airport. He had taught himself English and spoke Burmese, his local dialect of Thai, and some Chinese. He was a quiet and reflective character who had an ease about him, simultaneously radiating both confidence and humility. But beneath that calm exterior was someone not to be underestimated, something Finney would learn firsthand soon enough.

The visit to the local bus station revealed very little. It was bustling and crowded with both Thais and foreigners, with buses going in all directions, some with air conditioning and some without. Nobody recalled seeing the trio, but they also made it clear there were so many tourists with the same profile they may well have passed through there unnoticed. Just another group of young backpackers, hard to distinguish one from another. Banjob suggested a visit to the local newspaper. He had contacts there who may be able to provide some useful information, he had said.

Walking into the offices of the Chiang Mai Times was like stepping back in time. The place shook with the clatter of printing presses and was full of cigarette smoke, mixed with ink chemicals. The smell of ink was to be expected, but the cigarette smoke was not. Thailand had strict laws banning smoking in workplaces, banks, bars, and restaurants. The laws were widely obeyed but not here in the newspaper office. Banjob was recognized immediately and greeted warmly. It was clear Banjob's contacts may turn out to be more valuable than his language skills.

They were ushered into a large meeting room, offered bottles of ice-cold water, and asked to wait. Banjob explained they were to meet with the editor and a journalist who covered news along the border with Myanmar. Shortly after, a battle-hardened journalist in his fifties and a young woman entered the room. Introductions were made and the group sat down at a large boardroom table, fashioned from local teak wood. The man, a heavily accented Thai national named Arun, spoke first.

'The word is you've lost the daughter of someone very important in Australia. Is that correct,' he said.

The man was straight to the point and Finney was caught off guard. He didn't want this kind of information circulated, especially after the warning from the ambassador in Bangkok to be discreet. Finney crafted a story which downplayed the gravity of their mission. They were simply keeping an eye out and trying to determine what Jane Gordon had been doing in Chiang Mai. They had some idea who she may be travelling with, and they may have gone onwards to Mae Sai.

'Come on, be honest,' said the grizzled-looking Thai journalist, 'do you want our help or not? I've got plenty of other things I could be doing.'

The journalist was prickly and slightly hostile, but they needed his help. 'This needs to remain confidential,' he said.

Arun made a gesture of sealing his lips.

'The girl we are looking for is the daughter of a prominent public official. To be honest we don't know if she is missing or if she has simply gone off the radar for a few days. We are trying to keep this investigation as low-key as possible and I would be grateful for any assistance that you can give us,' said Finney.

Arun let out a long, weary sigh. 'Have you any idea how many backpackers come through Chiang Mai every year?' He didn't wait for a response. 'Millions. And last year, our government, in all its wisdom, decided to legalize cannabis. Do you know what this has done to our tourism industry?' Arun's question was rhetorical. 'This law has created all sorts of problems. Now most of our news stories report foreigners doing stupid things while stoned out of their minds. I'm not saying that is what has happened to your friend Jane Gordon, but it may well have had something to do with it. It's certainly the response you will get from our police force. I think it's more about the company she's keeping. My sources tell me this current group of peace-core volunteers is getting a little bit too involved with what's happening across the border in Myanmar. I would start by looking there.' He stood up, signalling the end of the conversation. 'Good luck. If we hear anything I'll get back to you. In the meantime, have a chat with my colleague here, she is a little bit more tuned into this generation.'

As he left the room Arun shared a few words with Banjob, they both chuckled. These two men know each other well, thought Finney.

Introduced as Piraporn, the young woman spoke with an accent that appeared to have evolved in a British boarding school. 'Just call me Pip', she began. 'I know some of the group Jane was staying with in Chiang Mai. Jessie Cheeseman is well known as a guy with strong connections to the Burmese freedom fighters. He works closely with resistance groups here and along the border.' This was information they already had but it was obvious this young journalist might be helpful in finding Jane Gordon.

Pip described how Chiang Mai had long been a haven for Burmese dissidents. Generations of opposition figures from Myanmar had made the town their base. Newsletters were produced in Chiang Mai and there was even a Burmese language radio station. For years before the 2015 elections, the military had been flexing its muscle, trying to shut down dissenting voices in Chiang Mai but never quite succeeding. 'There are plenty of spies around,' she warned. Social media had made it so much harder for the military to silence dissent, but now they used other tactics. They targeted the families of dissidents still in Myanmar.

'There are also many illegal Burmese immigrants working in Chiang Mai,' said Pip. 'Go to any construction site or market and you will see what I mean. Likewise, most of the domestic workers are Burmese women. We joke about how we've been warring with our neighbours for a thousand years, but it's OK for them to come and help us raise our children.'

###

Leaving the newspaper office, Finney wanted to better understand the city of Chiang Mai. Despite his fatigue, he suggested Banjob take him on a short tour around town. It was late afternoon but there was still some daylight left. The driver began by taking him to the top of a nearby landmark, known as Doi Suthep. It was a lookout point near the newspaper office. As they made their way there Banjob provided more background on the city.

It was the capital city of the country's second-largest province, with a population of over a million people. Established in the 13th century, it had been the capital of the ancient Lanna Kingdom. They arrived at the viewpoint, exiting the vehicle Finney noted the large numbers of tourists. Banjob explained how this temple held strong religious significance for many Buddhists, not only Thais, and many made a pilgrimage here.

As they stood looking out over the city, Banjob pointed out various significant landmarks including Chiang Mai University which sat at the base of the mountain and then further away a large hospital, temples, schools, and markets. The city had grown along both sides of the Ping River, its banks dotted with restaurants and hotels. The driver also pointed to the airport on one side of the city and suggested that they should take a drive over there.

'I've already seen the airport,' said Finney.

'Look around the airport at all the construction sites,' said the driver, pointing at the many cranes in the area adjacent to the airport. 'We call the area Little Burma.'

'I'm in your hands,' he said, climbing back into the vehicle.

The traffic had started to get heavier, so Banjob veered off into the side streets.

'You seem to know your way around here quite well,' said Finney.

'After I finished school, I spent four years living in Chiang Mai.'

'That makes sense, so what did you do here for four years?'

'I studied electrical engineering at Chiang Mai University. It was the best four years of my life.'

'Hence your knowledge of the city and your network of contacts, Banjob?'

The driver nodded as they navigated their way through the traffic and out towards the airport. The houses thinned out and the quality of the road deteriorated. The traffic was now comprised of trucks, large and small. There were rows of tin shacks, with men milling around. Smoke rose from small fires and washing hung from makeshift clotheslines strung around the shacks. There were carts selling all manner of food, some prepared and sold in plastic boxes and some being cooked on portable stovetops and barbecues.

In the near distance, the construction site was in full swing. As the light faded, a multitude of spotlights illuminated scaffolding, neat stacks of building materials, and a long stretch of metal reinforcing encased in formwork readied for the arrival of a convoy of concrete trucks. It looked like a shift change had just taken place, with a column of men streaming back towards the tin sheds.

According to Banjob, the site was Chinese-owned and destined to be a row of about three hundred shophouses, retail on the ground floor and residential above. These, combined with a modest twenty-five thousand square meter shopping centre and a couple of hotels, were destined to service the nearby airport. It was part of a major expansion as the city geared up for the increasing number of Chinese tour groups arriving on charter flights.

Banjob parked the van adjacent to the tin shacks. The air was thick with dust from the building site, the smell of food, and diesel fumes from the gaggle of machinery operating not fifty meters away. The noise was deafening. Finney winced at the assault on his senses. Recognizing this, Banjob took his arm and led him into a small alleyway between the shacks. It was no more than two metres wide, but it was packed with even more people, food stalls, and vendors selling clothes and household products. It was only then he became aware there were whole families there. Children played in spaces between the shacks and chased each other through the laneways. It was bedlam.

He trailed along behind Banjob until they popped out into an open area. Here there were plastic tables and chairs with people sitting eating food purchased from the vendors. 'Let's eat,' said Banjob. Before he could answer, Banjob was sitting him down at a table with a group of men who looked like they had been pouring concrete five minutes earlier. They were caked in dust and sweat. Banjob spoke to the men, and they moved their chairs to make room for Finney and greeted him with smiles.

The driver returned to the table with bags of sticky rice, satay sticks, and a bowl of curry. He sat and ate while Banjob talked with their table companions, occasionally including him in the conversation.

The driver explained how for most of these migrant workers from across the border in Myanmar, this was a better life. The work was regular, and the area was safe. Many had come from places that had been attacked by the Myanmar army because they suspected rebels were hiding in their villages. Some had come with their families; some had left them behind. One thing they all had in common was they all looked exhausted. Still, for most, their temperaments were good, and they were friendly.

Finney was tired and sleepy. It was only 7 pm in Chiang Mai but felt much later for the Australian with a second-day hangover, heat-stressed and confused. Banjob suggested it was time to head back to the hotel and Finney needed no persuading. All he wanted was to curl up in bed and get some rest.

Returning to the hotel, he didn't bother contacting Barry Quinn. He knew at some point he and the burly cynic from the embassy would lock horns, but it would have to be another time. He simply left a note under his door requesting him to meet them in the lobby at 6 am for the trip to Mae Sai. As he entered the hotel room, he was relieved to find the AC on high. The room was cool and dark. He had no energy to send text messages to Ella. It could wait till the morning. Instead, he lay on the bed, listening to the hum of traffic on the street outside, and tried to make sense of the case. Tracking down Jane Gordon was going to be harder than he first thought, and keeping the mission a secret, even harder.

He fell asleep almost immediately but then awoke with a start some two hours later, unsure what had woken him, but he knew the feeling. He was wide awake and unlikely to get back to sleep anytime soon. He stood at the window looking out over the city. The embassy had put them up in the downtown Movenpick Hotel. While not as upmarket as the Intercontinental Hotel in Bangkok, it was still better than anything he was used to. He decided a short walk might be the best remedy for his sleeplessness. He slipped on the same clothes he had been wearing all day and made his way down to the front of the hotel. He had no idea where he was, but he was confident his sense of direction was good enough he could safely go out for a short walk without getting lost. Just to be sure, he took a business card from the reception desk.

Once again, the heat and humidity hit him as he walked out onto the street. He was sweating immediately. The humidity felt even worse in the evening than during the day. There was a weight about it, like wearing a heavy leather cloak on his shoulders. He was struck also by the cacophony of noise as he walked out onto the street. There was loud music coming from a band at a nearby restaurant, the screech of motorbikes, the chatter of hawkers, and the piercing sound of whistles being blown by guards at his and nearby hotels. It was a game of dodgem navigating through carts, chairs, tables, stalls selling tourist trinkets, and, of course, his fellow pedestrians.

Finney opted to stick to the road, figuring it was the safer choice. He walked against the flow of traffic, keeping an eye on what was headed his way—until he quickly learned that motorbikes here paid no mind to lanes or logic. Having been to Thailand before, it wasn't a complete surprise, but he had to pay close attention to his surroundings. Before long he was exhausted again and was looking for somewhere to take refuge. Without noticing, he had walked into a small bar precinct, and he heard his name being called.

Turning toward the voice, he saw Barry Quinn, seated at a bar, beer in hand, with a young Thai girl by his side. It was one of those faux Irish-themed bars with an Irish flag and posters of windswept landscapes. By the time he had made his way across the street to the bar, Quinn had ordered him a beer. A large beer. The last place I want to be, with the last person I want to be with, and the last thing I should be drinking, thought Finney. He tried to look pleased to see Quinn. The bar was sparsely occupied, and the patrons were mostly local with a sprinkling of tourists. The local expats were easily identified as they sat hunched over their drinks, mostly beer, eyes glued to whatever sport was being shown on the numerous TV sets spread around the bar. There were no more than a few tables, with a few girls lingering behind the bar itself, serving drinks.

Quinn looked happy with all the attention he was getting from the all-female bar staff. It transpired he had all the attention because he was buying rounds of drinks for them. He was a different person. He was beaming.

'So, you finally came to your senses,' said Quinn, over the din of the music.

Finney couldn't hear a thing. He leaned in toward Quinn and shouted in his ear.

Quinn, in turn, shouted at the girl, 'Turn the music down, honey.'

Even with the music turned down they had to shout at each other to be heard, so they moved to a quieter corner of the bar. As they settled at a table, Quinn began waving his hands in the air across towards where they had just been seated. Finney turned to see the honorary consul, Jamie Owens, walking towards them.

'Here he is,' the consul exclaimed and extended his hand, 'welcome aboard lads.'

Finney shook his hand without enthusiasm. He'd had enough of Jamie Owens earlier in the afternoon and wasn't in the mood for another round. Had Quinn arranged for them to meet, he wondered.

'So how are you enjoying our fair city,' asked the consul. 'It's great, isn't it? I love it here. I mean it gets a little dull in the low season. But when the high season comes, there are plenty of tourists around with plenty of money. Everybody's happy. I bought the wife a restaurant so you can see we are very happy when there are plenty of tourists around. No tourist, no money. No money, no honey,' he went on.

Quinn burst out laughing.

'Well, that's what the Thais say,' said the consul. 'And they even put that slogan on T-shirts. At least I can get out on the golf course more easily at this time of the year, even if I do have to slush through some puddles and get my feet wet.' To say Jamie Owens was smug and self-satisfied was an understatement.

'Hey Finney, do you want one of these,' said Quinn, leering at the girl seated on his lap.

'I'll pass,' he said, shaking his head. She can't have been more than eighteen, he thought to himself, spoke barely any English, and looked distinctly uncomfortable. Quinn, on the other hand, looked right in his element.

'Suit yourself, partner,' said Quinn. He lit a cigarette as he balanced a beer in his other hand.

'So do you two know one another, I mean other than our meeting earlier today,' asked Finney, looking from Quinn to Jamie Owens. He was trying to be polite, but he wasn't sure why.

They looked at each other. 'Let's just say we have a mutual friend or two,' said Owens. 'We're waiting for one of them to arrive. He arranges to meet at 9:00 pm but that means any time *after* 9:00 pm. Harley Dowsett is one of the legendary characters of Chiang Mai. A complete reprobate with a reputation in tatters. Does he care about his reputation? Not one bit. When I spoke to him earlier, he sounded a little bit the worse for wear. I've no idea where he was but it sounded very noisy. He loves hanging around those ladyboy bars. I don't think he's that way inclined. He just likes to tease the hostesses. Are you that way inclined Mr. Finney,' he asked, 'is that why you don't want one of these little lovelies on your knee?'

He ignored the question.

Another man, short, fair-skinned and with a mop of brown hair, approached the table.

'Dan Pendergast, I wondered when you might show yourself,' said Quinn, looking at his watch. 'Just coming on board for the evening shift?'

The man nodded at Quinn before shaking his hand.

'You know this guy here,' Quinn said, pointing at Jamie Owens. The two men acknowledged each other, without any sign of friendship.

Quinn introduced his colleague to the bar owner, Dan Pendergast. 'This bloke runs the best bar in Chiang Mai,' said Quinn. 'Aside from the great beer they do some pretty good grub in here as well,' he went on.

Finney stood from his barstool and shook the man's hand.

'Not another bloody Australian,' said Dan Pendergast, with a pronounced New Zealand accent. 'I think we've got our quota of you blokes in Chiang Mai already. What's your business here?'

Thinking on his feet, Finney suggested his visit was to observe what was happening on the Thai-Myanmar border regarding drug smuggling.

'So, he's one of yours, Quinn,' the bar owner frowned, 'you come all the way here to do that? Surely that could be easily done through a bit of good desk research.' Turning to Quinn, he gestured for them to go to the other side of the bar. 'A quick word Barry, if I may.' The two men walked away.

Huddled together at the other side of the bar, they both looked back at him. It was obvious they knew each other well enough. Their body language said as much. A few minutes later Quinn returned to the table, but his mood was less jovial than before.

'It's been a long day Jamie,' said Finney, turning toward the honorary consul, 'and my body clock is telling me it's past midnight in Sydney. So, if you gentlemen will excuse me, I'll head back to the hotel.'

'Don't be a wowser,' said Quinn, as he returned to the table. 'There's plenty of fun to be had here.' Jamie Owens chortled in the background.

Finney left half his beer on the table as he rose from his chair. 'I'll see you bright and early in the morning, Quinn. Jamie, it's been a pleasure, and thank you for your help.' The two men shook hands. As he turned to leave, a bear of a man came into view. It was Harley Dowsett. Before he could move, the other two men were on their feet, shaking hands and introducing Finney.

'I was just leaving,' he said.

'Sit down and have a drink,' the man said. 'Otherwise, I'll get a complex, and think you left because you don't like me. That would be catastrophic because I've never in my life met anyone who didn't like me.' He gestured across to the bar for drinks all around.

The man's accent was indistinguishable. He certainly wasn't Australian, English, or American, but Finney couldn't pick his lilting tone. He must have been 190cm tall. He had narrow shoulders, which made him look even taller. He was barrel-chested with unusually long, skinny arms, which hung limp by his side when he wasn't using them to emphasize something he was saying. He was a very odd shape.

He had jet-black hair, with just a few flecks of grey on his temples that betrayed his hairdresser's attempts to keep him looking younger than he was. He looked to be in his early fifties, but some hard living had made him look older than his years.

Four large bottles of local Thai beer with four shots of clear liquor were placed carefully in front of them. 'Vodka with a beer chaser,' Harley Dowsett beamed. 'Bottoms up!' And with that, he downed the vodka shot, followed by several large gulps of beer from the bottle. 'Oh, don't you just love Leo beer? The Thai truck driver's beer of choice right across the country. None of this yuppy Tiger beer from Singapore or Dutch colonial Heineken, we will have the working man's beer every time,' he said loudly. He spoke Thai to the girls in the bar and left them giggling and looking embarrassed.

Dowsett was a writer of sorts. He was a stringer for several newspapers and did some other, unspecified, 'consulting', as he called it. Before moving to Thailand, he had lived in Cambodia, which he left in dubious circumstances, according to Jamie Owens. 'Nobody quite knows what happened but let's just say he won't be returning there anytime soon.' This information was whispered during one of Harley Dowsett's trips to other tables to catch up with friends and acquaintances. He knew most of the regulars and even made it his business to stop by the tables of the tourists and introduce himself.

He was loud and gregarious. It was all a bit theatrical, especially at this time of night. Finney was, however, too polite to rush off. He patiently cradled his untouched beer for much longer than the others. When Quinn got up to go to the bathroom he saw his opportunity. With excuses of jet lag and an early morning start, he escaped when the chance presented itself.

He left the men crouched over their drinks, talking over the top of one another and occasionally crashing into howls of laughter. The latter being the result of some funny anecdote shared by Harley Dowsett. They were embellished but it didn't matter, because they were funny. Not the kind of bawdy, blokey funny which was the preserve of the likes of Barry Quinn and Jamie Owens. Harley Dowsett's sense of humour was an observation of the absurd. It was picking apart the self-important official, the digital nomads, or mocking the cultural commandos, as he described them. Those were typically NGO staff or Westerners in Thailand doing a meditation retreat. Those who sat in cafes sipping a chai latte and lamenting the corruption of the Thai culture by modernity. They longed for the good old days before mobile phones, Facebook and Instagram, all the while sharing their thoughts via their mobile phones on Instagram and Facebook. Oh, the irony, he had drawled. He had just returned from a trip to Nepal and waxed lyrical about the experience. He had gone on a three-month retreat in a Buddhist temple, complete with Ayurvedic healers and self-administered daily colonic irrigations. His story was vivid, truly funny, and had the group in hysterics. It had been a silent, three-month retreat, meaning there was no talking allowed. It perhaps went some way in explaining his almost manic storytelling. Yes, Harley Dowsett was a character. Finney wasn't sorry to have shared an evening with him. It was also a very useful insight into the psyche of a different type of expat.

It was late and well past his bedtime. He admonished himself for not just getting up and leaving when he wanted to. There was another part of him that had enjoyed the experience. Harley Dowsett was a breath of fresh air and a great foil to the other two. The three men were having a love-hate relationship with their chosen country. For Quinn, it was different. His posting was nearing the end, and he was starting to come to terms with the prospect of his return to Australia. Dowsett and Owens, on the other hand, didn't look like they were leaving Chiang Mai any time soon.

Being so close to his hotel he wouldn't get lost. Nearing midnight, midweek and the streets were still alive with people. Mostly Thais, with a mix of foreigners, they had flocked to the bars and restaurants adjacent to his hotel.

Smoke rose from small barbecue stalls selling satay sticks, grilled squid, and numerous other unidentifiable pieces of protein. A long queue of people waited patiently for banana rotis. There were hill tribe people who sold trinkets straight off the sidewalk, while others trolled the streets with infants strapped to their backs also looking to sell their handicrafts to the few tourists in the city. There was live music and dancing. Would he get any sleep with all this noise? He need not have worried. His hotel room was well insulated from the noise and mayhem outside. He took a long, cold shower and once again he fell asleep quickly, if only for the next few hours.

Border Town

The wakeup call came but Finney was already up and on his second beverage. Instant coffee with a non-dairy creamer and two sugars. Another healthy start to the day, he thought. He had never really been a great sleeper, and it only got worse as he got older. Lying awake listening to the fan whirring above his head at 4.00 am he thought coffee was better than ruminating on what he was doing with his life. As he stood looking out onto the street from his hotel room window, coffee in hand, he saw the young girl from the bar the night before, exiting the hotel. He had a hunch he knew where she had stayed the night. Removing one of his recently purchased shirts from its wrapping, he experienced post-purchase dissonance almost immediately. He hated checked shirts, and this one smelled of chemicals. He would wash the others as soon as he had a chance, but for now, he had no choice but to wear this shirt.

Barry Quinn kept them waiting in the dimly lit, and unattended lobby for a good half hour later than their agreed departure time. Appearing in the same clothes as he had worn the night before, he reeked of cigarettes and beer, looked rough and was in no mood for talking. He gestured for Finney to take the front seat while he got himself comfortable in the back of the van and promptly fell asleep.

As they set off on their journey, the driver began the first of what would be numerous history lessons. He started way back in the Vietnam War years and described the transition away from the growing of opium poppies to the production of the new party drugs, as he called them.

Banjob knew the area well and provided useful information on the more recent exploits of traffickers from Myanmar and their network of Thai partners. Corruption, it seemed, was deeply embedded in the local police force, and immigration officials, bribes trickled down and oiled the wheels of commerce and crime.

Traffic was light as they made their way out of Chiang Mai but became busier as kids on motorbikes and in buses began making their way to school. Finney wondered what Ella would think about starting school at 7.30 am. Ninety minutes out of Chiang Mai, without saying a word, the driver suddenly swung off the road and stopped in front of a collection of ramshackle huts, and announced it was time for breakfast. The driver explained they were still another four hours from their destination of Mae Sai, and this was his regular place to stop and eat. The landscape had begun to change as they headed into more mountainous countryside.

The ground around the small cluster of shacks was dry and dusty, with stray dogs loitering in the hope of food scraps being thrown their way. Vendors greeted them as they entered, and Banjob was well-known here. Smoke from barbecues hung in the air, and woks sizzled as lorry drivers and locals tucked into a bewildering array of food. Metal trays were brimming with stir-fried vegetables and various curries. Large pots with rice porridge and steamers full of sticky rice were on offer. Cauldrons of soup bubbled away furiously next to large bowls containing noodles and all the condiments to go with them. Quinn, still in no mood for conversation, stayed in the vehicle and slept. He was happy for the driver to order the food and was content to eat anything that reached the table. Well, almost anything. He regarded himself as an adventurous eater but had to draw the line at the porridge with liver, squares of congealed blood, and intestines. It was still only very early in the morning.

Their noodle soup, when it arrived at the table, was complete with lumps of offal, funk-flavoured herbs and rubbery beef balls. He tucked in and felt memories of his trip to Thailand with Sarah all those years ago flooding back.

The five-hour drive to the border of Thailand and Myanmar allowed plenty of time for nostalgia. Despite the new highway and the gleaming pitstops of gas stations along the way, rural life was languid and timeless. Verdant green fields of rice were interspersed with orchards and water buffalos took refuge from the heat in small ponds. Banjob continued a running commentary describing the changes in agricultural practices as they snaked their way along the mountain roads. Longans and lychees gave way to citrus, papaya, bananas, jackfruit and more. What an abundance of food, he thought to himself, nobody was going hungry around here.

A further two hours into their trip they made a stop in Mae Salong, another opportunity to stretch their legs and grab yet more bottles of water. This small town had been settled by Chinese refugees fleeing the civil war in China between the communists and the nationalists in the '30s and '40s, Banjob explained. The town showed numerous hallmarks of that heritage with many signs in Chinese and an entrance gate designed in the image of a dragon. The inhabitants of the small town spoke mainland Chinese and a local Chinese dialect, according to the driver. Mixed with the ethnic Chinese were numerous hill tribe peoples.

Barry Quinn had finally risen from his slumber to complain about the heat, the noise, and the driving habits of the Thais. On the latter, he had to agree his nerves were more than a little rattled by the recklessness of other drivers. Seemingly relaxed, gentle and civil in most circumstances, once behind the wheel of a car they became impatient risk-takers. Overtaking on blind corners, running red lights, ignoring give-way signs, and tailgating were common practices. Stop signs and pedestrian crossings seemed entirely ornamental and motorcyclists exhibited a kamikaze recklessness. There seemed to be an almost fatalistic approach to driving from their fellow motorists. When quizzed about this, Banjob merely shrugged his shoulders. 'We believe in reincarnation,' he said, 'and we will be better drivers next time around.'

As they settled into the last leg of the journey from Mae Salong to Mae Sai, Finney took the opportunity to go through some of the notes provided by the Australian Embassy staff. Much of it seemed too old to be of any value. The notes included descriptions of drug warlords, corrupt public officials, and convoys of opium and methamphetamines ferried across the Mekong River in the Golden Triangle. The produce was protected along the way by a network of gangs, friendly farmers, police officers, and customs officials just seemed too fanciful in 2023. The return of the military to power in Myanmar in 2021 turned the clock back in more ways than one. He was soon to discover just how much things had changed since the army had taken back power in Myanmar.

Arriving in Mae Sai, both men were content to allow the driver to book them into their hotel. He wasn't sure what he was expecting but it wasn't anything as modern as the Orassa Hotel. It was all glass and grey rendered concrete on the main street in town and less than a hundred meters from the Myanmar border crossing. It was nestled between a pharmacy shophouse and a laneway leading to a market. A bakery, coffee shop, and a small bar occupied most of the ground floor entrance. Further along was an open-air restaurant, a guesthouse, with other shops selling clothes and homewares. Across the road was the Above Coffee Shop. He registered this as his go-to coffee fix getaway from Quinn and Banjob.

The dusty street was busy with vans, tuk-tuks, pick-up trucks, motorbikes, and cars coming back and forwards from the border. Many pedestrians were doing likewise. The curb was full of parked motorbikes and a sidewalk jungle of vendors selling deep-fried chicken, fruits, drinks, clothes, and handicrafts. Motorbike taxi drivers, dressed in numbered high-vis jackets queued patiently under umbrellas for their next passenger. The driver explained the system to him. Each rider had a special license which was displayed on their vehicle and a particular number on their vest which identified them. There was a system for queuing among them and it was far more orderly than it appeared to the casual observer.

'Is it always this busy,' enquired Finney.

'Seven days a week, and even busier around 9 pm when the border closes.' replied Banjob.

'What is your preference, gentlemen,' Banjob asked. 'Front or back of the hotel?' Finney asked for a quiet room while Quinn was happy with any room provided it was close to the bar. A sign of things to come.

It was early afternoon, and the heat was oppressive, he had always thought Sydney was humid but compared to this it was nothing at all. Quinn mooched around and sulked, he didn't want to be there and was not concerned about hiding his feelings. Finney looked around and was surprised to see any foreigners at all. For some reason, he thought this would be the end of the earth but there were still a few young backpackers and middle-aged couples shopping at the street stalls and eating at the open-air restaurants.

The driver suggested lunch, but it was so hot Finney declined, indicating instead he would settle for some fruit and more water. Banjob obliged and led him to a roadside vendor outside the market who was selling fruit, already peeled, and chopped. It was a small handcart mounted on bicycle wheels which could easily be moved from one location to another. Atop the cart was a glass case containing crushed ice on which lay a variety of fruits including watermelon, pineapple, guava, and papaya. He asked for a bag of each and Banjob made the order. The vendor carefully cut each of the fruits into bite-sized pieces before sliding them gently into individual bags with a wooden skewer. B120, about AUD $5. It seemed like a bargain. The cold fruit was perfect, and he picked his way through it as they made their way back to the van and on to their next destination.

The next stop was a meeting with the Drug Enforcement Administration (DEA). Unsurprisingly, Quinn had declined to go with them. Too hot and a waste of time, was Quinn's excuse. He would catch up on some real work while Finney and the driver went to meet with them, he had said. Banjob navigated the back streets of Mai Sai to an innocuous-looking building wedged between a cement factory and a ceramic tile outlet. It looked like a warehouse of some kind with no signage at all. Next to a roller door, there was an intercom. 'Please use the door on the left side of the building,' said a voice. The camera above the door allowed the occupants to see them arriving well before the doorbell rang.

Walking around to the side of the building, Finney found an open door and was greeted by a woman in her early thirties who introduced herself as Rosie Betts. Dressed in jeans, boots, and a khaki shirt, she was the North Thailand Field Leader of the DEA. With her were three grizzled-looking men, all dressed the same way, who were her subordinates despite two of them being much older. The DEA males all looked like ex-marines with crew cuts and black baseball hats, buffed biceps, and attitude.

The meeting had been hastily arranged through the Australian Embassy the day before. He introduced himself as a new AFP officer on secondment from Sydney, looking for intelligence on methylamphetamines coming from Myanmar through Thailand. Betts looked him up and down. Having been advised of his visit by the Australian Embassy, she had done her homework.

'First official visit here,' she asked.

He nodded

'Please follow me and instruct your driver to wait in the vehicle,' she said, as she turned and walked into the station. Following her into the building, he observed three modest-sized offices set in the sprawling warehouse. Hers was the largest and the walls were plastered with maps, press clippings, printouts, and satellite photos. A large whiteboard contained lists of place names and a to-do list with staff assigned to each item. Three computer screens and a laptop sat atop the large, L-shaped desk. Three filing cabinets lined up on another wall. 'Take a seat, Mr. Finney,' she said. 'Let's get started, shall we? I divide my time between here and Chiang Mai. You could call this the coalface but there is still plenty of action in Chiang Mai and I have a place there. I have five agents here. The three you met earlier, and two who are on a reconnaissance mission with the Thai military right now. Occasionally, they allow us to tag along on a mission, usually when they want some good press coverage. Most of the time we do our own thing. Keep in mind we are guests here and everything we do is about gathering intelligence. The same applies to you. Rule numbers one, two, and three, keep your head down.

'If you have an office in Chiang Mai,' he asked, 'what goes on there?'

'I have a couple of administrative staff, and we listen, and prepare reports. They listen to gossip and rumour amongst the Thais. I also have a daughter in Chiang Mai, and it allows me to spend some time with her,' she said.

Agent Betts had a grim assessment of the region. Drug activity on both sides of the border was so ingrained, nearly everyone had a connection to it. In Myanmar, it was all about production and packaging; on the Thai side, the focus was distribution through the major ports of Bangkok, Laem Chabang, Rayong, Sattahip, and Sri Racha. The old guard had been replaced, shifting from a chaotic Wild West to something far more business oriented. Drug money was being funnelled into resorts and tourist businesses and that was exactly where the DEA was looking. There, and of course the casinos across the river in The Democratic Republic of Laos. 'Always follow the money,' said Agent Betts.

Years earlier, the drug kingpin was Khun Sa. He was long gone. But as they say, the apple never falls far from the tree. Recently returned from studying in Australia, one of Khun Sa's grandsons had decided to try his hand at drug trafficking. His headquarters was a large regional town called Keng Tung in Shan State, Myanmar, some three hours away. His main point of exit for the product was in Tachileik, a border town right opposite Mae Sai. Betts pointed down toward the river and suggested they go take a closer look at Tachileik.

The embassy driver protested that he would accompany them on their tour. Betts declined and pointed Finney to her nearby four-wheel drive. 'No need to worry,' she said, 'I'll make sure he doesn't get into any trouble.'

'We can have a more honest conversation without the Thai staff around,' she said when they were in the car. 'We are never quite sure where allegiances are in this country.' Agent Betts took him first to the border entrance, a large concrete edifice across the small river.

'We have no idea exactly how many people cross this border every day, but we know it's substantial, along with many trucks and pick-ups. It's impossible to check every one of them and it's not our job anyway. We get regular reports from the Thais about how many busts they make but the information is unreliable, so we get our information in other ways,' she said, without elaborating. They then drove along the river with Betts pointing out the large number of people crossing the border illegally.

They sat on stools at a small bar perched on the riverside, across which they could see Tachileik township only a stone's throw away. The river in between was less than waist deep in parts, and for those not inclined to cross the official bridge, it was easy enough to walk back and forward that way, especially in the dry season.

During the day the drug product was brought across in trucks and vans. In the evening it was ferried by boat further down where the river was deeper and there were fewer police and customs officials. He quizzed her on the resistance fighters and soon discovered there were close ties with the drug traffickers. Was there a connection to the drug trade and Jane's disappearance, Finney wondered? Betts suggested they meet up again for dinner. She had intel to share, but right now she had other commitments. Returning to the DEA base, they agreed to meet later.

Banjob was standing by, as he called it, when they returned to the DEA warehouse. 'Where to next, sir,' he asked.

'Maybe time to take a breather,' suggested Finney. 'Let's go back to the hotel and I'll check some emails and do some housekeeping,' by which he meant he would have the chemicals washed from his newly purchased clothing. The hotel room was fine, but it overlooked the street and had all the attendant noise that went with it. He had no enthusiasm for changing rooms and would simply rely on his industrial-strength earplugs to block out any noise. With a couple of hours to spare before the dinner meeting with Rosie Betts, he took a stroll to get a feel for the place.

Not surprisingly, Quinn opted to prop up the bar in the hotel.

Mae Sai was a world apart from Chiang Mai. The town had the rough edges of a frontier, a place where the usual conveniences of Thailand – the ubiquitous 7/11s – gave way to a different kind of bustle. There were fewer tourists, and the faces in the crowd told a different story. Hill tribe people in vibrant traditional dress mingled with weary Burmese labourers making their way across the border after a long day's work. The local Thais seemed less affluent than their Chiang Mai counterparts, but they shared the same warmth and friendliness which he had come to appreciate in Thailand.

As he neared the border crossing, he noticed the uptick in activity. It was approaching 6 pm and a long line of cars was inching its way across the bridge, while a steady stream of people, mostly migrant workers by the look of it, crossed on foot. Over 90% of the foot traffic was heading back to Myanmar. The river, a shallow ribbon of water marking the border, was busy too. People bypassed the official crossing altogether, wading through the shallows from Thailand to Myanmar. The immigration officials didn't seem to mind, their attention elsewhere, as if this was just another routine evening in Mai Sai.

He enquired about the cost of crossing the border. Foreigners, U.S. $10 per one day, was the terse reply from the disinterested immigration official. In different circumstances, thought Finney, he would do a day trip across to the border town of Tachileik in Myanmar. But not this time. He returned to the hotel and made more detailed notes from his conversations with Rosie Betts. He also sent an email to Stacey Harmer and requested any updates she might have. Harmer, obviously still working, even at 9 pm Sydney time, shot straight back with a detailed email on some not-so-encouraging updates. Still no contact from Jane Gordon, and no activity on her credit card or phone.

Around 7 pm Rosie Betts arrived at the hotel to meet Finney and Quinn. Once again, Quinn had no interest in meeting with the DEA agent. He knew this was a blessing and he left the man nursing yet another large bottle of beer in the hotel bar. Betts suggested a little place on the edge of town. She wasn't keen to be recognized as her job required a low profile.

The daughter of expats, she had weathered a nomadic childhood across the Middle East and India. Her parents' work was a mystery he didn't press to solve. After five years in Chiang Mai, she'd been transferred to Mae Sai. Her Thai was better than average— more than enough to order food and exchange pleasantries with restaurant staff.

Over some fiery local Thai food, she gave Finney a very detailed overview of what life was like for the DEA station chief in this part of the world and what the War on Drugs had become. The U.S. Government was happy to be off the front pages of the newspapers. CNN and their counterparts had moved on and now it was all about pandemics and terrorism. The drug trade, however, continued unabated. Heroin was still being produced in Myanmar and distributed through Thailand but in much smaller quantities than in the past. He sensed he was being given a carefully curated picture of the situation on the ground.

As part of her narrative, was a detailed history lesson and the name of Khun Sa came up repeatedly. He had been born to a Chinese father and a Burmese mother, a native of the Shan state in the north of Myanmar bordering China. With no formal education he grew up fast and was drafted into the military by way of the Kuomintang in the early 1950's at the tender age of sixteen. The Kuomintang had fled to Shan State, northern Thailand, and other places, following their defeat at the hands of Mao's communist forces in 1949.

Through the 1960s and '70s, heroin trafficking became the funding source for private militia right across the region and beyond. A shifting marriage of convenience was secured with the government in Burma (as it was then known) and Khun Sa's reach, wealth, and influence flourished. Right through until the 1990's, he was the man. With a massive network of locals working for him and business deals with governments and militia, he was the world's biggest heroin trafficker. With that kind of reputation, it was not surprising he attracted the attention of the American government. Pressure from other governments naturally followed and internal changes in his organization saw him surrender to the Burmese Government in 1996. This came with a pardon, in exchange for a promise by him of no further illegal activities. He was allowed to quietly retire in Yangon, after having laundered tens of millions of dollars through legitimate businesses.

Khun Sa had a known family of eight children, all of whom were educated in very good schools abroad. They went on to have their own families and this was where the story became interesting. According to Betts, a grandson of the former drug lord, was busily resurrecting the empire through the production and sale of methamphetamines. He was also trying to establish a partnership with the resistance movement which had sprung up since the army takeover of Myanmar in February of 2021. The grandson, known as Zhang Sein, had been educated in Australia and was based in Shan State with meth factories dotted around the region. Unlike heroin, methamphetamines were easy to produce and distribute and required very little in the way of land or manpower. Zhang Sein's group had their security apparatus but also provided funding to the resistance fighters. Striking similarities between grandfather and grandson.

According to Betts, the focus of the DEA was the distribution points along the northern border between Thailand and Myanmar. The DEA had been hearing rumours about some of the other activities of Zhang Sein. He had been trading girls along the border with Laos and China. These girls were being trafficked as young brides into China and prostitutes for the casinos popping up on the Laos border with Thailand. This, combined with drug sales, was attracting a lot of interest from both the United Nations and the DEA. 'Not such a nice guy, by the sound of it,' offered Finney.

It was now his turn to do some talking. He realised that if he was to get help from Agent Betts, he had to come clean on the real reason for his presence in Northern Thailand. He wasn't here on secondment to the AFP, but of course, she already knew it.

He carefully crafted the story and omitted the fact Jane Gordon was the daughter of a prominent public figure. Agent Betts, however, knew there was more to the story.

He soon found himself having to divulge more than he wanted, pleading with her to keep it a secret. Her phone vibrated on the table. 'I'll have to take this,' she said, standing and walking a short distance. She stopped and turned to look back at him, nodded her head, muttered a few words into the phone, and then ended the conversation.

Returning to the table, her mood had changed. Her posture was different, she sat bolt upright and stared at Finney. 'OK Finney, why are you here? That was one of my colleagues on the phone. A body has been found near the Sai River. We believe it is the young American Peace Corps volunteer. It looks like he's been murdered. So, do you want to tell me what's going on?'

He knew he had to be honest. He left out the part about rescuing Jane Gordon in Sydney but the rest of it he told her, confidentially of course. He needed her help. He needed her contacts and most importantly he needed her trust. It was clear to him Betts had an extensive network across both sides of the border. She offered to put the word out amongst her network for any news on Jane Gordon. Two days in, and he was getting nervous. He needed to find Jane Gordon fast. He had three missed calls from a Bangkok number, it was sure to be from the embassy, he thought. They agreed to meet again the following morning. Betts had indicated she thought it would be easy enough to find out where Jane Gordon and Jessie Cheeseman's friends would be staying. Three choices roughly and they would hit those first thing the next day.

'In the meantime,' she said, 'I've got to get myself to the police station here tonight. The embassy staff will be here in the morning, but I've been ordered to try and smooth this over before they get here. There is some dispute with the Thais about where his body was found. They claim he was killed in Myanmar. Murders are bad for the tourist trade, or something along those lines.'

They agreed to meet again for breakfast at his hotel early the following morning. It was after 10 pm, and he was asleep on his feet. Returning to the hotel he found Quinn half comatose in the outdoor hotel bar, surrounded by empty beer bottles and an overflowing ashtray.

'Any luck with Betty Betts? You realise I know her,' he slurred. 'Bloody Americans, you can't trust them, that's for sure.'

Don't come back without Jane Gordon, and preferably with her still breathing, the ambassador's last words as they left the embassy in Bangkok, were ringing in his ears. This case just got a whole lot more urgent. He relayed the news about the body of the American Peace Corps volunteer to Quinn. This was bad news for Quinn, and he reacted accordingly.

'Oh Christ,' he said, 'don't jump to conclusions. We don't know for sure it is Jane Gordon's friend. She's probably smoking a joint right now somewhere in Chiang Mai.'

Finney disagreed and told him so. 'If she was still in Chiang Mai and still had her life and liberty,' he said, 'she would be using her credit card and talking to her parents. Neither of those things are happening.' They argued for a while until he realised it was futile to talk to Quinn in his current state. Drunk and obnoxious, he was making no sense.

'Just tell me again,' said Quinn, 'how long have you been here? So now after less than two days, you're the expert. You think you know what's going on. Bullshit,' he roared, causing the staff to look their way, 'you know nothing. And from what I hear, you don't have such a great record when it comes to keeping people around you alive. Yes, I know all about you, Detective Sergeant Finney. I know more about you than you realise. I know for a fact you don't have many friends back in Sydney and let me tell you, you have even fewer over here.'

He departed after telling Quinn his attitude would not be appreciated by the brass in Bangkok. That got his attention, and he agreed to be there in the lobby at 7 am when Agent Betts arrived. But he never made it.

Day 3 On the case - Mae Sai

Finney was wide awake, he looked at his phone, it was 3 am. He couldn't face the hotel's powdered coffee and non-dairy creamer this morning, so he made do with bottled water and exchanging text messages with Ella. With a three-hour time difference, she was awake and happy to tell her dad what she was up to. Ella knew he was working out of town but was unsure where and for what purpose. **It's all good Dad, having a sleepover at Charlotte's place on the weekend. Time to get ready for school. Later Dad.**

Their messaging was always like this. He wondered whether Ella knew she and her mother would move overseas with Charles Drayton. He knew Sarah would be expecting a call from him. Not today, he thought. He had other priorities. This had always been the problem, his top priority was work, not family.

He was meticulous and as some of his work colleagues remarked, an obsessive note-taker. He always carried a notebook with him, slipped inside a bruised leather binder his father had given him for his 18th birthday. So, as he went back over his notes, he was disappointed to see he had made little progress.

He needed to clear his head. It was still dark outside, but dawn was nudging the horizon, and motorbikes and pick-up trucks disturbed the peace. Low voices, haggling, laughter and the occasional shout, drifted up from the street. He remembered it about his previous visit to Thailand, it was a country that slept late and rose early. As he descended the stairs to the lobby there was only one security guard by the front door. The man was dozing in a small plastic chair and awoke abruptly, leaping to his feet with a salute, as Finney brushed past him. He opened the door, sucking in a rush of hot and humid air. I love the tropics, he thought to himself, but only briefly. Across the street from his hotel and a short walk away was the morning market, with a constant stream of vehicles delivering produce. Vendors were setting up as he arrived, selling all manner of fresh goods including fruits vegetables, herbs, curry pastes and what looked like freshly slaughtered chickens, pork, and beef. Different cuts of beef were hung on large hooks and men were wielding huge cleavers and breaking up the beasts on rickety tables. Buckets of offal were overflowed with hearts, kidneys, liver, and stomach entrails, and blood ran off the tables into puddles around the butchers. They were bare-chested with plastic aprons, shorts, and long plastic boots. Further along, fish vendors were standing amidst large plastic tubs full of live fish and eels. The ground around them was awash with fish guts, scales, and lurking felines. He dodged motorbikes, laden with goods, as they went up and down the narrow aisles of the market. Towards the back of the market, he could see smoke coming from a BBQ and he could smell the charred meat.

Following his nose, he headed towards the back of the market; he saw people gathered around on small stools eating what looked like rice porridge, some were eating rice topped with curry. Flat trays were brimming with stir-fried vegetables, curries of all sorts, steamed tofu, grilled fish, and a bewildering array of things he had never encountered before. He drew attention as the only Westerner in the market. This was not a tourist stop, and certainly not at this time of the day. The small, stout, female vendor looked at him as if to say, *order some food or move on.* It's a bit early in the morning he thought to himself, but what the hell, when in Rome? So, he pointed at the pot of rice, the stir-fried vegetables, and a red-coloured curry. He handed over B100 and received B70 change. In return, he received a plastic plate laden with food. He tried to crouch down onto one of the small stools. His legs were just too long, so he stood in a small corner out of the way. There was giggling from some of his fellow diners, but in a good-humoured way, he thought. The curry was fiery, and he knew he might regret this later in the day. He didn't usually eat breakfast, but this felt more like lunch, given he had been up for three hours already.

Returning to the hotel dining room around 6.30 am., he went straight for coffee. As he did so he saw his driver, Banjob, watching him from a corner table. As he approached the table the driver appeared sullen and almost hostile, in contrast to his usual happy demeanour. Finney sat down and greeted him.

'Good morning, sir, you are up early this morning, and I see that you have already been to the market.'

'You're very observant, how do you know?'

'That's my job to know where you are going and what you are doing. I also know last night you had dinner with Agent Betts from the DEA. Would it surprise you if I told you I have been reporting your movements back to staff at the embassy in Bangkok?'

'Well probably not,' he said, 'is it part of your job too?' He didn't like it, the feeling he was being spied on. But as the man had said, that was his job.

'Have you seen anything of Mr. Quinn this morning,' the driver asked.

He shook his head.

'You could look in on him. It is better if I drive you to and from your meetings with Agent Betts. The embassy will be much happier with that arrangement. I have been instructed to let you know it is the case.'

'Agreed,' said Finney. 'Agent Betts will be here shortly. We are going to meet with Jane Gordon's friends. Just so you know, we think their hotel is within walking distance, is it OK with you?'

'Yes, it is,' said the driver. 'It's my job, sir, I hope you understand. On the surface, this place is quite safe, but things are not always as they appear. This can be a dangerous part of the world. You would be well advised to keep it in mind.'

Finney simply nodded his understanding.

Right on the dot of 7 am, Agent Betts walked through the door. Looking tired and drawn, she declined breakfast and settled for coffee. Banjob absented himself and left them to it. Betts explained she had been at the police station until late. Other than an international driver's license tucked in his back pocket, which enabled identification, the young man had no other belongings. It was Jessie Cheeseman. As there was no sign of Quinn, he rang his room from reception. No answer. They would go without him. They went first to the Top North Hotel, just a short walk along the road leading to the border. Bingo.

The morning shift at the hotel was still settling in, chatting and drinking iced coffee, which seemed like the most popular beverage for the Thais. It made sense, with the weather always hot. Betts spoke to the reception staff in Thai, asserting that she and Finney were the team leaders for the group, and she requested their room number. The reception staff looked sceptical.

'Do you have B500 on you,' asked Betts. He searched around in his wallet, examining each note as he had yet to work out the Thai currency. The exchange rate was about B24 to one Australian dollar, or so he thought. 'I'm going to need it to get this information,' Betts went on. 'Nothing is free in Thailand.' There was a lot of awkward smiling from the Thai hotel staff, giggling but also a head gesture that said no. 'Apparently, they can't tell us if the others are in the hotel, but the B500 might just change their minds.' And sure enough, it did.

As they made their way to the second floor, Betts related the group was sharing a dorm room for six people, but the staff had noticed the group had shrunk to four. That made sense. Jessie Cheeseman was in the morgue at the local hospital awaiting a visit from U.S. Embassy staff, due to arrive that day from Bangkok. And Jane Gordon, whereabouts unknown. As it was so early in the morning, the group was most likely still asleep. The young woman who opened the door a few inches couldn't have been more than twenty. Groggy and half asleep she was wide awake by the time Betts had introduced herself and told her why they were knocking on her door so early in the morning. The other three were soon awake. Betts was in control, all business and authority figure. It worked a treat. All four of them were up and heading to the hotel coffee shop for a proper interview.

As they led the group downstairs, they attracted the attention of the other hotel guests. They were mostly young backpackers readying for another day of adventure on the Southeast Asia trail. No doubt some would be headed east toward the Golden Triangle at Chiang Saen on the Thai side. From there they might go on to Chiang Khong and take a slow boat down to Luang Prabang in Laos. The rest would travel in the other direction back down toward Chiang Mai or Chiang Rai.

Rosie Betts shot Finney a look that said, *too many people in here*. He nodded. 'Mr. Finney will buy you a coffee while I organize somewhere more private for us to chat,' she said. Making her way to reception she arranged for the use of a small meeting room, where she assembled the group.

The young man and three girls seated before them, heads bowed and nervous, knew what this was about. When told that Jessie was dead, three of the group began to cry. Amy Bescher, the girl who had opened the door, did not. She was the unofficial spokesperson for the group. 'I told him so many times,' she said loudly. 'What he was doing was dangerous.

According to the young woman, he had been interviewing some of the rebel fighters and broadcasting it on his podcast. He had also been writing articles on his blog site, The Myanmar Struggle, as it was known. Jessie Cheeseman had promised to keep the names of the fighters and their supporters a secret but had accidentally mentioned some of them by name in a recent blog post. This had upset them. He had gone in the evening, three days before, to try and set things straight.

'Do you remember the name he mentioned in the blog,' asked Betts.

'I don't remember exactly,' said Amy, 'and Jessie had deleted the name on the post. It may have been Dang or Shang, or something like that.'

'It wasn't Zhang, by any chance.'

'That's it, Zhang Sein. That was it. I don't know which is the given name or which is a family name. It's not the same as we use in the States. I don't know anything about him, only that he was kind of a big shot. I don't think Jessie knew him; he had just heard about him. He was someone important.'

Jane and Jessie had 'hooked up' in Chiang Mai, Amy explained, and Jessie had persuaded her to go with him to meet the rebel fighters. Of course, they were worried when they didn't return but they didn't know what to do. They had decided the night before, if they didn't return today, they would go to the police and report them missing.

They all sat in silence for several minutes, with one of the girls still quietly sobbing at the table.

'You will be interviewed by the U.S. Embassy staff when they arrive later today,' Betts told them. 'Do not leave the hotel until then. Do not speak to anyone about this and do not post anything on social media. Do you understand,' she said forcefully. They all nodded. 'Is there anything else at all you can tell us,' Betts went on.

'There was a guy who came looking for Jessie yesterday,' said Chuck Bowers. 'He said he wanted to borrow his laptop, but we said no.'

'We will need the laptop right now,' said Betts. Amy went off to get it and returned with the laptop and a phone. Both were locked.

'Try *myanmarstruggle* for the laptop,' said Amy.

They were logged into the laptop. With the U.S. Embassy staff on their way, they had to get as much as they could from the laptop in the next few hours.

Finney also decided to remove and examine Jane Gordon's belongings. 'Chuck, maybe you can help me,' he said. He wanted a few minutes alone with the boy to see what else he might know. The young man had been quiet during the interview and Finney had a hunch he might be hiding something. 'So now you can give me your side of the story,' he said, as they entered the room.

'This belongs to Jane,' said Chuck, as he pulled out a small blue satchel from under the bed and handed it over to Finney. 'I think her passport and other documents might be in here. There's nothing more I can tell you, Sir,' he said nervously. 'Jessie never talked much about what he was doing.'

'Did you ever meet his friends across the border,' asked Finney.

'I might have gone across a couple of times.'

'Chuck, I can see you're scared, but we need to find Jane. You've got to tell me everything you know.' Finney's voice was soft, but firm. He knew the boy was holding something back.

'Jessie was in too deep,' he began. 'Some of those guys wanted more from him than some free publicity about their fight with the government. We met further along the border the last time we went together, just outside of Tachileik. We hired a motorbike and rode east along the river and crossed by boat. They picked us up and we drove to the meeting. It's in a place called Wan Narr. There was someone else with them. He was driving a flash car and wore lots of jewellery. He was different from the other guys and did all the talking. He wanted information from us about the DEA. We told him we didn't know anything, but he didn't believe us. He accused us of working for the DEA.'

'It was Zhang Sein, wasn't it,' said Finney. 'The man you met was Zhang Sein.'

He nodded. 'We weren't exactly introduced. It wasn't that kind of meeting, but I heard some of the Burmese guys call him Zhang. We were at a warehouse about twenty minutes' drive from Tachileik. There were trucks coming and going and armed guards everywhere. Just young guys, but they all had rifles. It was scary. I told Jessie I wouldn't go back with him again.'

'Could you show me where the place is?'

The boy's eyes widened. 'No way, it's too dangerous. I'd never go back there.'

'I need you to show me where you crossed the river?'

'Sure, I can, but I'll never cross the river again.'

They returned downstairs, Finney carrying Jane Gordon's backpack and satchel.

'Agent Betts, could I have a word,' he said, as he took a few steps away from the group. 'Do you know a place across the border called Wan Narr?'

'Well, I know where it is on the map. I've seen it from across the river. What's your sudden interest in Wan Narr,' she asked.

'Chuck has just told me he went there with Jesse Cheeseman and that they met Zhang Sein. It puts him together with the freedom fighters and it sounds like he has a warehouse in the area as well. But you already know that.'

She nodded. 'Let's discuss this in private.'

It was nearing 9 am, 'you guys go and get some more sleep,' said Betts. 'We will stay here and try and get some information from this laptop. When we're done, I'll leave it at reception for you.'

'If the U.S. Embassy staff is coming to see us, who are you guys again, exactly,' asked Amy.

'Mr. Finney is from the Australian Embassy, and he is trying to locate your friend Jane Gordon. It would be helpful if you didn't mention our visit to the U.S. Embassy staff. We don't want to get in the way of their investigation.' She stared at each of them until they all nodded. 'OK, off you go and thanks for all your help.'

They decided it was best to move to another location and go through the contents of the laptop. They figured they had two or three hours before they needed to get the laptop back to the Top North Hotel and avoid bumping into the U.S. embassy staff. It was a complication they could do without.

As they walked out through the lobby, a voice called out, 'Hey Finney, we meet again.' As he turned, he caught sight of the young journalist he had met in Chiang Mai but didn't recognise. 'It's me, Pip, from the Chiang Mai Times. Have you found Jane Gordon yet,' she asked. Finney walked towards her; Betts walked in the opposite direction.

'Hi Pip, he said, 'Of course I remember you, what are you doing up here,' he asked.

'Well, I think you know why, it's about Jessie Cheeseman.'

Of course, he thought, news would travel fast, and it would be of interest as Cheeseman was based in Chiang Mai, and he was a foreigner. 'I'm just on my way out,' he said, 'but we could talk later. I've still got your phone number, are you staying here or just doing a day trip?'

'No, I'm pretty sure this is going to be more than a day trip, why don't you call me later and we can chat, maybe I can help you out,' she said.

He turned and caught up with Betts as she walked towards a coffee shop across the street and just far enough away so they could avoid prying eyes. 'Be careful with her,' she said. 'Very cute but also very indiscreet. Don't let on you and I know each other. Got it?' she said.

He nodded.

'Before you ask,' she said, 'I'll tell you straight. Of course, we knew about the place in Wan Narr. We've had surveillance on it for some time, but we can't do much about it. It's close enough to the Mekong River to be a very useful distribution point for the traffickers. I had no idea about those peace core volunteers being there, otherwise, I'd have said something.'

He took her at her word. What else could he do? The seeds of doubt about Agent Betts had been sown.

As they trolled through Cheeseman's laptop, they came across his blog posts in one folder and podcast audio files in another. The naming terminology was hard to follow so they concentrated on the most recent files. Soon enough they came across the file mentioning the freedom fighters and Zhang Sein as a 'financial backer'. There was mention of the link with drug traffickers and how they provided financial support to the freedom fighters. There was a reference to Zhang Sein, drug trafficking and freedom fighters all in the same post.

'Was this what got him killed,' she wondered out loud.

This was not news to Betts, 'this has been going on for some time,' she said, 'and it's in the best interests of the drug traffickers to support the rebels. This doesn't mean the rebel fighters support the drug traffickers. It is a marriage of convenience and that's all. The government soldiers don't try to suppress the traffickers, but they do extort money from them.'

What was news was the confirmation it was Zhang Sein, grandson of the infamous Khun Sa who was busily building himself an empire.

'Now I can see where things may have gone wrong. This is serious,' she said. 'I'm going to have to talk to my people about this and if Zhang Sein is involved, you had better tread carefully.'

Khun Sa was well known in these parts despite having died more than two decades earlier. If his grandson was back in business, it would be in the meth trade, not heroin this time. The Thais were doing all they could to stem the flow of methamphetamines from Myanmar down through Thailand into the Western world, but it was no use. They were fighting a losing battle.

Much of this he already knew from his work in the drug squad in Sydney. He knew where the meth amphetamine was coming from. More importantly, where did Jane Gordon fit into this? Had she been killed too, and they simply had not yet found her body? If she was still alive, what had they done with her? A call would have to be made to his colleagues at the Australian embassy in Bangkok. They needed to know this, but not just yet.

Turning their attention to the laptop they found a folder marked 'maps'. It was encrypted and they couldn't access the files. 'This could be important,' said Betts. 'I need to get one of my team to look at this. We can't hand this back to those kids, and we certainly can't hand it over to staff from the US embassy.'

'Well, how can we manage it,' he asked. 'Those kids are frightened and will buckle under any kind of interrogation.'

'Leave it to me. I think I know a way to get around this. This could give us some leverage with the drug traffickers if they are holding Jane Gordon. Whichever way we look at this, the laptop is valuable. It's my property now and there will be no interrogation regarding this laptop.'

He finally built up the courage to call the ambassador in Bangkok. He tried to sound positive and began by giving him an update on who he had spoken to and what they had gathered so far.

Clifton-Blythe interrupted, 'Have you found the girl or not? Are you any closer to finding her?' Finney admitted progress had been slow, but he felt they were on the verge of finding out what happened to her. A small lie but he had to give him something, and this could explain the link between Jane Gordon's friends and the Burmese rebels.

'Well, it looks like she may have been kidnapped by Myanmar rebels, or worse still, drug traffickers,' said Clifton-Blythe. 'Oh great, how the hell do I tell Bill Gordon his daughter is a captive of drug traffickers? Get out there and find out where the hell she is. Whatever it takes.'

'I'm going to need some cash to get this information, Sir.'

'Sure, I know how it works. It will be wired to Quinn. B250,000 should be enough to get you started, but there's plenty more. It doesn't matter what it costs. Now get on with it.' With that, the call ended.

He made his excuses to Betts and headed back to see Quinn. He tried calling Quinn's room from reception. When he got no reply, he went to the man's room. At first, he knocked gently and by the time Quinn finally answered the door he felt like he would wake the whole hotel up with the banging on the door. Quinn squinted into the light and reeked of alcohol. 'What the fuck do you want at this time of the day,' he roared.

'Well, it's nearly lunchtime and I need your help.'

'Downstairs in thirty minutes' said Quinn, as he slammed the door shut.

Banjob approached Finney as he sat waiting for Quinn in the hotel lobby. 'There is something you need to see and someone I want you to meet. I know you are an early riser and so am I. I'll meet you here in the lobby tomorrow at 5 am. It will be worth it.' The driver shuffled off into the far corner of the lobby and sat himself down. Standing by.

It was an hour before Quinn appeared, Finney wasn't bothered, it had given him time to think. He had to assume if Jane Gordon was alive, she was a captive of drug traffickers, across the border in Myanmar. She could be just across the river, or she could be hundreds of miles away. He had called Stacey Harmer back in Sydney and asked for help. He needed to know if there had been any activity on Jane Gordon's phone. Did the parents have a tracker on it? Anything at all. 'I'm on it,' said Harmer, 'I'll get back to you.'

Quinn snapped at the waitress that his coffee wasn't hot enough, leaving her terrified. 'Make me another one and this time make it hot,' he scolded. Finney tried to give

Quinn an update on what had been happening, but he realised the man was simply uninterested. He did agree, however, to go to the bank and retrieve the money being sent by the embassy.

'I'm going back to Bangkok,' said Quinn. 'This is a waste of time; the girl's probably dead and you need to face up to it.'

'Well, it's up to you if you return to Bangkok,' said Finney, without emotion. I will be better off without you; he thought to himself.

'Yeah, I'm out of here tonight,' snorted Quinn, 'and you can stay here and make a fool of yourself. Don't trust Betts and her crew. They will do you over. They will claim ignorance when it comes to this young volunteer guy. You wait and see.'

Quinn was puffing and wheezing as he climbed the stairs to the bank entrance, his face flushed red and sweat saturating the back of his shirt. It didn't help he was sucking on a cigarette the whole time. To add to his bad mood, he was forced to go to the counter as he could not withdraw such a large sum from an ATM. 'Bloody Thai banks,' he said, 'they're hopeless. It was a full twenty minutes of transaction but finally, Quinn came away with the cash and handed it over to Finney, minus B10,000. 'That's for me,' he said, 'for all the trouble you've put me through, and it should pay for some liquid refreshments in Bangkok this evening.' Returning to the hotel, they went their separate ways. Quinn went looking for Banjob to drive him back to the airport in Chiang Rai, which was only an hour away.

Finney decided to call Rosie Betts. 'Any news?'

'I'm sorry it's been a busy morning. I'm free now and there's something I think you should see; I'll pick you up in twenty minutes at the hotel.'

As he climbed into her four-wheel drive, he breathed a sigh of relief at a blast of cold air from the AC. The heat outside was oppressive, as was the air quality. 'I don't know how you deal with this heat,' he said.

'Well, you never really get used to it, you just get used to feeling hot and sticky all the time.

'So where are we going?

'We're going to drive down to Sop Ruak and the Golden Triangle, you may have heard of it.'

'Well of course I have, who hasn't?'

She explained how it might be useful for him to see it and understand what they were dealing with there.

They drove off in silence for a few minutes. Finney was once again impressed with the quality of the roads and said as much.

'Road building requires procurement of materials and contractors, and where there is procurement there is money to be made, especially for politicians and civil servants. If the Thais spent as much on law enforcement and border control as they do on road building, I would be out of a job' shrugged Betts.

Soon enough they drove into the small town where the speed limit said 50 kilometres, but nobody seemed to be obeying that rule. Sop Ruak, in Chiang Saen province, was a small town on the banks of the Mekong River as it emerged from Myanmar near the border between Thailand and Laos. The town had a long history dating back a thousand years and had been inhabited by both the Burmese and the Thais. It had a population of around 10,000 people but there were not many along the waterfront on this day. There was a small ferry pier, and then numerous smaller boats called long tails scattered along the riverfront. They parked the car adjacent to a large public building, The House of Opium it was called, it looked dated and unloved.

'Stop, not that way,' said Betts, pointing across the road. 'We will get a better view from up here.'

He followed her across the road where they arrived at the base of a steep set of stairs. He felt tired and thirsty before they even began the ascent.

'Come on, it's not too far,' she said as if reading his mind. She was right, and when they reached the top, he could see out over the Mekong to where the smaller river, The Sai, joined the Sop Ruak River as it emerged from Myanmar. It wasn't exactly a triangle but the proximity of the three nations gave it the name. Finney could see how easy it was to travel between Thailand, Myanmar, and Laos and how difficult it would be to manage the traffic. The Mekong was the largest of the waterways, coming all the way down from the Tibetan plateau and it was truly impressive. At this point, it still had a long way to travel through Laos, Thailand, Cambodia, and Vietnam before it spilled out into the South China Sea.

They stood and stared out across the water, Finney remarking at how brown and muddy it looked.

'It's the wet season,' said Betts. 'December through till about June, in the dry season, the river is much clearer, but with these daily storms washing silt into the river, this is what you end up with.' Pointing down the river from the place where the three countries merged, 'that's where we're headed,' she said. 'Come on then, we haven't got all day,' and they walked back to the car. 'It's just a couple of kilometres down the road, that's where the real fun begins.'

Walking along the promenade adjacent to the ferry pier in Chiang Saen, he looked across the river and saw a large multi-story building rising high above the flat landscape around it. 'That's the Chinese-owned Kings Romans casino,' she said. 'It is all part of a special economic zone agreed to by the Chinese and the Lao governments more than a decade ago. Gamblers come down from mainland China by air or by road and a lot of Thais crossed the river here to gamble in the casino. At this point, the river was only about three hundred meters wide. Betts suggested they take a boat across the river for a closer look. He had no objection.

Betts spoke briefly to one of the boat drivers and then turned to Finney, 'this is going to cost you 500 Thai Baht' she said. He handed over the money and they got into the small boat. Long Tails, as they were known, was a flat-bottomed boat with a motor at one end with a long metal pole attached. As they settled in, the boat suddenly roared to life, and off they went out into the river at high speed. Betts turned to the driver and shouted a few words above the noise of the engine, he immediately slowed down to a more reasonable speed. Betts explained the drivers of these boats typically drove them at top speed, and she had merely asked him to slow down a little.

Despite the noise of the V8 eggbeater, as Betts called it, they still managed to have a conversation. She pointed across to the left at what was Myanmar and straight ahead was Laos and behind them Thailand.

'You can see how porous the borders are here, and how easy it is for goods to be transported back and forward without any customs or border checks. It's impossible to control a river border with three countries so close to each other,' she said. 'It's challenging enough during the day but after dark, it's almost impossible.'

Finney could see plenty of activity on the water and along the riverbanks. On the Myanmar side there were scattered dwellings and what looked like warehouses along the riverfront. In the distance toward the casino building in Laos, he could see smaller buildings dotted around it, and in the background, rows and rows of apartment buildings about ten stories high.

Small fishing boats bobbed around in the still water of the Mekong, with fishermen casting small nets. Betts suggested that even though they appeared to be fishing, some were waiting for an opportunity to drop their modest cargo of meth on the shore to be picked up by the couriers on the Thai side. The cargo of these smaller-scale operators was most likely destined for the local Thai market rather than the more lucrative markets of Europe, North America, Australia and New Zealand. The cargo would be rolling across the border bridge at Mae Sai in lorries camouflaged with anything from timber, plumbing supplies or fresh produce. The guards on the bridge either didn't have the resources to check every vehicle or were being paid to look the other way. In either case, huge amounts of drugs were coming across the land bridge.

As they approached the Lao side of the river, he could see small piers dotted along the riverfront. There were also much larger ferries taking people back and forward between Laos and Thailand. They headed towards one of the smaller piers. As they came in adjacent to it the boatman jumped out and held the boat steady as his passengers climbed onto the pier. The driver was soon back in the boat where he brought the engine to life and took it out a short distance away from the pier.

'Don't panic, he'll wait for us for about an hour and then take us back.'

'All that for 500 Thai Baht,' asked Finney.

Betts nodded, 'he's probably living on about that much per day, and supporting a family.'

As they ventured onto the promenade adjacent to the pier, they were approached by a uniformed official. Betts flashed a document toward him, and he waved them through. He assumed it was a U.S. diplomatic passport or similar. Whatever it was, it was enough for them both to enter the country without any fuss. As they walked on, they were approached by numerous taxi drivers. Again, Betts engaged in conversation with them and shortly they were in a rickety tuk tuk hurtling towards the casino building which was about 1/2 mile away.

'So, you speak the language here as well,' he observed.

'No, I just speak Thai to them, most people in Laos speak Thai. It's mainly because they grow up on a diet of Thai soap operas.'

The tuk-tuk dropped them on the street outside the casino. As they stood there, Betts suggested it was better if they went to the back entrance, as she didn't want to be seen too close to the building. As they stood on the street and looked around Finney realised the street signs as well as the car and bus number plates were all in Chinese language. When he pointed this out to Betts, she explained that most things here were under the control of the Chinese. They brought in their own police force and the currency was also the Chinese yuan and of course U.S. dollars.

Betts had been in the casino the year before. Granted, it had been at the tail end of COVID, but she described the place as cavernous but deserted of gamblers. The staff, comprised of waiters, croupiers, security, and female 'attendants', as they were described, outnumbered guests by twenty to one. This further reinforced her view the place was just a giant money laundering operation with some gambling and prostitution thrown in for good measure.

She detailed the establishment of the zone agreed to and operated between the Laos Government and a private corporation, run by a drug triad, headed up by Zhao Wei. He had been sanctioned by the U.S. Government in 2018 and identified as the leader of an organization involved in money laundering, human and wildlife trafficking, and most notably, the global distribution of meth amphetamines, heroin and other narcotics.

From their vantage point just inside the entrance, he took in the vast expanse of the casino floor. Roulette, blackjack and poker tables stretched out before him, interspersed with row after row of flashing slot machines. Despite the sparse crowd, the noise was overwhelming, loud music clashed with incessant announcements blaring over the loudspeakers. Betts had been right; there were more staff than guests. The décor was garish and ostentatious with bright red carpet, oversized chandeliers and gaudy statues mimicking ancient Roman and Greek styles. It was a sensory assault, and Finney could already feel a dull headache forming.

'Seen enough,' asked Betts, not waiting for him to answer.

Leaving the casino, they crossed the street and headed toward a row of gleaming new shophouses with stores selling identical goods. These were the usual tourist shops with fake designer clothes and bags. Further along, stores were selling local tea, coffee and exotic Chinese medicines. There was liquor made from animal parts including bears, tigers and crocodiles. He pointed these out to Betts who nodded and suggested that many of the rare animals were being farmed in the areas adjacent to the main town, known as Van Pak Len.

They bought water from one of the shops and sheltered in the shade to escape the burning sun. It had already been a long, hot day and Finney was feeling the effects. 'I need some AC,' he said, sounding suddenly desperate. They found a small, air-conditioned restaurant, and ordered food, despite not being hungry. Finney's phone pinged; it was a message from Stacey Harmer. **Jane has made contact. Call me,** was all it said. Despite being in another country his Thai SIM was working. He made his excuses and moved away from Betts for the call. He noted the time, almost 4 pm.

'We've had a text message from Jane Gordon,' said Harmer. 'Well, it's was from her phone and to her parents.'

'When was this?'

'Late last night, at almost midnight.' **All good,** was all it had said. 'Still no activity on the credit card. I'll call you if anything else comes through. Keep your phone handy.' And she rang off.

'Maybe some good news,' he said, as he returned to the table. 'We have another text message from her phone.' Betts suggested the fact she had sent a message, rather than calling, meant someone else had authored the message.

'My daughter is a few years younger than Jane Gordon,' he said, 'she never calls or leaves audio messages. Always texts, not just to me but to her friends and even her mother. The kids don't make phone calls anymore, that's for old folks like me,' he laughed. He felt odd, having laughed. It seemed wrong given the circumstances, but he had managed to forget for just a few seconds what he was dealing with.

After cooling off for half an hour, it was time to journey back to Mae Sai. The visit to Van Pak Len had been enlightening and deeply disturbing and had left Finney feeling uneasy. He was forced to put emotion aside for the time being, until he could give it his full attention. For now, he would have to talk again with Jane Gordon's travelling companions. He knew he was yet to get their full story. The U.S. embassy staff would have finished their business and moved on, leaving him the task of joining the dots. They allowed their boat driver to crank the throttle for the return journey. The river breeze was a relief from the oppressive heat, and the cool spray of river water was welcome on their sunbaked faces.

Their focus now would be on Chuck Bowers, Jessie Cheeseman's best friend, and fellow Peace Corps volunteer. Bowers and Jane had also been close, and

Finney had a gut feeling he might know more than he'd let on so far. A lot was riding on this conversation. He hoped it would provide the missing piece of the puzzle or at least point them in the right direction. The stakes were too high to leave any stone unturned.

As they pulled up outside the group's guesthouse, they saw them gathered in the reception area, bags packed and ready to leave. There was a van parked outside, presumably waiting for them. Betts strode in and commanded them to sit. Once they were seated, Betts changed her tone and softly enquired as to whether Jane was their friend. It was a great strategy. 'Well of course she is,' they said in unison.

'If that's the case I need to talk to all of you, especially you, Mr. Bowers,' said Rosie Betts. She shot him a glance that said, do not make a move. Betts and Finney took turns walking them through the events on the day Jessie Cheeseman and Jane Gordon disappeared. There were more tears. Chuck Bowers sat quietly, staring at the floor. 'You carry on here,' said Betts, as she motioned for Bowers to follow her through to the coffee shop behind the reception. He did so without objection.

'Ok, Chuck, it's just you and me and this is off the record. Just tell me what was going on with Jessie and his Burmese friends.'

It came out in a tsunami of guilt. Both Chuck and Jessie had been involved in meetings with the Myanmar freedom fighters, as he called them. They usually went across the border clandestinely, either here in Mae Sai or at another point near the small town of Mae Salong. It was close to the Myanmar border and easy to go back and forward without bother from border controls. But this time they wanted to meet here in Mae Sai. Chuck wanted to spend time with a new female friend so had asked Jessie to do the meeting on his own. That was no big deal, he said, they had done so before. With this arrangement in place, it was Jessie Cheeseman's idea to invite Jane to go with him. It had never appeared risky, the boy asserted. They were just collecting stories, writing about them in their blog, and doing the occasional podcast.

There was a long pause. Betts had done this kind of thing before and knew what she was doing. She was giving him time to take it all in, to realise the importance of giving the full story.

'He had written about the connection with the drug traffickers,' Chuck began. 'I tried to tell him it was a mistake. The last blog was about how the sale of drugs was financing the rebellion against the government and how it was wrong and would undermine their struggle. I thought he was just going to meet the usual guys but there may have been others there too,' said Chuck.

'What other guys,' she asked. 'Have you met them before? Did you get their names?'

'At our previous meeting, there had been this older guy there. He didn't say much, and he wore a mask, but when he did speak, his English was way better than the others. He didn't need an interpreter. He seemed angry. That's all.'

'Did you get a name,' Betts prompted.

'They called him Zhang.'

'So, this man's name was Zhang Sein?' Betts shifted in her seat. 'Tell me more about the meeting, Chuck. What did they want from you and Jessie?'

'They wanted a positive story from us,' he said. 'They showed us maps of where their camps were and the cities that they planned to attack. Jessie took photos of them. They wanted us to tell the world, but especially people back in the States, about how they needed support. They were angry all this money was going to the Ukraine to fight off the Russians. There was no help coming their way to fight off the army who had overthrown the government.'

The Captive

On the third day of her captivity, Jane Gordon's strength finally gave out. Her body was spent from the relentless wailing, the desperate cries for help, and the frantic pounding of the door that had bruised her fists. Her refusal to touch the unappetizing food had left her feeling weak and listless. She was isolated now, separated from the other four young women who had been with her, without warning they had simply disappeared after the second day. She was left alone in a windowless room, under a harsh, unyielding light which denied her the comfort of sleep.

The room was sparse and dirty; a ceiling fan struggling to move the stifling air, a grimy mattress on a rusty wire frame, and a filthy toilet in the corner adding insult to the misery of the place. Food and water came twice daily and slipped through a gap under the door, but she hadn't touched any of it. The watery rice soup with its small, sad pieces of chicken was the least of her concerns.

The noises outside her room were a cruel reminder of life, continuing beyond her prison: Trucks growling in and out at all hours, muffled conversations she couldn't make out, the crowing of roosters, and even the laughter of children at play. It was surreal, as though the world had forgotten her existence.

Then came a sudden banging on the door, jolting her out of her exhausted stupor. A voice followed, harsh and full of authority: 'Be still and sit down on the bed. Someone is coming to talk to you.'

Too weary to resist, Jane obeyed, sinking onto the edge of the bed. She was beyond fear now, her spirit dulled by exhaustion and despair. All she could do was wait for whatever came next.

The door creaked as it was opened, slowly. A boy of no more than 16 years old poked his head around the door and stared at her, and she stared back. He closed the door again and there were words spoken and the door reopened, and an older man entered.

'Hello Jane,' he said, 'my name is Zhang Sein. You can call me Sein.'

She wanted to leap from the bed and hit him, but she had no energy, and she was shackled to the bed base.

'Just try and relax for a minute, I want to talk to you,' said the man.

'How can I relax while I'm chained here like an animal,' she said.

'Well, let's talk first, and then perhaps we can do something about the chain around your leg' he said. 'I understand you are an Australian. I studied in Australia and lived in Sydney for four years. Is that where you're from, Sydney?' She nodded. 'So, what were you doing with the young American guy' he asked.

'I just met him,' she spluttered, 'where is he?'

Zhang Sein just stared at her without saying anything.

'You killed him,' she shouted, and burst into tears again, straining against the chain that held her leg.

'Well, *I* didn't kill him, and I didn't order the killing either. It was a mistake and I'm sorry. But the real problem we have here is, what are we going to do with you?'

Sitting there silently trembling, Jane Gordon was exhausted and had nothing to say.

'Are you working for the DEA,' he asked, 'or are you working for the Australian government? Who are you working for,' he demanded in a raised voice.'

'I don't work for anyone,' she said, 'I am a student, I'm just here on holiday. I'm a backpacker. My father will be looking for me, he's a powerful man, and he will have been in contact with the embassy in Bangkok, I'm sure he has.'

'You say your father is powerful, is he in the army or is he a policeman? What is he? What does he do?'

She paused, unsure what to say about her father. 'He is a senior official in the government of New South Wales,' was all she said.

Zhang Sein had spent long enough in Australia to have some idea of what his position might be. He might be powerful, but not so powerful in Myanmar. And he said as much to Jane Gordon.

'Well, he would have been in touch with the ambassador, they know each other. They went to university together and they will be looking for me,' she said.

Zhang Sein's expression changed. 'Well, that is interesting news,' he said. 'You look hot and dirty. How would you like to have a shower?' She said nothing. 'You will have to behave yourself if we let you out of here.'

She nodded, 'I will behave myself, please just let me go and I won't say anything to anyone.'

'Let's just start by getting you cleaned up, shall we?' He said, leaving the room.

A short time later she could hear the door being unlocked. A young woman wearing a traditional Myanmar dress consisting of a long, folded skirt with a simple white blouse entered the room. She was holding a towel with a bar of soap on top, she said nothing as she handed this to Jane Gordon and motioned for her to follow. Stepping out of the windowless room into a large warehouse, she could see now where all the noise was coming from. There were forklifts, trucks, and rows of tables. In one corner there were boxes stacked ten meters high. Young men were loading them into trucks and pick-ups. There were also men with rifles standing near the doorways. The young woman spoke to her, but Jane didn't understand. She followed her to the other side of the warehouse, past young men who stopped and stared at her.

They came to a small room, a simple concrete shell. Jane entered and the door was locked behind her. In one corner was a large, blue plastic barrel filled with water and a small plastic bowl bobbing around on the top. There was a red sarong on a railing, a plastic bottle of soap and green mould on the floor and walls. There was a small, frosted glass window on one wall. Jane stood and stared at the room for a few moments and then removed her clothes and began to ladle the water from the barrel over her. It was cold and she shivered but was grateful anyway. She hadn't showered for days, and the weather was hot. It was a far cry from the luxury of her bathroom in Sydney, crammed full of designer shampoo, conditioner, moisturizer, perfume, and more. But still, she was grateful.

Finishing her shower, she wrapped herself in the sarong and gathered her clothes in one hand. Her hair hung in a mess, clean but unbrushed. She suddenly felt hungry. She tapped on the door and the girl opened it slowly and took Jane Gordon's dirty clothes from her. She followed the girl back across the warehouse to the chatter of the young men and women packing boxes onto trucks. She lowered her head and looked away. This time she was led to a different room. As they entered, she felt a rush of cool air and saw her captor sitting behind a desk. He motioned for her to sit.

'Don't be afraid,' said Zhang Sein, 'we are civilized people here. We have morals too, just like people in the West.' The wall behind him was dotted with photographs, mostly portraits and many in black and white. Family members no doubt. There were also several certificates and a bachelor's degree certificate from The University of Technology, Sydney. He offered her water, which she accepted with gratitude. He turned toward the wall behind him, 'this is my family,' he said proudly. He pointed to a black-and-white portrait of a stern-looking older man. 'My famous grandfather, Khun Sa, maybe you have heard of him,' he asked.

She shook her head.

He then pointed to his bachelor's degree certificate. 'Do you know it,' he asked, 'The University of Technology, Sydney, (UTS), is my alma mater. I didn't do much work there,' he laughed, 'mostly done by my friends, but I learned a lot during my time in Sydney. One whole year learning English and three years having fun.' He laughed again.

His face was boyish and fair-skinned. He could have been sixteen, she thought, but she knew he was much older. He was dressed in a business shirt, with designer jeans and rubber sandals. Clean-shaven, with hair that looked recently cut, the young man looked more like an accountant than a drug trafficker.

'Are you hungry,' he asked. She nodded. 'We have Burmese food. No McDonalds or KFC here. Sorry about that.'

Having not eaten for several days; she was hungry. He spoke to the young woman who was standing quietly by the door, and she scurried away, returning shortly after with a tray containing a bowl of rice, what looked like a bowl of curry, some flatbread, and a banana. Zhang Sein raised himself slowly from his chair.

'I'm going to leave you to eat your breakfast. I will be back shortly, and we can talk more about your future. Nong Bak will stay with you. Please do not try and escape,' he said as he was leaving, 'there is nowhere to run to.' He closed and locked the door behind him.

The young Burmese woman moved toward the only window in the room which looked out over the warehouse and drew the curtain. Jane hungrily devoured the food, all of it. Afterwards, she felt exhausted and fell asleep in the chair. When she awoke, she was alone in the room. Unsure of how long she had been asleep she sat upright and scanned the room. There was no computer, no phone, or any other communication device that she could see. There was, however, a television in one corner. Lying next to the television was a remote control which Jane grabbed and began pressing buttons randomly. The T.V. came to life and blared music at a loud volume. She heard the key in the lock of the door and the young girl entered, holding an outstretched hand for the remote. Her captor did not return, and she was taken back to her room. This time she was not chained to the bed.

###

#Know Your Enemy

The fan hummed softly overhead and the aircon droned from its perch on the wall, creating an oasis of cool comfort in the hotel room. Despite the climate control and his trusty earplugs securely in place, Finney still couldn't sleep. Being a light sleeper, he always carried earplugs. Once he got to sleep, he wanted to stay that way. He had forgotten how noisy Asia could be, with the relentless buzz of motorbikes and the ceaseless barking of dogs. Oddly enough, the dogs saved their noisiest barking for nighttime. During the day, they blended into the background of the city's chaos, but at night, their howls echoed uninterrupted through the streets.

This was simple insomnia; the kind that just kept sleep out of reach, unlike the other, more insidious version that usually plagued him. The other kind tricked him into falling asleep at a reasonable hour, only to jolt him awake at 2 or 3 a.m. From there, his mind would spiral into a frenzy of irrational thoughts, making sleep impossible until just before dawn, when he would finally drift off, only to be rudely awakened by the morning light.

But tonight was different. Finally, sleep began to wash over him, bringing with it a jumbled wave of thoughts and images: Jane Gordon's terrified face, Ella's smile, the stern gaze of Ambassador Clifton-Blythe, and the enigmatic presence of Pip Tan. These faces swirled together, blurring the line between his waking anxieties and the dreams which began to take hold. Finally, exhaustion got the upper hand, and he drifted off into a restless sleep.

He managed to sleep until 4.30 am. Was this a good sign he was getting in the groove of the local time zone, and he was almost getting enough shuteye. He opened the door to his small balcony and was hit by a familiar wall of hot, humid, and gritty air. Even at 4.30 am, it was 30 C, and the small town of Mae Sai was coming to life. Vendors in the street began to set up their stalls, goods being delivered, and the sound of brooms sweeping courtyards and roadways. This is where the overlapping night shifts of the hotel security guards mixed with the day shift of market vendors, labourers, and the rest of the workforce who didn't have to endure the challenges of staying awake all night. He had done his fair share of night shift work at the beginning of his policing career, that was the beginning of his struggles with sleep, or more accurately, the lack of it.

He took in the wisps of smoke from the numerous charcoal fires and the smell of food being prepared. Finney remembered back to his first visit with Sarah all those years ago. The tagline from the Tourism of Thailand Authority at the time had been, The Land of Smiles. It could be more appropriately described as The Land of Smells. In one short stretch of street life, his sense of smell would be beguiled by the intoxicating aromas of great food, incense, flowers, and perfume, and then assaulted by the pungent odours of fish sauce, diesel fumes, and putrid drains.

Gulping down a half-bottle of water, he pulled on some shorts and a T-shirt. Banjob had said to dress casually. He took the stairs to the lobby and met Banjob and another man, deep in conversation in Thai, at least he assumed it was Thai. He was introduced to the man, known as Kyle Mint. The van was parked at the front of the hotel, and they climbed aboard, the temple was not far away and there was no need for seatbelts, Banjob had said.

Sure enough, less than five minutes later they were entering the parking area of Wat Phra That Doi Wao. 'Just call it Wat Phra That,' said Banjob. As they exited the vehicle, Finney noticed a long, steep set of stairs with a large Buddha statue at the top. 'Yes, that's where we are going,' laughed Banjob. 'It's a good thing it is still so cool.'

They started up the stairs and Banjob was taking them two at a time, as was his friend. Both men were at least ten years older than Finney but more fit than he was. As they disappeared up the stairs, he was reaching for his water bottle, puffing and out of breath. I've got to get back to the gym, he thought.

As he reached the top of the stairs to a large flat area, scattered with numerous Buddhist statues and altars, he realised they were the only people there. 'We shouldn't be here this early,' said Banjob, 'it doesn't officially open until 8 am for visitors but I had a chat with one of the monks yesterday and he said it was no problem to come in early. 'It is a temple, like 7/11, open 24/7,' he chuckled.

All three men walked to the edge of the platform and took in the view. They must have been a few hundred meters above the town. 'So, are we looking at Mae Sai down there?'

'Well, no, it is Mae Sai and Tachileik,' replied the driver.

'So where is the river?'.

'It's down there, you just can't see it,' said the man from Myanmar.

Banjob pointed out it was impossible to see where Mae Sai finished and Tachileik started. 'The border is very ill-defined around here,' he said. 'The Thais spoke Burmese as well as Thai and the Burmese spoke Thai as well as Burmese. It is difficult to distinguish one from the other and the police couldn't pick the drug dealers from the labourers.'

Now it was the turn of the other man to speak. 'My good friend here hasn't even introduced us properly. Yes, my formal name is Kyle Mint, but please don't call me Mr. Mint. It makes me sound like some kind of confectionery,' he chuckled, no doubt he had used that line before. 'Just call me Tura, and I am Burmese, or Myanmar if you prefer.'

His accent was British private school. The two men shook hands and Tura looked hard at Finney. 'I am Burmese,' he repeated. 'All this nonsense with Myanmar. I still don't know why we had to change the name.'

'Why was the name changed, I'm confused between the use of the words Myanmar and Burma,' he said. 'You seem to use them interchangeably.'

'I am Bamar,' said Tura, his voice steady but laced with a quiet intensity. 'We make up more than 70% of the population of our country. The next biggest group, the Shan, are around 10%. Even though we have many ethnic groups, most are very small in numbers. Look at where we are on the map, and you'll see why—people from China, Tibet, Bangladesh, Laos, Thailand, and India have all mingled here. The names Myanmar and Burma have both been used for centuries. Some academics think the word Burma is a derivative of Myanmar. It's complicated for foreigners, but for us, either name works, and no one gets too offended by it. It's not important, so please don't worry about it.'

Tura paused, allowing his words to sink in. Then he continued, his tone shifting to something more solemn. 'What is important to understand about my country is that it is complex. I mean it is not black and white. I was schooled in England in my early life, so I understand Westerners like to put things in boxes, to make things neat and convenient to categorize. But my country cannot be put into a neat little box.

We fought the Thais for more than a thousand years and retained our freedom. We were colonized by the great Moghuls. Then the British came in the late 1800s, deposed our King, took away our royal family, plundered our resources, ruined our great nation, and left it broken. The Japanese came and went, and then finally, we got our country back.'

His voice carried the weight of history, the pride of a people who had endured and survived. Finney could feel the layers of pain in Tura's words, the tenacity of a nation that had seen so much tragedy, yet still held onto its identity, however fractured or complex it might be.

'We are made up of many ethnic groups,' he went on, now in full stride. 'We speak multiple languages and eat different foods from one place to another. Now we fight amongst ourselves while we hold the door open for the Chinese to come in. Of course, the Chinese won't colonize us as the British did but colonize us they will.' His eyes were moist with tears, and his cheeks shook.

He turned on his heels and strode toward the temple, gesturing for them to follow. As they reached the entrance, he removed his sandals and turned to Finney and Banjob. Tura had been carrying a small daypack which he removed from his shoulder and opened. He took out a folded piece of cloth and shook it to unravel what looked like a sarong and handed it to Finney.

'Wear this over your shorts. We call it a longyi.'

It was a piece of material about 80cm in length and sewn along the middle like a skirt. The man from Sydney fumbled, and Tura stepped forward, asked for the longyi and demonstrated the right way to put it on and tie it up. Finney eventually got the hang of it, and they entered the temple together.

The temple was much cooler than outside, much to Finney's relief. It was decorated with gold and adorned with numerous statues. He followed the lead of his two local companions, lit three incense sticks and knelt in front of the largest Buddha statue. They bowed three times before placing the incense in a container full of sand at the base of the large statue.

Walking him around the temple the men explained the meaning of the murals covering the walls. They also discussed the subtle differences between a Thai Buddhist temple and one in neighbouring Myanmar.

'Of course, ours are more beautiful,' laughed Tura.

'So where are all the monks,' asked Finney.

'They are out doing their morning alms,' Banjob explained. 'The monks rise early and meditate before walking through the adjacent neighbourhoods, offering prayers to people and accepting food in return.'

As they walked toward the car, Tura suddenly stopped in the middle of the sunny temple courtyard. The three men stood in a circle. He opened his hands towards the other two men.

'But finally, we're not fighting amongst ourselves anymore,' he said. 'Now we are united against a common enemy. Do you know who our enemy is,' he asked rhetorically. 'The army. They are the enemy of the people, and we have finally realised that. More importantly, we have decided to join hands with all our brothers and sisters in this great country and together we will defeat the army,' he said with a grand gesture.

'Are you familiar with the writings of Sun Tze,' asked Tura.

'The Art of War,' replied Finney, 'that's the only one I know.'

'It's the only one you need to know. The first principle is that every battle is won before it is fought.'

He nodded, 'Yes, I seem to recall that.'

'Make sure you adopt the same approach with your adversary. If it is who I think it is, you will need to know his weakness. Let me tell you what it is. He seeks adoration. He wants to be seen as a winner, someone who gets what he desires. If you make him feel that way you will also get what you want. You must know your enemy, and only then will your war be won before it begins.'

The heat was getting to Finney. With sweat trickling down his back and off his forehead, he suggested they retreat somewhere for a cool drink. It was still only 6.30 am but already it was hot. He jumped in the passenger seat and once again delighted in the rush of cold air from the car's AC.

'What is connecting the drug traffickers and freedom fighters,' asked Finney. 'Is it simply a convenient alliance? What happens if democracy is reinstated?'

'The resistance fighters call themselves the People's Defence Force here in the Shan State,' said Tura. 'There are parallel and unconnected groups in other states. Many are in hiding, in various places in Thailand and especially along the Thai/Burma border. The rebels have recently changed their tactics. There are more and more military informants in the big cities and the government is conscripting any young man under twenty-five years old to fight, so many young men are going into hiding and joining resistance groups. They believe if they must fight, they would rather fight against the government, rather than fight their friends and neighbours. The increasing number of atrocities against civilians, perpetrated by the army, is another reason why so many people are joining the resistance movement.'

Tura explained how he travelled daily across from Tachileik to Mae Sai, and he observed many things that would go unnoticed by the casual visitor. Finney knew that comment was directed at him. I can pick a labourer or a rebel fighter from a drug mule, Tura had said. It was their clothes, and their expressions, the drug mules were often nervous and agitated. Tura had worked for the UN and had done so for many years, he also confided that he knew a lot of people working on different projects in Myanmar, some of them clandestinely. 'I do what I can to make the world a better place,' he laughed, but not because what he said was meant to be funny.

Finney wondered whether he also did some work for Rosie Betts. What he came to realise was that all was not as it seemed with his companions.

Tura suggested they stop at the morning market on their way back to the hotel. 'I can only take so much of that hotel food,' he said, 'I need some rice porridge with some grilled pork skewers for my breakfast this morning.'

As they walked into the markets, Banjob suggested he might give the visitor a short tour of the market.

'I've already been here,' said Finney.

'Well, I know you've been here,' replied the driver, but I don't think you've had a proper look at this market just yet.'

The driver then proceeded to lead him around the market pointing out the numerous varieties of fruits; lychees, longans, dragon fruit, rambutan, papaya, pineapples, oranges, and a bewildering array of chillis and fresh green vegetables. Banjob seemed happy to pick up fruits and vegetables and explain what they were to his guest. The vendors seemed unperturbed by this behaviour and in fact, laughed and joked with Banjob as they walked around. The sights and smells were very different to what Finney was used to, there were sweet and sour foods, the smell of wood smoke and sizzling woks, pots of boiling soup, and grilled fish. It was busy, dirty, hot and smelly but somehow, he loved it. He was taken in by the relentless movement of people coming and going, pushing carts, delivering produce, and the ceaseless chatter between vendors and early morning customers. Banjob pointed to the ground which was a mix of asphalt and concrete with water everywhere. 'This is why we call it a wet market', he said.

There was a mix of customers but most of them were female, observed Finney. The majority carried just a simple basket and came every morning and bought enough food for a day at a time, but then some had helpers following them with a trolley and were buying large amounts of meat, fish, and vegetables. As he saw him looking at others in the market, Banjob explained that they were restaurant or food vendors buying up for today's trade, the housewives are regulars, and many start their day with a visit to the market. Some of them are maids and this is also part of their job. Well, it is certainly colourful and more fun than my weekly visit to the supermarket in Newtown, thought Finney, how dull my life is.

'People seem so happy and smiling in this market,' Finney suggested.

Banjob paused before responding. 'A smile can mean many things, not always happiness. Sometimes a smile can mean nervousness, fear or submissiveness, wouldn't you agree,' he asked. He turned and walked away toward another food stall, not waiting for a reply.

Tura joined them eventually, clutching five or six plastic bags of food. 'Breakfast is served,' he shouted. 'None of that boring English breakfast for us this morning gentlemen,' he said. 'Just look at this bounty. Let's get back to the hotel, I'm starved.'

The three men settled at a table in the hotel dining room. None of the staff seemed bothered that they had brought their food with them, with several coming to their table to peek at what they had to eat.

Seated together Finney took the opportunity to quiz Tura further on his knowledge of Tachileik and the activities of the drug traffickers. 'Were they somehow involved in Jane Gordon's disappearance,' he inquired.

'Not beyond the realms of possibility,' was Tura's response. 'That would be my guess. I could do some digging around for you if you have the resources.' Finney assumed that this was a reference to funds to cover the source of information. He had been around long enough to know that if you wanted information of this kind, it would cost you money. In Thailand, Australia, or Myanmar, it would cost money.

'How much are we talking about,' asked Finney.

'Well, let's start with B50,000 ' said Tura.

That seemed like a lot of money and Finney said as much.

'How much do you want this girl back,' asked Tura.

He dutifully handed over the cash. Whatever it takes, was his unspoken answer. 'I'd like to make a trip across the border,' he said, 'just to get a feel for the place.

Tura looked doubtful. 'I'm not so sure that is a good idea. Unless of course you just go across as a tourist, in any case, I couldn't take you there. I can't be seen with you; I know too many people.'

Now it was Banjob's turn. 'I'll take you across sir,' he said. 'I can pose as a tour guide easily enough and my face is not known over there. We might have to get you a disguise of some sort.' He looked the man up and down. 'You look too much like an undercover cop. No tourist would be wearing those clothes in this heat. I'll get you something from the market,' he said, holding out his hand, 'B500 should be about right.'

Finney knew he would need another trip to the bank as his funds were dwindling and he had a feeling there would be more to pay. Way more.

Tura took his leave and returned across the border. 'I'll take the shortcut and wet my feet,' he said, meaning to say he would wade across the river rather than take the official route across the bridge.

Man Down

Seated in the hotel restaurant, his phone pinged; it was a message from Stacey Harmer. **Jane has made contact. Call me**, was all it said. He made his excuses and moved away to make the call. There had been a message from Jane Gordon's phone late the night before. The Gordons had called it in at about 6 am Sydney time. All it said was. **I'm OK, I'll call you.** There had still been no activity on her credit card and the feeling was that the message may have been from someone other than Jane. 'Call me as soon as you hear anything,' he said, and abruptly ended the call.

'We really should be getting Mr. Quinn involved,' said Banjob, 'the ambassador called last night and said as much.'

Finney was surprised by this. He had assumed that Banjob had driven Quinn back to Chiang Rai the night before for his onward journey to Bangkok. But the driver revealed that Roger Clifton-Blythe instructed Quinn, in no uncertain terms, to remain in Mae Sai until Jane Gordon was found. Quinn had been furious and had gone off in search of a bar to quell his fury.

He tried calling Quinn on his mobile, but there was no answer. He asked reception to call Quinn's room, but still, there was no response. Growing concerned; he asked the reception staff if they had seen Quinn that morning. They had not. He asked if Quinn had checked out or organised transportation to Chiang Rai. The staff confirmed that it was impossible Quinn could have checked out or left without them being notified.

With a growing sense of unease, he headed for the stairs.

He climbed to the second floor, his mind racing through possibilities. Reaching for Quinn's door, he pounded on it, each knock echoing in the otherwise quiet hallway. But there was still no answer. Finney felt a cold knot in his chest. Something was wrong. He tried the door handle and found it unlocked. Tentatively, he turned the handle and slowly pushed the door open, half expecting a torrent of abuse from Quinn. It was eerily quiet and pitch black. 'Quinn are you in here,' he called out. There was no reply. The cool air from the AC rushed out into the hallway, along with a smell. A putrid smell. It was a mixture of nicotine, stale beer, uneaten room service food, and death. He felt inside the door for the light switch and turned it on.

Sprawled out on the bed was Barry Quinn. Eyes wide open and bulging, naked from the waist down, his body was bloated and contorted. On the bedside table was an overflowing ashtray, Quinn having ignored the No-Smoking signs plastered on the wall behind the bed. Alongside the ashtray were several empty beer bottles and an open packet of condoms. He's had company, thought Finney. After checking for a pulse, which he knew he would not find, he recoiled back into the hallway and gagged. It was not his first corpse, but it was certainly one of the worst that he had ever seen. Quinn wasn't pretty when he was alive, and death had certainly not improved his looks.

Clicking the lock and pulling the door shut behind him, he descended the stairs back into the coffee shop. Banjob was still sitting there, cradling his coffee. Finney, as calmly as he could, sat down opposite Banjob. The embassy driver saw right away that there was a problem.

'What is it sir,' asked the driver.

He paused for a moment. 'It's Barry Quinn,' he said, 'he's dead.'

He needed time to think. Who to call first? The ambassador. That was the only call he had to make. The embassy would handle it after that. That was *their* job. He would need a back story for the police, or did he just check into another hotel and avoid that altogether? Call the embassy. He knew that Clifton-Blythe would be none too happy with this news to start his day. Finney suddenly needed a drink. A strong drink. Even this early in the morning that didn't seem to matter. He was startled from his thoughts as he felt Banjob's hand on his shoulder.

'Come on, sir, you need a shower and a change of clothes before we call this in. With that, he led Finney to his room and waited in the hallway. 'I'll give you twenty minutes and then I'm knocking on your door.'

Banjob had been right, the shower and change of clothes were good, but he stared at the phone and was still unable to make the call. He had time to think about what to say to the ambassador. Just tell it like it is. It will be messy, and they will need to get someone from the embassy here as soon as possible, but he could carry on with the search for Jane Gordon. He was making progress. They would find her. Yes, sir, you can be sure of that. He had the script. Now for the call.

Finney was surprised at how easy the call was, and how short. He had been right, Clifton-Blythe seemed more concerned about the progress of the Jane Gordon case than he was about the death of Barry Quinn. And yes, he would send someone up and they would be there by lunchtime. Banjob would get them to Mae Sai from the airport in Chiang Rai. The repatriation of Barry Quinn to

Bangkok was not his problem and on no account was he to speak to the Thai police. If questioned, he would pose as a tourist who had nothing to offer about the death of a serving Australian Federal Police officer. It was a suspected heart attack, simple as that. That would be the explanation. The embassy would arrange an autopsy in Bangkok. Diplomatic status and all that. Case closed. 'Get on with finding Jane Gordon,' were the ambassador's last words.

Clifton-Blythe had advised him to let the hotel staff find Quinn so that he could stay as far away from the incident as possible. It would only complicate his real work in finding Jane Gordon. He felt guilty doing so, as he knew how bad it looked up there, but the ambassador was right. So, yet another lie was his to tell. As he approached the two young Thai receptionists, he was crafting yet another script. 'I cannot seem to get through to Mr Quinn, perhaps one of your staff could check in on him,' he suggested as an afterthought. The older of the two receptionists called over the security guard from the front door and spoke with him in Thai before handing him a key. It was time to get out of there and he did just that.

Relocating himself to the café across the street, he seated himself at a table near the window where he could view the hotel entrance without being seen. Quinn's body would remain in the hotel room. That had been the instruction of the police after contact from the ambassador's office. The hotel staff, on the other hand, wanted him gone as soon as possible.

Finney needed to speak with Rosie Betts, and he desperately wanted news from Tura. It was midday by the time he got a hold of Betts. She was busy she had said, the previous evening there had been a gun battle near a remote border post, sixty kilometres from Mae Sai. Thai army officers had killed twenty-one traffickers, all mostly small-time mules, and the Thais had sustained casualties of their own. He held back the news about Quinn, and they agreed to meet that evening. Finney was checking emails when he heard his name being called. It was Pip, the Chiang Mai journalist. Pip, who had contacts everywhere, had already heard the news about a suspicious death at the Orassa Hotel.

'I thought you were over at the Orassa Hotel. Any luck finding that girl you were looking for,' she said. Pulling up a chair she began to chatter about the excitement across the street. 'There's some dead foreigner over there but I can't get any information from the police, even after I offered them money,' she went on, 'and that is very unusual.'

He still had trouble adapting to the look of Pip and the way she spoke. She looked like a Thai and spoke English like a lily-white BBC TV newsreader. Finney found it disconcerting and worse still, he did not know why he reacted that way.

'There's been a gun battle at a border post last night,' she continued, 'multiple fatalities, so I've got something to can report. Months go by and we hear nothing out of Mae Sai and in the space of a few days we have a dead Peace Corps volunteer, a border gun battle, one dead westerner in the hotel here, and another missing.' She shot him a glance and a wink. 'Come on, tell me what is going on with Jane Gordon.'

He had to decide. Pip was well connected, she knew people, she had sources and there were things she could uncover that were beyond him. That said, she was a journalist, and his experience had taught him that journalists would do anything for a story. He had to keep this under the radar.

'A few of us are getting together tonight for a drink,' said Pip. 'Why don't you join us? Don't worry, it won't just be boring journos, I know a bunch of people here, some Westerners, some Thais, Burmese. Come on, it will be fun. 9 pm onwards. We will be at the Bamboo Bar, everyone knows it, just a few minutes' walk from here and overlooking the river. Hope to see you then.' With that, she was gone.

There is something about Pip Tan, but that would have to wait. He needed to get back to thinking about Jane Gordon, and then there was still the matter of Barry Quinn. Would they send up another officer to assist him?

Around 2 pm, and right on point, Banjob appeared with Richard Hanlon from the embassy. Hanlon had been Finney's pick-up man at the airport at what seemed a lifetime ago but was only three or four days. He had lost track of time. 'We meet again Mr. Finney,' said Hanlon. He looked like he would rather be anywhere else than standing on a dusty street in Mae Sai. Hanlon needed the back story before he faced the mayhem across the road where Quinn lay prone and half-naked in his bed on the second floor.

He explained to Hanlon that he had no idea what had happened to Quinn. 'To be honest, I've hardly seen the guy these past few days,' he said. Banjob nodded in agreement. 'The only time I saw him he was propping up the bar at the front of our hotel. He refused to help me in any way.'

'That sounds like him,' muttered Hanlon. 'The key thing is we need to keep you out of this. There is no way you are answering any questions from the Thai police. I don't even want them to know you are here. We will book you into another hotel for tonight. Do not go back to the hotel until after we get him out of there. A couple of days should be enough for things to settle down. Banjob, you take care of that if you would. Finney, you stay here until I return.' With that, Hanlon turned on his heels and headed over toward the hotel.

Finney heard the van door slide open, and Bart Guthrie emerged and headed straight towards him.

'What happened across the road there,' he yelled.

Banjob stepped forward, 'Mr Guthrie, please stay calm,' he said.

'My best friend is dead in that hotel,' Guthrie continued, pointing at the Orassa, 'and I want to know what happened. I want to know the truth.' He was almost yelling and people in the street turned and stared.

Once again Banjob spoke, 'Mr Guthrie please, let's discuss this in private. Mr Finney, please step into the van for a moment.' Both men did so with Guthrie in the front seat, and Finney in the back.

'Give me the whole story,' demanded Guthrie.

No one had told Finney that Barton Guthrie would be travelling to Mae Sai. It caught him by surprise but the best he could do was to just tell the truth, he had nothing to hide. Quinn was reluctant to be involved in the investigation to find Jane Gordon and he had made that very clear. He had barely seen him during their time in Mae Sai and every time he did see him, he had a drink in his hand. Finney did not characterize it in those exact words. He was more tactful. What he wanted to say was that Quinn was a belligerent drunk who did as little as possible and all he wanted to do was to get back to Bangkok. Of course, he omitted that last piece of information.

'So where was he last night,' demanded Guthrie.

'I have no idea; I haven't seen him since yesterday lunchtime. He took me to get some cash from the bank and I did not see him again until I found him dead in his room this morning.'

Guthrie flinched. 'There must be more to this than meets the eye,' he said.

'Did he have any history of heart problems,' asked Finney. 'It looks like a heart attack to me.'

'So now you are a doctor are you,' spat Guthrie. There followed a long silence. 'No heart issues that I know of,' said Guthrie finally, 'but the autopsy will tell us that. It is my job to get him home and that is what I intend to do.' He glared at the other man for a moment before opening the van door and making his way across the road to where his friend lay dead on the second floor of the Orassa Hotel.

Finney was relieved as he saw Guthrie disappearing into the distance.

'Don't worry about him too much,' said Banjob, 'he treats everyone like that. Don't take it personally.'

Banjob was a paradox. He was polite and deferential, but at other times he could be very blunt. When he was being blunt, he still sounded polite and diplomatic. After twenty years at the Australian embassy, some things had rubbed off or perhaps that was just his character. Whatever it was, he diffused a tense situation and Finney was grateful. He needed to know if the driver had heard from Tura.

'He'll get back to us when he has something,' said Banjob, 'and don't worry, your money is well invested with Tura. He knows everyone worth knowing on both sides of this border. While that was reassuring, he needed results fast. As if reading his mind, Banjob said reassuringly, 'Our friend can be trusted. He will get back to you as soon as he has something.'

Finney went back to his emails. There was the usual smattering from the human resources people, training courses were available, stress support, and preppy platitudes about how to enjoy work. But there it was, the email from Stacey Harmer, the subject title was **'Hit and Run'.**

The incident had occurred a few weeks earlier, not long after the rescue of Jane Gordon in Newtown. Funny coincidence there, thought Finney. According to his colleague, a young international student from Myanmar had been arrested following the death of a pedestrian in the inner city of Sydney on the night of the 6th of September. The man was still in custody and the case was ongoing. There had been one application for bail shortly after his arrest, but it had been rejected. There was another scheduled in a few days. According to the email it would be opposed by the NSW police. The young man's name was Zhang Win. OK, so that made sense. Could this man be related to Zhang Sein, a young, but high-profile drug trafficker and grandson of the infamous Khun Sar.

'Can you get me the name of the officer managing this case,' he asked his colleague.

He was still seated outside at the hotel across the street from the Orassa. There were four police pick-up trucks outside and a small crowd still gathered, no doubt speculating on what was going on inside. As he watched, a black van with heavily tinted windows rolled into view. An elderly Thai man emerged with a small black duffel bag.

Finney figured this was either a doctor or undertaker, about to ready Quinn's removal and repatriation back to Bangkok. There was another flurry of activity as police conferred with the man before he entered the hotel. Twenty minutes later a group emerged from the hotel with a large, black body bag on a hospital trolley. The body of Barry Quinn was loaded into the waiting van. He could also see Hanlon and Guthrie in conversation with the police. Hanlon was a Thai speaker, so he did not need assistance from Banjob as an interpreter. Soon enough the doctor exited the hotel and after conferring with the police, got into the van and it sped off. It was his understanding that the body would be flown to Bangkok from Chiang Rai. Hanlon and Guthrie headed back across the road, no doubt to speak with him again.

Hanlon looked exhausted and Guthrie just looked angry. They pulled up chairs and both sat down, with Hanlon requesting a more detailed report of what had occurred over the preceding days. Finney had explained that he had seen little of Quinn, he knew nothing about his movements, and that they would get more information from the hotel staff. 'We are unable to interview them,' said Hanlon, 'that is the job of the Thai police'. He also advised that the ambassador wanted an update on the progress of the search for Jane Gordon. Finney explained that he had sought information from a Myanmar national, Tura, and that he would speak to him again that evening. He was also working closely with the DEA and was sure that Myanmar drug traffickers participated in the abduction of Jane Gordon.

'Listen,' said Hanlon' that is all very well, but do you have anything concrete on where she might be and how soon we might get her back?'

He shook his head, 'I am afraid not, but we will find her.'

'I'm not sure the ambassador shares your optimism,' said Hanlon, 'our work here is done, and we are on the 9:00 PM flight from Chiang Rai to Bangkok. Hanlon called over to Banjob, 'OK let's get going, there are things that we will need to do when we return to the embassy.'

'This case is not over yet.' Guthrie glared at Finney, 'This case has a long way to go.'

He was relieved to see the two men leave. The hostility from Guthrie was palpable. He suddenly felt completely wrung out, it didn't help that he had been sitting out in the heat for three hours and had had nothing to drink. He ordered a large bottle of water and some ice, and as an afterthought, he ordered a bottle of beer. He gulped down the beer first, followed by the water. As he sat there gazing across the street, he saw Rosie Betts arriving in her jeep. A friendly face, and a welcome distraction. Unaware of what had occurred, Betts seemed visibly shocked by the presence of the police outside the hotel. Finney picked up the phone and called her, as he spoke, she turned around to face him and then began to walk across the road. With her hands upturned as if to say, what is going on here, she saw his empty beer bottle on the table, 'I think I will be needing one of those too,' she said.

He explained the events that had occurred that day. As he heard himself speaking, he really could not believe it either. 'Well, let's face it,' she said, 'Quinn was kind of a walking heart attack; all those cigarettes, overweight, and who knows what else.' She sounded less than sympathetic. What was of more interest to her was the fact that Finney had met Tura. Of course, she knew him, he should have realised that straight off. Betts seemed encouraged by the fact that Tura was now also helping on the case. 'He is one of the good guys,' she said, 'he knows everybody. I'm not sure why I didn't think of contacting him myself. Sorry about that.'

He also explained the arrest of the Burmese student in Sydney. Could it be too much of a coincidence that he could be related to Zhang Sein? Betts picked up her phone and began crafting a text message. When she was finished, she put the phone back down on the table.

'Tura will know for sure and if he doesn't, he will find out if they are related. We will know soon enough.' And they did, in less than fifteen minutes her phone pinged, and she read the text message. 'Boom,' she said, 'they are brothers. If Zhang Sein does have Jane Gordon, we now have some leverage to get her back.' Suddenly Finney didn't feel so exhausted. This was the first bit of good news that he had since arriving in Mae Sai. He wanted another drink, and Betts joined him.

The alcohol loosened the conversation and soon enough they were sharing their private lives. Betts had been married to a Thai man in Chiang Mai and had a daughter, who was living with the ex-husband there. That explained a lot, thought Finney. Why she had been content to stay in the job so long and to live in this dusty outpost? Mae Sai was only five hours from Chiang Mai, and she could see her daughter every week. The ex-husband was rich and so was his family. She was not a Thai national and her ex-husband's family had money, power, and influence. She would never win custody of her daughter and never get her back to the States. Her eyes moistened with tears as she told her story, coming to Thailand as a young woman and immersing herself in the culture. The next minute she was married with a young child and an abusive and neglectful husband. To make matters worse for her was the fact that her ex-husband had remarried. He had married a Thai woman from a prominent family, which of course had made his own family very happy. They had had a child of their own and now Betts was feeling marginalised as a mother. Finney shifted uncomfortably in his seat as an image of Charles Drayton flashed before his eyes.

He realised they had a lot in common.

The pause in the conversation told Finney that it was his turn to share his story. He left out the part about Charles Drayton and his feelings of animosity and tried as hard as he could, to paint a brighter picture than existed. He saw as much of Ella as he could, he and Sarah were civil toward one another, and Ella was doing well at school. Their daughter also seemed to have accepted the fact that her parents would never reconcile. They settled in at the bar, ordered some food, and continued their conversation. It had been a long time since he had a conversation quite like this, where he felt so relaxed and open. It had always been one of Sarah's criticisms of him. You are a closed book, she used to say, and he was.

As they were deciding whether to order yet more drinks, he remembered the invitation he had received from Pip Tan. He mentioned it to Betts, and she frowned.

'You might want to think twice about socializing with that crew,' she said. 'They are a mixed bag.'

'Yes, I thought that myself, but then again, I thought we might pick up valuable information. Pip and her friends have good contacts in this region.'

'True,' she said, looking a little sceptical, 'OK I am up for it, so long as you can tolerate reggae music because that is all they play at The Bamboo Bar. We can walk from here, it is just around the corner, on the riverside. So, watch out for mosquitoes.'

Finney settled the bill, and they moved on.

They could hear it before they could see it, Bob Marley blasting out on a crackly stereo and the sounds of conversation and laughter. This might be fun, he thought, it had been a long time since he had sat in a bar and listened to Bob Marley and the Wailers. Along with the music came the smell of cannabis. Well, it's the whole package. Pip leapt out of her seat to greet them as they arrived. Pip and Rosie were well acquainted, Rosie having previously lived in Chiang Mai. 'So great you came,' gushed Pip Tan, 'let me introduce you to the gang.'

The bar had a relaxed, almost laid-back vibe that Finney found unexpectedly comforting. As he scanned the room, he noticed a couple of travellers whose origins he couldn't quite place. They blended into the mix of patrons, some young Thais, most likely locals, perhaps with a few from Bangkok, and a smattering of Western tourists. Most of the Westerners were young, but a few older faces stood out, looking slightly out of place, as though they were still figuring out how they ended up in a bar like this.

Among their group was Clarke, an earnest young American doing research for his PhD on traditional Thai music, who was based in Chiang Mai. Anka, a thirty-something Dutch woman, was working on a gender development project funded by the United Nations. Both seemed deeply invested in their respective causes, yet they fitted seamlessly into the relaxed atmosphere of the bar.

Then there was Pip, accompanied by another colleague from her Chiang Mai newspaper. Pip, her colleague, and Rosie were chatting quietly in Thai, their conversation punctuated by occasional glances in Finney's direction. Each time Pip looked over, he couldn't help but wonder what they were discussing. Was it about him? And if so, why?

Despite the undercurrent of curiosity, the overall atmosphere was friendly. Jugs of beer made their way around the table, and the conversation flowed with ease. He found himself loosening up, the tension that had been knotting in his chest all day slowly unravelling as the night wore on. For a moment, surrounded by a mix of people who all seemed to be on some kind of journey, he felt good, maybe, just maybe, things would work out.

People were moving around the table and chatting. Clarke, the young PhD student sat down next to Finney. 'So, Declan, what brings you to Mae Sai,' he asked.

He was keen to keep the real reason for his visit a secret. 'I am doing some field work through the Australian Embassy' he said, 'I'm in law enforcement so this is a bit of a fact-finding tour for me.

Clarke raised an eyebrow, 'so I assume you're working with the DEA.'

'Well not exactly, Agent Betts has been showing me around but that is just a courtesy. A lot of the drugs that end up in Sydney, which is where I am from, come out of this part of the world. It is good for me to see what this looks like and it gives me a better understanding of what we're up against.' He saw the look on the young man's face. 'I am not here looking at cannabis,' he said. 'I am more interested in harder drugs, methylamphetamines mostly. But not tonight, I am just looking to relax, make some new friends and have a fun time. So, cheers,' and he raised his glass. So that was Finney's cover story for the rest of the evening, and like any effective agent he had to believe his own cover story.

Beer started flowing faster and vodka shots were consumed. People had interesting stories to tell. Realizing it had been a long time since he had met such a diverse group of people, he was enjoying himself. Time got away. The demon was getting a hold of him, and he knew it. That was normally how it unfolded. He could see it but couldn't seem to alter the course of what was happening. Agent Rosie Betts also saw it.

'Hey Finney,' she said, 'it is closing in on midnight, I think I'll head off.'

'Just one for the road,' he said.

'Not for me, it is a school night remember, and you still haven't found your girl.'

I think I have, he thought, looking across the table at Pip Tan. He was smitten. At that same moment, in the distance, he saw Banjob standing by the doorway. He knew it was time to leave.

The driver had booked him into another hotel. There were still police stationed at the Orassa Hotel, and he couldn't be seen there, especially not in the condition he was in. 'You might join us, Agent Betts, this news will be of interest to you too,' said the driver. They made their way back to the hotel. It was the Baan Teuk Homestay, a small guesthouse with no more than ten rooms. Finney barely registered the owner as they arrived, and they made their way through to a small courtyard.

'So, what have we got,' he said, slurring his words. Banjob and Tura looked at one another, Tura spoke first.

'The word on the street in Tachileik is that Zhang Sein was behind the killing of the young American boy, Jessie Cheeseman. At the very least it was his men who carried out the killing.'

'Well, I've also got some news,' said Finney, and went on to tell them about his email from Stacey Harmer and the arrest of Zhang Sein's brother.

It was at this point that Rosie Betts decided to leave. 'Finney,' she said, 'I need to give you those documents from the car, can you come and collect them?'

He didn't remember having to get any documents from Rosie but followed her to the car anyway.

'I know you have had a few drinks, and you've let your guard down, but you shouldn't be sharing that intel with Tura. You don't know him well enough. You need to keep your cards close to your chest around here. Call me in the morning and we can talk then.'

He was not so drunk that he couldn't see he had said the wrong thing. He was trying to apologise as she jumped into her jeep and headed off into the night.

It was time to call it a night. He struggled upstairs to his new hotel room and promptly passed out. He was awake again a few hours later, full of remorse for his lapse of judgement. He also had a raging thirst and was disoriented in his new lodgings. He devoured a half-litre bottle of water and managed to get himself back to sleep.

He was woken at 6.30 am by the phone ringing next to his bed. It was Banjob. 'Good morning, sir, can you meet Tura and me for breakfast as soon as possible?' He did not remember making any arrangements to meet for breakfast but agreed to be downstairs in fifteen minutes. Panadols, loads of water, and thoughts of a full English breakfast got him down there even faster.

As he descended into the lobby of the guesthouse, he had a vague recollection of the man greeting him there. An older Thai man with grey hair and a straggly beard who spoke with a strong American accent.

Lofty Ambitions

Jane Gordon waited all day, expecting him to return, but she contented herself with a shower and some food for the first time days. With a full stomach, she found it easier to sleep. She still had no idea what time it was or how many days she had been in captivity. What Jane did know was that Jessie, her friend and lover, was dead. Would she be next, she wondered. She lay on the bed staring at the ceiling fan as it spun slowly, moving hot air from one part of the room to the other.

She had spent the first forty-eight hours of her captivity shaking, sweating, vomiting and unable to sleep. All of these were classic withdrawal symptoms. On top of that, she was irritable, anxious, and had aches and pains all over, and worst of all she couldn't sleep. After finally getting some sleep, she awoke feeling calm. Afraid, but calm. Jane thought about her parents, they must be worried about her and would have people looking for her, surely, they would. Her father was a powerful man, but would his power be of any use in this part of the world, she wondered. The young woman, whom Zhang Sein had referred to as Nong Bak, came and went from the room with food and water, but she never spoke. Was it because she had been ordered not to, or that she simply could not speak English? Jane began to wonder about the life of that young girl in contrast to her own life of privilege. She felt remorse for the way that she had spoken to her parents, the way she had let them down. She lectured herself. If she made it out of here, she would turn her life around, stop taking drugs, go back to university, and reconnect with her old friends. She would treat her parents better and tell them how much she loved them. It wasn't just that she was being held captive, this was the first time that she had been straight for months, maybe even years. Jane had been in a cycle of drugs and alcohol for as long as she could remember, even before she had left high school. That was where it all began. A boarding school that was less than fifteen minutes from where her parents lived. She had lost contact with her friends after school finished, she was captive of the feeling she had when she was high. It helped her forget; it made her feel numb.

Having been drug-free for almost a week, she was thinking more clearly than she had done in a long time. Did I have to come to Thailand and be kidnapped to realise how good my life could be, she questioned herself. The irony was obvious to her. No longer was she captive to the drug but to the drug traffickers. It is the same thing, she thought. There was a way out. She stood up from the bed and tapped gently against the door. She heard the key go in the door and it opened a few inches and Nong Bak peered through the gap. I want to speak with Zhang Sein, she said. She repeated his name several times. The young girl nodded and then closed and locked the door again. Jane knew she had to be patient. All she could do now was wait.

During this time, she went back over her bad behaviour at home and the events that had occurred during her time in Thailand. Advice from friends had shaped her decision to travel to Bangkok and Chiang Mai. She encountered the group that included Jessie Cheeseman at the hostel, and they had taken her to the iconic Riverside Bar in Chiang Mai. Located on the Ping River, it was popular with both Thais and foreigners. After a meal there, they moved on to several other bars before settling in at one of the many clubs that stayed open till around 5 am. It was there that they got to know each other, despite the mind-numbingly loud house music. They agreed to meet again the following day. Jane was intrigued by Jessie's passion for the people of Myanmar, fighting an unjust military regime. Despite having never been interested in politics, she felt drawn to the struggle through her affection for Jessie Cheeseman. The youngest of three sons, Jessie's parents were both academics and the family lived in California. He was raised in a liberal environment where he was encouraged to be independent and curious. After graduating from UCLA with a degree in geography and politics, he wanted to see the world. First, he went to South America for six months as a volunteer in a village school. He had the travel bug. After successfully applying to become a Peace Corps volunteer, he was posted to Thailand, where he studied the Thai language and became a volunteer teacher's assistant in a school on the outskirts of Chiang Mai.

It had only been a few days, but Jane and Jessie became inseparable. They toured the town and its surroundings on Jessie's motorbike. Jane felt liberated. Visiting Thai temples, orphanages, youth development projects and elephant camps, she was enthralled. A whole new world opened before her. They spent most evenings out with his friends, listening to northern Thai folk music, clubbing and indulging in the local cannabis which was widely available. Jessie had explained that it was only a year earlier that you could get thrown in prison for possession of even a small quantity of weed. Suddenly the law changed, initially for the production and use of medicinal cannabis, but then that was extended to recreational use. Before long, retail outlets were popping up all over the country. Franchises with names like Big Bud Dispensary, Blow, Cannibalize, Up in Smoke, and The Budtender, became popular. The Thais were nothing if not creative and opportunistic.

The trip to Mae Sai was a bonus for Jane. She hadn't planned to go there but was persuaded to go by Jessie and the others. 'Come along,' he said, 'it's a fascinating part of the world and there are not so many tourists.' Jane had not told her parents; she knew it would worry them. For her, it was an opportunity for a bit of extra independence, adventure, and some more time with Jessie. They had taken the local bus, no air conditioning, and very hard seats. It had been a six-hour trip with numerous random stops in small villages along the steep, winding roads. They were the only foreigners on the bus, which for Jane, made it feel even more exotic.

After checking into a dorm room at the Top North Hotel, the group made their way to a small bar, raised on stilts above the river, to watch the sunset. It was already late in the afternoon and the sun had slipped behind a wall of tropical haze. There was not much sunset to see but they still soaked up the atmosphere of being in the northernmost part of Thailand gazing across toward Myanmar. For all but Jessie Cheeseman and Chuck Bowers, this was their first glimpse of the country. Pointing across the river, Jessie leaned in and whispered to Jane, 'If you want to, we could go over there later this evening.'

She smiled and nodded her head. It had all happened so quickly. They left the group at the bar shortly afterwards, just as the light was fading, and they made their way along the unpaved road, down to the river. It was quite shallow, less than thirty centimetres deep. They removed their shoes and waded across. Waiting on the other side were three men. The two younger men wore the traditional Burmese longyi and tee shirts, with the third, older man, in jeans and a polo shirt. The two younger men knew Jessie as they smiled and shook hands. The third man stood back a little.

Just wait there a moment, Jessie had told her, as the men walked a few steps away along the riverbank. Jane stood there taking in her surroundings, scattered shacks just a few meters up from the water's edge and young children playing nearby. She could hear chatter in the distance and there was the smell of wood fires and food being cooked. Suddenly, she heard a thud, a shout and she turned to see Jessie falling limply into the river. The man in the jeans was holding a piece of metal pipe. 'Run away,' shouted one of the younger men as the older man moved toward her. She didn't have time to react, the man had his arms wrapped around her with one hand over her mouth. The next minute she was being thrown into the back of a pickup truck. The rest was a blur.

Jane was brought out of her thoughts as the door opened and Nong Bak walked into the room and gestured for Jane to follow her. They walked back to the office where Jane had first met Zhang Sein with the girl opening the door and ushering her inside. He was seated at a desk typing furiously on a laptop, 'sit down,' he said, without lifting his eyes from the screen. She sat quietly and waited.

Finally, he stopped typing and looked up at her, 'you look well,' he said.

'I'm OK,' she said, 'I just want to go home.' At this point, she began to cry.

'Please don't cry,' he said, 'I need to talk to you about something. You say that your father is a powerful man, well

I want to know how powerful. I have a problem. My brother is in Sydney, and he is in trouble with the police, and I want to get him home. Is your dad powerful enough to help with that? What exactly does he do?'

Jane realised that it was her only hope of getting out of there. 'He's a senior government figure,' she said.

'What do you mean,' he asked, 'is he a politician? I'm not sure how useful a politician would be to me right now. I know your political and legal system in Australia is quite different from what it is here. If he were a politician here it could be useful, but not so useful in Australia. Your politicians cannot be bought as easily as ours.'

'He's the Governor of New South Wales,' she said finally. 'He has many important friends, who include politicians, but also the police as well. He has helped me out of trouble a few times with the police.'

Now she had his attention. 'My brother's in jail in Sydney. I spoke to his lawyer, and they've taken his passport.'

'I'm sure my father can help; he knows powerful and influential people. Give me my phone and I'll call them.'

'So, your father is Sir William Gordon?' Turning the laptop around to face her. There was a picture of her father and mother at an official function.

Jane was startled by the image, bursting into tears, and pleading with her kidnapper. 'Yes, that's my mom and dad. Please let me call them, I'll ask them to help your brother.'

Zhang Sein had been searching the internet looking for her father and he had come across Sir William Gordon. Bingo, he thought to himself, this could be exactly what he needed. He needed to know more about this man.

'Would you like to get some fresh air, Jane?'

She nodded and followed him out into the main part of the warehouse, where there was still a hive of activity. There were two large roller doors, but they were both closed. Over to one side was a small door leading outside into bright sunshine and heat. Jane squinted, as she had been locked in the windowless room for many days. The young girl, Nong Bak, followed them out carrying bottled water, which she handed to Jane Gordon and her captor. The warehouse sat on a large clearing on the side of a hill. There was a dusty road leading through a forested area to the warehouse, the whole area was surrounded by wooded hills as far as she could see.

Jane stood and gazed around her for a moment, 'where are we,' she asked. She immediately knew her captor would not give away their location.

'Let's just say we are somewhere in Shan state,' he said. 'There is no way anyone will find you here and no way for you to escape if that is what you are thinking. This is all mine,' he said, sweeping his arm in a large arc. 'My family has owned this land for generations. This is our homeland. I know everyone and everyone knows me.

'Now let's talk a little bit more about your parents, and particularly your father. How often have you been contacting them since you have been in Thailand?'

'I normally text them every couple of days. Provided I let them know where I am and I'm OK, then I think they're happy. But I am sure they will be worried about me because I haven't been in contact with them since I left Chiang Mai. I don't know what day it is.'

'It is Wednesday, you have been here almost a week. I am sure it feels longer. I will give you your phone and you can send them a message but we will have to change the internet somehow so it cannot be tracked. It could take a couple of hours. We must keep our location a secret.' He spoke to Nong Bak, and she scurried off back to the warehouse.

'Where are we? I just want to know.'

'We are in Shan State' he told her again. 'Let's just say we are closer to China than Thailand.' They were just outside Keng Tung, a large regional city in Shan State, home to his ancestors and about three hours north of Tachileik, but he was not sharing this with the girl. 'From here we will defeat the army and bring democracy back to Myanmar,' he said as he gazed out over the mountains. He turned to look at her, 'do you think I am just a drug dealer,' he asked. Jane simply stared at him.

'We are working together with the freedom fighters to restore our elected government. Dictatorship is bad for business. We want democracy here; we want to be recognized as a progressive country. For those few short years we had a proper government in power, tourists came and foreign investors as well. The world took us seriously. Now we are back in the dark old days of military dictators and the mafia. Worse still, we have allowed the Chinese back into our country and they will take everything from us and leave us with nothing. Look around you, we are a country rich in natural resources but what we do not have is the freedom to develop as our own independent country. The British took it from us, and we have never really recovered. But we can see a better future,' he said. 'I give some of my profits to the resistance fighters and now we have unified, we can defeat the dictators. I plan to go into politics, and one day I want to be Prime Minister.'

'The dictators have kept us captive because they kept us divided. Do you know we have more than 100 different ethnic groups in Myanmar,' he said, 'with as many different languages. The military has exploited this to divide us and have us busy fighting among ourselves. But now we are united under the banner of the Peoples Defence Force, which we simply call the PDF. We have more than 100,000 soldiers. We are taking back key towns and cities.' He looked out over the mountains again and pointed into the distance. 'We control all of this and as far as you can see all the way south to Mandalay.'

'So, you want to be Prime Minister,' Jane asked, 'will people want a drug trafficker as their leader?'

He frowned. 'People have short memories,' he said, 'if they can see their lives are better, all will be forgiven. I try to keep a low profile. Right now, I do not do much directly with the PDF. I do what I do, and I give them money. That is what matters. This is not Australia; we do things differently here. We see it all the time in politics. One minute, two groups are enemies and fighting one another. The next minute they are in a coalition government. Our last government, led by The Lady, was a coalition of several different political parties and of course representatives from the military. They were in government for almost six years and things were going well.'

'Who exactly is the lady,' asked Jane, 'I'm not sure who you're talking about. To be honest I do not know much about Myanmar.'

'Please,' said Zhang, 'can we just refer to it as Burma?' That is the real name of our country, not this Myanmar nonsense. The military changed our name from Burma to Myanmar back in the late '80s for public relations purposes. When I say The Lady, I am referring Aung San Su Kyi. Surely you must have heard of her?'

Jane nodded.

'Well, now she is in prison and getting old as well. We need a new generation of leaders who can get our country out of this hole we have been in for decades. The only way it will happen is to overthrow these dictators and take control. We will have to do whatever it takes. I want to send a message to your family. Would you be able to do that for us,' he said. 'I want them to know you are OK and in good health. Then we can negotiate your release.'

'Can I call my parents,' Jane asked.

'I'm afraid it won't be possible. We will make a short video and all I want you to do is to tell them you are OK and that we will be in touch. It's all we can do right now.'

They had written a script for her to follow when they made the video, using a mobile phone. The video was finalized, and the girl was returned to the room, accompanied by the young Burmese housekeeper.

Self-Loathing

The morning after the night before Finney was feeling unsteady on his feet as he approached Banjob and Tura. The Burmese man began by going back over what he said the night before. The word on the street was Zhang Sein's men had killed Jessie Cheeseman. The details and motive were incomplete.

'Where do we go from here,' asked Finney, 'do you have contacts who could confirm he has her?' There was a long silence.

'We know he has her. We need to put the word out we are prepared to negotiate. Would your government negotiate over the jailing of his brother,' asked Tura.

Immediately, he regretted sharing the news about Zhang's brother the previous evening. Rosie Betts had been right; he should have kept it to himself. He would need to speak with the ambassador, he told the men, and he rose to make the call. He knew this was someone else's decision to make. It was well above his pay grade.

The call went straight to voicemail, so he called Richard Hanlon, who answered immediately.

'Good morning,' he said, 'are you calling to check we made it home safely with Barry Quinn's body,' he asked sarcastically. 'Have you managed to find Jane yet?'

'Well, not exactly, I am trying to get a hold of the ambassador and he's not answering his phone. I need to talk to him as soon as possible,' he pleaded.

'Let me check where he is, I'll call you,' and he rang off.

Returning to the table he found the two men deep in conversation, which ceased as soon as they saw him. He needed to move fast. 'Do we know where Zhang Sein is,' he asked Tura.

'He has several locations, one near Tachileik and another near Keng Tung, further north in Shan State. My hunch is, if he has her, he is in Keng Tung. It is further away and more secure.'

'Until I speak with the ambassador, it is best if the brother isn't mentioned,' said Finney. 'We could offer a reward to get her back. Could you make some calls?' Tura nodded. 'Great,' said Finney, 'give me an hour to make some calls to Australia, and let's talk then.' He needed another coffee before he headed back upstairs to his room, his laptop, and, hopefully, a conversation with Stacey Harmer.

The small guesthouse did food off the menu and likewise the coffee. The owner, the man he had seen earlier with the straggly grey hair and American accent was a jack of all trades. Banjob had introduced him as Somchai, he was the barista, as well as waiter, receptionist, and head chef. Approaching the man, he ordered another coffee.

As he waited, Finney admired the eclectic furnishings in the reception and restaurant. There were dozens of old cameras lined up on a bench along one wall. Nearby was an antique Remington typewriter, old record turntables, a gramophone, telephones, and an antique barber's chair. There were wagon wheels, and candy dispensers from the 1940's and the walls were dotted with old black and white photos.

Parked in the courtyard outside the guest house were a Land Rover and two old jeeps. 'Do those vehicles out there belong to you,' he asked.

'They belong to my family. The one over there is the oldest,' he said pointing at an old British Land Rover. 'It was manufactured in 1948 and belonged to my dad. The other two are jeeps. They are a little older, but my favourite is the Landy,' he said, referring to the Land Rover.

'Do you drive them at all,' assuming they were just for show.

'I sure do,' said the man, proudly. 'I drive the Land Rover every day. I could take you for a spin if you are interested.'

Finney declined politely, 'I'm quite busy today.'

'Tomorrow,' the man said. 'I've got you booked in for two more days.'

He knew then a decision had been made to keep him away from the scene of Quinn's death for at least a few days. It didn't bother him at all. He was in no hurry to go back to the hotel. He gratefully accepted his freshly brewed coffee from his new friend, Somchai, and returned to his room for a conversation with Stacey Harmer.

'You sound a bit rough,' she said, as he spoke into the phone, 'Big night?'

'I need your help,' he said, sounding desperate.

She could tell he was agitated; this case was dragging on and he had much pressure on him from Jane Gordon's parents.

'We've only got a few days before this bail hearing,' he continued. 'This could get messy here. The brother may be the bargaining chip we need, but it must be kept under the radar.'

'Are you saying what I think you're saying?'

'I guess I am,' he said. 'I think it's clear that Zhang Sein has Jane Gordon, if she's alive. If so, the case he's going to want something in return, and that could be the brother. From what I'm hearing he could sell Jane Gordon across the border into the Chinese economic zone in Laos. If that happens that would be the end, we will never see or hear of her again. Our government does not recognize any legitimate government in Myanmar now, so we have no choice but to negotiate directly with Zhang Sein. We must hope he wants to get his brother back. It's all we have.'

'Leave it with me,' said Harmer, 'I'll call the arresting officer and see what they have planned for the next bail hearing.' The call was over.

He sent a terse text message to Rosie Betts.

I need your help. Please call me.

His phone pinged almost immediately.

Give me 15 minutes.

He felt a flood of relief, that was a bridge he could not afford to burn.

There were different ways they could approach this. If they put the word out on the street there was a reward to find Jane Gordon, it could set off a nightmare of timewasters, not to mention attracting publicity and the attention of the Thai police. They didn't have the resources or the time. No, they had to target Zhang Sein directly. He needed to know they were looking for the girl and they would pay for her safe return. There was no need to say exactly how much they would pay, just a willingness to pay. He needed Tura to help him with this, but before he asked for his help, he wanted to run it past Rosie Betts. It was clear Betts respected Tura, but would she trust him in this situation? All he could do now was wait for her return call.

It was almost 10 am as he set off to meet Banjob and Tura. His phone rang. It was the ambassador. 'What's going on Finney,' he barked, his tone clipped and unforgiving.

'I am sorry to bother you, sir,' he said apologetically. He explained the need to talk directly with the traffickers, and they had reliable intelligence they were holding Jane Gordon.

'I'm listening,' said Clifton-Blythe.

'We need to contact them and make an offer for her safe return. We know we have the brother in custody in Sydney, but I don't want to bring it into the conversation right away. We simply reach out and say we are prepared to negotiate. Can I count on your support for this?'

'I'll have to talk to my people in Canberra,' said the ambassador. 'I will get onto it straight away, keep your phone close.'

Almost immediately, his phone started ringing again. It was Betts. Banjob raised his eyebrows as if to say, *you are a popular man.* Walking away from the table yet again, he took the call. He started on the apology when she cut him off. 'Let's just get on with the job,' she said. It was all business in her voice, so he proceeded to fill her in on his conversations and his plan.

'It's a good plan, so call me when it's in place,' was all she said.

Finney stood for a moment, thinking about what a fool he had made of himself. It was the alcohol, yet again. He just could not take it steady like most others seemed able to do. Once he had the momentum of a couple of drinks in him everything just seemed to accelerate. It was a downhill slope. He downed drinks faster, he often moved onto hard liquor when all those around him were going in the other direction. I must get on top of this, he lectured himself. The simple solution, for now was to stay off it altogether until this case was solved.

Returning to the table, he began quizzing Tura on how hard it would be to get a message to Zhang Sein. Finney explained they were prepared to offer a ransom payment, but he was waiting for official confirmation on how much it would be.

Tura would need more money to get the message out. He also suggested they should do it sooner rather than later, as he tapped the face of his wristwatch.

'How much is this going to cost us?'.

'20,000 baht should cover it,' said Tura, looking across towards Banjob.

'Leave it with me to organise,' As he stood, he turned to Banjob, 'I need you to take me across to the office of the DEA.'

The driver looked surprised but did as he was instructed.

Finney turned to Tura; 'I'll get back to you as soon as I hear from the ambassador. He took the B20,000 cash from his wallet and handed it to Tura. 'In the meantime, let's see if we can get a message to Zhang Sein,' he said as he and Banjob stood and walked out towards the van.

They sat in silence in the van as they headed across town to the DEA station.

'What's going on,' asked the driver. 'We're not going to see Agent Betts, are we?'

'No, just park up here,' said Finney.

Banjob and Tura were close, it was obvious. They often spoke in whispers and Finney needed to know Banjob was working in his best interests, but he was not sure how to raise the subject with him. He wondered whether Banjob was sharing intelligence with Tura which he should not have been. He had to clear the air.

As they pulled up by the side of the road, Finney's phone began to ring. The name on the screen made his pulse quicken, it was the ambassador. Without a word to Banjob, Finney exited the vehicle into the car park, the gravel crunching under his feet as he walked away from the car. He answered the call, his voice steady but with an edge of anticipation.

The line crackled briefly, and then the ambassador's voice came through, sharp and commanding, cutting through the muggy afternoon air like a knife. 'Whatever it takes, that's the response from our guys here. Bill Gordon is beside himself with worry. Keep it under the radar. We cannot afford to alert the Thais to this and even more importantly, we cannot alert the press. If they get a whiff we are operating a clandestine operation in Myanmar with the drug traffickers, we are toast.'

'I'm going to need more cash, and where are we on the brother who is in custody in Sydney?'

'Sort the cash out with Hanlon,' said the ambassador, 'whatever it takes and whatever it costs,' he went on. 'This thing with the brother is going to be more complicated. There has been a development. The NSW police is your wheelhouse, so I will let you deal with that. Talk to your colleagues, you will find out soon enough. If the brother is our only bargaining chip, then so be it. First, get the message to them we want to negotiate. Have you got that Finney,' said the ambassador.

'I'm on it,' he said. 'While I've got you here sir, I've got another question. How much can I trust our driver, Banjob? I have a hunch that he has divided loyalties. I also need to know if you have authorised him to keep an eye on me and if is he reporting to you on my activities.'

'Well of course I asked him to keep an eye on you, who else have I got up there? He has been with us a long time,' said the ambassador, 'and all I can say is my predecessors held him in very high regard, and so do I. Do you need me to send Bart Guthrie up there to help you out?'

'We have this under control, sir,' was all he said, hoping to avoid Guthrie joining him in Mae Sai. It was the last thing he needed. He would not be of any help. Quinn had stayed out of his way, but Guthrie was a different proposition altogether. Finney did not want him anywhere near this case.

'Well, get on with it then,' said the ambassador, 'the next time I hear from you I want good news.'

He then contacted Richard Hanlon and arranged for a money transfer to his private account. His next task was going to be much tougher. Returning to the van, Finney joined Banjob in the front seat.

'I need your opinion on something, Banjob,' he said.

'I'm not sure how useful my opinions are,' said the driver.

Searching for the right words, he began tentatively. 'I'm worried about our negotiations with these Burmese traffickers. We are completely reliant on Tura.'

'What are you concerned about?'

'We have no visibility on what is going on between Tura and his contacts in Myanmar. I'm not used to operating this way. I am usually at the front line and doing this kind of thing myself, rather than having to do it through a middleman.'

'So where are we right now,' asked the driver.

'We are waiting for Tura to get a message to Zhang Sein.'

The driver stared at Finney for longer than was comfortable. No,' he said, slowly and deliberately, 'where are we? Are we in Australia? Are we in Sydney? No, we are in Thailand. And we are trying to negotiate something happening over the border in Myanmar. We cannot cross the border and negotiate. So, what do we do?'

Finney looked at him, knowing he was not yet finished.

'We work with what we have,' the driver continued. 'I do not think you trust our friend Tura. Would I be correct? You hardly know him, but can you afford not to trust him? That's the question you must ask yourself. Let me tell you how I see it. He is all we have right now. He is well-connected and has a good reputation. Do you think he would risk all of this by doing the wrong thing with us? We should try and see it from his perspective. He is from Myanmar, not Thailand or Australia. So, he has different allegiances, but he is also working with foreign agencies, including with your friend, Agent Betts. He also must worry about his safety. He has children and grandchildren. Did that occur to you?'

Of course, Tura would be mindful of not alienating people on his side of the border. He had to tread carefully. Still, Finney said nothing but simply nodded, indicating to Banjob he was listening.

'My advice to you is to put your trust in Tura. It is the most important thing right now. Can I also suggest you focus on negotiations with the people who have Jane Gordon? We need to see it from their perspective as well. Of course, they would accept money, but the release of

Zhang Sein's brother would be a much better bargaining tool. The ambassador has said money is not a problem, but what about getting the brother out of jail? That won't be easy. I know Australian law works differently to this part of the world, but you will need to find a way to get him out,' said Banjob.

Finney nodded his agreement, and he knew the driver was right. He had to approach this differently. Tura was in a difficult position. He was also relying on trust, from his people and this stranger sitting here in Mae Sai. Finney had been sceptical of Tura, especially when it came to money. He had been paying Joey Rivers to collect information for him, so why was he reluctant to do the same with Tura. His phone pinged. It was Stacey Harmer. **Call me NOW!**

It was 3 pm in Sydney when Stacey Harmer picked up the phone after one ring. 'I've spoken to the officer in charge of the brother's case. They will oppose bail as he is a flight risk, and they are confident he will not be released. They are still preparing the charge sheet but at this stage, it looks like manslaughter and culpable driving. Both are serious charges, as you know and will carry a hefty custodial sentence. But the big news is,' she went on, 'the Gordons received a video message early this morning at around 2:00 AM. I'll send it over to you but let me summarise for you first. It is from Jane Gordon and she's reading from a script. She is upset but physically she looks OK. They are demanding a ransom of U.S. $250K and the release of the brother. They are giving us twenty-four hours to respond. How are we going to play this,' she asked.

There was a long pause before he answered. 'Well, the ransom will not be a problem but the release of the brother, where do we even start? Forward me the video,' he said, 'I need to see it for myself. I will call you back.'

Less than a minute later the video arrived and again he exited the vehicle, wanting to view it on his own. Jane Gordon looked exhausted, her eyes were red and puffy. The video was shot just showing her head, he could not see what she was dressed in but her hair looked clean and brushed but there was no denying she was distressed. Harmer was right, it was also clear she was reading off a script of some kind. She spoke in a stilted, halting voice. There was a moment at the end of the video where she had finished the script and her voice began to tremble as she said, 'Mum, Dad, I love you.' Suddenly, the video went black. Jane Gordon made no mention of where she was or who was holding her. For that, he would rely on Tura, who was at that very moment meeting one of his contacts across the border in Tachileik.

He sent a text message to Stacey Harmer. It said simply, **Put me in touch with the officer in charge of the Zhang Win case.** In less than a minute the contact details arrived. Detective Inspector Jodie Coppins from NSW Police City Central. He didn't know her but called anyway.

He knew he should have called DCI Burrows first, but things were moving too quickly, and he would have to bypass the protocols. Stacey Harmer passed Jodie Coppins' mobile number on to Finney, and she answered the call on his third attempt. DS Coppins sounded irritated. Knowing he had to drop Sir William Gordon's name into the conversation to get her attention, he did so, and it worked. It was best to give her just enough information to get her cooperation. He explained the connection between the young man, Zhang Win, and the abduction. He also suggested a delay to the bail hearing would be helpful. It would allow him time to finalize his plan and contact the kidnappers.

DS Coppins was unconvinced. She explained the complexities of granting bail and how the process could not be manipulated. The hearing had been scheduled, and it would not be easy to have it cancelled. The best she could do was to seek a postponement for a maximum of seven days, and she also advised him to go higher up the chain of command.

He knew exactly what she meant. The governor of New South Wales would have contacts within the judiciary, including judges. He would need to contact the ambassador again and ask for his assistance, being an old friend of William Gordon was an important connection. Clifton-Blythe would have to be the go-between, whether he liked it or not. Getting the brother out on bail would be the bargaining chip they needed, but he knew it wouldn't be easy. He sent a message explaining the situation and asked for his assistance in getting the governor to pull strings.

Feeling dehydrated, hungry, and hungover he needed sustenance. Banjob ferried him back to a modest little Thai place down by the river. The driver left him there with the excuse he had to go and refuel the van. Finney knew the man had another agenda, but didn't care. He had been here the day before with Rosie Betts. It felt like a lifetime ago. His phone was pinging. Text messages from the ambassador, a missed call from Stacey Harmer, and most importantly a message from Rosie. **Where are you, let's catch up**, was all it said.

The call to her was his priority. I will join you for lunch was her reply when he told her where he was. His day brightened. He needed to atone for his poor behaviour the night before. Thankfully, he had not gone completely off the rails, but just enough for her to see his weakness. He felt a connection with Rosie, but most importantly he needed her help, so he did not want to ruin it this early on. Soon enough she arrived and took over the duties of ordering food.

He took the opportunity to bring her up to date with developments. They had all but confirmed the identity of those holding Jane Gordon. If it was Zhang Sein, he had a strategy in mind. They had a bargaining chip with the brother in police custody in Sydney, but that wasn't easy to navigate. As the food arrived Finney was again surprised at the variety of things that she ordered, and the quantity. 'How many people are coming for lunch,' he joked.

Smiling, she told him you can never have too much food in Thailand. 'An old Thai proverb states that the eating story is big, and the dying story is small. This explains their obsession with food,' she said.

There was a fiery papaya salad and an even hotter clear fish soup, accompanied by sticky rice, grilled beef salad and a Thai omelette. He had always thought he had a reasonable tolerance for spicy food, but this was next level. His eyes watered, his lips were numb, and he could feel a rebellion building in his gut. He almost felt dizzy, was it the hangover or the spicy food, he wondered.

Seeing him struggle she told him to mix the salads with the sticky rice and omelette, which might help to cool it down a little. As if the weather was not hot enough, he was sweating profusely as he ate the lunch. He drained glass after glass of ice water. His dining companion looked amused. They ate in silence for a while, with Finney occasionally complimenting her choice of food.

'This food is delicious and like nothing I've ever tasted,' he said, 'but my stomach is on fire.'

'The food in the north is unique. There is a famous noodle soup called Kao Soi, unique to the north, you must try it.' Calling the server over, she went ahead and ordered it.

'About last night,' said Finney, 'I just want to apologise.'

She raised her hand as if to say, 'Let's just enjoy lunch for now and talk about it later.' That was fine by him, but he knew there would have to be a conversation. If not now, over lunch, before they parted company. While the atmosphere was cordial, there was a veil of tension he could only attribute to his behaviour the night before.

The conversation turned back to Tura and his role in the negotiations. 'You have to trust him,' said Betts. 'You also need to try and understand him.' Finney nodded.

'No, I mean you *really* need to understand him. He is trying to keep his people on his side, and this is a remarkably diverse group. It includes strange bedfellows including the resistance fighters, the drug traffickers, the Myanmar army, and local Shan state politicians. The alliances are shifting, but he must balance them and keep them talking and listening to each other. You should also know he lost his son earlier this year in the struggle against the army. Despite this, he still works with the army. Because he must.'

Finney listened intently but still had questions he needed to ask. 'I feel like he is not being straight with me,' he said finally. 'I feel like there is so much going on I'm not aware of.'

She laughed out loud before covering her mouth with her hand and apologizing. 'I'm sorry, but can you hear yourself? You've just arrived and already expect to know exactly what's going on. Forget it. Be thankful if you understand ten per cent. I've been here almost ten years and the longer I'm here the more I realise I don't know. Try and work on a few simple principles.'

'And what might they be?'

'Well for starters you could acknowledge Tura is not on your payroll, well not officially anyway. It means you have to reimburse him for the work he is doing and the risks he is taking. Can you imagine what might happen to him if either the police or military across the border find out what he is doing for you? Try to get a pile of money ready as soon as you can and work out a way to get the brother released. Whatever it takes, isn't that what your ambassador said?' Before he could interrupt, she went on. 'You will have to get the brother back here. I know you think it is impossible, but you might be surprised at what can be done when there are VIPs involved.'

His phone pinged alerting him to a message from DS Coppins. **You have friends in high places. The bail hearing was postponed seven days. Call me.** Finney excused himself to make the call. The phone rang and she picked up immediately.

'You got my message,' she said.

'Well, I guess you are right DS Coppins,' he said, 'I do have friends in high places. I think we're going to be talking quite a bit; can I call you Jodie?'

'Well, I guess so,' she said, 'does that mean I have to call you Declan?'

'Call me whatever you want,' said Finney, sounding blunter than he had intended. 'So, can you run me through what happened at the hearing this morning?'

'It was all over quickly,' said Coppins. 'The judge expected the postponement application. So did the boy's solicitor, he made no objection which I found to be strange. He announced during the hearing he wanted to call other witnesses and needed time to organize this. Therefore, he had no objection to the postponement. The solicitor seemed very upbeat to be honest. The boy was not in court, but he was beamed in by video link and said nothing during the proceedings. Are there any developments at your end you would like to share with me,' she asked.

There was a long pause, there was nothing else he could tell her, but he tried anyway. 'We are still trying to identify the main players in this whole saga. It is proving difficult, but we are hopeful for some good news later today.'

Jodie Coppins knew this was a brush-off. She also knew she would not have divulged any information either, had she been in his position. 'We expect the solicitor to come back to us in the next few days,' she said. 'I will keep you posted.'

'I'd like to be able to give you more information,' he said, feeling guilty. 'You know how it is.'

'No problem. I know how it is. We will be in touch.' She ended the call.

Returning to the table he shared the contents of the call.

'Good news,' said Rosie. 'This buys you time and I have a feeling you are going to need it. You should accept your driver's offer and make the trip across to Tachileik. Primary field research, as they call it, can be enlightening.'

'Why don't you come along, he suggested, 'I'm sure we could benefit from your local knowledge.'

She shook her head. 'I have problems of my own.' There was a young tech wizard in Washington looking at the encrypted files on Jessie Cheeseman's laptop and she wanted to know if he had made any progress. She had a feeling there was something on the laptop, valuable to them both. She would also call Tura on his behalf, to try and get a little more action from him. They needed to make progress today and he was the man to make it happen, she had emphasized. She urged him to take the opportunity to get across the border and look around Tachileik. 'Get your feet on the ground over there and get a feel for the place,' she said, 'the next few days might be fast and furious.'

They went their separate ways, after agreeing to meet again in the early evening. Finney called the driver and arranged to meet at the border crossing. Banjob would be parked nearby in the van with a change of clothes for Finney. Do not return to the hotel, he had said. There were still too many police around.

True to his word, the driver had purchased a loud, flowery shirt for Finney to wear across the border. He had also bought a pair of bright green shorts and flip-flop shoes.

'There is no way I am wearing this,' he said. 'I will look ridiculous.'

'Look around at the other tourists,' said Banjob. 'You will fit in very easily.'

He was right of course. He looked at the motley flock of tourists wearing the ubiquitous bright flowery shirts. At least he was not compelled to wear those Thai elephant pants, so popular here and in Chiang Mai. Reluctantly, he climbed inside the van and changed into the new clothes. There was even a baseball cap with 'Dodgers' printed on the front and a pair of fake Ray-Ban sunglasses.

'This is what we were looking for,' said the driver, as Finney emerged from the van. 'Just another tourist making a day trip across to Myanmar.' As they approached the bridge, Banjob strode straight toward the checkpoint and turnstiles. Realizing he didn't have his passport; he looked across at the driver and knew it had been taken care of. 'Good thing I got a hold of your passport,' said the driver. 'I took the liberty of getting it for you from your suitcase. It is all part of my job,' he said as if reading Finney's mind.

'Just follow me if you will, sir.' Banjob greeted the immigration officials with a Wai, and pointed at Finney, trailing along behind him. There was chatter between Banjob and the officials and both men were waved through. No paperwork required; a cash payment would be sufficient. Banjob had folded up two five hundred Baht notes into a small square and slid them across the counter to the immigration official. A slight nod and it was done. Not corruption, Banjob had said, just bypassing needless paperwork. They crossed the bridge in silence along with a mix of Thais, Burmese, and a handful of Western tourists. Mid-afternoon, it was not too busy. Dark clouds gathered in the mountains surrounding Tachileik. A storm was brewing.

Loitering amongst a group of tourists on the Burmese side of the bridge, with a broad grin, was Tura. 'Welcome to Myanmar,' he said quietly, 'follow me at a short distance, please.' He led them toward a nearby coffee shop. They walked through to the back of the shop to a small kitchen. 'Take off that silly hat and shirt,' instructed Tura, handing him a large straw hat, a blue, long-sleeved shirt and a blue-coloured Burmese longyi. 'Do you remember how to put these on,' he asked.

'I think I will manage. What's going on? I thought I was supposed to blend in with the rest of the tourists.'

'You did blend in with the tourists here, but where we are going now, there are no tourists. Try and pull the hat down as far as you can and turn up the collar of your shirt. It is a pity you are so tall. We are going to exit through the rear door, please climb into the back seat of the pickup truck and lie down on the seat,' said Tura. 'Do not ask me any questions right now. When we are out of town, I will give you a signal.'

Exiting through the rear of the coffee shop they found the doors of the pickup truck open, and Finney climbed in, lying down on the back seat as instructed. Tura climbed in behind the wheel and Banjob in the passenger seat and off they went. It was hot and dusty, and the car smelled of farm produce. There was a chemical smell like fertilizer and something resembling poultry manure. It was not unpleasant, thought Finney, but he wasn't sure how long he would last without some fresh air. He could hear other vehicles and chatter until they had exited the busy area adjacent to the border. The road was rough and potholed. Gradually it became quieter and there was less noise from other vehicles. He heard a plane overhead, but close by. He assumed they were passing the airport. 'You can sit up now but keep your hat on.'

He was relieved to sit upright and take in some fresh air. There was no air conditioning but thankfully the windows were open. Taking in his surroundings, he saw they were on the edge of a small village. There were houses dotted along one side of the road and people working in the fields of fruit trees on the other. Children played by the roadside and the occasional motorbike whizzed past them. 'We are heading east,' said Tura, 'toward the Laos border. There is something I want you to see. In the meantime, if I say so, lay back down on the seat. Your pass to come across the border limits you to stay in Tachileik but I am taking you down to Wan Narr, we cannot allow you to be seen out here.'

'Wan Narr, the name is familiar,' said Finney. 'Chuck Bowers and Jessie Cheeseman had been taken to a compound in Wan Narr where they met Zhang Sein. He related the story to Tura and Banjob.

Tura nodded, 'Yes, he has a base there. We don't think there is any meth manufacturing going on there. It is strictly for storage and distribution, and large quantities go across to Thailand by boat.'

'Do you think Zhang Sein might be there in Wan Narr? How close can we get? Have you heard anything from your contacts?'

'Slow down a bit there, I was about to give you an update. I heard from my contacts in Tachileik, and nobody has seen him for more than a week. If he is in Tachileik he is usually quite visible. He drives around in a pimped-up red jeep. Likewise, when he is in Keng Tung. I know for sure he has not been around here. I hope to hear back from my contacts in Keng Tung today. We cannot get too close to the compound at Wan Narr. It is well-guarded, and they have eyes on the street as well which is why we cannot allow you to be seen here.'

'I get it, but I am feeling the heat from my embassy colleagues about this. We are worried if we don't make contact soon it might be too late.' The other men knew what he meant.

'Don't worry,' said Tura. 'You have something of immense value to Zhang Sein, and he knows it. The word is he is desperate to get his brother back home. My contacts in Tachileik have known about the brother since he was arrested. The last time Zhang Sein was here he was ranting about it. Ranting about how he would go over there himself and break his brother out of prison if necessary. We know he is not that stupid.'

'Have you ever met him,' asked Finney.

'I have not met him,' said Tura, 'but I've seen him in action, a few times here in Tachileik, and once across the river in a Lao casino. He and some of his boys frequent a hotel pub in Tachileik, known as the 1G1 Pub. He has a special table and spends a lot of money there. He also likes to throw his weight around and show off to the locals. Let's just say he likes to put his power on display. I saw his goons beat up a waiter there one evening after he offended the big boss.'

'I don't see you as a pub kind of guy,' he said, as a joke.

'As I have said to you before, not everything is as it appears. My various jobs take me to all sorts of places, and I meet all sorts of people. Would you be surprised, for example, to learn one of my favourite genres of modern music is rap? Admittedly, I like my rap done in my native Burmese language. It is a great insight into the attitudes of young people here in my country. It is used very effectively as a political tool. In my day it was The Rolling Stones and Bruce Springsteen, but of course, it was all long time ago.'

They drove through another small village with nothing more than a few shophouses, a modest temple and some scattered cottages. A short distance away, he saw a large concrete building set back from the road on a small incline. 'Get down again please,' said Tura. The car turned into the driveway towards the building and the guard at the entrance ushered them through. The building was surrounded by a large, empty carpark. Tura pulled the car into a space as far away as possible from the building. 'Stay where you are,' he said, getting out of the vehicle slowly, and taking a good look around. He stood next to the rear window of the car.

'You can sit up now and take the hat off. Look down and across to your left and you will see a large building with a mahogany brown roof about two hundred meters over there. Do you see it?'

Finney saw it off in the distance. Tura handed him a small pair of binoculars. They looked like military issue. Through these he could see the warehouse situated inside a compound, it was as large as a football pitch. Surrounded by a high wall, topped with barbed wire, there was a secure entrance with a boom gate and armed guards. It was well fortified. It looked more like a small prison than a warehouse compound. Whatever was being stored there was valuable. There were several vehicles including two medium-sized trucks and four or five pick-ups. Along one fence there were also more than ten motorbikes.

'That is quite an operation,' said Finney, 'by far the biggest building in the whole town. Plenty of security and vehicles. I can't see a red Jeep though.'

'I am guessing our man is in Keng Tung, his ancestral home, and where he has a much bigger operation. It is one of his main production sites, along with others, scattered around the Shan state. I just thought it might be useful for you to see this. That warehouse is more than two thousand square meters in size. It is only a short drive from here to a small pier on the Mekong River and from there, it is ten minutes by boat across to Chiang Saen in Thailand. Zhang and his team also cross there to the casinos in Van Pak Len. Banjob tells me you have already been over there with Agent Betts.'

'Your source is well-informed,' said Finney. 'You say there is surveillance on this property, are you able to tell me how it is being carried out and by whom?'

'Surely you already know the answer to that question. I would endanger my colleagues if I gave away their identities. Let us just say they are local, and they have dirt under their fingernails.' He took this to mean they may have been farmers in the local areas. Tura went on, 'People keep watch and pass on information. We cannot use drones either, they would be too easy to spot. It is old school, eyes and ears, on both land and the river.'

'What are the chances of Jane Gordon being down there,' he asked.

'As I said before, Jane Gordon is more likely to be in Keng Tung. Even though this base is well fortified it is too close to the border, and he would not risk keeping her here. No, it must be Keng Tung or somewhere further north in Shan state.'

'What is this building behind us,' asked Finney, pointing to the two-story, whitewashed concrete building. He had noticed there were several small trucks and pieces of earth-moving machinery parked on one side of the building.

Tura went on to describe the village hall, built by the army as a vanity project and it was largely vacant. The army seemed to think large construction projects were good for their image. The villagers would have preferred to have a new water system, but they had no real choice in the matter.

'We need to get you back to Tachileik before we attract any attention.' Tura slid in behind the steering wheel and began the short drive back to Tachileik, with Finney again forced to lie down in the back seat to avoid being seen. Tura explained if he were to be seen, there would be someone waiting for them at the bridge crossing well before they got there. 'We are not the only ones with eyes and ears in this place,' he said.

The army, while not in complete control, had plenty of informants on the ground. He felt as if they were simply retracing their steps and soon enough, they were going through the back door of the restaurant and this time they were stopping for a cool drink. The place was simple. Tiled floors and Laminex tables and red, plastic chairs. Overhead ceiling fans pushed the humidity around just enough for it to feel cool. Finney was back in his loud floral shirt and ready to look the part of the tourist again.

Banjob ordered fruit shakes as the storm clouds continued to build outside. The humidity was rising, and he heard thunder off in the distance. 'We will get some relief from the heat shortly,' said the embassy driver, passing an umbrella to Finney. 'Let's finish up these drinks and see if we can fit in a short tour before we head back across the bridge to Mae Sai.' Tura chose not to go with the two men, not wanting to signal his association with them.

B200 got them a one-hour tour of a temple, a market, and a couple of other nondescript landmarks in Tachileik. Finney was disoriented at first as the traffic was on the right side of the road, in contrast to Thailand where it was driven on the left. The town appeared to have more than the officially published population of 50,000 inhabitants, but there had not been a census for over a decade, so the figure was likely to be higher. They finished off their tour with a visit to the local market adjacent to the border bridge. The products were almost identical to the market on the Thai side, but the atmosphere was different. Finney found it less friendly and the vendors a little pushier than their Thai counterparts. Banjob's explanation was simple. Life was much harder over here. The government didn't help its citizens, and they had to fend for themselves.

'Let's get you back across the border before 6 pm, have you seen enough?' he asked. Finney nodded and they headed back across the bridge, with Banjob taking the lead once again and negotiating immigration on Finney's behalf.

The clouds descended quickly. By the time they were halfway across the bridge, the heavens opened. Both men were startled by the first thunderclap and then they came in rapid succession along with flashes of lightning a short distance away. The rain was torrential. They took shelter under a small eave outside the immigration checkpoint. In moments their feet and legs were saturated by the splashing rain. The noise was deafening. Other travellers around them scurried to take cover. Standard umbrellas were inadequate for the volume of rain. In no time at all there was three or four inches of water running across the concrete bridge. Banjob was trying to speak to Finney, but he couldn't hear a thing. He turned his hands up as if to say, let's just wait it out here, there's nothing else we can do. Such was the quantity of rain; visibility was down to less than ten meters. The immigration officials, and other locals, looked relaxed. They had seen it all before. As quickly as it had started, the rain stopped completely.

The two men folded their umbrellas and shook off the excess water. Finney removed his rubber flip-flops and shook water from them as well. Despite having been undercover, his shirt was wet as were his shorts. People emerged and began queuing for the crossing again. Finney followed Banjob off the bridge and back down to the nearby market. Small rivulets of water hurried in all directions, but their destination was the river. It had become an angry torrent of muddy, foaming water leaping over boulders and washing large clumps of soil and rubbish away down toward the confluence with the Mekong.

There had been several storms since his arrival, but nothing like this one. Looking around the market near the base of the bridge crossing, he saw the vendors getting to work clearing the water. Some were sweeping water away while others were removing the reams of plastic they had used to cover and protect their goods from the downpour. Food vendors were returning to the street and charcoal barbeques came back to life. It seemed that within minutes, order was restored.

By the time they got back to the van, the clouds were clearing, and the sun emerged. Vapor began to rise from the wet bitumen. The temporary relief from the heat was replaced by muggy humidity causing trickles of sweat to run down his back. 'I might walk back to the guesthouse,' he informed the driver, 'I could do with the exercise.'

'Will you be going straight back there,' asked Banjob. 'I can go back to the guesthouse, change and shower if I know I shouldn't be following you somewhere else.'

'Well, yes of course. Have you also changed hotels,' Finney asked.

'I was always at the Bann Tuuk Guesthouse. Somchai is an old friend of mine,' said Banjob.

'So, you've been there all along,' asked Finney.

Banjob explained it was cheaper than the Orassa and the ambassador disliked wasting money. Somchai was an old friend from Chiang Mai University, and the driver was happy to support his enterprise. They had studied engineering together. Somchai had gone on to be a professional photographer and Banjob, a driver. They and their families had known one another for over thirty years, and as far as Banjob was concerned, he was like a brother.

Returning to his room, he received several text messages. Rosie Betts, Tura, and Sarah had all left him messages. Had something happened with his daughter, Ella, he wondered. **We have things to talk about. Call me. Sarah.** She picked up the phone as soon as he called.

'What's going on, he said, is Ella OK.'

'Everything is fine,' said Sarah, 'I told you Charles is being transferred to head up a new office. Well, it's been confirmed, and we are going to Singapore. He is leaving next week. Ella and I will join him in four weeks.' There was a long silence. 'Are you there'

'I'm here,' he said. 'I don't know what to say. When we spoke about this a few days back you told me you wouldn't be going until next year. Why are you pulling Ella out of school now? This will be so disruptive. How does she feel about it?'

'I spoke to the school in Singapore, and they are on a different schedule than our schools here. They advised me it would be better for her to start now. We have talked about it, Ella and I, and I think she is OK with it. Sure, she might miss her friends, and it might take time to adjust but I think this will be good for her. For all of us.'

'Really,' he said, trying not to sound sarcastic, 'for all of us? When will I see her? You guys will be halfway across the world. I can't just jump on a plane to Singapore every weekend. Not on my salary.'

'Charles and I are negotiating for three monthly visits back to Australia. You can still see her but just not as often. Listen Declan, I don't want to get my solicitor involved in this, but I will if I must. This opportunity is too good to pass up and that's all there is to it.'

He knew better than to get into an argument with Sarah, especially about Ella. They had been here before, and it had not ended well. While their separation had not been acrimonious, Sarah had always had the upper hand when it came time for negotiations. She was a trained lawyer after all. He knew his best course of action was to agree to the proposition.

'I won't stand in your way. I just want what's best for Ella. We will have to work out a way around it. I can come to Singapore during those three months and spend some time with her then,' he said, trying to sound positive. 'Can I call and talk to her about this.'

'Sure,' said Sarah, 'but only if you understand this is not up for negotiation. We are moving to Singapore in a month. I hope you will be back before then.'

'I get it,' he said. 'I won't stand in your way. I just need to talk to my daughter.'

'So long as you are not trying to change her mind about this. We have been planning this, and Ella has been part of the planning all along. To be honest, I'm surprised she hasn't talked to you about it already. Maybe it says something about your relationship with her.'

That hurts, he thought, but she was right. 'I'll call her in the morning. Maybe then you and I can have a longer conversation about the school as well. I'll call you tomorrow,' he said and hung up. Sitting for a moment, his head in his hands, he felt overcome with pessimism, and remorse. Ella, Sarah, his parents, his career. Things looked bleak. With perfect timing, he was jolted from his thoughts by a knocking at the door. It was the driver.

Face to Face

Answering the door, he found his driver, clearly excited and panting from having run up the stairs. 'He's here, Zhang Sein is in Tachileik,' said Banjob. 'Tura has been trying to call you but couldn't get through, so he called me.' He was still preoccupied with the news from Sarah, and now this. He needed a few minutes to think and told Banjob as much. Instructing the driver to wait for him downstairs, he stood in the middle of the hotel room and wanted to scream at the top of his lungs. Looking at himself in the mirror he saw a bedraggled, middle-aged man clad in loud, wet clothes. He showered, shaved, and changed back into a less provocative outfit. At least now looked the part, even if he didn't feel it. He checked his phone to see three missed calls from Tura. Returning the call, he began by apologising but the man cut him off.

'I've had a call from one of my contacts,' said Tura, 'Zhang Sein arrived late this afternoon and went straight to the warehouse location in Wan Narr. Given the lateness of the day, I assume he will stay overnight in Tachileik.' Tura had put out another message to him and was sure he would make contact sometime in the next few hours. He told Finney to be ready to cross the border at short notice. 'Pick up my call when you see it,' demanded Tura, 'we may only have a small window here. Tura hung up the call. Finney prepared to make his next call, to Agent Betts.

'You're a hard man to get a hold of,' she said. 'How was your sightseeing trip? Better still, tell me in person. I'm on my way to Chiang Mai tonight to see my daughter but I'll drop by to see you on the way. I'll see you in fifteen minutes.'

He descended the stairs to the lobby to be greeted by the beaming smile of Somchai, the guesthouse owner. 'Good evening, Sir, can I get you anything, a nice cold beer or a coffee perhaps?' Banjob, seated outside in the courtyard and engrossed in his mobile phone, did not even look up. 'I'll take some cold water,' said Finney, taking a seat, he realised how dusty the place was. Being open to the elements it was no surprise there was a thin layer of dust across all the various knickknacks and collectibles.

Soon enough, he saw Rosie pull up in her 4-wheel drive pickup truck, which blended perfectly with the dozens of other similar vehicles so popular in the region. She joined him in the lobby of the guest house, where he brought her up to date on his visit across the border and the arrival of Zhang Sein.

'So, I guess you hope to hear something from him tonight,' she said. 'I haven't had any direct dealings with him, but I understand he can be a bit of a tough guy, despite his young age.'

'I've heard the same thing myself,' he said. 'It will be hard to know unless I get an opportunity to meet him. Tura seems confident we can get our message across to him and he will agree to meet. How do I even set up such a meeting and what things should I look out for? I was hoping for some advice.'

She thought for a moment before answering. 'It would be safer to have him come across the border and talk to you here in Mae Sai, but I can't see him agreeing to it. Likewise, not a clever idea for you to meet him in Myanmar. We don't want you being kidnapped as well, and we don't want the Burmese authorities catching up with you.'

'I was thinking the same thing myself,' he said. 'A face-to-face meeting is essential. I need to gain his trust and get a feel for what he is really like. I need to talk with my ambassador again. He won't be happy about me operating in an unauthorized jurisdiction. He's already paranoid about the Thais finding out what we are doing, let alone me getting caught up with the Burmese.'

'This might sound a little crazy but just bear with me for a moment. I've never done this myself, but I do know that occasionally meetings happen on the river. It's a neutral zone and it's possible to bring two boats together side by side and have the meeting there.' She could see him frowning. 'Not the kind of boat we took across the river,' she went on, 'something larger with a roof, more private and more discreet.'

'Maybe it could work. Zhang Sein won't come across to Thailand and hopefully, Tura can get him to understand why I can't go over to Myanmar. I'll talk to Tura about it. What's with the trip to Chiang Mai? How long will you be away,' he asked.

'My daughter has a school performance tomorrow. I try and get down there most weekends, but I missed last weekend because of work. You know how it is.' He did. 'It's complicated. My ex-husband and his new wife have been taking Angie away on weekends. We had an agreement I would have weekends with her, but my ex is a Thai, and the law is on his side. He's rich and influential. What hope do I have?'

He wanted to share his news about Ella moving to Singapore, but this wasn't the time. He had to stay focused on saving a daughter, even if it wasn't his own. He had to count himself lucky. The Gordons must be suffering. That thought brought him back to the reality of what he was doing in Mae Sai.

She set off to Chiang Mai leaving Finney to make some big decisions about meeting with Zhang Sein. In the back of his mind though he was thinking about his conversation with Sarah. *I don't want to get the solicitors involved*…neither did he. He didn't have the money but more importantly, he didn't want the aggravation. He wanted an amicable relationship with Sarah, but it was proving difficult. Then he thought of Rosie Betts and her situation, so like his.

As he watched her walk back to her car, he realised there was something different about Rosie Betts today. Was it that he had never seen her dressed in civilian clothes? Or was it the way she talked about her young daughter? She briefly described her breakup with her former husband without giving too much away. He could see something in her eyes this evening. Sadness and resignation. He knew those feelings as well. Was he giving up too easily? How can I make this thing with Sarah and Ella work, he wondered.

He had one more phone call to make. Again, he gave himself a few minutes to craft a script. The ambassador appreciated an economy of words. Just cut to the chase, was his catchphrase. Eventually, he took the plunge. He thought his argument had been convincing, but it wasn't the way the ambassador saw things. He had grave doubts as to whether a swap between Zhang Sein's brother and Jane Gordon was possible. Of more immediate concern was Finney's plan to meet with the kidnappers in person.

'Too risky,' the ambassador said, 'way too risky. If anything happens to you, it's just more shit on my desk.' Finally, after much debate, the ambassador agreed for him to meet with Zhang Sein, but only if the meeting occurred on Thai soil. There was to be no travel across the border to Myanmar. Well, I guess a meeting in the middle of the Mekong River was still not technically in Myanmar, thought Finney. It was best he didn't mention it to the ambassador. Better to ask for forgiveness than permission. It was also clear Banjob had yet to report their visit to Tachileik earlier that day. He had to make sure the driver kept the visit a secret.

He moved back to join Banjob and updated him on developments. Having done so he broached the subject of their trip across the border and the need to keep it a secret. After all, it had been Banjob's suggestion, and he agreed the ambassador didn't need to be told. The driver was meeting up with his friend Somchai for dinner. There was no invitation extended to Finney, and he was glad of it. He needed time to reflect on the events of the day. Was it too late to call Ella? It was midnight in Sydney, it would have to wait until tomorrow. He decided on a walk. A short distance from the guesthouse he received a call from Tura. This is it; he thought, the kidnapper had made contact.

Sure enough, he had. 'I got a call just now,' said Tura. 'Zhang Sein is here until lunchtime tomorrow and wants to meet with you here in Tachileik.'

'I can't meet him in Tachileik. It's too dangerous. I can't afford to be caught by the Burmese police or military. What about the option of meeting on the river somewhere, do you think it's possible?'

'Well, I could ask. I don't see why not, and I know it's happened before. Leave it with me and I will get back to you, but you will need to be ready to move at short notice.

The best thing for us is to aim for early morning, around dawn.' He rang off.

Finney continued his walk around the neighbourhood adjacent to the guest house. It was suburban and quiet but only two blocks away from the bustling street leading to the border crossing. There were shophouses with small gardens, with the occupant's doing business from the downstairs front room and living out back and upstairs. There was a small tailor shop consisting of little more than an old-fashioned sewing machine and an ironing press. Next door was a small-scale laundromat and a convenience store where kids were doing their homework in one corner of the shop. Mom and Pop stores, they were called, according to the driver. He turned into another street and came across a makeshift market laid out along the roadway. Traffic had been blocked off and vendors had simply laid their goods out on mats along the street. It was mostly fresh produce but there were also people selling ready-made food and some household goods. It was clear this was mostly neighbourhood locals buying and selling from each other. Many of the children, already dressed in their pyjamas, played amongst the stalls.

It had a different feel to the tourist market near the border crossing. There were no tourists here. He bought some satay sticks and sticky rice, which he ate as he walked along the street. People smiled and waved at him as he passed by. Finney liked the atmosphere of the place; it was a community. He thought of how different his Sydney neighbourhood felt. It was transient, edgy, and abrasive. By contrast, this community had very deep roots, often with three generations living under one roof. As he rounded another corner, he found himself down by the river again and opposite The Bamboo Bar. The reggae music was blasting out into the street. As he looked across to the bar, he saw Pip and the group he had drinks with the previous evening. Not tonight he thought, not tonight. As he turned to walk away, he heard his name being called.

'Come and join us for a drink.' He turned and waved, then walked back across the street to where Pip was standing at the front of the bar. 'I've had a long day,' he told her, 'And maybe I had one too many vodka shots last night.

'Oh, come on, just the one drink can't hurt.'

'No, seriously, I'm on these antibiotic medications and I shouldn't be drinking any alcohol at all,' he lied.

Before he could go on, a booming voice came across from the bar, 'Finney as I live and breathe.' He looked over to see Harley Dowsett, arms spread, gesturing for him to join him at the bar.

'You know Harley?' asked Pip. 'Well of course you do, everyone knows Harley.' She grabbed his arm and led him to the bar.

He accepted Harley Dowsett's outstretched hand. 'What can I get you partner,' said the man.

'Just make it a soda water. I'm feeling a bit out of sorts today,' he said.

'I know a cure,' said Dowsett. 'A double vodka. Neat. Followed by a large bottle of Leo beer.'

He protested, but it was pointless.

Pip moved back to the table nearby and sat with her friends. He remained standing at the bar with Harley Dowsett. 'So, what brings you to Mae Sai?'

'Just getting to know the area a little better,' said Finney.

'Tell us what you're doing up here. I've heard the news about our mutual friend Barry Quinn. Sad news indeed. Was it the old ticker,' he asked. 'Thirty years smoking those Marlboro Reds will do that to you, I guess. Your visit up here wouldn't have anything to do with the young Peace Corps volunteer being killed, would it? Or the major offensive by the Thai army against drug traffickers a day or two back?'

He shook his head. 'Out of my jurisdiction, I'm afraid, both of those events.'

'From what I hear there was an Australian girl up here with the American.'

'As I said before this is strictly a fact-finding mission for me. I'm new to the job in Sydney, and we are just trying to get a fix on the origin of the meth amphetamines that are arriving in Australia. All this other stuff is pure coincidence.'

'Well said and very convincing. You know what they say, an effective agent always believes his own cover story and it sounds like you certainly do. Well done,' said Dowsett.

'May I ask what brings you to Mae Sai,' said Finney. 'Or put another way, what's your cover story?'

'I wear many hats, at least that's what people say about me. It's quite true. I write for a few publications, including a music magazine out of New York City. It's not quite Rolling Stone but it's the same genre. The Yanks love this kind of story. You know the one, young peace core volunteer brutally murdered in an exotic part of northern Thailand known as The Golden Triangle. Was it the Chinese Triads? Was the CIA involved? They just lap this stuff up. I'm here working on that. It's my cover story and

I believe it,' he winked! 'When I get desperate for work, I also teach English.'

'You are quite versatile, by the sound of it,' said Finney. He knew in the back of his mind this man was involved in all sorts of other things he was not prepared to share.

'I just do whatever I can to make some money so I can continue living in this part of the world. I came here years ago. I was a young fellow looking for adventure. I was a fresh graduate with an arts degree and not many prospects in England, so I did one of those English teaching courses and off I went. I started in Vietnam, then on to Cambodia and landed here a couple of years ago. I've been away too long to go back now. I mean, come on Finney,' he leaned in, 'who do you work for? I've met plenty of spooks in my time and you reek of it.'

'You've got me all wrong. I'm just a regular civil servant. So where is home,' he asked, trying to change the subject. 'You said you were from the UK, is that right?'

'Well, I guess I am. Dad was in the Foreign Office, so we moved around a lot. He did a stint in your neck of the woods. We spent three years in New Zealand, and while we were there, we made many trips to Australia. Mom used to joke that we went to Sydney and Melbourne to do some shopping. Before that, my dad was posted to Kenya and Greece. I guess you would say I'm a bit of a gypsy.'

'So, you're doing a story on the young peace core volunteer who was found dead here a few days ago, is that why you're here?'

'Yes, that's it pretty much,' he said. 'I'm trying to work out a way I can spin this offensive by the Thais against the drug traffickers into a story, but I don't think my readership needs any more stories like this right now. The Jessie Cheeseman story will do me for the time being. As a bonus I get to hang out with this fine bunch of young people over here,' he said pointing at the table where Pip and her friends were sitting. 'They are a fun crowd. This will be a late night for sure. You should join us; you'll pick up all sorts of interesting information,' he said, tapping the side of his nose.

Finney could see it was heading in that direction. Not for me, he thought. He caught Pip's attention and signalled his departure. She leapt from her chair and walked to the bar, grabbing him by the arm. 'Just where do you think you're going,' she demanded.

'I have another commitment,' he lied and moved away toward the door. 'Another time.' He waved and walked out as quickly as he could. The ephemeral night market had all but disappeared. The last of the vendors were packing up their small stalls and the street was returning to normal as he made his way back to the hotel.

Back in his room, he began drafting an email to Sir William and Lady Gordon. He would offer reassurance their daughter would come home to them, safe and well. The sudden realisation Ella was soon to be moving overseas gave him a better understanding of what the Gordons were going through. They needed hope. He kept the email brief. He mentioned nothing of the death of Jessie Cheeseman. They had a good idea where Jane was, he said. He was preparing to meet with the captors, and he was confident they could negotiate her safe release. He also mentioned he may need Sir William Gordon to exert his influence to achieve her freedom. This was done without specific mention of what exactly may need to be done. The email was sent to the ambassador, Roger Clifton-Blythe, with a request to forward it to the Gordons.

He then sent a text message to his daughter, suggesting they chat early in the morning. From his room, he could hear the chatter of his driver and the guesthouse owner from the courtyard below. He descended the stairs to speak with Banjob about the meeting with Zhang Sein, planned for the following morning.

Tura had already brought him up to date on this development, the driver told him. 'This is good news, sir,' he went on, 'but we must be careful. My friend Somchai suggests we use a boat driver who is a close relative of his. He can be trusted. Do you have a weapon,' he asked.

He was shocked. 'Do you mean a gun,' he asked. 'If so, no I don't. Do we need to take a gun? How big is the boat? Do you know where we will meet?'

'We have an approximate location for the meeting. It will be near where the Sai River reaches the Mekong River. It is quiet with not much traffic and very little police activity. Tura is trying to set the meeting for early in the morning. The earlier the better, if we want to go unnoticed. Of course, we will need a gun. Fortunately, I have Mr. Quinn's weapon. Neither Mr Guthrie nor Mr Hanlon seemed interested in his bag, so I have it in the van, along with his gun.'

Finney didn't even want to know about the legalities of having a weapon. He knew it was illegal; however, they had diplomatic immunity if push came to shove. For the time being this was the least of his worries.

'I suggest you try and get an early night,' said the driver. 'We will need to be ready to leave around 4:30 am. Will I need to come and wake you up?'

'That won't be necessary. You must know by now I am an early riser.' His main concern was about actually getting to sleep. 'I would be lying if I said I wasn't a little nervous about meeting Zhang Sein. Can you also let me know how much cash I will need to cover this trip tomorrow? I'm assuming we will need to hire the boat. Will there be any other costs,' he asked.

'I'll let you know. I also suggest you don't mention this meeting to anyone, especially Agent Betts. The last thing we need is for the DEA to put surveillance on us. We don't want to scare away Jane Gordon's captors. Who knows how they'll react if they think we are working with the DEA?'

It was good advice. Banjob was proving he was more than simply a driver and occasional translator. There was no doubt Betts wanted to keep an eye on Zhang Sein, but her motives were vastly different from his. With a bit of luck, he would not hear from her again tonight and could simply explain how things had moved too quickly for him to have updated her before the meeting.

He barely slept, his mind relentlessly churning over the scenarios that could play out. Each one felt like a trap waiting to be sprung. The darkness of his hotel room did little to calm his nerves, and the distant hum of traffic outside was a constant reminder of the world continuing, oblivious to the dangers he was about to face.

The stakes were painfully clear. If this meeting with Zhang went sideways, he could easily become another of the man's hostages. He had no illusions about the ruthlessness of the people he was dealing with. He couldn't let his guard down, not for a second. His survival depended on his ability to think quickly and act decisively.

Their ace card was Zhang Win, the kidnapper's brother. The man was already in custody, and that gave Finney a glimmer of hope. If he could convince Sein that he had the influence to get the brother released and returned to Myanmar, it might just buy him enough time to get Jane out of this mess alive. But that was a big 'if.' The uncertainty gnawed at him, making sleep difficult.

Then there was the ambassador. Finney knew he was walking a tightrope by not informing the embassy about the meeting. It was a calculated risk, one that could backfire spectacularly if things went wrong. But right now, he needed every edge he could get, and sometimes that meant keeping things close to the chest.

'Let's cross that bridge when we come to it,' he muttered to himself, trying to push the worry aside. But even as he said it, he knew the bridge was looming closer with every passing minute.

Finney was awake at 3 am. He figured he may have had three hours of sleep. Hearing movement downstairs he observed Somchai and Banjob drinking coffee in the courtyard. He dressed quickly and joined them, gratefully accepting Somchai's offer of coffee. He was concerned that he had not heard from Tura, but the driver had. They would leave at 4.15 am, for the short trip to the river. The boatman would meet them at the designated pier, just off the riverbank at 5 am. They would contact Tura who would guide them to the meeting point. It would still be dark, which would provide cover from the police and the army. They did not expect the meeting to last long and hoped to be back at the guesthouse no later than 6:00 am.

Realising that he now had time to call his daughter, Finney excused himself and returned to his room. It was almost 7:00 am in Sydney, and Ella would be up readying herself for school. He made the call, and she picked up the phone quickly.

'Dad, you said you would call this afternoon, is everything OK?'

'Everything is fine Sweetie,' he said, 'it's so great to hear your voice. I've been talking to Mum again about your move to Singapore. She told me that you guys will be moving earlier than we first thought. I just wanted to check in with you, everything is OK. How are you feeling about the big move?'

'It's fine Dad. It will be fine. We are packing already. To be honest I'm excited. I know I'll miss my friends, but I am excited. Mum said there are already some family friends living in Singapore and there is a girl I went to school with a few years ago. I don't remember her, but Mum says we were friends before, so it's good news.'

On the one hand, he was relieved. He knew this was a wonderful opportunity for Ella, and he didn't like the thought of her being unhappy about the move. Quite the opposite, she genuinely sounded excited.

'Well, that's great Sweetie. I'm sure you will make friends quickly.'

'Will you be back before I leave? I don't want to leave without saying goodbye Dad'.

'Sure, Ella, of course, I'll be back before you leave. You don't need to worry about. I'll take you to say goodbye to Grandad and Uncle David before you leave.'

'Hey, I must go, I'm meeting some friends before school. Love you, Dad.' That was it, a three-minute call. He didn't have time to dwell on it.

Somchai was in the front seat with Banjob. Finney climbed into the back of the van and slid the door shut. As he did so he noticed the shotgun on the back seat along with Quinn's holstered pistol. The shotgun looked old, which didn't matter, it was just for show. 'You will need to put the holster on, sir,' said the driver, 'and I will carry the shotgun.'

'Do you think this is necessary,' he asked. 'I am not sure about the shotgun, and should I conceal the pistol.'

'They need to see the weapons. If they see the weapons, they will know we are serious. They will be armed; I can guarantee it. These guys do not mess around. Do not be fooled by their youthful age, or how friendly they might appear. If they have ideas about kidnapping you, they will think twice about it when they see this shotgun and pistol. Believe me, do not underestimate these guys, and do not forget they murdered Jessie Cheeseman.'

Of course, he was right. It would be dangerous to underestimate these men. As they exited the guesthouse the neighbourhood was eerily quiet. A few stray dogs skulked along the road and the early risers amongst the nearby poultry began their morning chorus, breaking the stillness of the dawn. It was only a few kilometres to the river, but every meter felt like a countdown. They veered off the main road to avoid prying eyes. 'It is a small town,' muttered Somchai, 'people notice things.' The road was sealed and smooth, and theirs was the only vehicle on it. Soon enough the river came into view. First, it was the Sai River, a narrow winding stream about to merge with the much larger, more imposing Mekong River. The Sai was nothing more than a trickle compared to the Mekong's vast, unyielding presence. The dawn breaks quickly in the tropics, and they were racing against it, eager to reach their destination before the light betrayed their presence.

They pulled into a clearing, and there, waiting by a small wooden pier, was their boat. It was not the usual longtail boat Finney and Betts had taken across the river to Laos. This was slightly bigger and had an area covered by canvas. It looked like it could accommodate a minimum of ten people. It also had an inboard motor which made it much quieter than the noisy longtail boats. Without a word, they eased away from the shore, slipping into the darkness. The dawn was creeping up fast, revealing silhouettes of boats moored in the distance. As the light broke, another boat appeared, speeding toward them.

'This will be them,' Banjob muttered, eyes on his phone. Tura had just sent a message – **Zhang Sein is on his way**. His pulse quickened. He could see now they had been skirting the Thai shore, trying to stay hidden. The other boat was closing in fast, and their driver, sensing the tension, slowed the engine to a mere whisper, sitting stiffly in his plastic chair, eyes darting nervously toward the approaching vessel.

The other, slightly smaller boat, paint peeling from it, pulled alongside, and ropes were thrown across to fasten the two vessels together. Words were exchanged and a light turned on in the other boat. They would not need it for long. The dawn had broken. He could see five men in the other boat, all but one were wearing masks. They were all very young. One man stood out from the others; he was better dressed, seated at the front of the boat with an automatic rifle resting across his legs. He assumed the man was Zhang Sein.

'Please stay seated,' said Banjob. Somchai sat quietly on the other side of the boat not saying a word. Banjob spoke to the men in the other boat and pointed across toward Finney. Banjob stood slowly in the boat and motioned for Finney to take his seat, which was nearest the man he knew was Zhang Sein. Banjob introduced the two men. There was tension in the air. The men surrounding him were also carrying rifles, but not of the kind their boss had. Theirs appeared to be old and were not automatics.

The man looked different from the photos Finney had seen. He was clean-shaven and well-groomed. He looked more like a boy band pop star than a drug trafficker. He most certainly didn't look like a killer. His skin was smooth, and his hair was recently cut. He wore clothes more appropriate to an urban shopping mall than a boat bobbing around on the Mekong River in the Golden Triangle. He looked out of place. His voice was soft, and he spoke slowly with little accent, and appeared well educated. They sat opposite one another, not a metre apart. The two wooden boats bumped against each other in the gentle current. Zhang Sein's crew, guns by their sides, stared straight ahead at Banjob and Somchai while one of them scanned the horizon for any other vessels. There were none to be seen.

Finney was sweating. The air was heavy with humidity as the dawn broke and slivers of sunlight began to cross the water. It wasn't just the heat and humid air that had Finney in a sweat. It was pure nervous energy. He found his hands trembling. The stakes were high.

'May I call you Declan?' the man said, sounding calm.

'Of course, what shall I call you?'

'Just call me Sein.'

'Nice to meet you, Sein. Can we get down to business?'

'No time for small talk?' asked the younger man. 'I love the river at this time of day. So quiet and peaceful. In an hour, it will be crowded with boats. It's also the best time for us to meet. Not so many people around. I would shake your hand, but I understand why you might not want to board my boat. It is for the same reason I would not want to board yours. You are from the embassy in Bangkok, correct?'

'Yes, I am,' he said. 'I'm here to take Jane Gordon home to her family.'

'We all want our family close by. What makes you think I have Jane Gordon?'

'My sources are telling me you took her after the young American was killed.'

'That was very unfortunate. He wasn't meant to die. Of course, you realise I wasn't there, and I didn't order his killing. I am in no way responsible and those who are, have been punished. You're right, Jane Gordon is currently my guest, just as my brother is your guest in Sydney. We both want the same thing then.' He said, smiling. 'We want our families reunited with their loved ones.'

'We need to know she is safe and well. I've seen the video you sent. When was it made,' he asked.

'She is safe and well. The video was made a few days ago. What about a video from my brother? How do I know he is OK?'

'You must have spoken to his lawyer,' said Finney. 'Surely, he can verify his well-being. I understand you were a student in Sydney,' he said, trying to establish some rapport.

'I was a student in Sydney. I like Sydney. I want to go back there but now it is not so easy. Visas take such a long time. So, let's get back to business, shall we? I've got something you want, and you've got something I want. I want my brother back, U.S.$250K in cash and I also want the boy's laptop. Jessie Cheeseman. I want his laptop.' Zhang Sein was smug and self-assured. He knew he had the upper hand.

'Your brother is charged with a serious offence. We can't just spring him out of jail. You already know it's not that simple.'

'He is innocent. He wasn't driving the car that killed that poor old man. I think the person responsible will come forward soon and this can all be resolved.'

This was news to Finney, but he let it slide. 'If that is the case, then perhaps Jane Gordon can be released. As for the laptop, I'll see what I can do.'

'I think we both know that your legal system in Australia is slow and rigid. But let's wait and see what happens today. You might be in for a surprise,' he said, grinning. 'These are my three conditions for the safe return of Jane Gordon. The release of my brother, the ransom and the return of the laptop belonging to Jesse Cheeseman. My brother is innocent. He wasn't driving the car. The person responsible will come forward soon and my brother can be released.'

'Perhaps when we're done here you should make a call back to your colleagues in Sydney. I know you can't negotiate through the Burmese government. The way I see it; you and your government have no other option. I will keep Jane Gordon for as long as it takes to get my brother home. At present, she is in good health and is being well looked after. I would hate for anything to happen to her as she is a nice girl, but if my demands aren't met then I can't guarantee her safety. Is that clear,' he demanded, his voice suddenly becoming louder.

'I understand,' said Finney, 'but can arrange for Jane to speak to her parents? If we can do that, we can get you talking directly with your brother. Could we agree on that?'

'Let's do it,' said Zhang Sein.

He passed across a piece of paper. On it, there was a phone number and an email address. They used a sophisticated VPN and encrypted telephone system, so there was no point trying to trace either the email or telephone number, the younger man explained.

'I will give you twenty-four hours, and in that time, I want to talk to my brother. Are we clear, Declan? One last thing and this is especially important. Do not get the DEA or the Thai army involved. At present the Thais are making life very difficult for us and the DEA is always a menace. I'm warning you, do not get them involved.'

Finney nodded.

'I think we are done here,' said Zhang. 'It is now almost 8:30 am in Sydney. This would be a good time for you to start talking to your colleagues. You will find the situation regarding my brother has changed and another bail hearing will be brought forward. I'll give you a few hours and then I expect to hear something from you.' He turned and spoke to the other men in the boat. The ropes holding the two vessels together were untied. The motor on the other boat came back to life and it disappeared into the distance.

The boat containing the men from the Thai side motored gently back to the mooring by the riverside, only a short distance away. Finney's phone pinged. It was Jodie Coppins requesting a return call. As they disembarked from the boat, he made the call. The reception was poor, but he got the message. A young Burmese student had come forward earlier in the morning. He claimed to be the one driving the car which killed the pedestrian. Zhang Win's solicitor had immediately petitioned the court for an urgent bail application. It was under consideration from the court and the police were deciding whether to oppose bail.

This was what Zhang Sein had been referring to. Another student would come forward to take responsibility for the accident. There was no doubt the other young student had been coerced to do so. Most likely he had been offered money or his family in Myanmar was pressured. Tura had suggested something like this could happen. There was a high chance bail would be granted, and the young man would walk free. If that happened, Finney's bargaining power was significantly diminished.

He decided it wasn't too early to call the ambassador, though he was less than impressed with the news Finney delivered.

'I'm no lawyer,' he said, 'but if he is granted bail, we have a big problem. Leave it with me, Finney, I'll get back to you.'

He then left a message with Betts. There was something on Jessie Cheeseman's laptop the kidnappers wanted. Had her tech colleagues been able to get into those encrypted files, he enquired.

Returning to the van, he instructed the driver to return to the guesthouse immediately. I'll organise some breakfast for you, sir, Somchai had said, when they arrived. Finney was grateful but unable to show it. He had hit a brick wall. He hadn't foreseen this scenario at all. He grabbed his laptop and began crafting an email to Stacey Harmer. He needed expert legal advice on their options for bail. Zhang Win's passport would have been seized. They needed to keep a hold of it. He also considered the option of an ankle bracelet. Having him out on bail was not a bad thing provided they could keep him in the country. He listed these options in an email to his colleague. He finished the email; *I'll call you in a couple of hours for a catch-up.* **Urgent** - went in the subject line of the email.

There was a gentle knock on his door. It was Somchai there to inform him Agent Betts had just arrived and was waiting downstairs to speak to him. 'I'll serve your breakfast in the courtyard,' said the man.

Rosie Betts sat at one of the corner tables in the small dining room of the guest house. Her head was bowed as she stared into her coffee.

'I thought you were in Chiang Mai for the whole weekend,' said Finney, as he approached the table.

'Things didn't quite work out as planned,' she said. As she looked up at him, he could see that her eyes were red, and she had been crying. 'My ex-husband decided spontaneously he needed to go and visit some friends in Bangkok, and he took Angie with him.' She gathered herself and sat upright. 'So, what's happened,' she said, putting an end to discussions about her private life.

He brought her up to date on the meeting with Zhang Sein. At least they knew for sure she was being held captive by them. They now knew they wanted to trade Jane Gordon for the brother.

'What about the laptop,' said Finney, 'do we have any news on what it contains?"

'We do, why do you ask?'

He detailed the demand of Zhang Sein that he gets a hold of the laptop. 'I didn't tell him you had it,' he said.

'That was smart. I spoke to my tech guy in Washington who has the files. He managed to get into some of them. There were audio recordings and images of several hand-drawn maps. These contained locations in Shan State. I'm assuming these belong to Zhang Sein and it's what he is looking to get back. We haven't analysed the audio files just yet. They are in Burmese, and they will need to be translated. I guess these files led to the death of Jessie Cheeseman,' she said.

'We need to hand over the laptop. I'm not sure how we will convince the kidnappers we haven't made copies of those encrypted files.'

She nodded. 'This is going to be complicated by people up the line in the DEA,' she mumbled, to herself.

'You sent the files to your tech guy, right, not the actual laptop.'

'I did,' she said. 'Am I thinking what I think you are? Should I just deny I ever had the laptop?'

'Or we give Zhang Sein a dummy laptop with the files on it.'

'No, it's too risky. He is tech-savvy and if he realises what we've done we could be in trouble.'

'I'm headed to my office. I have other work I need to get onto, especially this Thai army action taking place along the border. I'll need to prepare a briefing for my colleagues back in Washington. We have the files, so I no longer have any use for the laptop. I can get it back to you later today.

Better still, send your driver over to pick it up,' she said, standing from the table. 'I hope you realise I'm sticking my neck out for you here.'

He did and said as much.

She looked exhausted.

'Have you just arrived back from Chiang Mai,' he asked.

'It's been a long night. I haven't slept. But I need to keep busy otherwise I'll go crazy.'

Events were moving quickly back in Sydney. Zhang Win's solicitor had petitioned the court for a bail hearing. With the young man surrendering himself to police and claiming to be the driver who killed the pedestrian, his legal team had a compelling case for Zhang Win to be released. It was possible the hearing could be held that day. In ordinary circumstances, given that it was Friday, they would have a weekend to come up with a solution. Finney felt sure however that the boy's solicitor would agitate for an immediate bail hearing. He had to buy some time.

He picked up the phone and called Stacy Harmer. 'You're up early this morning DS Finney,' she said as she answered the phone. 'I got your email, and I have been working my way through it. We've got a few options when it comes to Zhang Win. Firstly, I'd like to hear about your meeting with the kidnappers.'

He briefed her on the meeting, carefully curating the parts he did not wish to share, especially that he carried a gun in an open holster. That would have been far too difficult to explain. The good news was they talked directly to the kidnappers of Jane Gordon and had a better plan to get her back. The surrender of this other student may have made life a little easier if anything.

'Yes and no,' said Harmer. 'It is a setup, and the court will likely see it for what it is. Unless of course there is a conversation with the presiding judge. The other thing we discovered is Zhang Win is in the country illegally. His student visa expired a couple of months back. We suddenly have extra leverage.'

'We will have cause to deport him,' suggested Finney. 'Or better still, put him in immigration detention. We will need advice from an immigration lawyer. There will be people much higher up the food chain making those decisions. Ideally, we have him out on bail but under strict conditions. We can't afford for him to get out of the country. That means an ankle bracelet, daily reporting to a police station and even some surveillance. I'll talk to the ambassador and see what he says.'

'Just a heads up for you,' warned Stacey Harmer. 'DCI Burrows is on the warpath again. It might be a clever idea to check in with him. He is angry you haven't contacted him since you arrived in Thailand. Just a short email update,' she suggested.

'Thanks, Stacey, I appreciate the warning, and I'll get onto it straight away.'

He ended the call and crafted a carefully worded email to his boss, DCI Burrows. He was more concerned about what he left out of the email rather than what he included. Burrows would already know about the sudden death of Barry Quinn. It would not have gone down well. He was also careful to omit any mention of a face-to-face meeting with the kidnappers. He sent the email and hoped it might buy him some time. He needed Burrows on his side. He would eventually be back in Sydney and under his supervision. He needed more friends and fewer enemies.

If Jane Gordon is released unharmed it will reflect well on Burrows as well.

A call was also made to the ambassador in Bangkok. Clifton-Blythe, aside from the occasional pompous bluster, was a highly experienced professional, and knew the region well. He had a reputation as a shrewd diplomat. He knew how far he could push the system and not create waves. He believed diplomacy was best conducted in a still pond, not a stormy sea. More importantly, he was well-connected. At first, he was annoyed about the meeting with the kidnappers, but he was pragmatic enough to realise it had gone well and, now it was over, presented no risk. They moved on. 'So where are we up to,' he had asked, 'with the brother in Sydney.' Finney explained the situation and sought advice on how much he should share with Sir William Gordon.

'He needs to be brought into the loop,' said the ambassador. 'I'm not suggesting in any way he could alter the course of this case, but he might just be able to have some influence over the terms and conditions of the bail. It will be better for us if we get this guy out of jail as quickly as possible. The kidnappers will see this as an act of goodwill for sure. It should be our top priority. Let me talk to Bill Gordon. In the meantime, you concentrate on working with your team in Sydney and make sure you get a hold of that laptop. I'll get Hanlon onto some logistics here as well.'

The momentum was changing, he could feel it. For the past five days, he felt like he was running on the spot, now he was caught in a tidal wave.

His phone jolted him back to the present. It was Stacey Harmer. The Department of Immigration had been notified the boy had overstayed his visa, and they wanted in on the case. There was concern their involvement could derail his plan. If he was released on bail, immigration would bang him up in a detention centre and he could be held there indefinitely. They had to ensure that didn't happen.

Finney needed to speak directly to William Gordon. There had been a delay to the bail hearing which would buy them some time. How would they get Zhang Win back to Myanmar without falling into the morass that was immigration detention in Australia? Illegal migration was a hot political topic in Australia, as it was in many other Western countries. If governments were seen to be weak on people in the country unlawfully, it was electoral suicide. As a result, political parties of all persuasions were tough and unyielding. The processing and appeals systems were clogged with people who had been in detention for years. The ambassador was the conduit to get a hold of Sir William Gordon, and he also insisted on him being on the call. Finney didn't mind that at all. Clifton-Blythe was proving to be a critical part of the process and more helpful than some of his team at the embassy in Bangkok.

It was the ambassador who took the lead in the call. He detailed the possible whereabouts of Jane and her captors, but more importantly the status of the brother in Sydney. The governor immediately understood the importance of keeping Zhang Win out of the immigration detention centre and sending a positive signal to his daughter's captors.

'What can we do in the short-term,' asked the governor.

'We could start by setting up a video call between the two brothers,' Finney suggested. 'That can be done from the jail cell. The next step is to have a deportation order ready, so the moment bail is granted, he's taken straight to the airport. We'll need to get him on a flight to Thailand. After that, it's a border crossing into Myanmar.'

'It would be nice if we could just commandeer a Royal Australian Airforce (RAAF) plane and have it land directly into Chiang Rai,' chuckled Roger Clifton-Blythe. 'I'm sorry Bill, I know it's not funny but to be honest, getting this kid through Bangkok and then onto Mae Sai will be a nightmare. We have no jurisdiction over a felon here.

There was silence from all three men. Finney had no experience with this kind of thing. Clifton-Blythe, on the other hand, would not have suggested an RAAF flight if he hadn't seen such a thing in the past.

'We can make this happen,' said the governor. 'You've seen it before Roger, and so have I. We brought a bunch of miners out of Timor-Leste on an RAAF plane. It was all hush hush of course but it happened.'

'We saw it here in Thailand and Indonesia after the Tsunami in 2004 as well,' said the ambassador. 'Friends in high places Bill, it's what we need right now.'

'Leave it with me,' said Gordon, confidently. 'I know who to call. Stay by the phone, both of you.' And he was gone.

Finney was feeling more confident, but he knew that there were still way too many moving parts in this case. Firstly, they had to get Zhang Win out of custody and then out of the country. That would be the easy part. Getting him through Thailand and into Myanmar would be the most difficult. Where would the exchange take place, he wondered. First things first, he had to put the brothers in contact with one another as he had promised Zhang Sein.

Midday in Mae Sai meant it was getting late in the day in Sydney, and he knew he had to act fast. He picked up the phone and called Jodie Coppins. He was desperate and she was pessimistic about whether the video call could be organised.

'I don't make the rules in the prison,' she said, 'but I'll give it my best shot.'

Technically Zhang Win wasn't in prison, he was on remand. It was different. Finney knew there was more latitude, and he also knew if the order came from high up the ladder it would be approved. He was right. It was less than ten minutes before he got the call from Jodie Coppins.

'It's done. It was as if they were expecting my call.'

'They *were* expecting your call,' he said. 'Send the prison details through to me and I'll make the contacts on this side. This will buy us some time while we get the repatriation happening.'

'You are joking, right? Do you think you can just get him released and deported? There are still some big questions about his case needing answers.' There was anger and frustration in her voice.

'Sorry, of course, you're right. I was just thinking out loud,' Finney said, trying to placate her. 'I appreciate your help with this whole thing Jodie, thank you very much.' Jodie Coppins didn't know the whole story. She knew little about what was going on behind the scenes and Finney needed to keep it that way.

He needed to talk again with Zhang Sein. He wasn't sure of the best way to do that. Forget the text messages or emails, straight talking over the phone would be his choice.

He sat for a while thinking what he wanted to say. Of course, he was trying to set up a video call between the two brothers. He also wanted to tell him he could have the laptop and would be able to give it to him. What's the impression I want to leave with this guy, he wondered. Declan Finney is the guy who can make things happen. That was the impression he wanted to get across to the kidnappers. It's not an ego thing, he told himself. It's just they know me, he has met me, and I need him to trust me. Returning to his room he made the call.

'Declan, nice to hear your voice again,' said Zhang Sein. At only 26 or 27 years old, he had so much self-confidence. He spoke to Finney as a peer and was not at all intimidated.

'I've got some good news for you,' said Finney, trying to sound positive. 'We've been able to set up a video call for you and your brother. That can take place anytime in the next few hours.' They spent the next few minutes discussing the details of what platform they would use. They settled on a Zoom call.

'What about the laptop?'

'I think we can make this happen,' said Finney, holding back a little.

'It's a package deal. The release of my brother, the ransom and the laptop.'

'We can make this happen, but it will just take time. The most important thing is to get your brother back home. Am I right?'

'I want Win back as soon as possible. He is not very happy where he is right now. We are not used to being treated this way.'

'Let's start with the video call. I'm working as fast as I can, I truly am,' said Finney, and he meant it. 'What about you give us something? Jane's parents want a video call, just like we are arranging for you and your brother.'

'I see you've done your hostage negotiation course. You give me something, I give you something. That's how it works, right? No, I can't do t. I know you will try and trace the call, and I know your preference is to free Jane Gordon without releasing my brother. Would that be right Declan? I know it is,' he said without waiting for a reply. 'I've got a feeling this is your first hostage negotiation. You might be surprised to learn it's not mine. No video call today.' Zhang Sein ended the call.

He was right, this was his first hostage negotiation. He knew he was out of his depth. His room was dimly lit and dusty. He needed light and fresh air. As he descended the stairs, he saw Banjob cleaning the van in the courtyard. 'Going somewhere, sir,' he enquired. 'I can take you in the vehicle, it's freshly cleaned.'

Finney shook his head, declining the offer. 'I'm just taking in a little fresh air, and I won't go far. If I need you, I'll call.' As he exited the courtyard, he turned left to the road which led back to the border. Phahonyothin Rd. was packed with vehicles, and in the distance, he saw the Orassa Hotel. He was happy to be staying elsewhere and his new accommodation, while a little more rustic, would do fine. He wanted some air, but he also wanted to be surrounded by people. It was mid-afternoon, a storm was brewing, the humidity was rising, and the Mercury was well past 30 C.

After a fifteen-minute walk, he decided to take refuge in the Brew Whale & co. Coffee Shop. He took a window seat where he could watch the world go by but also enjoy the air conditioning. The place was a riot of knick-knacks, mismatching furniture and bold colours. He ordered a mango shake and settled in to check his messages.

He went through them one by one. They were all important. *Care To Comment,* was the subject line from Pip, the Chiang Mai journalist who was never far from his thoughts. Before he could check the others, he got a call from her.

'Did you get my message,' she said straight off.

'I just saw it. Comment on what?'

'You don't know, do you?'

'Know what? What don't I know?' He was tense and irritable. He'd been up since 3.30 am after little more than three hours sleep.

'You sound grumpy,' she teased. 'If you don't know what I'm talking about I'm quite sure you won't want to comment. Can I suggest you call your colleagues at the embassy? There's something you need to know. Afterwards, you can call me. We've decided to spend the weekend here. It is Friday, and you know where we'll be tonight. Why don't you join us for a drink any time after about 6:00 pm,' she said and ended the call.

Now he was intrigued. His problem was he didn't know who to call at the embassy. He certainly didn't want to call the ambassador and ask an open-ended question like, is there something I need to know? He decided to call Richard Hanlon instead.

'I was about to call you,' said Hanlon. 'We've got the autopsy results back on Quinn and they don't look good. He died of cardiac arrest just as we thought he had.'

'What's the problem exactly,' said Finney.

'The problem is his blood contained temazepam, cocaine, and methylamphetamines. We have a forensic pathologist's report which asserts he was given the temazepam to render him unconscious, and then the meth and cocaine, which triggered the cardiac arrest, were administered intravenously. The needle was inserted at the base of the skull. Extremely hard to find, but our guy did. Meaning, the heart attack was induced. So far, we've managed to keep the Thai police out of this. Bart Guthrie is flying to Chiang Rai first thing in the morning to investigate further. We figured he could help you out with this Jane Gordon thing as well. How does that sound?'

It was the last thing he wanted to hear, and he was clear about this to Hanlon. 'We are at a delicate stage of negotiations, and I don't want that jeopardised. Guthrie is like a bull in a China shop, and I don't want him anywhere near the kidnappers.'

'It's not my call; you will have to speak to the ambassador about that. Guthrie is head of the AFP here at the embassy and he is a senior officer to you. I think that kind of makes him your boss. Does that sound about right?'

'Technically yes,' he had to concede, 'it does, but my understanding is that I am the lead on this case. I'm the one negotiating with the kidnappers. I was hand-picked by Sir William Gordon to come and find his daughter. Does that sound about right?' he said mockingly. He didn't care about offending Hanlon. All he knew was he didn't want Bart Guthrie anywhere near him right now.

Unknown to him, Guthrie had already met with Roger Clifton-Blythe and suggested he take control of the whole kidnapping operation in Mae Sai. Fortunately for Finney, the ambassador had confidence in his abilities, and he was no fan of Guthrie. Or for that matter Barry Quinn. He had no direct jurisdiction over the AFP team within the embassy, but he didn't like the way they operated. Their behaviour often reflected badly on his team and the embassy more broadly. They had a reputation. He had made it clear Guthrie was to stay away from Finney, but he also knew Guthrie would do whatever he liked.

He finally spoke with the ambassador late in the afternoon, and felt reassured by the conversation. He'd decided to send Hanlon along to keep an eye on Guthrie. Annoyingly fastidious, like a school prefect, at least Hanlon at least followed the rules-unlike Bart Guthrie, who seemed to invent his own as needed.

So just how did Pip get this information so quickly, Finney thought. She certainly was well-informed, and it would be only a matter of time before she worked out what had happened to Jane Gordon. This would cause problems. Should he bring her into his confidence? Rosie Betts had warned him about her, and he also had his prejudice about journalists from years in the police force. But she wasn't a regular journalist. He would meet her at The Bamboo Bar for a drink. What harm could it do?

The bigger question, which was hard to ignore, was who killed Barry Quinn, and why. He would have enemies, and there was no doubt about that. But up here in Mae Sai, thought Finney. Would his enemies come after him up here or was it just easier to get to him while he was away from the embassy? He knew Banjob would have all the background on Quinn but was he prepared to ask Banjob about him? He decided against making inquiries with the embassy driver. It was all too complicated. Focus on the job at hand, he told himself. There were questions about Quinn's death that needed to be answered, but they would have to wait.

Brotherly Love

On remand, he was still dressed in his designer-label clothing. The young man was cocky. He had swagger which only comes with youth. He smirked at the prison guards as if to say, *I'm the winner now.* The news from his solicitor, while overdue, had been good. He would be free in the next few days, and he got to talk to his brother. As he was being walked to the interview room he started whistling.

The video call was monitored, of course, but the boy had the room to himself. Shackled to the desk, he beamed a broad smile to his brother when he appeared on the screen. For most of the conversation, the two brothers spoke in their native language. The call would have to be translated, but expectations were low. The police knew the confession of the other student meant Zhang Win was off the hook. The prosecution could make a case they were both involved but it was unlikely.

'We will have you home soon little brother,' Zhang Sein had said. 'Just keep your head down for the time being and let me handle things from this end. Don't talk to anyone.' The younger brother was jovial, but his brother was not. 'Don't do anything stupid,' the older brother lectured his younger sibling. 'When you're released you stay in the apartment and don't go out anywhere. You are not safe until we have you back home.' The police allowed them ten minutes only, but it was more than enough. They were done after five, with the boy calling out to the guards he was finished, and he was returned to his cell. For those monitoring the call, there was little optimism anything useful would come of it.

The humidity surged, the storm clouds came rapidly, and the rain started with thunderclaps and lightning bolts. The rain pounded on the tin roof and was deafening. Jane Gordon sat with her knees tucked under her chin on the floor of her cell. The atmosphere had changed over the last 24 hours. Zhang Sein was absent. The background noise of the men in the warehouse was louder than usual. There was more chatter. More laughter. And the previous evening they had been drinking and playing loud music. It sounded like a party. When the cat's away…….

She had not left the room for more than 24 hours now and felt restless and depressed. The young Burmese girl, Nong Bak, had brought her food in the morning and again in the evening, but the hostage had little appetite. Nong Bak sat with her and encouraged her to eat, through gestures. Soon she heard a commotion outside as a convoy of vehicles arrived. The Burmese maid quickly jumped up and left the room. Soon enough Jane could hear voices, one of which sounded like Zhang Sein, but she couldn't be sure.

Back in Mae Sai, it was getting late. The rain had come and gone, with Finney sitting it out in the small cafe working on his laptop but mostly just thinking. He got an email from Jody Coppins confirming the video call between the two Burmese brothers. Well at least it's something, he thought to himself. It was time to reach out to Zhang Sein again. This time he decided to do it using text messages. He preferred a voice call, but he was dealing with a generation which thrived on text messages.

Hi Sein, I hope the call went well. Please let Jane speak to her parents. We need proof she is alive and well. Bail hearing in the morning when your brother

will be released from custody. We will then get him back to Myanmar.

Unfortunately for Finney, Zhang Sein had other things on his mind. Returning from his trip to Tachileik he learned several of his storage locations and couriers had been hit by the Thai army offensive along the Thai/Myanmar border while he had been away. He was furious. Jane Gordon, locked in the small room under the same roof as Zhang Sein's office, cowered as she heard him shouting and screaming. He didn't know it just yet, but the video call between Jane and her parents was not happening anytime soon. Unlike Finney, Zhang Sein couldn't afford to focus on just one thing. He had shipments which had to be made. He owed money to powerful people. He didn't want to think about his brother right now, but he knew he had to get him home sooner rather than later. He sat down and got details of the raids on the Thai border. They had lost seven men, but more importantly, they had lost over 100 kilos of meth.

He left the other men sitting in the warehouse, walked out onto the large terrace outside and gazed out over the mountains towards the West. This always calmed him down. Was the connection between these raids and the young Australian girl he had locked up inside the warehouse? Could these two things be connected, he thought to himself. If so, could he use Jane Gordon as a bargaining chip with the Thai army as well as the Australian government? A smile came across his face as he concluded that perhaps he could.

He had not responded to Finney's text message. Now was the time to add just one more demand for the girl's release. The Thai army had to cease their offensive along the border and allow the shipments to go through. He sent a message to this effect to Finney.

Just when he thought he had set up the makings for a successful exchange, Zhang Sein's message arrived. His first impulse was to pick up the phone and call Zhang Sein, and he did so.

'It looks like I've got your attention,' said Zhang Sein, 'you put a stop to these raids by the Thai army. Get your ambassador to speak to them.'

'I think you already know I can't do that. I'm not even here in an official capacity. The Thais aren't interested in your brother or Jane Gordon. Their activities are not connected to her and there's nothing I can do to stop their raids against your men.'

'You haven't even had time to talk to your people about it. How can you be so sure?'

Finny tried to take some heat out of the conversation. 'Sein, you must listen to me, we will pay the ransom, get your brother home, and hand over the laptop because those things are under our control. What the Thais are doing on the border is out of our control.'

There was a long pause. 'What about the bail hearing, when is it.'

'Tomorrow, and we could have him on a plane and on his way home by Sunday. What do you think about that? I have another suggestion. I will trade you the laptop for a video call between Jane Gordon and her parents. But it must be tomorrow morning. People on my side are doubting your sincerity. So, what about it?'

The young man took his time. 'Ok,' he said finally, 'it's a deal. I'll send someone to pick up the laptop from the river. Tomorrow at 6 am, and when we have the laptop, we can do the call. You set it up on your side.'

'If you let me down on this, I can't guarantee we can trust you any further,' he said. Another long silence followed.

'I get it,' said the kidnapper, and ended the call.

Hurrying back to the guesthouse he found Banjob cleaning the van. He needed the laptop.

'It's already done,' said Banjob. 'As instructed sir, I went over there, and Agent Betts handed it to me herself. Whatever you have on the machine, it must be important,' said the driver.

He took Banjob aside from the courtyard where there were other guests and staff. 'I need to speak to you in private,' he said. 'We need the boat again in the morning, at around 6 am. We will meet the Burmese at the same place and hand over this laptop to them.'

Banjob raised his eyebrows. 'Does our ambassador know about this,' said the driver.

'Of course, he does,' lied Finney. 'Do you think I'm stupid enough to do this without permission?' He figured by the time Hanlon arrived mid-morning and discovered he had handed over the laptop, Jane Gordon would have spoken via video link to her parents and all would be well.

The sun was setting, and the mosquitos were out in force. Finney decided to retreat to his room. It had been a long day, and he needed to gather his thoughts and even grab some rest. The overhead fan in his room was on high. He flipped the AC on and flopped onto his unmade bed. Seconds later he was fast asleep. He dreamed of Ella. They were walking home from school together; she couldn't have been more than seven or eight years old. His daughter was chattering about all her friends and her favourite teacher, Miss Molly. She read books to them every afternoon. They skipped together along the pavement and then stopped by their local store to buy ice creams. The dream was vivid, and he woke up with a strong recollection of it, but no memory of ever walking Ella to school. His conscience was playing tricks on him. He knew he was a prisoner of his past.

Watch Your Back

His mouth was dry, and he was hot and sticky. The tropical heat made him lethargic. The air was thick and heavy. He felt irritated by the people around him, Banjob, Tura and especially Bart Guthrie, whose imminent arrival left him with a feeling of dread. As for Zhang Sein, he was conflicted. In some ways he liked him. He liked his self-assurance, but he also found himself despising that same character trait. It came from a privileged upbringing funded by the violence of his grandfather. He is a drug trafficker, for Christ's sake, he reminded himself.

Finney needed a drink. He would settle for water to begin with. He drank thirstily from the minibar. Firstly, he drank two bottles of still water without effort. He then turned his attention to a litre bottle of sparkling water. By the time he was done with, his mood had brightened. I'm just dehydrated, he realised. Every local he had met so far had lectured him on the importance of drinking plenty of water. He had foolishly ignored the advice. He'd always fantasized about living on a tropical island. He was now having second thoughts.

When he looked at the Thais, he saw a kind of languid relaxation. Was it simply they were pacing themselves in the relentless heat and humidity, he wondered, or had a more leisurely rhythm to their lives? He had noticed people took naps, whether it was motorcycle taxi drivers sprawled out on the seats of their vehicles in between customers or vendors dozing next to the stalls during quiet spells, people seemed to nap. I'll be more relaxed after this is all over, he muttered to himself. He could only hope so.

He showered and changed his clothes. It was nearing 9 pm. He found Banjob downstairs and confirmed all was in place for the laptop to be delivered early the following morning. Realising he had not eaten since breakfast he made his way to the local night market in search of food. He stopped at the same stall as the night before and was greeted as if a long-lost friend by the vendor. Does he recognise me, Finney wondered, or are all his customers treated this way? Yet again he noted how hard it was to read people in this part of the world. A smile can mean many different things, Banjob had told him a few days earlier. He was right.

All along he knew where he would end up and why. He wanted to see Pip Tan again. He told himself he was simply curious, but he was captivated by her. It was only a five-minute walk to The Bamboo Bar. Once again, he heard it before he saw it. He could also smell it. The acrid odour of cannabis emanating from the bar was unmistakable. He had dabbled in some weed smoking in his youth but had never liked it. It made him feel even more socially awkward and shy while he was stoned, and he felt depressed and fuzzy-headed the following day.

Balloons and ribbons hung from the ceiling, swaying gently with the movement of air in the crowded bar. A table of Thais nearby was deep into a birthday celebration, the sound of their laughter mixing with the clinking of glasses and bursts of chatter. But Finney wasn't here for the festivities. His eyes were fixed on the table by the river, where six people sat, framed by the flickering lights dancing off the water.

Pip was there, sitting alongside two other young women, her face lit up by the glow of the lanterns strung overhead. Across from her, holding court with his back to the river, was Harley Dowsett. The man was animated, his arms slicing through the air as he recounted some story which had his audience enraptured. On either side of Dowsett were two men, and his eyes narrowed as he recognized one of them—Dan Pendergast, the bar owner from Chiang Mai. The sight of him made Finney uneasy.

From his vantage point at the entrance, he hesitated. The scene before him was raucous, Dowsett's group was loud enough to draw the attention of other patrons. Empty beer bottles cluttered their table, evidence the party had been going on for a while. Finney felt as if he was walking into some kind of trap. This could either be a stroke of genius or a colossal mistake.

As he deliberated, Dowsett's gaze caught his. There was a moment of recognition, and then Dowsett was on his feet, a broad smile stretching across his face. He waved Finney over, his voice booming above the din of the bar, welcoming him with the kind of enthusiasm which suggested he had been expecting him all along.

He took a deep breath, pushing his doubts aside. There was no turning back now. He approached the table, preparing himself for whatever might come next.

'Well, well, well,' said Dowsett, 'if it isn't the enigmatic Agent Finney.

'It's just plain old Finney,' he said.

Dan Pendergast eyed him suspiciously. 'You certainly get around,' the man said, looking at Finney.

'I could say the same of you,' said Finney. 'What brings you to Mae Sai? Shouldn't you be in Chiang Mai running your bar down there?'

'I'm looking into buying a business up here,' said Pendergast.

'Please tell me you're not looking at buying The Bamboo Bar.'

'Not my style,' said Pendergast.

He was offered a seat next to the men, but Pip insisted he sit next to her as she patted the small space on the bench seat. 'Come over here Declan and tell us all about your day,' she said cheekily. 'It must be more exciting than mine, that's for sure. Trying to get information out of the Thai police is harder than getting blood from a stone. How is your fact-finding tour coming along?'

'Fact-finding tour,' Dowsett boomed. 'Come on Agent Finney it's time to confess. What are you doing up here? Guns, drugs, revolution or simply recreation. Which is it?'

'A very boring fact-finding visit, I'm afraid,' he said, sticking to his script. 'I wish it was a little more glamorous. Even some simple recreation would be good. What you folks are up to sounds far more interesting,' deflecting attention away from himself. 'And it's just Detective Sergeant Finney. I'm nobody's agent.'

'It's great to see you sticking to your cover story,' said Dowsett. 'What can I get you to drink,' he said as he stood and headed towards the bar.

'Soda water will be fine,' said Finney.

The man returned with a soda water and a vodka shot. This guy knows me too well already, thought Finney, ignoring the vodka shot. The group had been drinking for some time. The girls sitting with Pip were both slurring their words and giggling at something only they found to be funny. They were both Dutch exchange students from Chiang Mai University enjoying a weekend road trip.

Finney was sitting opposite thc man with Pendergast and Dowsett. He had been introduced as Joel, a visiting academic with expertise in environmental science, and he fixed Finney with a cold stare. The man was in his late forties with a physique which screamed mercenary rather than an intellectual. Finney wasn't convinced he was who he said he was. He was also thinking the three men knew each other very well. Was it a coincidence they were all here together?

'So, what's on for you this evening,' said Pip as she leaned in close to Finney. 'We are going back to my place after this if you want to join us.'

'Which hotel are you staying in,' he asked, shifting uncomfortably in his seat.

'My parents have a house here on the edge of town towards Chiang Saen. I'm staying there. Would you like to come and check it out?'

'Do your parents live here?'

Pip went on to explain her father lived in Bangkok with a new wife. Her mother and siblings, who lived in Chiang Mai, maintained the pretence their father lived in Bangkok solely for work purposes. Though her parents had been separated for many years, it was never discussed.

'It's a Thai thing,' she said, 'we don't get divorced. We just don't talk about it and the new wife keeps a low profile.' The house here had belonged to her grandparents. 'It's on the river and has a beautiful view. You should come and see it,' she suggested.

Shaking his head, Finney explained he had another early start in the morning.

'You sure are playing hard to get. What does a girl have to do,' she laughed.

He liked her. She was fun, and she was beautiful, but she was also a journalist. He had other things on his mind.

'We could catch up tomorrow,' he said. 'Can I call you around lunchtime?'

'Sure, why don't you do that.' She turned her attention back to the men across the table. 'Can you believe this guy,' she said, pointing a finger at Finney. 'I invite him back to my place for a nightcap and he declines.'

'Ask me back to your place for a nightcap and I certainly will not decline,' sniggered Harley Dowsett.

'We both know that's not happening, Harley. I'm surprised you're still even here. Mae Sai is a bit tame for a man with your tastes. Am I right?'

'My tastes in all things are varied and exotic,' he said, affecting a posh English accent. 'I also appreciate the tranquil atmosphere of this charming little border outpost. There is intrigue hidden here behind a façade of tranquillity. Agent Finney would know that better than most, despite his recent arrival.' He shot a look toward Finney indicating he knew more about his work in Mae Sai than he wanted to let on.

Finney let the comment slide. It was bait, and he wasn't biting. Time to move on. He carefully slid the untouched vodka shot across the table toward Dowsett. 'I will have to politely say no to the vodka this evening,' he said. He stood up and said his goodbyes. As he was making his way to the exit he heard Pip behind him.

'You will call me tomorrow,' she said, as she stood on her tiptoes and pecked him on the cheek.

'Of course,' he replied. He could feel himself blushing. He felt like a teenager. He saw for the first time her perfectly formed almond-shaped eyes and silky, jet-black hair. As he walked back to the guesthouse he regretted saying no to a nightcap. This kind of thing doesn't happen to me, he thought. He reflected on being the only sober person at the table, which was an unusual experience for him. Usually, he was the first guy to the table and was well-lubricated by the time the others arrived. Friends had told him booze made him more talkative and confident. He could only hope he wasn't one of those boorish, loud drunks.

Arriving back at the guest house at around 11:00 PM, it was eerily quiet. There was no sign of either Banjob or his friend Somchai. There was no one to be seen. The van was parked out front so perhaps they had gone out in one of Somchai's classic cars, he thought. Either way, he didn't care, there would be no interrogation from the driver this evening. He made his way up to his room and decided to check his emails one last time before turning in for the night.

He went straight to the email from Stacy Harmer which had been sent hours earlier. The subject line was titled, BAIL HEARING SET. His colleague went on to explain there would be a bail hearing at 10:00 am the following day, Saturday. A bail hearing on a weekend was unusual but not unheard of, especially in a case like this. Finney already knew the outcome; the young man would be released, no question about it. He was nervous that when Zhang Sein's brother was released from prison there was a chance, he could escape the country. It would depend on the bail conditions. He would need to speak to Jodie Coppins and ensure they had a watertight plan. The call would have to be made no later than 5:00 am.

He tried to sleep but with no success. He tossed and turned and thought of Ella, Pip, and the impending arrival of Bart Guthrie, but most of all he thought of Jane

Gordon. Held captive now for more than a week, what shape would she be in, he wondered. Had she been treated well?

At around midnight, he heard a commotion downstairs. Drawing the curtains slowly, he saw Banjob and Somchai in the courtyard. Both appeared drunk. The driver appeared aggressive, wagging his finger at his friend. They began shouting at each other.

Finney opened his door and stepped out onto the landing. 'Everything OK,' he called out to the two men. Hearing his voice they both looked up and took a step away from one another.

'Politics,' said Somchai, 'never discuss politics while drinking Thai whiskey.'

'He's right,' said the other man. 'It can only lead to disagreements.'

Even in the dimly lit courtyard, embarrassment was evident on Banjob's face. 'I'm sorry if we have disturbed you, sir,' the driver went on. 'It's time we called it a night Somchai, what do you say?' The other man nodded.

'We have another early start tomorrow Banjob,' said Finney, 'I'll see you at 5am sharp. Goodnight.' Perhaps Banjob wasn't such a saint after all. As he returned to his room, Finney's phone buzzed with a stream of urgent messages—all from Pip.

Need to see you. Urgent. Dangerous. Please help.

The last thing he needed right now. Before he could think further, his phone lit up with her incoming call. He answered, reluctantly.

'Hi, Pip. I got your messages.'

'Declan, I need to talk to you now,' she said, her voice shaky. 'I'm standing outside the Orassa Hotel, but they told me you'd checked out, where are you? Are you back in Chiang Mai?'

'I've moved hotels—figured you'd know why.'

'Why didn't you tell me about your colleague's death?'

'There's a lot going on, Pip. What's so urgent?'

'I can't talk about it over the phone. Can we meet?'

Against his better judgment, he agreed, suggesting she come to his guesthouse. Within minutes, he spotted her near the gates, visibly agitated. Without a word, he led her to his room, hoping they wouldn't be seen.

She slumped on the bed, reeking of alcohol, her hands shaking. He handed her a glass of water.

'I feel sick," she muttered, shaking her head.

'One too many drinks, perhaps?"

'It's not that.' She glanced up, eyes filled with terror. 'It's what I overheard at the bar. After you left, I heard Harley Dowsett and Dan Pendergast talking about Barry Quinn's death. Pendergast kept saying, 'It had to be done,' as if they'd planned it.'

'What exactly did they say?'

'Pendergast said, 'We're better off without him around.' But it was more than that. I spoke with someone at Chiang Mai police—Barry Quinn was murdered.'

Finney tried to hide his reaction, but she caught on.

'Don't give me that look,' she said, her tone sharp. 'You knew. And now I hear there's an embassy agent here investigating. Is it true?'

He nodded slowly, unsure how much he could reveal.

'Why would they kill him?' she demanded.

Her expression hardened as the pieces seemed to fall into place. She stood, moving toward the door before turning back. 'I can't ignore this, Declan.'

"Sit down, Pip," he urged quietly. "I need your help."

They stared at each other in silence, and he realised she wouldn't back down. After a pause, she continued. 'Pendergast and Dowsett mentioned going to the casino in Laos. I lost track of them after that.'

'So, you're certain Pendergast hinted at killing Quinn?'

'He didn't say it outright, but he sure implied it.'

Finney nodded. 'It's okay to be upset. You've been through a lot. What are you planning to do with this?'

She pulled out a notepad, pen in hand. 'Is there an active investigation into the embassy staffer's death?'

He couldn't help but laugh. Moments ago, she was falling apart; now, she was back to being a tenacious reporter. Pip started laughing, too, and soon they were both bent over, laughter cutting through the tension. They finally quieted, locking eyes.

"Ridiculous, isn't it?" she said. "What is going on?"

She pulled him into a hug. He didn't resist, the moment stretching until his phone buzzed again, interrupting them.

'I can't confirm anything,' he said. 'All I'll say is, I'm not involved in the investigation. Take this to the Thai police, not the embassy. It's their jurisdiction.'

She gave him a long, searching look. 'You're a terrible liar, Declan. I know you're looking for Jane Gordon. And I think I know where she is. This thing with Quinn's death must be connected.'

'Go on.'

She explained her theory—how Jane had gone to meet Burmese rebels, only to fall into the hands of Zhang Sein's cartel. 'They're holding her in Shan State, demanding a ransom.'

Finney leaned forward, nodding as he pieced it together for her. 'And Zhang Sein's younger brother is locked up in Sydney. That might be leverage.'

She nodded. 'Am I getting close?'

'There's some truth in there.' They sat in silence before she spoke again, her tone softened. 'I know you're trying to keep this out of the public eye, and I won't publish until it's over. But I want the story.'

He sighed, recognizing he had little choice. 'Deal.'

'So… how's the swap happening?'

'Can't discuss it now. Once Jane's safe, I'll tell you everything. Just… trust me.'

She nodded, understanding. 'And Barry Quinn's death?'

'Tell the Thai police—anonymously.'

Finney leaned in. 'We'll get through this, Pip. But we have to be smart. Whoever's behind this won't hesitate to keep their secrets buried.'

Pip's eyes held a mix of fear and determination. 'You're right. But I'm not backing down.'

'Good,' he replied. 'Neither am I.'

It was nearly 2 a.m., but he made coffee anyway. When he turned back, Pip was fast asleep, stretched out on the bed. He lay down beside her, knowing he needed rest. When he woke, she was curled against him, slowly coming to as she took in her surroundings.

'What time is it?' she muttered.

'Just after 4:30. I have to head out, but you can stay and sleep.'

'Did we…?' she began, her voice trailing off.

'No,' he said with a smile. 'We just talked. You fell asleep.'

She looked relieved. 'Thank you, Declan. I feel better after our conversation last night.'

'Glad to help. And Pip… be careful.'

They kissed and shared a lingering embrace before he left, the earlier awkwardness replaced by a new, unspoken affection and understanding. A bond.

As he made his way downstairs, he began making a list of things to discuss with Jody Coppins. At around 5:00 AM, 3 hours later in Sydney, he sent her a text message asking if she was free to chat. Almost immediately, his phone rang.

'So, you got the email from Stacy Harmer. There was some frantic activity yesterday afternoon. I have never seen the system work so quickly but of course, now I know why. You want to talk to me about our strategy this morning,' she went on, not waiting for him to respond. 'We will agree to bail, with strict conditions. These include forfeiting his passport, twice daily visits to the central police station, an ankle bracelet and no contact with the other young man or his family. We will also have a team conducting surveillance on his apartment. We are going to be all over this kid like a cheap suit. There will be a red notice at all airports. That's being managed by the Department of Home Affairs. So how does that stand with you,' she asked.

'You've managed to tick off all the conditions on my list, but I'm still nervous. Will he be released immediately?'

'Pretty much, I'd say. I can't see any reason why we could delay his release. I figure you have forty-eight hours, Declan, in which time, you need to get him out of the country, escorted of course.'

'That's a whole other world of pain,' he said, 'and fortunately for me, it is someone else's problem to organise.' There wasn't anything else he could share with Jody Coppins, certainly not the delivery of the laptop. He ended the call by wishing her good luck with the bail hearing and requesting an update once it had concluded.

Finney and Banjob set off with the laptop to meet the boat driver. This time Somchai did not accompany them. No need to bother him this morning, the driver had said, they knew where to go. They drove in silence and Finney sensed it was not the only reason his friend wasn't coming along. He took the battered-looking Dell laptop from its case. It was plastered with stickers, including Give Peace A Chance, Black Lives Matter, and I Love Thailand. He would have to deny any knowledge of a password and hope the bluff worked. Despite Banjob's objections, he insisted on handing over the laptop himself. This time he had no gun.

As they motored the short distance out to the nearest buoy, he was nervous, unsure if Zhang Sein would be there or whether his men would behave themselves. This time they didn't bother lashing the boats together. Zhang Sein had sent his underlings to collect the computer, and Finney simply passed it over without conversation and they sped off back in the direction of their base. Returning to the hotel a short time later he parted company with the unusually subdued driver. Banjob was headed to Chiang Rai to collect Richard Hanlon and Bart Guthrie from the airport. Finney was hoping they would not be staying at the guesthouse. There was still no sign of Somchai so no chance of coffee either. Sitting in his room he reflected on the night before. The revelations from Pip were disturbing but he would put them to one side. What he couldn't put aside were his growing feelings for the young journalist.

It was still too early to call either Zhang Sein or the ambassador, so he decided to make a call to Ella.

He always started with the same text message, **Free for A Chat with Dad?** There was no reply. It was the weekend, and he figured Ella had plans with her friends. He would call again later. Knowing he could buy a coffee at the market; he headed off in that direction. As he rounded the corner from the back street onto Pahoyothin Rd, he saw in the distance Harley Dowsett and Dan Pendergast deep in conversation outside the Top North Hotel. Both men looked unsteady on their feet and looked as though they had pulled an all-nighter. Dan Pendergast was jabbing his finger into the chest of the much taller man. Dowsett turned and saw Finney in the distance and began waving and shouting. It was too late for him to pretend he had not seen the two men. As he began walking towards them, they stopped their argument immediately.

'Well, if it isn't our old friend Agent Finney,' said the taller of the two men. 'What brings you out so early in the morning or is it you are still on your way home,' he laughed. 'Maybe you took young Pip up on her offer of a nightcap after all.' The other man said nothing but simply stared at Finney.

'I'm just looking for some coffee,' he said. 'I thought I might find something at the local market. I'm still working on Sydney time so I'm seeing a lot of breaking dawns these last few days.'

'Seeing a few of them down by the river is what I hear,' said the New Zealander. 'Word has it you've been making some boat trips. Any truth in the rumour,' he smirked drunkenly.

It was obvious to Finney both men had not slept and had been drinking all night. Bloodshot and slurring their words they wouldn't be vertical for long, he thought. 'It looks like you fellows have had a long evening,' he said, trying to lighten up the conversation. 'This must be your hotel here,' he said, pointing to the Top North Hotel.

'Do we look like backpackers to you,' Pendergast barked aggressively. 'Do I look like a cheapskate of some kind?'

'Settle down there Dan,' said Dowsett, putting a hand on the other man's shoulder. 'Our friend is just being polite.'

'Polite,' spat the other man, animated and teetering on unsteady legs, 'he's a spook. Look at him. What are you looking for Finney,' he said raising his voice. 'You want to keep out of other people's business if you know what's good for you.'

Finney didn't bother responding.

'It's time we got back to our lodgings,' said Harley Dowsett. With one hand on the other man's shoulder, he turned him around and they both staggered along the street away from the border crossing, presumably in the direction of their hotel. Finney turned and walked towards the market and hopefully some coffee. He was shaken by the hostility of Dan Pendergast but now he understood where it was coming from. Of more concern was how they knew of his movements near the river. He would have to be careful in the company of those two men.

The market was now familiar territory to Finney. He navigated his way through the narrow alleys to a stall selling Thai coffee. Kopi as it was called, in Thailand. The vendor poured boiling water through a long sieve filled with coffee grounds into a small metal jug. It was then poured into a tall glass containing condensed milk. The coffee and the condensed milk stayed separated until stirred with a long spoon. It was sickeningly sweet, and Finney loved it. He bought himself three small Chinese Donuts to eat with the coffee.

Sitting on a small stool drinking his coffee he pictured the young Burmese student being taken to the court in Sydney at that very moment. He would wait for confirmation of the student's release from Jodie Coppins before calling the ambassador. He hoped arrangements would already be in place for the transfer of the student back to Thailand. He was happy not to be responsible for that part of the process. His phone pinged. It was Ella. **Sorry Dad, Out with Friends. Later. XXX**. She would call back when she could, she always did.

The phone pinged again. This time it was from an unknown number, but Finney knew who it was. **Thank you for the laptop. We need to talk. Stand By. I will call you in fifteen minutes.** It was Zhang Sein, who was also, no doubt, picturing his brother being liberated from his jail cell.

It was also getting hot and noisy as the market filled with people. It was not the best place to take the call from Zhang Sein. Making his way out of the market he saw Somchai, the owner of the guesthouse. Finney carefully avoided making eye contact. It would be better for both men if they did not speak. He knew Somchai would be embarrassed about the events of the previous evening. Some things were better left unsaid, Tura had told him several days earlier. He had been right, and this was just such an occasion. Finney made his way further down the street toward the Twenty-Seven Mae Sai Brew Café. It was just opening, and he was the first customer.

'The coffee machine is not turned on yet,' said the young girl setting up tables on the sidewalk.

'I'll just take some water for now,' said Finney. 'May I sit here,' he pointed to one of the tables tucked in a quiet corner outdoors. She nodded as he sat down. His phone rang and as expected, it was Zhang Sein.

'Declan, good morning,' he sounded cheerful.

And why not, thought Finney, in a couple of hours his brother will be free. 'Good morning, Sein. Are you in Tachileik,' he asked.

'It's not important where I am. What is important is how long it will take to get my brother home.'

'One thing at a time. Let's get him out of remand,' he said, trying to avoid using the word jail. 'I need you to set up a call for Jane to speak to her parents. I think I've shown you enough goodwill by now, don't you agree?'

'Sure thing, Declan,' said Sein, sounding upbeat. 'I'm not with Jane right now but I think we can make it happen. Stay by your phone and give me a couple of hours. I also want something else from you. I want to know by the end of today when my brother will be back home. Are we clear about that?'

Finney was nodding. He was reluctant to make a commitment, but he knew he had no choice. 'I'll talk to my colleagues and get back to you.' They ended the call.

He also had other things on his mind. Well, other people. Harley Dowsett and Dan Pendergast. He shot off a text message to Stacey Harmer. It was Saturday but he knew she would be thinking about work. He needed some research done and she was an expert. I am a web ferret, she had said. If the information were out there, she could find it. Soon enough he had her on the phone. Finney gave her the background on the two men but carefully avoided mention of the news from Pip. It had been clear in the bar in Chiang Mai that they knew Barry Quinn and were not just acquaintances. At least he now knew why the two men suddenly appeared in Mae Sai so close to the time of Quinn's death.

'See what you can get on them,' he asked. 'It might be easier with Pendergast as he is a Kiwi.' He was reluctant to ask his friend to do some snooping on Barry Quinn, but it had to be done. Finney had seen his file and knew his background in the fraud and drugs squads. 'Be thorough,' he told Harmer, 'But please be discrete. Don't leave any fingerprints or we will both be in it deep.'

'Sure thing,' she said, 'I know all the shortcuts. This case with the Burmese student sure is ruffling some feathers. They've managed to keep it out of the press so far, but you just never know,' her voice trailing off.

'We get him out of the country ASAP, it's the only answer. Even if we park him somewhere for a few days, so long as it is outside Australia.'

'It presents another set of risks,' she said, stating the obvious. 'Once he's out of our jurisdiction we can't control what happens. Getting him through Thailand will be tricky.'

He didn't need to be reminded of this. He had spent a lot of time going through the various scenarios. He thought it was fanciful, but the ideal scenario was a direct flight from Sydney to Chiang Rai. He got the impression from the ambassador anything was possible if you had the right connections. All of that would be the responsibility of Bill Gordon and Roger Clifton-Blythe. His job was to make sure Jane Gordon was still alive and able to be traded for Zhang Win. Right on cue, he received a message from Zhang Sein. He was prepared to set up a short video call between the girl and her parents. It was to be no longer than two minutes. The kidnappers would send through the Zoom meeting details. Don't bother trying a trace, the message said, if you do, you jeopardize her safety. She will be moved to another location after the call, he added.

Finney was juggling phone calls and text messages. To add to the mix, he saw Tura walking towards him. The man seemed to know Finney was there. This was no chance meeting. There was no time for pleasantries.

Taking a seat opposite Finney, the man started firing questions. Is the brother out of jail yet? Has Zhang Sein agreed to allow the daughter to speak to her parents? Do you know they have already moved her? 'The girl has been held on the outskirts of Keng Tung, as we suspected,' said Tura. 'Last night she was moved to another location on the other side of the city. I understand it is a monastery. There are now armed guards patrolling the new location.'

He answered the questions as best he could. Tura was well-informed on the movements of Zhang Sein and his men. I have eyes and ears everywhere, he had said. He also explained that the government was sending the army to several locations within Shan state. 'People are nervous,' he said. 'Be careful Mr Finney.'

When they had first met, he had been wary in his dealings with Tura. He now realised it was all or nothing. The man had shown himself to be reliable and that would have to be enough to trust him. As they edged closer to making the deal with the kidnappers, Tura was more important than ever. Finney quizzed him about Dowsett, Pendergast and Quinn. Had he had dealings with them? Had he heard anything?

Tura looked surprised at Finney's change of tone and his apparent candour. 'Do I finally have your confidence,' he asked.

Now it was Finney's turn to look surprised. 'You always had my confidence,' he said.

'We both know that's not true so now we can be honest with one another. What I say to you now is strictly between us. If you quote me, I'll deny it. What you do with the information however is up to you. Your man, Barry Quinn, has been a very naughty boy. He has been working on both sides of the fence. He's bent, is it the correct expression?'

Tura launched into an epic monologue describing the activities of the three men, Quinn, Pendergast and Dowsett, The Three Musketeers. Or the three stooges would be a better description. Pendergast had a network for drug distribution back in New Zealand. He was a bikie, not that he looked like one now. Over the years his boys had expanded into Australia. They started in Sydney and Melbourne but now they are in Perth, Adelaide, and Brisbane. Quinn was his man on the inside. He kept Pendergast informed and made sure the occasional bust happened without too much collateral damage. He has also helped Pendergast get rid of most of the competition. Somehow, they get busted, and he never did. In Chiang Mai, they call him Pendo. He was once a very promising tennis player but then he had some kind of injury. This was his cover in Chiang Mai. He supports the tennis players at the Gymkhana Club. He knows everyone and people think he is just this sports nut who also happens to run a bar. The bar is a great cover. He washes some money through it, and it attracts a diverse crowd. So, if the occasional group of bikers come through, nobody notices. He explained how the organisation was low profile. Dan Pendergast was a family man, married to a Thai, with whom he had three children. He also supported their school and was well-behaved. He saved his bad behaviour for trips to Bangkok, Chiang Mai and even Mae Sai. Tura went on to explain how he and Dowsett had slipped across the river the night before and squandered thousands of dollars at the casino in Laos.

Putting two and two together, Finney explained to Tura his encounter with the two men earlier that morning.

'I'm surprised you didn't encounter them when you were having your little riverboat trip this morning,' said Tura. Seeing his look, Tura explained, yet again, he had eyes and ears everywhere. 'It's why I'm so useful, right,' he said.

'I can't argue with that,' he said, 'it's just you seem to know everything before I do.'

'Why does it seem so hard to accept? This is my 'hood and these are my tribes,' he said as he swept his arms out across in front of him. 'Not your 'hood, Mr Finney, not your tribe.'

Tura was right. Why was Finney finding it so hard to accept? His phone was pinging with messages coming thick and fast.

'So where does Dowsett fit into all of this,' asked Finney.

'Harley Dowsett has a reputation stretching from Tokyo to Jakarta. He has been kicked out of Japan, Vietnam, and Cambodia. He'll never be able to go back to any of those places. Let's just say he has a predilection for the strange, exotic and sometimes illegal pursuits. He is also particularly good at extortion. I think the current term is sextortion. Apparently, over the years he has compiled quite the dossier on all sorts of people. Judges, diplomats, politicians, police, teachers and on it goes. He gathers up nasty facts about people and then uses it in exchange for money and favours. I think you can see where this is headed, Mr. Finney'.

He could see where this was leading. He didn't know exactly in what sequence the formation of this trio had occurred, but he had an idea. Dowsett gets something on Quinn and in return for keeping it a secret, Quinn becomes their man. He and Pendergast had been working together. At this point in the inquiry, it didn't matter very much. The point was Quinn was helping them get the product out of Thailand and into Australia with minimal disruption and suspicion. It wasn't too much of a stretch to believe this led to his ultimately death. Had he refused to continue to cooperate with Pendergast and Dowsett? He knew he had to share this with someone, but who? His mind was racing but it was brought to a sudden stop.

'Before you get carried away, Mr Finney, you might like to consider the possibility some of Barry Quinn's colleagues may also be involved in this little conspiracy. That's not too much of a stretch of the imagination, is it,' said Tura.

The first thing which came into his mind was the imminent arrival of Bart Guthrie. Banjob had gone to Chiang Rai to collect him and Hanlon. Just focus on Jane Gordon, he told himself. Then the other voice in his head was saying, what if her disappearance is connected to Quinn's death? He had seen it too often in the past to simply ignore the possibility of a connection. More importantly, might this affect the release of Jane Gordon?

That left Rosie Betts. Surely, she was aware of all of this, how could she not have been, and why hadn't she shared the information with him? His head was spinning. Lack of sleep, the heat, dehydration, and stress overwhelmed him. Suddenly he felt dizzy, and the next minute he was slumping forward off his chair and onto the concrete pavement. Just in time, Tura grabbed him, propping him back up in the chair and pushing his head between his knees.

'Let's get some blood back into your brain,' said Tura, sounding like a doctor. 'Take a deep breath and keep your head between your knees' he said in a quiet voice. He called the waitress over and spoke softly to her. The next minute she emerged from the café with a cold towel and another bottle of icy water. 'Put this over your head,' said the man, draping the cold towel over Finney. Removing the lid from the bottle he first poured a small amount of water over Finney's head before passing the bottle to him. 'Be careful in this heat. It gets the better of you before you know it. I see it all the time, especially with white people like you.'

White people like me, thought Finney. He was imagining someone saying that back in Sydney. The outrage would be instant. Here it didn't seem to matter. He rested his head back against the wall of the café and took a deep breath. Tura suggested they return to the guesthouse where Finney could take a cold shower and recover in his air-conditioned room. He didn't need much persuading. Despite Finney's protests, Tura called over a tuk-tuk driver and they both climbed aboard for the two-minute drive back to the guesthouse. Finney was glad not to be walking.

Somchai was watering plants in the courtyard. He and Tura made sure Finney made it to his room safely. The cool air inside had an instant effect. Taking Tura's advice, he took a long cold shower and then flopped onto the bed. It was less than an hour, but the short nap had the desired effect.

He awoke refreshed and revived. As he looked out his window and saw Hanlon and Guthrie emerging from the van, he realised he had done the right thing. At least now he had the energy to deal with what was to come. His first thought was the men had been booked into the same guest house. Thankfully, he was wrong. They were here because Finney was the first person they wanted to speak to. Guthrie paced the courtyard aggressively, chest out, head cocked, looking up at Finney's room. He gave himself a few minutes to compose himself before descending the stairs into the courtyard.

Guthrie headed straight for him, 'take a seat over here,' he said, 'I've got a few questions for you.'

'Do I need a solicitor,' he said half-jokingly and immediately regretted it.

'You think this is funny,' said Guthrie. 'It is anything but funny. One of my men, a good man, is dead, murdered, and you think this is funny.' His blood pressure was up. Finney could see his face was flushed and a vein in his neck was throbbing.

'I have nothing to hide,' said Finney, 'I told you all I know a few days ago. I didn't see Quinn before his death. The last I saw of him he was happily sitting in the hotel bar surrounded by beer bottles.'

Guthrie glared at him. 'A little respect Finney, the man is dead, and his widow and children are grieving. We need answers.'

Hanlon stepped forward. 'Detective Finney, we need your full cooperation,' he said, trying to calm the situation.

'Leave this to me, Hanlon,' said Guthrie. 'This is my jurisdiction, not yours.' Hanlon retreated to another table, as Guthrie stood over Finney and started firing questions. 'Was Quinn with anyone? Did he seem worried about anything? Who did he mix with in Chiang Mai? Did you see him with a woman at any time?' Finney decided to drip-feed information to Guthrie.

He relayed the events of their night in Chiang Mai, where they were and who they were with, in precise detail. He told Guthrie about the young woman leaving the hotel in Chiang Mai without his own opinion she had spent the night with Quinn. It was implied. He mentioned Jamie Owens, Dan Pendergast, and Harley Dowsett. Finney tried to take in Guthrie's reactions at the mention of these men. He wondered whether Tura was right, Quinn's colleagues were involved. Did that include Guthrie, he wondered, as he answered the questions. It took no more than a few minutes for him to recount the past few days events. Had all of this occurred over such a brief time, he thought to himself.

'Why wasn't Quinn with you during these meetings with the DEA,' Guthrie demanded.

He explained how Barry Quinn had declined to accompany him to any meetings except those which occurred in Chiang Mai. They had met with the Honorary Consul and interviewed the staff at the guesthouse and that was it. He looked across at Banjob for confirmation.

'It's true sir,' said Banjob.

'I'll get to you shortly BJ,' snapped Guthrie, not even bothering to turn and face the driver. 'So, what about this bar you were in? Name and location.'

'It was some kind of sports bar near our hotel. Banjob will know the name and address, I'm sure. I didn't go to the bar with Quinn,' he said. 'I couldn't sleep so I went out for a walk. I passed by the bar which is where I saw him and the other men. I stayed for one drink and then I returned to the hotel. That was it.' He decided not to mention he had seen Dowsett and Pendergast in Mae Sai. Guthrie would know that soon enough.

'Did he have any visitors in the Orassa Hotel during the time you were there? Did you see anyone coming or going?'

'I didn't see a thing. The only time I saw Quinn was in the bar of the hotel and that was it. He told me the day before he died, he intended to return to Bangkok. I just assumed he was doing so.'

'What about the visit to the bank? Quinn made a withdrawal and handed over B250,000.'

'He only handed over B240,000 baht. Quinn pocketed B10,000 baht for his expenses.'

'Noted,' said Guthrie. 'I recall approving that expense claim,' he lied. 'What about the DEA, did he meet with them at all?'

He confirmed that, to his knowledge, Quinn had not met with them. 'I have to say I was surprised.' Finney went on. 'They are our colleagues up here, right? I know they were acquainted with each other, Quinn said as much, but he refused to speak with them.'

'Colleagues' snorted Guthrie. 'The DEA? They're not our colleagues. They share intel with us when it suits them. They do their own thing, and we do ours. They are publicity hunters. They just want to be seen to be doing a great job. Front page of the Bangkok Post with the Thai army,' he scoffed. 'Don't tell me you've been taken in by Betty Betts as well.'

There was the mocking again, thought Finney, if only you had half her brains and acumen. He explained he had met with Agent Betts several times and that she had been extremely helpful. He decided to leave it there. It was clearly his opinion the DEA and the AFP were not working closely together at all.

Guthrie was becoming frustrated, pacing backwards and forwards in front of Finney, firing questions and accusations. 'You are holding back on me Finney; I can feel it. You better tell me everything you know or there will be trouble.'

Finney had enough. He stood from his chair and walked closer to the man, 'I've told you everything I know,' he said. 'I don't work for you DI Guthrie, and this isn't my case. I answer directly to the ambassador and Sir William Gordon. I have one job here and that is to get Jane Gordon home safely. I'm sorry about your colleague Barry Quinn, but it's just not my problem right now and it certainly isn't a priority for me.'

Turning away from Guthrie, Finney directed his attention to Richard Hanlon. 'Please set up a time for me to speak with the ambassador in the next hour. The kidnapper's younger brother will be released from prison today. We need a plan to get him back here.' Finney walked up the stairs back to his room. He was shaking.

Moving the Cargo

He had three unread messages, Jodie Coppins, Rosie Betts, and Zhang Sein. He read the last message first. *Zoom meeting at 1pm. Code Z23897635 Password freeatlast24.* Very funny thought Finney. Walking out onto the balcony he called down to Hanlon to join him upstairs. He'd written the meeting code and password on a post-it note, which he handed to the man from the embassy. 'Get this to Sir William Gordon as fast as you can,' said Finney. 'The ambassador will have his direct line.'

'Who do you think I am Finney, your secretary,' he said.

'Just get the message to him. I'm not messing around here Hanlon; we need to get things done fast and yes, if you want to be my secretary for a few days, that's fine. I'm sure the governor will appreciate it.' Finney closed the door in the man's face.

The next message was from Jodie Coppins. **Bail Granted. Processing will take one hour. Then he is free. Bail conditions as discussed. Check your email.** Well, at least that's something, strict bail conditions would make it harder for the boy to get out of the country. He sent a text message to Zhang Sein confirming the video call between Jane Gordon and her parents. He also confirmed what he was sure Zhang Sein already knew; his brother had been granted bail and would soon be free.

Flipping open his laptop to check for Jodie Coppins's email, she had copied part of the bail hearing judgement referring to the boy's expired visa. It outlined a condition whereby the boy would be deported at the first available opportunity. Whatever that meant. It was deliberately vague and would allow for a charter flight if it was an option. Or even a possibility. To hell with Hanlon, thought Finney, I need another conversation with Clifton-Blythe.

'Jesus H Christ', said the ambassador as he answered the phone. 'What is going on up there? I've just had Hanlon on the phone, describing a war zone between you and Guthrie. You two should be working together on this.'

'I don't want Guthrie anywhere near my case. As far as I'm concerned, he is up here looking into the death of Barry Quinn.'

'Are you sure you can handle this on your own Finney,' questioned the ambassador.

'There are other things happening I don't have time to talk about right now. All I can say is we need to keep Guthrie as far away from this as possible. His presence could endanger the life of Jane Gordon. Can I be any clearer?' he asked.

Clifton-Blythe took a moment to digest this. 'OK, what do you need me to do?'

That's more like it, he thought, I've got his attention now. He explained to the ambassador the outcome of the bail hearing and the conditions set by the court. 'We need to get him back here ASAP,' he said, 'has there been any decision about how it will happen?'

Clifton-Blythe's tone was calm, but the weight of his words pressed down on Finney. 'The boy will be removed later tonight,' he began, his voice steady. 'We've arranged for a flight to take him into Chiang Rai. The logistics are tricky, there's a lot of high-level government-to-government negotiation happening behind the scenes. But we'll make it work.'

Finney understood well enough, and the complexities were clear in his mind. This was a delicate operation, balancing the glacial pace of diplomacy with the urgency of the mission.

'Fortunately for us,' said the ambassador, 'there's still a strong reservoir of goodwill in Thailand, thanks to the cave rescue a few years back.' His voice softened slightly as he mentioned the event that had gripped the world. 'You remember, of course, how the rescue of those boys and their coach from the flooded cave captured global attention. It was a tense operation, but what stuck with the Thai people was two Australians played a crucial role in its success. The connection has lingered in the national consciousness, and it's something we're leveraging now.'

He reflected on the significance of those words. The rescue had been a rare moment of international unity and heroism, and it had left an indelible mark on the relationship between Australia and Thailand. The goodwill generated then was now an asset, and it could help navigate the safe return of Jane Gordon.

'The Thais remember,' Clifton-Blythe added, almost as if reading Finney's thoughts. 'And it's what's giving us the edge we need to make this operation possible. We're not just outsiders meddling in their affairs; we're partners who've stood by them in a moment of crisis.'

Absorbing the information, he felt a mix of relief and anxiety. The plan was risky, but the groundwork had been laid, and there was no turning back. The night ahead would be critical, and Finney knew the success of the mission hinged on the careful execution of every detail.

The ambassador reminded him again of the need for secrecy.

'Sure,' said Finney, 'I get it. I've been talking to the brother. How do we get the boy from Chiang Rai back across the border into Myanmar?'

'At this stage, no plan whatsoever,' said the ambassador, I was relying on you.'

He paused and thought for a moment, he had a vague plan, but he wasn't ready to share it just yet. He bought some more time and reassured the ambassador he was in control. Hanlon was responsible for setting up the call between Jane and her parents. His next problem was finalising a plan for the exchange. Finney stayed in his room with the TV on and the sound turned down. Thai PBS channel was covering the offensive of the Thai army against the drug traffickers. The subtitles were sketchy but that was the gist of the footage. There was also footage of the Myanmar army offensive against the rebels in the eastern part of Shan state. How could these two events impact the release of Jane Gordon, he wondered. He knew that Rosie Betts would be well-informed, but how much would she share with him? Surely, she must know about Quinn, Dowsett and Pendergast. Now he thought he knew why Quinn had no interest in meeting with her.

The Plan in Place

It was now late afternoon. Finney's phone started to ring, it was Clifton-Blythe. 'It looks like we've got him on a Hercules sometime just after midnight, Sydney time,' he said.

'Meaning we should see him around 7 am tomorrow,' he guessed.

'We're still working through that. Not sure if we can land the plane in Chiang Rai. Something about the runway being too short. I'll get back to you about it. Now it's time for you to do your thing.'

They went on to discuss the organization. Where could they do the swap? It was Finney's job to organise it. How to keep the Thai police at bay. He made no mention of Dowsett, Pendergast and their involvement in the death of Barry Quinn. It could only complicate matters. The living have preference over the dead, he thought. They wound up the call and immediately Finney's phone started ringing again. It was Ella. Could he afford the time to take the call? Could he afford *not* to take the call? Picking up the phone he injected his voice with unnatural enthusiasm. Ella saw straight through it.

'What's up Dad, you sound weird.'

'Sorry Sweetie, loads of noise around here so I had to shout.'

Ella was in the mood for a rant. Her father was not, but he let it roll as he always did. It was usually about her mother but today it was about Charles Drayton. He had admonished her for some minor misdemeanour, and she had taken offence. 'He's not even my real father,' she said. He simply listened while she complained about Charles and her mother. Eventually, she calmed down, as she always did. 'When are you coming home Dad, I miss you.'

'I miss you too, Sweetie. With a bit of luck, I'll be home mid-week.'

'We leave for Singers in three weeks, just make sure you're home before then.'

'Singers?'

'Singapore, Dad, Get with the program!'

'Of course, Singapore,' he echoed.

'Anyways Dad. Gotta go. Lola is coming for a sleepover. Later.' And she was gone.

He made his way back past the bedlam of the border crossing. It was a Saturday with a throng of tourists mixed in with migrant workers crossing back and forth. They looked mostly like Thai tourists, but he had to admit he wasn't sure. It didn't matter. What mattered to him most was that Guthrie and Hanlon had left the guesthouse. Finney had things to do. The first order of business was getting a hold of Zhang Sein. Should he be contacting Rosie Betts, he wondered. She had been on his mind since the morning conversation with Tura. He knew her priorities didn't align with his but for the first time realised they might be incompatible.

The timing of the Thai army offensive had him intrigued. Betts had told him it was part of a political tug-of-war in Bangkok. Did the kidnapping of Jane Gordon offer an opportunity, where they could get Zhang Sein across the border and have him arrested by the Thai police? The U.S. could then have him extradited, which is exactly what they had tried to do years ago with his grandfather. It hit him like a bolt of lightning. Betts wasn't concerned about Jane Gordon. She was simply a lure to hook the fish.

If anything, he needed to keep her out of the loop now. 'It's called an epiphany,' he muttered to himself. Tura had been trying to point him in that direction all along and he hadn't seen it until now. Better late than never.

Returning to the guesthouse, he made straight for his room. He made the call to Zhang. It was obvious to Finney the brothers had been talking, despite it being forbidden under the bail conditions. He knew it was too late to worry about it now. Once they had him in custody again and on the way to the airport, they could confiscate his phone.

'Where is Jane Gordon,' he asked.

'You know I can't tell you. She has chatted with her Mama and Papa, and she is ready to go home. So how will we exchange our people,' he asked.

Finney had given this little thought. He knew Zhang wouldn't come across to Thailand and he couldn't take the brother to Myanmar. Both options were far too risky. 'Could we use the boat again in the same way I handed over the laptop,' asked Finney.

After a long pause, 'I'm not sure I like the plan,' said the man. 'It would be too easy for the DEA to have one of their boats there on standby. I know you have been talking with the DEA team,' he went on. 'There is nothing they would like better than to lock me up in a U.S. prison.'

'Of course, I've been talking to the DEA, but you have my word the DEA know nothing of our plans for this exchange.'

The man laughed. 'The DEA are listening to this call right now,' he said. 'That is why you are going to hang up now, walk to your nearest 7/11 and buy a new SIM card. When you've got it, call me back,' he said ending the call. Finne did as he was instructed. When they spoke a short time later, the kidnapper outlined his plan. They would meet at the boat pier near Kings Roman Casino in Van Pak Len, across the Mekong River in Laos. Technically it was neutral territory, but Finney knew it was risky.

Now it was a waiting game, and they would rely on news from the Australian ambassador. It was now early evening and Finney hoped Zhang Win and his minders were already en route to the airport in Sydney.

###

This time Jane Gordon was travelling in the cabin of the pickup truck. Seated in the rear alongside Nong Bak and a young man, she was blindfolded. Zhang gave a running commentary of the trip from the front seat. Jane wished she could see the landscape, and she said so.

'This might be my only trip to Myanmar,' she said, 'and this blindfold is making me feel sick.'

'OK, what's the harm,' he said, and the blindfold was removed. Jane Gordon blinked at the sunlight. The sun was low in the sky but still bright and hot. They were still in Shan state, he explained. They were taking her to a safe place and, if things went to plan, tomorrow she would be on her way home to see her parents.

The young woman began to weep. Her captors looked embarrassed for her. 'I know I should be happy,' she said, 'but I've caused everyone so much trouble. I can't stop thinking about Jessie and what his family must be feeling.'

'We're all sorry about Jessie, it was not meant to happen, and I want you to tell your people that. It was an accident and people have been punished.

Silence descended over the occupants and Jane stared out into the countryside. They drove through small villages and her companions covered the windows with pieces of cloth as they did so. 'Shortly, we will pass through an army checkpoint. We pay them off to let us through, but it's better if they don't see you. Nong Bak will cover you with a sarong and you are to stay perfectly still and say nothing. Do you understand,' he asked, firmly.

She nodded her understanding, having no desire to jeopardize her release, and they passed through the checkpoint without incident.

As they neared Tachileik she was blindfolded again. She could see nothing but knew they were near another town. The traffic increased and she could hear motorbikes and honking horns. Shortly after, the vehicle rolled off the bitumen road and onto loose gravel which she heard crunching and crackling under the wheels of the pickup truck. Exiting the vehicle the blindfold was removed, and she recognised her first place of captivity. She was back in Wan Narr, although she didn't know it by name.

Back in the small, locked, and windowless room, she wondered how long it would be before she was freed. Her spirits should have been lifted but all she could feel was sadness, guilt, and fear. Sadness about the death of her friend, Jessie Cheeseman, and guilt at the distress she had no doubt caused her parents. How can I make it up to them, she wondered. The fear came from the realization this could all go wrong. This was a dangerous place. Zhang Sein was a dangerous man.

###

Back across the river in Mae Sai, Finney was restless and needed to get out of his room. He peered out the window, the courtyard was empty. The van was gone, and he assumed Banjob was with the two men from the embassy, Guthrie and Hanlon. A few guests were moving around but it was largely quiet. This was his opportunity to get out of there unseen. Or so he thought. Descending the stairs he held his phone to his ear, always a reliable strategy to get out of a conversation. The owner of the guesthouse was fussing around behind the coffee machine and called out to Finney. He simply pointed at the phone next to his ear, pretended to be talking and made a hasty exit out onto the street.

The neighbourhood street vendors were in place, and the nightly local market was well underway. He wasn't in the mood to interact with stallholders tonight. He had too much on his mind. As he walked out toward the main road, he decided to turn left rather than walk back toward the river. Many of the shops had closed and metal roller doors had been drawn down. The nighttime food stores had appeared and were crowding the sidewalk. Many customers simply pulled up and ordered food to take home without dismounting their motorcycles. Bags of noodle soup were prepared by the vendors, poured into bags, and tied at the top with rubber bands. The air was thick with BBQ smoke. Some stalls had a small cluster of chairs and tables.

He wanted alcohol but had the willpower and commonsense to resist the urge. He walked past a few small restaurants and cafes and of course the ubiquitous 7/11 stores. He had counted three in the short walk he had taken along Phaholyothin Rd. Suddenly, out of nowhere, a large black pickup truck pulled beside him with a screech. The window slid down from the passenger side, and Tura ushered him into the vehicle. The man in the driver's seat was unknown to Finney. They drove away a short distance and turned into a dark, quiet side street. Tura spoke to the driver, and they pulled over under a tree in front of a vacant block between two large, walled houses.

Tura turned around in his seat to face Finney, who was sitting in the back. 'Zhang Sein arrived back in Wan Narr about an hour ago. He has the girl with him.'

Finney looked at the driver and then back at Tura.

'Don't worry about him,' said Tura, 'no English at all.'

'I'd rather we spoke in private.'

Tura spoke to the driver, and he got out of the vehicle, walked a few metres away and lit a cigarette.

'How do you know he's back in Wan Narr,' said Finney. Tura had put his contacts on the lookout for Zhang and sure enough, he had been told of their arrival.

'The brother should be back in Thailand sometime tomorrow. I'm waiting for confirmation from the embassy they have left Australia,' he said.

'How do you plan on getting him across the border?'

He explained the had a plan to meet across the Mekong River in Van Pak Leng.

Tura was shaking his head. 'This is too dangerous. Once they have you over there you have no protection. They take the brother and keep the girl and what can you do then? They might even take you as well. No diplomatic immunity over there, everything is controlled by the Chinese, not the Lao,' he said.

Finney was aware of the risks. He had been through it in his mind a dozen times, but what else could he do? He told Tura as much. 'Should I be contacting Agent Betts,' he asked the man.

Now Tura was shaking his head furiously. 'On no account should you bring her into this,' he said forcefully. 'I know she has spoken to the Thai military about this kidnapping, and she wants to trick Zhang into coming to Thailand.'

Just as he had suspected, the DEA had their agenda. They do have a reputation, he thought, how could he have been so naïve? He would keep the DEA out of it, he assured Tura. But what alternative was there to the swap in Laos? 'Could it be done on a boat or a barge,' he asked.

Finney's phone pinged. Who else but Agent Rosie Betts, Northern Thailand Team Leader, DEA. Finney ignored it. 'It's Betts,' he said, 'she knows we are close and wants an update'.

Another ping on his phone. This time it was the ambassador. **Flight delayed out of Richmond Air Base. Problem with Immigration**, was the message. Just as he had suspected, the immigration officials were objecting to the boy's deportation. His only hope was Bill Gordon could pull in a few favours. He had plenty of influential friends. The problem was immigration was now such a political hot potato, favours for influential friends just didn't cut it anymore. The last thing any politician wanted was to be seen to bend the rules for some 'illegal' student. He did not bother passing on this news to Tura.

'At the end of the day, where you meet the kidnappers is your decision. But steer clear of the DEA-they've got their own agenda. I do some work with Agent Betts; you know she will always put the interests of the DEA ahead of yours. I'll come with you,' he said. 'You are going to need someone like me. I have the language skills, and I know these people. They are my people, even the traffickers.'

Finney nodded. 'When they've left Australia, we will have about twelve hours to get this set up. We hope to land him in Chiang Rai. I'll arrange for Banjob to meet the plane. The ambassador will be there and two AFP guys from Australia.'

'That is quite a posse you've got right there. Those AFP boys won't be coming across the river, it will be just you and me. You will have to act quickly; it won't take the DEA long to find out your plane has landed in Chiang Rai.'

Finney knew he was right. The details will be resolved in the coming hours. 'So, you will stay in Mae Sai?'

Tura nodded. 'I have many friends here,' he said, pointing to the other man who was walking back towards them. 'Best if you make your way back to the guesthouse from here without us. Too many prying eyes.'

The men drove off as Finney walked back toward the main road. There was a more direct route back to the guesthouse but there were too many stray dogs prowling around in the shadows of the dimly lit streets. As he approached the guesthouse, he could see two vehicles parked in the street. One van was driven by Banjob, and the other, a dual cab pickup truck belonged to Agent Betts. He almost turned on his heels and walked away but thought better of it. He could only avoid her for so long and he hoped Banjob had returned without the men from the embassy.

Walking into the guesthouse, he saw Banjob first, seated in the corner with his friend Somchai. He gave them a nod. Seated across in another corner was Rosie Betts reading something on her phone. She looked up to see him as he entered.

'Hey stranger,' she called out, 'it's Saturday night, will you join me for a beer?'

He shook his head as he sat down, 'just a soda water for me,' he said.

'You're a hard man to track down. I've been calling you. Are you trying to avoid me,' she said, only half-jokingly.

He made a show of looking at his phone. 'I've been out walking, and I must have missed the call.' As a distraction Finney turned to Somchai and raised his hand, signalling a wish to order his soda water.

'You don't get off that easily. What's going on with Jane Gordon? Have you got Zhang's brother back over here yet?'

The DEA agent was fishing for an update. He tried to be vague. 'We've got some roadblocks back in Australia,' he started, 'problems with the bureaucrats we can't just sweep aside.'

'From what I hear, your ambassador and Governor Gordon can make things happen,' said Betts.

Shaking his head, Finney stuck to his story. 'It might be a few more days before they can get him out of the country. Even then, we are still working on the details of the exchange. It's complicated.'

His drink arrived and gave him another opportunity for a distraction. 'Maybe you can give me an update on the Thai army offensive. I've seen a lot of military vehicles around the town and the word is they are planning something very big.' The distraction worked.

She gave him details of a planned Thai military offensive scheduled for the coming days. It would take place along the Thai/Myanmar border near a town called Fang. They would hit the area hard. It was very mountainous countryside and hard to monitor. Small-scale drug mules could come and go as they pleased but the Thais were determined to wipe them out. It might be just the cover we need, thought Finney. If the arrival of the brother coincided with those raids, the Thai army would be too busy to go after Zhang Sein.

'It's getting late Rosie, and I'm beat,' he said. 'It's been a long day, and I need some rest. Can we pick this up again tomorrow?'

'I think you're throwing me out,' she joked. 'Sure thing, let's catch up tomorrow.'

Finney nodded, knowing it would not happen. His phone was ringing, it was Clifton-Blythe.

'You had better take that,' she said, as she stood from the chair and turned to leave.

He waved her goodbye as he answered the call. 'Yes sir, where are we up to?'

One Last Hurdle

Located about thirty kilometres from the Sydney CBD, Villawood Detention Centre started its life as temporary migrant accommodation back in the 1950s. It had recently become the place of last resort for many of the miserable souls seeking asylum in Australia. It was also a detention centre for those who had overstayed their visas and were appealing deportation orders. Some of its occupants had been here for years. To Zhang Win, it looked like a prison. In many ways, it was.

The walls surrounding it were over four metres high and topped with razor wire. Walking through the metal detector, the boy was being watched, not just by the centre guards but by the AFP officer accompanying him and the unblinking eye of a security camera. He was herded through several more security doors before finally being placed in a holding cell. It was made of reinforced Perspex walls, so he was under constant surveillance, with the AFP officer removing the handcuffs before he was led inside.

It contained a bed, fixed to the floor, a basin in one corner and a toilet in the other with a small waist-high screen for privacy. No TV, nothing else at all in the room. It was all hard, white, moulded plastic surfaces. The cell was in the observation block and was designed for high-risk occupants. Some of the staff referred to them as the suicide rooms. The AFP officers sat on a bench seat opposite his cell and stared at him.

'What's going on,' he pleaded. 'What am I doing here? Where's my phone? I want to call my solicitor.' Nobody responded. The Centre staff went about their business., having been told the kid wasn't their responsibility, and the AFP guys would take care of him.

The boy slumped on the bed eventually, exhausted. It was late, nearly midnight. He fell asleep without touching the food that had been pushed through a small slot at the base of the security door to his cell.

He'd only been asleep a short while when his solicitor arrived, accompanied by two officials from the Department of Home Affairs (Immigration Division). The boy was woken and removed to an interview room. It was crowded with all of them in the room, but they all needed to be there. There was a JP, the boy, his solicitor, two immigration officials and two AFP officers. The Justice of The Peace (JP), Richard McIntyre, dishevelled and clad in a crumpled coat and blue jeans, looked like he'd rather be somewhere else. What have we got here? I left a warm bed and it's late. Get on with it,' he ordered.

The immigration officer looked nervous. 'It's a Notice to Deport, sir,' he said, directing this advice to the JP. He then produced a wad of paper with several pages with stickers marked, 'Sign Here.'

These were first given to the solicitor, Brian Stevens, who gave them a perfunctory glance, and then slid them along to the boy sitting next to him. 'Sign there,' he said, handing him a pen. The boy did as he was told. His solicitor lent over, flicked a couple of pages forward and stabbed at another page, 'Sign here as well.' The boy followed the instructions. It was done.

'Now can my client get on a plane as promised,' the exasperated solicitor said. 'This wasn't part of the agreement; I don't even understand what we are doing here.'

'We are observing due process, Mr Stevens,' said the JP. 'It's called due process and as a man of the law, I would expect you to understand and respect that.' Stevens began to object when the JP simply raised the index finger of his right hand as if to say, be quiet! 'Now, if we are done here, I will return home and resume my sleep.' With that, the JP turned and exited the room.

The immigration officials handed one copy of the Notice to the solicitor and returned the other to a blue folder which they kept. 'You are free to go, Mr Zhang,' said the more senior of the two and with that they left.

'Could you give me a few moments in private with my client,' said the solicitor.

'I'm afraid that won't be possible,' replied Sergeant Adams, one of the AFP officers. 'Our instructions are clear. Mr Zhang is to be always under observation until he arrives in Thailand.'

Exasperated, the solicitor spoke to his client. 'The paperwork is all done. Because you overstayed your student visa you will be excluded from traveling back here for a period of three years. After that time, you can re-apply for a new visa. These gentlemen will now escort you back to Thailand. I understand that there is some arrangement for them to take you to the Myanmar border but that is between you and them. Once you leave here you are under their control. Do you understand,' he said, a little too forcefully.

'Can I talk to my brother,' the young man said.

Now it was the time for the AFP officer to speak. He explained that he was now under arrest and would be taken to an airfield where he would board a plane bound for

Thailand. During that entire time, he would have no access to any electronic devices, phone, laptop or otherwise.

The boy nodded. 'I just want to go home,' he said eventually. 'I want to see my family.'

You will, son,' said his solicitor, patting his shoulder. 'Good luck' and he turned and left the room, not waiting for a reply.

After having been given time to gather his meagre belongings and visit the bathroom, the boy was handcuffed to Sergeant Adams. The place was quiet at this time of the night as he passed through security to the exit of Villawood Detention Centre.

Once again, they were in the back of the black van with heavily tinted windows. As they sped through the night toward Richmond Airforce Base the boy thought about his reunion with his older brother. He was afraid. Keep your head down and behave yourself,' his brother had told him. 'If this works well, you can set up a base for our business there.' He knew his brother would be angry. They set off on the one-hour journey at 1 am. There was no hurry. A decision had been made to delay the flight till early morning at around 9 am. That way they would be arriving in Northern Thailand late afternoon. The plan was to transfer the boy to Mae Sai and then across to Laos. The trip across the river would be made after dark and they didn't want there to be too much time between his landing and doing the swap. This would be the riskiest time. If the DEA had plans to get a hold of Zhang Sein, it would be then.

The boy would be held in a cell at the airbase. There was only one prison cell. A drunken and belligerent recruit was happily being released to make way for the new inmate.

Guards looking on. The boy slept.

Clifton-Blythe briefed Finney on the departure time of the flight. They had arranged a smaller civilian plane on lease to a senior government minister. Thai officials would not need to be notified of the arrival of this plane and that would make it less likely the DEA would get wind of it either. Finney, Guthrie and Hanlon would meet the ambassador at Chiang Rai Airport mid-afternoon. Another vehicle had been hired to accommodate Zhang Win and the AFP officers accompanying him. The two vans would then travel in convoy back to Mae Sai.

They needed a base in Mae Sai. Finney delegated the job for Tura to manage. The boy must be kept out of sight and no hotel would be secure. He made the call, and it was agreed. I have many friends here, Tura had said. He had a place in mind on the edge of town. They could get in and out without raising any suspicions. Banjob could arrange the boat. Just be vague with him, he had instructed Tura. Tell him we will need him all day into the evening. We need him on standby. Pay whatever he asks. After agreeing to meet again early the next morning, he made his way upstairs to his room. He hadn't lied to Rosie Betts, he was exhausted. He'd not slept more than three or four hours each night he had been in Thailand. He could feel a crash coming but knew it couldn't be now. He needed sleep but he knew he wouldn't get it tonight, of all nights. All he could do was make sure he was ready for what was to come the following day.

He lay on the bed staring at the whirring fan above him. He thought of Ella and Sarah. He didn't miss Sarah so much anymore, but Ella was different. He missed her but when they were together, they struggled to talk. Too much time apart, he wondered. Not enough shared experiences. He thought about his father, Hector. Am I turning into my father? Does every man wonder this, he pondered. Was it too late to change that now? I won't turn into Hector, he promised himself. The past is a dangerous place, a friend had once told him. They were right.

The events of the day now had time to invade his thoughts. The revelations from Pip about Quinn's death. Was Guthrie involved; he wondered. What was so bad they had to kill him? Exposing them of course, he knew that was it. Had Quinn's conscience got the better of him? He knew it wasn't his problem right now, but it could become his problem soon enough if he wasn't careful. Watch your back, he told himself.

Had he betrayed the confidence and trust of Rosie Betts, he wondered. Was he being too careful by not bringing her in on his plans? He knew he couldn't risk it.

As always, sleep was elusive, fitful and begrudging. At 4 am he gave in to wakefulness and blinked as his phone lit up on the bed beside him. **Pick up Now.** It was Clifton-Blythe. Finney returned the call and got a blast of facts. The plane had left Sydney and was expected to arrive in Chiang Rai at 5 pm Thai time, after a brief stopover in Singapore. Finney was expected at the airport by 4 pm sharp. Was everything in place, the ambassador demanded to know.

Finney assured him it was, knowing full well there were things still to be done. He was still to confirm with Zhang the brother was on his way and the timing and location of the swap. Clifton-Blythe didn't need to know that right now. The man sounded irritated and deprived of sleep. Finney empathized.

Just be ready, the ambassador had told him and ended the call.

At 6 am he finally dragged himself out of bed and stood for longer than was necessary under the shower. Dawn was breaking outside. The morning neighbourhood chorus was in transition from howling dogs to crowing roosters. He could hear the housekeepers chattering while they swept the downstairs courtyard. The big day had arrived.

He had begun wearing the Burmese sarong as his pyjamas. The longyi, as it was called, was a gift from Tura a few days earlier. A few days ago, he thought, it feels like a lifetime. He paced the room scripting a message to Zhang Sein. He gave just enough information without letting on he knew they were back in Wan Narr. He agreed to meet on neutral territory without specifically agreeing to meet across the Mekong River in Laos. On Tura's advice, he would push back against it. Too dangerous, the man had said. There are floating pontoons scattered around the confluence of the Sai and Mekong Rivers, these would be better, he had advised, and safer. Finney was content with the tone of the message, it was good, and he sent it off. He didn't expect a reply, not at this time of the morning.

He made his way downstairs, following the fragrance of freshly brewed coffee. The guesthouse was coming to life and Somchai beamed as he fussed around behind the overly large coffee machine. It was commercial grade and would have been at home in a mid-size Starbucks coffee shop. Fully imported from Italy, he had bragged to Finney.

'The usual,' asked the owner, as he saw Finney emerge into the small dining room which faced the street.

He nodded and smiled, 'just a long black,' he said and took a seat nearby. There was a family of Thais who smiled as he walked by. Weekend visitors, he figured as he had not seen them before.

Soon enough, Somchai emerged from behind the counter. 'Sit down, sir,' said Somchai, 'I'll bring it over,' as Finney made to stand up and collect the coffee himself.

Somchai took the opportunity to introduce the family seated nearby. 'These are my relatives, visiting from Chiang Mai,' he said, pointing at the family seated at a nearby table. The two children gave Finney the Thai *wai,* while the parents simply nodded and smiled.

'Nice to meet you all,' he said, opening his laptop. It was for show only, it allowed him to sit quietly without having to make conversation. As he made a pretence of checking his email, one caught his eye. BEWARE OF GUTHRIE, was the subject line. It was from Stacey Harmer. It outlined news, or more accurately rumour, of an ongoing investigation into the death of an AFP officer in Thailand. A cloud hung over the whole of the team there, including Bart Guthrie. They are desperate to solve the mysterious death of Barry Quinn, she had said. Finney's name had also appeared as a potential suspect, according to Harmer. Be very careful, were her closing words.

This was the least of his worries right now. He knew he could be in the frame for Quinn's death. Finney had not been updated on the course of the investigation, neither was he particularly interested. He had a good idea who the perpetrators were. He had not heard from Pip since their meeting the previous day and nor did he want any contact with her until Jane Gordon had been freed. It would be an unnecessary distraction. He would keep the information about Pendergast and Dowsett to himself until then.

He had not noticed Banjob seated quietly near the van. The man had a knack for being unobtrusive. They acknowledged one another with a nod and Banjob approached his table. 'Anything I can do for you this morning' the driver asked. Finney motioned for him to sit down.

Banjob confirmed with Finney the boat had been booked and was on standby. It was now Finney's turn to brief the driver. The departure time to Chiang Rai was scheduled for 2 pm. He had also arranged with Tura for the boy to be held at the house of a friend until they travelled to meet with the brother. They would visit the cottage without Guthrie and Hanlon, Finney advised, wanting to keep them away from there until the drop off later in the day.

The cottage was set on a medium-sized plot of land surrounded on one side by an orchard of fruit trees and on the other by open fields. The house itself had a large parking area and a double garage. There were several motorbikes and a pick-up truck parked next to the house. Tura emerged from the house as they pulled up. After exchanging greetings, he took Tura aside and explained they would need the house to themselves for several hours early in the evening. The occupants would need to be out of the house between 5 pm and 10 pm. Pulling B3000 from his wallet, Finney handed it to Tura.

'This is more than enough,' nodded Tura, 'and my friends will be happy.'

Finney went on to outline the plan for getting the boy to the exchange point. 'The first vehicle would hold Finney, Tura, Banjob, the AFP guard and the boy. The other vehicle is a decoy, but they don't know that yet so let's keep it to ourselves,' he went on. 'We will need to lose the other van halfway there and I'm yet to arrange it with Banjob. Leave it with me,' he said. They would be back sometime between 6 pm and 7 pm and expected the house to be vacated by then.

Finney's phone was ringing. Unknown number, it was Zhang Sein.

'Where's my brother,' he demanded to know.

'Right now, he is in Singapore.'

'When are we meeting?'

'Sometime around 8 pm,' said Finney 'but there must be a change of location. We can't go across to Laos, it is too risky. The DEA has the place under constant surveillance,' he fudged the truth yet again. 'I suggest we meet near pontoon No. 636. You know it, right,' he asked. 'I handed over the laptop to your boys near there. It is out of the way and safe.'

Agreed,' said Zhang Sein. 'Finney don't try anything, or Jane Gordon will not get out alive. Do not bring anyone with you. Do you understand?'

'I'm bringing my friend Tura, you remember him. I need a translator. Agreed?'

The other man agreed and hung up.

He went back to his conversation with Tura. He was confident they had everything in place. Tura was concerned about the weather. If there was rain, it would be difficult to make the meeting, he suggested. The storms of the past few days had produced wind and waves on the river making it too dangerous to take the boats out. Finney had no backup plan. They just had to hope for the best.

He sat in the front seat of the van with Banjob. They were on their way to pick up Guthrie and Hanlon. Finney turned to Banjob, 'How much do you know?'

'What do you mean,' the driver replied.

'Come on Banjob, about the plans for this evening.'

'Very little,' the man said, shaking his head.

'Well, whatever it is, try keeping it to yourself. Can I trust you?

'What choice do you have?'

Finney knew he was right and nodded in agreement.

Guthrie and Hanlon were waiting in the hotel lobby. Finney didn't bother to join Banjob in getting them. He barely greeted them when they got into the back seat of the van. They had been booked into The Room Resort on the Chiang Rai side of the main highway into Mae Sai. It was isolated and difficult for the men to access anything, that had been Banjob's plan when suggesting the hotel. He also wanted them as far away from Finney as possible. He had told the embassy staff The Room Resort was the best option, and they had taken him at his word. Guthrie was his usual belligerent self. He complained throughout the entire trip about their hotel, the Thai police, the heat and anything else he could think of. Hanlon sat quietly and said nothing, as did Finney. He tried to interrogate Finney on the details of the exchange, but Finney pretended he couldn't hear him and eventually, Guthrie gave up and fell asleep.

Chiang Rai Airport, known as Mae Fah Luang, was on the northern side of the city of Chiang Rai. With a population of around three hundred thousand people in the metropolitan area, it was smaller than its big sister city of Chiang Mai. They were early and the ambassador was yet to arrive. Finney suggested they wait in the van to avoid being seen at the airport. The others agreed. Parking a discrete distance from the terminal, they sat in an awkward silence.

Shortly afterwards another van pulled up beside them. Again, it was a hired vehicle with no diplomatic plates. It was however being driven by an embassy driver. Finney received a message requesting him to join the ambassador who was seated in the rear of the other van. As he was exiting the vehicle Guthrie reached over and grabbed his arm from behind.

'Where the fuck do you think you're going,' he snarled.

'The ambassador wants a word,' he said, pointing to the van parked next to them.

'I'm coming too,' said Guthrie.

As the rear door of the second van slid open and Clifton-Blythe saw the two men standing there, he held up the palm of his hand. 'Just Finney for the moment,' he said, speaking to Guthrie. He climbed into the back seat with the ambassador leaving Guthrie fuming. Eventually, the man gave up waiting on the sweltering tarmac and returned to the other van. Gone was the pinstripe suit and gold cufflinks, Clifton-Blythe was dressed casually in a pair of Chino pants and a short-sleeved shirt. It was impossible to hide his patrician background and despite his weekend attire, he still looked very much out of place at a regional Thai airport. There were no niceties exchanged, and the two men got down to business.

They discussed plans for the rest of the day. The drive to Mae Sai and a short wait in the safe house until the sun went down and the river traffic decreased. It would be around 8 pm. The boat had been arranged, and Zhang Sein was standing by to take receipt of his younger brother. He made his case to exclude Guthrie and Hanlon from the operation and the ambassador shook his head, reluctantly. No fan of the AFP man, Clifton-Blythe knew there would be consequences for keeping Guthrie at a distance. 'We'll cross that bridge when we come to it,' he said.

Then came the bombshell. Bill Gordon was on the plane from Sydney with the boy and two AFP officers. 'He insisted on coming,' said Clifton-Blythe, 'and would not be denied.' There was a long silence.

'We can't have him involved in the exchange,' said Finney, 'it's too risky. To be honest, I don't even want the AFP guys there. I'll be taking our Burmese contact and the driver. At a pinch, I could have one of the AFP guys in the van, but he will not be coming on the boat.'

The ambassador let out a long sigh. 'I get it, I do,' he said. 'This is my second posting into this part of the world and while I've never negotiated a kidnapping, I know how it works. How do we keep these AFP guys at arm's length?'

'Misdirection,' he said. 'We will set off in two vehicles but only one would make it to the right location. Simple as that. I will take the boy in one van with Banjob, one AFP officer and our Burmese translator. Everyone else will be in the other van, including Guthrie. Somewhere along the way, the two vehicles would be separated. The plan is in place. If we turn up with a whole bunch of people, we will scare off the kidnappers, or worse.'

'You've thought this through.'

'I have sir, and I've met the older brother several times. He's no fool and he is ruthless. There's only one way to do this and ensure we get Jane out alive. Her father can't be anywhere near this either. It's the last thing we need.'

'And the drivers are aware of what's going on. Of course, they are,' the ambassador said, answering his own question.

The ambassador's phone pinged. He paused to read the message. 'They are about ten minutes out from here. The passengers won't come through the terminal. We will drive to the plane over there,' he said, pointing to a large hangar about one hundred metres from the terminal. 'We can drive into the hangar and remain out of sight. I've done some planning of my own,' he said and winked at Finney. The ambassador called Hanlon, advising him to wait in the carpark until they returned. Off in the distance they saw the small jet coming into land. Sure enough, it turned away from the terminal and headed toward the large commercial hangar. Their driver started the engine and off they went.

After being waived through the gate marked, NO ENTRY - RESTRICTED AREA, they made their way across and into the hangar. An airport security guard was standing by the main door, looking confused but disinterested. The engines had been turned off but still made plenty of noise as they wound down. Eventually, the door of the plane opened and one of the co-pilots lowered the small set of stairs. A plain-clothes AFP officer emerged first and looked around. Clifton-Blythe exited the van first, followed by Finney.

'Ambassador Clifton-Blythe,' the AFP officer enquired.

The ambassador nodded and extended his hand. 'How's your flight,' he said, not needing a response. The man merely nodded.

Finney stepped forward and introduced himself.

'Are we secure here, Sergeant Finney,' he asked.

Finney nodded. 'Do you have him cuffed?'

'Yes sir, at all times.'

'Let's keep it that way. There are two of you, right? I'll want you seated on either side of him in the rear seat. Let's bring him out.'

The young man shackled to an AFP officer looked bewildered as he emerged from the plane and struggled awkwardly down the small stairs. Finally, it was the turn of Sir William Gordon to disembark. He looked different to what Finney remembered. A big-framed man, with an air of authority was the picture of the man Finney had in his mind's eye. The man navigating the stairs, carrying a black duffel bag, now looked old and weary.

He was surprised to see him and Roger Clifton-Blythe embrace. They were clearly very close friends. He thought he saw a tear in the governor's eye, but he wiped it away and quickly regained his composure.

Walking up to Finney, Bill Gordon extended his hand and gave it a firm, warm shake. 'Thank you, Sergeant Finney. Here's the ransom money, don't let it out of your sight, 'he said, handing over the bag.

Finney nodded. 'We'll have you in the back here with the ambassador sir,' he said, pointing toward the van, with the police and the boy behind you. Bill Gordon turned and looked at the boy who was shuffling to the van locked together with his minder, AFP Sergeant Adams. 'Piece of shit,' the man muttered, as the two walked past them.

With the prisoner and the police in place, it was the turn of Bill Gordon and the ambassador to take their place in the vehicle. Finney took a final look around and climbed in the front seat with the driver. This is my operation from here on in, he thought to himself.

'The plane will refuel and be on standby to depart this evening,' announced the ambassador.

They cruised slowly back toward the carpark, the driver advising Banjob in the other vehicle, to be ready to leave. Banjob would lead the convoy back to Mae Sai. The hour-long trip back was silent and tense. Soon enough they arrived at the cottage. Tura directed them to park behind a small stand of trees adjacent to the house and just big enough to conceal the two vehicles. The occupants of the house had gone and taken their vehicles with them. One lone motorcycle, which Finney assumed to belong to Tura, sat outside the house. Tura had arranged for there to be food and water for the visitors, but nobody was eating. Anxiety and fatigue were great appetite suppressants. The boy was taken to one of the small bedrooms with an attached bathroom. He was kept there, shackled and under guard by the AFP officers.

The others gathered in the living room. The ambassador spoke first. Introducing everyone in the room he pointed at Bill Gordon, 'This man has had his daughter taken by drug traffickers and it's our job to get her back.' He then called on Finney to brief those present.

'What about our colleagues guarding that kid,' said Guthrie.

'The less they know, the better,' said Finney. 'Their job is all but over. From here on it's up to us to make sure we get Jane back home safely.' He outlined, in broad terms how they would extract Jane from the kidnappers at a place by the river, yet to be designated.

'It all sounds too vague,' said Guthrie in a challenging tone.

'That's just how it is right now, we are yet to get the details from the kidnappers.'

'Why are we pussy footing around with this scum,' said Guthrie. 'Why aren't we setting the terms here?

'We don't want to spook them,' said Finney. 'They have already shown how ruthless they can be. They killed Jane's friend and plenty of others, from what I 've heard. We can't take the risk. It's critical, anything said here doesn't leave this room.'

As Guthrie looked to stand from his chair, Bill Gordon beat him to it. 'Sergeant Finney is right,' he said, directing his comment at Guthrie. 'He has been dealing with the kidnappers, and he knows them. They know him and what's more, it looks as if they trust him.'

Guthrie, scowling, sat back in his chair without speaking.

Finney now had the authority from both Bill Gordon and the ambassador to lead the operation. He briefed both men accordingly. His plans were in place with Tura and Banjob. They, along with Finney, the boy and the senior AFP officer would travel in the first vehicle. Bill Gordon, the ambassador, Guthrie, Hanlon and the second AFP officer would travel in the other vehicle. The second vehicle would not arrive in time to board the small boat, but not everyone had this piece of information. He couldn't begin to imagine Guthrie's reaction when it occurred, and he didn't care. The voyage to the pontoon would take no longer than fifteen minutes. Finney had sent a message to the kidnappers outlining the details.

The boy was restless. He wanted to get out of there but was shackled to the bedhead. He had been offered food but had declined, drinking only water during the two hours waiting to leave. The AFP officer sat outside the room with the door open. Guthrie had advised Finney to give the boy a Valium, it would calm the lad down he had said. At last, something useful from Guthrie thought Finney.

'Here take this,' he said, passing two pills to the boy.

The boy looked doubtful. 'It will make you feel better,' said Finney, sensing the boy's reluctance to swallow the medications. Dutifully, he obeyed.

Just before 8 pm, they assembled in the living room of the small rural cottage one last time. The air was thick with tension, the kind that comes when plans are set into motion, and there's no turning back. Finney, with a stern expression, went through the plan again. Every detail mattered. He couldn't afford anything to go wrong, not with so much on the line. The room was quiet, save for the occasional nod of understanding or grunt of agreement from the others.

The vehicles were loaded in silence, and they set off toward their destination. The boy, handcuffed to Finney, sat silently in the rear of the first van alongside the AFP officer, his eyes wide with fear and uncertainty. Tura was seated in the front with Banjob. The road ahead was dark and fringed on both sides by tall bamboo trees more than three metres high, the night's silence only broken by the low hum of the van's engine.

A few kilometres into the trip, the second vehicle lost sight of the first as Banjob veered down a side track, turning off his lights as he pulled into a secluded driveway.

The sudden turn caught everyone by surprise. 'What the hell?' blurted out Sergeant Adams, seated in the rear of the van with Finney and the boy, his voice edged with panic.

'It's all part of the plan,' explained Finney calmly, trying to soothe the nerves of the anxious officer. 'This is a distraction for any prying eyes. We'll meet the others at the destination shortly.' His tone was steady, but inside, he couldn't shake the feeling that something could go badly wrong.

Banjob restarted the van after a few minutes, and they continued their journey along the darkened road. The night was eerily still, the only sound was the occasional rustle of leaves as the wind picked up. The humid air clung to Finney's skin, adding to his discomfort. As they approached a T-junction, Banjob turned left, and they began a slow descent toward the river. Even in the dim light of the van, he could see Adams was on edge. He understood the officer's concerns, this was no ordinary operation, and the stakes were high. As they pulled into a clearing, Finney could make out the silhouette of a small pier with a solitary lamp casting a dim light over the boat bobbing gently in the river.

'Stay with the van,' he instructed the AFP man, his voice firm but reassuring. 'We'll be back soon.' The boy remained cuffed to Finney as they made their way toward the boat. The river's surface was calm, reflecting the quarter moon hanging low in the sky like a silent observer of the night's events.

'We're lucky with the weather,' remarked Tura, breaking the tense silence. 'But it can change quickly. Let's get going before that happens.' Finney nodded, but his mind was elsewhere. The humid air, the dark waters of the

Mekong, the shadows shifting with every breath of wind, it all felt like a bad omen. But there was no room for doubt now. He had to see this through.

'What about me?' called out Sergeant Adams from the van, his voice laced with uncertainty.

'Stay with the van,' Finney repeated, trying to mask the anxiety in his voice. 'The others will be here shortly and keep it quiet from now on.' The van's engine shut off, and the night closed in around them, the only sound was the gentle lapping of the river against the pier.

Finney led the boy to the boat, which had a larger inboard motor than the one they'd used before. The engine came to life grudgingly, its low hum blending into the night. They chugged slowly into the darkness, the boat's bow quietly slicing through the water like a knife.

A short while later, they saw the pontoon come into view, the floating materialized out of the darkness. In the distance, another boat appeared, heading toward the same destination. Finney's heart raced as he heard a voice call out from the approaching vessel.

'They want you on the pontoon first,' Tura informed Finney, his voice low.

With the boy still cuffed to him, Finney moved toward the side of the boat and struggled onto the pontoon. The platform rocked gently under their weight; the movement almost soothing in the otherwise tense atmosphere. As their boat idled next to the pontoon, the other vessel glided silently closer.

Zhang Sein was there, issuing orders to their boat driver. Three of his men flanked him, their expressions unreadable, but their eyes sharp and alert. Seated in one corner of the boat was Jane Gordon, her head bowed, her body slumped as if the fight had been drained from her.

'Sit down Declan, and show me your hands,' Zhang Sein commanded from the other boat, his voice calm but threatening at the same time.

Finney lifted his hands, showing the cuffs which bound him to the younger brother. 'You don't trust me?' Sein asked, his tone laced with mockery.

'Just a precaution. 'You won't get any trouble from me.'

'I hope you're telling the truth,' Said Zhang, his eyes narrowing as he studied Finney.

'We just want Jane, and we will be gone.'

As the other boat pulled alongside, the kidnapper made his way from his vessel onto the pontoon, dragging his captive with him. 'Here is your girl, now give me my brother and the money,' he demanded, his voice leaving no room for negotiation.

Finney and the boy moved to stand, the weight of the moment pressing down on them. 'Hello, brother,' the younger man said, his voice soft as he addressed his older sibling. Sein responded with a curt nod before stepping toward them.

'You have caused me no end of trouble,' he muttered, his tone betraying a mix of anger and frustration. Without warning, he punched the brother in the stomach, sending him falling to his knees, and Finney along with him. The sudden movement jostled Finney, and Zhang caught sight of the gun holstered under his shirt.

'I thought I could trust you,' the man hissed, his eyes sharp with anger. Before Finney could react, he'd ripped the gun from its holster and pressed the cold barrel against his temple.

'Keys to the handcuffs!' he shouted, his voice sharp and demanding. 'Give me the keys!'

With shaking hands, he surrendered the keys. Zhang Sein struggled to unlock the handcuffs in the darkness, cursing his frustration, his gaze never leaving Finney. Behind them, Jane Gordon, unseen by her captors, crouching down she edged her way to the other side of the pontoon. This was her chance at freedom, and she would take it.

The boat containing Tura was in position next to the pontoon, the engine purring softly. 'Jump onto the boat, Jane!' Finney shouted, his voice cutting through the tension like a knife. In a split second, and with Tura's help, she leapt onto the boat, her body hitting the deck with a thud. Almost instantly, the vessel roared away into the distance.

Clutching the duffel bag, Zhang Sein and his brother froze as floodlights from the shore lit up the pontoon. The night erupted in gunfire, sharp cracks echoing through the air. The two brothers scrambled to their boat, which sped away, leaving Finney stranded on the pontoon. The kidnapper got what he came for but was angry just the same.

The thin wisp of cloud obscuring the moon evaporated and he was suddenly bathed in light. For a moment, Finney stood there, dazed, the water lapping gently around him like he was on some private stage. Then, a sharp, searing pain tore through his thigh, like a hot poker stabbing at his flesh. The impact sent him stumbling back, and he crashed into the water with a splash. The river water was warm, almost like a bath, but gritty and murky, filling his mouth and nose as he fought to keep his head above the surface.

His arms flailed in the water, panic setting in as he struggled to stay afloat. Gasping for air, he managed to grab onto the side of the pontoon, his fingers gripping the wet wood. The gunfire had stopped, and the only sound now was the soft lapping of the river against the pontoon and Finney's ragged breaths as he held on for dear life. He was in shock and had lost all his strength.

His leg throbbed with pain, the wound seeping blood that mingled with the muddy water. But he couldn't think about that now. He had to focus on getting out of there, on getting back to safety. The operation was over, but it hadn't gone entirely to plan. Clouds moved across the moon again, casting him back into near darkness.

The Good Doctor

The gunfire stopped almost as abruptly as it had begun. He could hear shouting from the Thai side of the river, but he could see nothing this far from the shoreline. At first, his leg was throbbing with pain. He knew he'd been shot, and his leg began to go numb. It was a bad sign, and he knew he had to get out of the water. This mighty river, The Mekong, beautiful and mysterious, was no doubt home to all manner of organisms hostile towards the human body. Soon enough he would discover the severity of his wound. He felt around for the ladder onto the pontoon. Eventually he found it, dragged himself up and collapsed in a wet, muddy heap of pain, with the handcuff still dangling from his wrist. It was suddenly quiet. The past few minutes had gone by in slow motion but now he was back in real time. He could feel warm blood oozing down his leg. He felt faint and knew he was losing consciousness Rolling on his side, he removed his belt, wrapping it around his upper thigh, pulling it as tight as he could and screaming in pain. He knew it would slow the bleeding for now.

He heard a vehicle in the distance. Was that Jane Gordon being whisked back to Chiang Rai, he hoped, unhurt and reunited with her father? He thought of Ella and wished he had called her before this madness had occurred.

He lay on his back and stared at the sky. It was black and starless. In the distance, he heard the first thunderclap of an approaching storm. Now he could see lightning on the shore across in Laos. Or was it Myanmar? He had lost his orientation. Even if he could swim, which direction would he take? Soon enough he heard the rain racing across the water. Tick, tick, tick, and then it was on him like sharp little needles. He covered his face with his hand as he rolled on his side. With the rain came a fierce, swirling wind which had sharp raindrops attacking him from all directions. He curled into a ball and felt the waves building under the pontoon. It rocked violently from side to side forcing him to grab onto the top of the ladder to prevent himself from being tossed back into the river. The tropical storm passed by mercifully quickly and he lay exhausted and motionless on the wet pontoon, he had no choice but to wait and hope his colleagues would come back for him

In and out of consciousness, Finney's head swooned as he lay soaked in blood and rain. He thought of his daughter, his father, his brother David, and Pip Tan. He saw the beaming face of Somchai offering a freshly brewed coffee. Finally, he came around and propped himself up on one elbow. He looked around in the darkness. Could he make it to shore, he wondered. He had no idea how far or in what direction he would have to swim. Safer to stay here and just hope, he decided.

It felt like hours later that he heard the low thump of the boat engine, it was not too far away, and it was getting louder. He tried to sit up again, and he shouted, 'I'm over here'. He couldn't see it until it was almost right next to him, it was Tura at the front of the boat. Finney cried out to him.

'Quiet,' called Tura, 'be quiet.' The man climbed onto the pontoon and lifted Finney to his feet. For a small man, Tura was strong. He dragged Finney to the steps of the pontoon and somehow supported him down into the boat. Slumping into the seat Finney heaved a sigh of relief.

'We're not out of danger yet, Declan, you've been shot by one of your colleagues, it was Guthrie who shot you. We must get you somewhere safe but not back to Mae Sai. Not until we get the bullet wound looked at.' The boat motored off slowly. Finney could feel the waterway narrowing, they were back on the river that divided Thailand from Myanmar, and he could see lights in the distance. Soon enough they were coming to shore at a small wooden pier. A set of stairs led to a small shack. Unable to walk properly the two men helped him up.

It was a small boat house with a makeshift bed and little else. They laid him down and covered him with a dusty blanket. Again, the two men spoke, and the driver of the boat disappeared.

'He's gone to get someone to look at your leg. In the meantime, you will need water. Just wait here,' said Tura.

'Just tell me,' He asked, 'did Jane make it safely to her father? Please tell me she's safe.'

She was safe. Right now, she was on her way to Chiang Rai with her father and the ambassador. Tura explained he would be back shortly. Finney lapsed into unconsciousness again. The men returned later with another man, carrying several plastic bags. Finney barely moved when they entered the room. He was completely drained.

'This is a friend of mine, he's a doctor and agreed to take a look at you,' said Tura. 'You can call him Doctor Min.'

'Let's get you cleaned up,' said the doctor. He handed Finney a water bottle and helped him to sit up in the bed. He then proceeded to remove some first aid items from one of the bags. Using a pair of scissors, he cut away Finney's jeans from below the belt tourniquet. After first giving Finney a needle with a local anaesthetic, he used antiseptic as he cleaned the wound of blood, mud and river water. 'You're a lucky man, the bullet has gone through your thigh with very little damage,' said the doctor 'I'll get this cleaned up as best I can and pack the hole, but you will need to have it looked at again in the next few days.'

'I don't feel so lucky,' he said, flinching at the burning antiseptic.

'Here, take these,' said Tura as he passed him over more painkillers. 'This should help, but it might take fifteen or twenty minutes to dull the pain.' He also removed Finney's phone from his back pocket. Holding it up to the light, he shook his head, 'I'm not sure if we can save this' he said, 'but we'll give it a try.'

'We need to get you out of these wet clothes,' said the doctor. He worked away quietly at Finney's wound, cleaning and bandaging it. The painkillers were beginning to take effect, and he started to relax. The doctor explained he had done as much as he could. Handing over several bags of pills he advised on what to take and when. Tura nodded and the doctor turned to leave.

Finney called to the doctor as he neared the door, 'Thank you, doctor, I'm very grateful.'

'You are welcome, sir,' was all the man said, without turning back. And then he was gone down the rickety steps and out into the darkness.

'My friend has taken a big risk in seeing you,' said Tura.

'How can we thank him?'

'Money, Mr. Finney, with money. Don't worry about it now.'

Tura had brought with him an oversized T-shirt and the very trusty Burmese sarong. Finney tried to laugh as Tura passed it over to him.

'I can't walk around in this,' he protested, 'I'll get arrested.'

'We will get you some proper clothes in the morning when Banjob is back from Chiang Rai.'

'I'm guessing I can't go back to the hotel tonight.'

'I'm not sure when you can go back to the hotel sir,' said Tura. 'Your colleague Bart Guthrie is the man who shot you. It looked deliberate to me. He was told not to fire by your ambassador, and he went ahead and did so anyway. Stay here until morning and we will decide then. Try and get some sleep. It will be dawn soon enough and we may need to move you.'

'Where would you move me to,' said Finney, realizing he didn't even know where he was.

'You are in Tachileik about half a mile from the border bridge. For once it might be safer to be in Myanmar,' said Tura

He fell asleep almost immediately while Tura and the other man sat outside guarding the shack.

The evening thunderstorm had cleared the sky of dust particles leaving it bright and blue in the early morning. It would be hazy again in a few hours but for now, the sky was as blue as a crocus flower. Finney woke to the sounds of boat engines and brooms sweeping dusty courtyards in the distance. He struggled out of bed and saw the two men sitting, sipping tea on the small pier.

Seeing that Finney was awake, Tura offered him a cup of the steaming hot, sweet beverage.

Finney nodded his gratitude, never had a cup of tea tasted so good. 'And some of those little green pills too, please. My leg is throbbing.'

Painkillers were administered and Tura brought him up to date on the events he had missed the night before. Jane Gordon had been safely delivered back into the loving arms of her father. Against the orders of the ambassador, Bart Guthrie had opened fire using the headlights of the car to illuminate the pontoon. In the darkness and confusion, it had appeared Finney had gone on the other boat. They are unaware he had been shot, and Guthrie was speculating Finney went willingly with the kidnappers. Nobody else was buying that story.

'It is essential you get in touch with the ambassador as soon as possible,' said Tura. 'Guthrie and Hanlon are back in Mae Sai investigating the death of Barry Quinn but also keeping an ear out for what has happened to you.'

'Oh Christ,' said Finney, 'what a mess.'

'You need to contact the ambassador and get out of here as soon as possible. He is your ally, you can trust him, according to Banjob.'

'Can Banjob get me back to Bangkok,' asked Finney.

'There's a small problem there. He has been assigned to Guthrie and Hanlon.'

Finney's head was spinning. Lack of sleep, the gunshot wound, and the painkillers weren't helping. He realised how dependent he had become on Tura and Banjob and without them, getting back to Bangkok would be a challenge. He thought of Pip Tan. First off, he would call the ambassador. Or would he? Could he rely on the ambassador not to give away his location to Guthrie and Hanlon? Better not to take the risk.

'How is my phone,' he asked.

'No time to fix it yet,' said Tura. 'Relax and drink your tea and I'll get onto it. It is best if you stay inside the building. We are seeing a lot of drones around lately and we know the army, the DEA and even your friends from the embassy might be using them.'

He went back inside and tried to rest and enjoy the cool of the morning. It would not be long before the blasting heat of the day returned. Again, he fell asleep, the fatigue catching up with him. The small hut was stifling, and eventually, he woke up in a ball of sweat. He struggled to get up and flung open the door. The sun was low in the sky, and he realised he may have slept nearly all day.

Tura turned from his seat near the steps, 'please stay inside' he said, 'people are looking for you.'

Tura had sent the other man away to get food. It was late in the afternoon and Finney would need to spend another night in the hut. According to Tura, there was too much police activity near the border.

'I've got your phone working.' Said Tura. He had thirty missed calls, many of them from the ambassador, several from Pip, Banjob of course, and international calls with no number.

'Do you want to try it out,' he said, getting up to give the phone to Finney.

Leaning forward to take the phone, Finney groaned as pain stabbed at his leg. 'I might need some more of those pills,' he said to Tura. The man obliged and passed over a handful of medications.

'This many pills will knock me out.'

'They're not all painkillers,' said Tura, 'there are some antibiotics there as well. The doctor prescribed those to be taken three times a day. And if you do make phone calls, only stay on the line no more than a couple of minutes. If someone wants to, they'll trace the phone back here.'

Taking the man's advice, he started with text messages.

To Ella – **Hello Sweetie. Really busy with work. Will call you tomorrow. Love you!!!!**

To Banjob – **Is it safe for me to come back to the hotel?**

To Pip Tan – **Are you still in Mae Sai?**

To Roger Clifton-Blythe – **Please call me. Urgent**!

Instantly his phone rang. It was Clifton-Blythe. 'Declan (he had never called him Declan before), where are you? Are you OK?'

'I'm OK, except for a small gunshot wound,' he said. 'I'm keeping a low profile and recovering.'

'What do you mean, gunshot wound? Where are you? You should be in a hospital. Can I send Guthrie and Hanlon to come and get you?'

'Not on any account tell them I have called, sir. Please. You saw for yourself Guthrie firing at us on the pontoon. He wasn't aiming for the kidnappers; he was aiming at me. I'm sure he is involved in the death of Barry Quinn somehow, but I'm not sure how to prove it.'

'It's not your job to do that. Your job was to rescue Jane Gordon, which you've done. Congratulations, Jane and her father are somewhere between Singapore and Sydney right now. Bill Gordon asked me to pass on his sincere thanks. We've been worried about you. We thought you were in the hands of those drug traffickers.'

'When the bullet hit me, I ended up in the water,' Finney reported. He would stay where he was and recover, before returning to Bangkok. He would make his travel arrangements. He implored the ambassador not to share their conversation with anyone, especially Guthrie. They would discuss the matter further at the embassy and he ended the call. Almost immediately the ambassador called back. Finney let the call ring out.

He received a text from Banjob. **Not safe to come to the hotel. I will get your bag and passport to you.**

Again, the phone rang, thinking it was Clifton-Blythe again, Finney ignored it. It rang again, it was Pip Tan.

'Are you still in Mae Sai' he said without any greeting.

'Hello to you too,' she said, 'I'm fine, how about you? I've heard some rumours about action on the river last night. You wouldn't happen to know anything about it, would you?'

'Nothing at all to do with me,' he lied. 'I was hoping I could ask for some advice and even some help. How would a white guy get out of Mae Sai and back to Chiang Mai without anyone knowing about it?'

There was a silence.

'That was you last night, wasn't it? Boats, gunshots, speeding vans heading towards Chiang Rai airport. You didn't make it onto the plane.'

'I didn't even make it to Chiang Rai,' he replied, 'but I'd sure as hell like to get back to Chiang Mai and then onto Bangkok. Preferably without attracting any attention. Any ideas?'

'You might be in luck. As it happens, I was hoping to get back there tonight. After dark of course. Let me call you back.'

Finney emerged again from the hut and motioned to Tura.

'Banjob called me already,' he said. 'Your belongings, including your passport, will be here soon.'

'Great,' said Finney. 'I need to get back across the river. What's the best way for us to do that?'

'Banjob tells me there's a lot of police and army activity on the Thai side after those gunshots last night. It might be easier if we get you back in the floral shirt and baseball cap and just walk you across the border. Your passport won't have the correct stamp but it's nothing US$50 won't fix.'

He realised he was out of cash. It would not be a problem, Tura reassured him. Banjob would take care of it. Finney explained his plan to get back to Chiang Mai with Pip and move on to Bangkok from there. The Burmese man, whom he now regarded as his friend, offered him some advice.

'Be aware that Guthrie and the others, Dowsett and Pendergast, might try and take another shot at you. Stay out of sight of the DEA as well. They have eyes everywhere and Rosie Betts would always act in the best interests of her employer.'

It was sage advice, Finney concluded. He even had his doubts about travelling to Chiang Mai with Pip, but who else could he rely on?

Food had arrived courtesy of Tura's friend. Curry, eggs and rice. Finney was ravenously hungry and greedily devoured two plates of food. He felt curry running down his chin. Lifting his head to wipe it away he saw the two Burmese men looking at him.

'I'm sorry,' he said, 'I don't always eat this fast. I haven't eaten for over twenty-four hours.'

Tura laughed, 'It's OK, it is always nice to see a man enjoying his food.

All three of them laughed. He realised he could laugh. Jane Gordon was safe. He was still alive. He just had to get back home safely. He felt his shoulders relax. Even the wound in his leg felt less painful. He felt the pressure and intensity of the last week falling away. He thought of Ella. He felt good for the first time in months, since the death of Joey Rivers. Things would be OK, he told himself.

The Long Road Home

A short time later a man arrived and handed over Finney's bag, including his passport. They then waited until late afternoon as the sun was setting and he had changed back into his tourist apparel. A pickup truck had collected them from the shack. Seated low in the back seat of the dual cab; his baseball cap was pulled low over his face. Exiting the vehicle at the base of the bridge they moved forward with groups of Thai tourists toward the immigration guards. The border crossing was busy. Tura walked slightly in front of Finney and passed both of their passports over at the same time, with the cash folded discretely into Finney's passport. Taking the passports the officer looked up at Finney slowly. He stood from his chair and retreated behind a waist-high screen to one of the other immigration officers. They stood in conversation, for several minutes, before the man returned. Finney held his breath. The man casually picked up the stamp, pressed it against Finney's passport and gave both documents back to Tura, accompanied by a brief comment.

'People have been looking for you. We need to stay out of sight. Don't look back,' Tura muttered, 'and follow me quickly'. They walked through the immigration post and into Thailand. They emerged off the bridge and Tura turned to the left and down into the nearby market alleys. He picked up a large straw hat from one of the stalls and paid for it. 'Put this on,' he said. They had arranged to meet Pip Tan at a nearby waterfront restaurant, but Tura realised it was too exposed, too many people around.

'Change of plans,' said Tura, 'text Pip and tell her to meet us at Wat Phra That Doi Wao. It's only ten minutes from here. Follow me and we'll get a tuk-tuk from one of the side streets.'

Finney did as he was instructed. Emerging from the market on a small side street they found a tuk-tuk and Tura negotiated the fare. Finney paid the driver. He now had cash courtesy of Banjob. When his bag was returned, he found B100,000 folded neatly in an envelope. Enough money to see him safely back to Bangkok, he hoped. As the vehicle pulled away Tura pointed down the street toward the border crossing and there it was. The black pickup truck belonging to Rosie Betts was parked opposite the border crossing. Betts was behind the wheel with one of her crew cut underlings in the passenger seat. In the back seat of the vehicle was Bart Guthrie. Finney knew they were looking for him. He had ignored the numerous text messages she had sent over the last twenty-four hours – they had become increasingly more forceful in their tone. She wasn't happy to have been left out of the loop on Jane Gordon. Finney had no regrets about that. Tura was right, she had a whole different agenda, but why was Guthrie there? What story had he spun to her? He knew it was time to get out of Dodge.

Arriving at the carpark in the temple grounds they found Pip waiting for them in the far corner. It was dark now and easier to move around unseen. They would travel back through Fang and Chiang Dao, Pip advised. We should be there in five hours. The car was full of fuel so there was no need to stop. The only thing they may encounter were police checkpoints, which had sprung up because of the army border offensives, she suggested. Fingers crossed they don't see one. They transferred Finney's bag to Pip's car. As they stood in the carpark

Finney realised just how much Tura had done for him. Not just helping him to navigate the release of Jane Gordon but saving his life the night before. Reaching into his pocket he pulled out the wad of cash Banjob had passed on to him. 'How much do I owe you?', he asked the man.

'Well, there's money for the doctor and the driver today,' said Tura. 'Let's just say B10,000 should cover it.'

Finney peeled off B30,000 and handed it over.

'This is too much. I said B10,000.'

'You saved my life,' said Finney, 'and risked your own. I know I can't put a price on it but at least take this extra cash for yourself.'

The man shook his head, as he handed back the balance of cash to Finney. 'I told you in this very place, in this temple, did I not? I do what I can to make the world a better place. With Jane Gordon back at home with her family, it is a better place. What will *you* do to make the world a better place, Declan? Think about it,' he said, as he turned to walk away.

He stood there in the fading light and watched Tura walking back towards the tuk-tuk. He hoped they would meet again someday.

They drove in silence, Pip realizing Finney was deep in thought about the events of the last week. It was not over yet, she knew. The death of Barry Quinn would reverberate for some time. How would she navigate her future with the knowledge she had of Quinn's death and the role of Pendergast and Dowsett? They were both relieved as they reached the outskirts of Chiang Mai without encountering any police checkpoints. It was nearing midnight, and Finney was worn out and exhausted.

Pip had suggested he avoid the Movenpick Hotel this time and choose somewhere far away from that part of town. He agreed. They pulled into a hotel just off Nimmanhaemin Rd. several kilometres away. The BED Nimman Hotel would do fine. A four-star place a few notches up from his guesthouse of the last few days. All modern and minimalist, Finney would be content to have a soft bed and some cold AC. They lingered in the lobby, not knowing what to say to one another. He was too tired to talk, and his travelling companion could see it. She insisted on taking him to the airport for a standby flight the next morning. After wishing him a good night's sleep she left after a short embrace and a peck on his cheek.

There it was again, thought Finney, he had strong feelings for Pip Tan. He had no energy to ask her to stay and the timing was all wrong. He watched as she got in her car and drove away. Declining the offer of assistance to carry his bag, he made his way to the room by himself. Still dressed in the floral shirt and bright green shorts he knew he should shower but that would have to wait. He fell into a deep sleep minutes after crawling into what felt like the most luxurious bed, he ever slept in.

It felt like he had just shut his eyes, and his phone was ringing. It was 7.45 am. He had been asleep for almost 8 hours. He blinked as he reached for his phone. It was Ella.

'Dad,' she yelled, 'what's going on? Are you OK? I've been trying to call you. They've brought forward our departure date for Singapore. We're leaving this weekend. Where are you? I need to see you.'

'Hold on there, Sweetie, slow down,' he said. 'I'm fine and I'm still in Thailand.' He paused. 'Now take a deep breath and tell me what's going on.'

Plans had changed. There was a place at the new school, and they had to take it. Charles was in Singapore and had found them an apartment, so the move had been brought forward. He knew his daughter was excited and ready to go but couldn't leave without seeing her father. Was it pity, in her voice, he wondered. Ella finally calmed down and her father gave an assurance he would be home before she jetted off to Singapore.

'I have to get back to class,' she said and ended the call.

Could he get back in time, he wondered. He packed and showered quickly, keen to get to the airport and back to Bangkok as quickly as possible. Taking coffee in the hotel lobby, he made the call to Clifton-Blythe.

The ambassador checked on Finney's well-being and sounded genuinely happy to hear from him. He was insistent Finney report to him in Bangkok as soon as possible. He also reassured Finney he had not divulged his location or movements. Outlining his plan to the ambassador, Finney advised him he would board the first available flight to Bangkok and simply transit there to Sydney. He needed to see his daughter. He wouldn't be stopping off in Bangkok. The ambassador objected, there were complications around the death of Barry Quinn. His counterpart from the U.S. Embassy had been on the phone. Agent Betts was making waves, and Finney had been called in to answer some sticky questions.

He wasn't happy and let the ambassador know it. 'I have fulfilled my end of the bargain and taken a bullet for my trouble,' he said. 'Quinn's death had nothing to do with me,' he asserted. He suggested Clifton-Blythe look more closely within his team at the embassy for answers about

Quinn's death. He needed to get back to Sydney. It was urgent and for once in his life he would put his family before his work.

After a long pause, the ambassador relented. 'They'll make my life hell here, but you do have a point. I'm sure Bill Gordon won't look too fondly on me if I hold you here against your will. Marley will organise the flights. There's a Thai Airways flight out of Bangkok to Sydney at 6.30 pm. Marley will call you about the Chiang Mai to Bangkok flight. Keep your phone handy.'

'I have no intention of coming to the embassy,' he repeated.

'No need, I'll have Marley meet you at the Thai desk at 3.30 pm. Don't be late. You did a fine job, young man. I'll be honest and say I had my doubts about you, but you stood up when it mattered. If you need any back up in Sydney just let me know, but you will be coming back to Bangkok to answer these other questions. Say your goodbyes to your little girl and be prepared to get on a plane back to Bangkok. Is that clear?'

'Clear,' he said and hung up.

It was 10 am by the time Pip arrived at the hotel and Finney was restless. 'I was about to order a cab,' he told her. 'Let's go, we can talk in the car, I've got a plane to catch.'

She brought out a plastic bag and passed it across to Finney. In it, he saw two pairs of neatly folded elephant pants. 'One green and one blue, that was the order, right?' she asked.

'You remembered,' he said. 'You are so thoughtful.'

'What will Ella think if you arrive home empty-handed?'

Pip had arranged for Finney to see a doctor at a local clinic on their way to the airport. According to him, the doctor in Tachileik had done a fine job. The dressings were changed, and he was advised to see a doctor again on his return to Sydney. That was reassuring.

They stood awkwardly in the terminal building after Finney had purchased his ticket to Bangkok.

'How can I thank you for getting me back here safely,' he asked.

'Take me somewhere nice for dinner,' she laughed. 'I know you're coming back here. Not next week but soon enough, I know you will come back. This place gets under your skin. In a good way.'

Finney nodded. He knew she was right. It was already under his skin. Finney suggested she stay quiet about the conversation she had overheard in Mae Sai between Pendergast and Dowsett. He would pass the information on. It would be safer that way. She nodded in agreement. They stood in silence for a moment, the weight of the goodbye hanging between them.

'This is harder than I thought,' Pip said quietly, her voice steady but soft.

Finney nodded; his gaze fixed on her. 'Yeah, it is.'

He reached out and took her hand, a simple gesture that felt natural. 'You'll be alright, Pip,' he said, his voice soft and low. 'You're stronger than you know.'

Pip looked up at him, a small, sad smile playing on her lips. 'And you'll stay out of trouble?' she asked, half-teasing.

Finney gave a short laugh, though his eyes were serious. 'I'll do my best.'

They stood there, hand in hand, neither wanting to let go just yet. There was no need for grand gestures or words. The connection between them, quiet and understated, was enough.

'Take care of yourself, Declan,' Pip said finally, squeezing his hand one last time.

'You too, Pip,' he replied, his voice barely above a whisper.

Without another word, they leaned in and kissed for the first time. It was brief and a little awkward, a moment neither would forget. When they pulled away, there was no need for further goodbyes. They simply nodded to each other and turned to walk in opposite directions, the noise of the airport quickly absorbing the sound of their footsteps as they went their separate ways.

Exiting through Bangkok to Sydney was a blur for Finney. His leg was throbbing, so he dosed up on painkillers. The ambassador's assistant handled check-in and immigration, before walking him to the Thai Airways lounge. She had offered to escort him to the departure gate, but he declined. As he nursed a soda water, he saw the message come through from Rosie Betts. **We will meet again DS Finney. You have enemies so watch your back. This isn't over yet.** Finney read the message over and over, trying to get the tone of it. It was full of ambiguity, and he was happy to be leaving the country right now. He would find out the true meaning of the message soon enough and he decided against a reply.

After an agonising two-hour delay, nestled in the business class cabin with a vacant seat beside him, Finney could begin to relax. The events of the past week had been like a dream. The sights, smells and sounds of Northern

Thailand had amplified the experience, and only time would allow him to distil what had been the greatest adventure of his life. By the time the plane hit the tarmac at Kingsford Smith Airport in Sydney, Finney was ready to stretch his legs. Cabin fever had set in at around the five-hour mark on a nine-hour flight. On the bright side, his new diplomatic passport had him through immigration and customs in no time. He emerged into the bright blue spring sky and shivered at the 21C temperature. He'd been away just over a week, yet it felt like a lifetime.

As the taxi glided through the familiar streets of home, Finney couldn't help but feel a strange dissonance. The cityscape, once so comforting in its predictability, now seemed sterile, almost lifeless. The orderly traffic, and the absence of the chaotic energy he had grown accustomed to, made him feel as though he had stepped out of a vivid dream into a grey, muted reality.

He found himself unconsciously scanning the sidewalks, half expecting to see a street vendor setting up a stall or the distant sound of motorbikes weaving through the traffic. But all he saw were the neat, clean lines of a city that now felt foreign to him. The bustling street markets, the cacophony of voices, the heady mix of scents from food stalls, and the relentless heat which clung to you like a second skin—all were now just memories, leaving behind an emptiness he hadn't foreseen.

They say travel can be dangerous, but routine can be fatal, and he realised just how true it was. The journey had changed him in ways he hadn't expected. The intense experiences, the brushes with danger, and the connections he had formed had left an indelible mark on him. The phrase 'this part of the world will get under your skin' echoed in his mind. He had heard it often, and now, he knew it to be true.

It wasn't just the sensory overload that had imprinted itself on him—the sights, the smells, the sounds, the heat—it was the people. The unyielding optimism, the kindness, and the warm smiles of the locals had chipped away at the hard exterior he had built over the years. Their friendliness had lifted him in ways he hadn't realised he needed, infusing him with a sense of hope he hadn't felt in a long time.

But was it all real, or was the jetlag playing tricks on his mind? He wondered if his optimism was genuine or just a fleeting illusion brought on by exhaustion and the disorienting effects of crossing time zones. He didn't have the answer, but one thing was certain—something within him had changed. The world he had left behind had gotten under his skin, and it would be with him, colouring his thoughts and his life, long after the jetlag had worn off.

After showering and changing his clothes, he headed straight to Balmain. He knew Ella wouldn't be home from school yet. It was Sarah he wanted to see. As she opened the door, she was shocked.

'What the hell happened to you,' she said. 'You look terrible.' It wasn't the usual wear and tear of a three-day bender; this was a look of exhaustion she wasn't used to.

'Well, are you going to invite me in,' he said.

She stood aside as he walked into the hallway and down to the small kitchen. The house was a jumble of half-filled cardboard boxes and plastic bags.

'The packers are coming tomorrow so I'm trying to get ahead of it,' she said. 'Are you OK,' she asked with genuine concern. 'I've never seen you look so tired.'

'Let's just say it's been a long week. I've also just arrived on an overnight flight so maybe I'm jet lagged as well.'

'So, was it a success? The trip, was it successful?'

'I guess you could say it was,' he said, looking around at all the half-filled boxes, 'So, it's true what Ella told me, you're leaving this weekend.'

She could hear the sadness in his voice. 'I'm sorry Dec, it just all happened so fast.' She pushed a chair toward him, 'Sit down and let's talk.'

'There's not much to talk about,' he said, gingerly lowering himself into the chair. 'You guys are leaving this coming weekend, right?'

She nodded and said nothing.

'How long are we looking at?'

'A minimum of three years, but to be honest, I'd like Ella to finish school up there so it's more likely it will be four.'

There followed a long silence with neither of them making eye contact.

'We can make this work Declan. I know we can.'

He agreed. They talked through the arrangement Charles Drayton had made with his firm. There would be three visits back to Australia each year, all paid for by the firm. Meaning he could see Ella reasonably often, especially if he made the effort to go to Singapore. There was no acrimony in the conversation. No spite. No hate. Just pragmatism. The two of them agreed they would do what was best for Ella. She offered him coffee, but he declined. He asked for permission to stay until their daughter arrived home from school.

'Do you want her to see you like this, Declan? You look terrible.'

She was right. It was best if he returned the following day after a good night's sleep. 'I'll collect her from school if it's OK,' he asked.

'Sure thing. Why take her somewhere for an early dinner?'

Finney hoped they would part company on good terms, as he handed over the bag containing the elephant pants. 'Give her these from me, will you, all the way from Chiang Mai.'

Opening the bag, Sarah looked at him and smiled. Reaching out her arms to him, they embraced for the first time in a decade. I remember this fragrance, he thought, and in a moment, it was gone. They both took a step back and knew that was it. The line in the sand. There had never been any real chance of reconciliation, he had thought, but now he knew for sure. What he also knew was he had to be a better father.

Despite the fatigue, he decided to walk along Darling Street, Balmain, before catching a cab back home. It gave him time to think. Normally, right about now, melancholy would descend upon him, even some self-pity. Not today, not after the week he had just had. His leg reminded him of that as he stepped off the curb. Where to from here? His career would now be secure. Even a promotion. He would have some credibility in the force, and some friends in high places.

He might also have Bart Guthrie breathing down his neck. He would go back to Bangkok; he also knew there was unfinished business there. Would he return to Chiang Mai? Of that, there was no doubt.

In the distance, he saw The Sackville Hotel, an old pub with which he was all too familiar. I might have that drink now, he thought to himself, but just the one.

THE END

Just somewhere........................

Author's Note

The crimes in this book are fictional, and all characters are products of the author's imagination. While certain organizations mentioned are real, the characters and any questionable practices associated with them are entirely fictional and do not reflect the actual standards or practices of these organisations in any way.

Made in United States
North Haven, CT
21 March 2025

67039457R00187